PENGUIN DEC

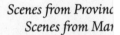

Scenes from Provinc
Scenes from Mar

William Cooper was the pen-name of Harry Hoff. Hoff was born in Crewe in 1910, and after studying at Cambridge he began teaching in Leicester – an experience which formed the backdrop of *Scenes from Provincial Life*. After the Second World War, when he served in the RAF, Hoff became a civil servant working, among other organizations, for the UK Atomic Energy Commission and the Crown Agents. His final novel, *Scenes from Life and Death*, was published in 1999. He died in 2002.

Harry Hoff had published four novels under his own name before adopting the pseudonym of William Cooper for *Scenes from Provincial Life*, which was published in 1950. Described as 'genre-busting' by the critic D. J. Taylor, it paved the way for a host of novels in the 1950s and 60s featuring ordinary provincial anti-heroes, from *Lucky Jim* to *Billy Liar*. Together with its sequels *Scenes from Metropolitan Life* and *Scenes from Married Life*, it is regarded as the best of his work.

Nick Hornby has written seven novels: *Fever Pitch*, *High Fidelity*, *About a Boy*, *How to be Good*, *A Long Way Down*, *Slam* and, most recently, *Juliet, Naked* (2009). He has also written the screenplay for two films, *Fever Pitch* and *An Education*.

Scenes from Provincial Life
and *Scenes from Married Life*

WILLIAM COOPER

PENGUIN BOOKS

PENGUIN BOOKS

Published by the Penguin Group
Penguin Books Ltd, 80 Strand, London WC2R ORL, England
Penguin Group (USA), Inc., 375 Hudson Street, New York, New York 10014, USA
Penguin Group (Canada), 90 Eglinton Avenue East, Suite 700, Toronto, Ontario, Canada M4P 2Y3
(a division of Pearson Penguin Canada Inc.)
Penguin Ireland, 25 St Stephen's Green, Dublin 2, Ireland (a division of Penguin Books Ltd)
Penguin Group (Australia), 250 Camberwell Road, Camberwell, Victoria 3124, Australia
(a division of Pearson Australia Group Pty Ltd)
Penguin Books India Pvt Ltd, 11 Community Centre, Panchsheel Park, New Delhi – 110 017, India
Penguin Group (NZ), 67 Apollo Drive, Rosedale, North Shore 0632, New Zealand
(a division of Pearson New Zealand Ltd)
Penguin Books (South Africa) (Pty) Ltd, 24 Sturdee Avenue, Rosebank,
Johannesburg 2196, South Africa

Penguin Books Ltd. Registered Offices: 80 Strand, London WC2R ORL, England

www.penguin.com

Scences from Provincial Life first published by Jonathan Cape 1950
Published in Penguin Books 1961
Scenes from Married Life first published by Macmillan 1961
Published in Penguin Books 1963
Combined edition first published with a new introduction in Penguin Books 2010

1

Scenes from Provincial Life copyright © William Cooper, 1950
Scenes from Married Life copyright © William Cooper, 1961
Introduction copyright © Nick Hornby, 2010

The moral right of the author and of the introducer has been asserted

Set in Dante MT Std 11/13pt
Typeset by Palimpsest Book Production Limited, Grangemouth, Stirlingshire
Printed in Great Britain by Clays Ltd, St Ives plc

A CIP catalogue record for this book is available from the British Library

ISBN: 978-0-141-04688-4

www.greenpenguin.co.uk

Penguin Books is committed to a sustainable future
for our business, our readers and our planet.
The book in your hands is made from paper
certified by the Forest Stewardship Council.

Introduction

My sister gave me *Scenes from Provincial Life* for Christmas, possibly in 1982 or '83. I'd never heard of either the book or its author before that. I don't know how she came across it, or why she decided I should read it, but it was a smart and very welcome gift; ten years later, when I began to think about writing my first novel, it became clear to me that William Cooper was one of the authors (along with Anne Tyler and Roddy Doyle, among others) who had helped me to think about the kind of fiction I wanted to write. Cooper was certainly one of the authors who helped me to think about the kind of fiction I wanted to *read*. I was not long out of university, and – like Joe, the narrator of *Scenes from Provincial Life* – I was teaching in a secondary school. Unlike Joe, however, I didn't think of myself as a writer yet. (One of the incidental pleasures of *Provincial Life* is its painful accuracy about a writing career in its infancy – the hope, the despair, the waiting for acceptance letters that never come, the constant vows to give up or to plough on.) I was reading very little, partly because of my workload, and partly because university had dulled my appetite for books. I didn't want to read the novels I felt I ought to be reading, and nor did I want to give up my pretensions, so as a compromise I just gave up on literature altogether. When I started in on my sister's Christmas present, I found I couldn't stop: Cooper's readability, his attractive, conversational style, helped me to remember why I had enjoyed reading so much in the first place, before lectures and essays destroyed it all.

Don't just take my word for it, though – I'm not the only person who loves the novel. *Scenes from Provincial Life* seems to me so simple, lucid, attractive, and funny that anyone who finds he can't read it probably ought to ask himself: 'Should I be trying to read books at all? Wouldn't it be better to sit and watch television or something?' This, I think, is as good a summary of the enduring appeal of the novel you are now holding in your hands as anything I could provide. True, this summary is provided by the author himself, on what would appear to have been a particularly bullish day, but this doesn't make it wrong. Unless you are one of those people who think a novel can't be any good unless it makes you weep with the effort of reading it, then Cooper's refreshingly immodest self-assessment is spot on.

Scenes from Provincial Life was published in 1950, and served an important function in post-war English literary history: without Cooper's novel, there may well have been no *Lucky Jim*, or any of the other '50s and '60s novels that deal with relatively ordinary people in relatively ordinary situations. Making a case for the influence of a particular work of art, however, is never a very persuasive or attractive argument – without *The Birth of a Nation* there may very well have been no *Pulp Fiction*, but the latter is a lot more fun to watch than the former, and the joy of Cooper's novel (which, despite bearing all the hallmarks of a debut, wasn't his first – he'd already written three or four under his real name, Harry Hoff) lies in its readability and freshness. It's funny and candid and surprisingly, disorientingly, modern.

It's impossible to read the opening chapters of this book without thinking of Philip Larkin's observation that sexual intercourse began in 1963. We always presume we know what Larkin meant – but the sexual conduct of Cooper's characters renders the observation meaningless in every way. The novel takes place in 1939, right before the outbreak of war. Joe, the schoolteacher narrator, and his friend Tom share – not altogether peaceably – a weekend cottage in the countryside outside the provincial town where they live and work. (Cooper himself lived and worked in Leicester.) Joe uses the cottage for assignations with his girlfriend Myrtle, and Tom uses it for assignations with his young boyfriend Steve. There is no archaic moral dimension to any of this, and Tom is not tortured by his sexuality. No outrage or even disapproval is expressed at any time, in the narrative or in the dialogue; it's just how things are. Similarly, there is no sense that the sexual relationship between Joe and Myrtle is in any way illicit. What troubles the narrator is the listlessness of the relationship – should they marry, should they part? – a dilemma which one has seen in fiction before, but rarely in a novel set before the war. And Joe's relationship with his pupils is bewilderingly contemporary, too. They call him by his first name, and encourage him to climb out of the classroom window so that he can escape the stuffy school air and clear his head. 'At one period the upper forms had devoted a few days of their attention to choosing theme songs for members of the staff. I was told that mine was "Anything Goes": it seemed to me fair,' Joe tells us, philosophically. His snobbish and unexamined dismissal of 'the soppy, drawling, baby-talk of the slum areas' is much more likely to jar our sensibilities than either his professional or his sexual conduct.

No novel set in 1939 could avoid a political dimension, of course, but in *Scenes from Provincial Life* the threat of war is brought up organically: the torrent in Europe is funnelled and tamed, and it reaches Joe's provincial town in much the same way as it would have reached any provincial town in the summer of 1939, as a trickle of intense personal anxiety and distraction. Throughout the book, Joe, Tom and their forbidding older friend Robert (based on the novelist C. P. Snow) talk about emigrating to America – they seem certain that Britain will lose a war, or fail even to fight one. Munich, and Chamberlain's piece of paper, we are told, was a particularly desperate moment. 'The essence was that we thought life for us would be insupportable in a totalitarian state. We did not argue very much; it went without saying . . . We had not the slightest doubt that were some form of authoritarian regime to come to our country we should sooner or later end up in a concentration camp.' America comes to perform the same sort of function as the farm in *Of Mice and Men*: it's a dream and a promise, and the reader knows that the young men at the centre of the narrative will never get there, not least because hindsight tells us they will have to stay and help fight the war – which is, of course, what they wanted to do.

At the end of the novel, Cooper provides us with updates on his characters – the wars they had, the marriages, the careers – as the decade or so between the events the book describes and its publication logically allow him to do. The postscript comes across as a neat – and, yes, very modern – fictional device, but actually Cooper wrote autobiographically in a way that would have surprised even the most literal-minded of readers. *Scenes from Metropolitan Life*, the sequel to this book, remained unpublished until 1982, for legal reasons: in *Metropolitan Life*, Joe's affair with Myrtle continues, but Myrtle is now a married woman, and the real-life Myrtle wasn't happy. The third book in the series, entitled *Scenes from Married Life* and included in this volume, wasn't published until 1961, and there is a suspicion that Cooper's career was damaged as a result. *Scenes from Provincial Life*, at least, will live on, I hope. It would be nice to think that its re-publication could influence a whole new generation of writers. And if you find yourself unable to read it, then you should take its author's advice, and go and look under your sofa cushions for the remote control immediately.

Nick Hornby

Contents

Scenes from Provincial Life   1

Scenes from Married Life   213

Scenes from Provincial Life

THIS BOOK IS DEDICATED TO PEGGY

Part One

I

Tea in a Café

The school at which I was science-master was desirably situated, right in the centre of the town. By walking only a few yards the masters and boys could find themselves in a café or a public-house.

I used to frequent a café in the market-place. It was on the first floor, and underneath was a shop where coffee was roasted. A delicious aroma drifted through the maze of market-stalls, mingling with the smell of celery, apples and chrysanthemums: you could pick it up in the middle of the place and follow it to the source, where, in the shop-window, a magnificent roasting-machine turned with a flash of red enamel and chromium plate – persistently reminding you that coffee smelt nicer than it tasted.

Two or three times a week I had tea in the café with a friend of mine named Tom. He was a chartered accountant, and the offices of his firm were in a building between the school and the market-place. By specializing in income-tax claims, Tom made a comfortable living: it could have been luxurious, had he accepted the invitation of certain townspeople to visit their business premises after hours and falsify their returns. Tom had other things to do in his spare time.

We had been friends for several years. Both Tom and I had literary ambitions. During my six years spent teaching in the town I had published three novels. Tom had published one. I secretly thought I was three times as good a writer as Tom. At this time, February 1939, I was aged twenty-eight and Tom twenty-seven.

For reasons of delicacy I will not disclose Tom's surname. Other things about him it will be impossible to conceal. With the best will in the world you could not help noticing immediately that

Tom was red-haired and Jewish – it fairly knocked you down. He had rich, thick, carroty curls and a remarkable nose. He was nearly a stone heavier than me; and he gave the impression that he would be a good deal heavier than that, were he not always engaged in bustling physical activity. He had a rounded head, with greenish eyes and a rather pouting mouth. He was intelligent and high-spirited, and I was very devoted to him. It was not apparent that he had a formidable personality.

Sometimes what a man thinks he is can be just as interesting as what he really is. In Tom's case it was just as interesting and decidedly more wonderful; it had an endearing romantic grandeur. Tom saw himself as a great understander of human nature, a great writer, a great connoisseur of the good things in life, and a great lover. He did not see himself as a great chartered accountant. Nor did he see himself as a great clown – in that respect not differing substantially from the rest of us.

Tom possessed a formidable capacity for psychological bustling. In an easy agreeable way he bustled other people into doing things they did not want to do. He was always trying to bustle me, especially for instance over our country cottage. Tom and I shared the tenancy of a cottage ten miles outside the town, and the arrangement was that we should spend alternate week-ends there. Now I had two very strong reasons for wanting to stick to the arrangement: one was my legal right, and the other was because I was visited there by a young woman, a very pretty young woman called Myrtle.

My desire to preserve my legal right was therefore unusually strong. Tom, made in a different mould, did not see it that way. In a style more heroic, more passionate, more expansive, more wonderful than mine, he systematically tried to bustle me out of my turn.

There was some basis for Tom's picture of himself. He was courageous and he had a great fund of emotion: he had a shrewd down-to-earth insight into human nature and tireless curiosity about people. He was the ideal listener to one's lifestory – the only trouble was that in order to encourage the next person to tell his life story Tom was liable to repeat under the seal of secrecy one's own.

I usually arrived in the café first. It was superior, and chosen by me because there were no cruets and bottles of tomato ketchup on the tables at tea-time. Tom thought this showed I was finicky. 'You wouldn't notice the cruet if you were interested in the human heart,' he said, with great authority.

As the café was superior Tom could never resist ordering his tea and cream cakes with a superior manner. He waved his hand, which was small and comely, in an aristocratic gesture. The waitress appreciated it.

Perhaps I might go so far as to disclose that Tom's name was definitely not Waley-Cohen or Sebag-Montefiore – alas! very far from it. He would dearly have loved to be an aristocrat. He might have carried it off with his hands, but his face was against him. There was nothing coarse about his features, but unfortunately there was nothing even faintly aristocratic. His red hair gave him no help at all, and he was sensitive about it. When he first read *A la Recherche du Temps Perdu*, and discovered that Swann's hair was red, he was overjoyed.

For Tom it was then but the smallest step to identify himself completely with Swann – red hair, aristocratic birth, peculiar sexual temperament and all. 'Ah,' he would say, sighing, 'How I know the torments of jealousy!' And his voice, though low, carried such tremendous emotional weight that I listened with my deepest sympathy.

As Tom came into the café I thought he had an unusually preoccupied expression, but it disappeared as he sat down. When he had concluded the artistic performance of ordering his tea, he said:

'Any news of the book?'

'Not a word.'

Tom was referring to the manuscript of my latest novel. Most young novelists decide somewhere in the early stages of their careers that they have written something a class better than

7

anything they have written before. I had reached this point with my fourth book. My publisher had naturally, but not promptly, turned it down. It seemed to me in my inexperience that my publisher asked one of two things from me: either to write my previous novel all over again just as it was, or to write it again with a stronger story, sharper characterization, deeper revelations of truth and much, much funnier jokes.

For the benefit of anyone who does not already know, I can say that the recognized thing to do, when a young novelist has written the first novel that he thinks good and it is turned down by his publisher, is to send the manuscript to a writer of distinguished reputation. This is what I did. An earlier novel had produced an unsolicited letter of praise from Miss X.Y.: she had consented to read the manuscript of my latest. Her secretary had acknowledged receiving it three weeks ago.

'Not a word?'

'I suppose she's busy,' I said, for some reason or other trying to excuse her. I think I felt I had to excuse my ally.

Tom raised his eyebrows.

'How's Myrtle?' he asked tactfully.

'All right.' As might be expected I was continually haunted by the possibility of Myrtle's not being all right.

I said diffidently: 'We had a very enjoyable Sunday together.'

Tom's eyes appeared to bulge a little with disapproval.

'Why don't you let her come out on Saturday night? You know perfectly well she wants to.'

I felt badgered, and tried to sound confident. 'Propriety, my dear Tom. I don't want to risk village gossip and so on.'

It was natural for Tom not to let pass an opportunity for getting the better of me.

'How completely unrealistic of you.' He shrugged his shoulders in the manner of a great understander of human nature. 'You introverts.'

Tom and I had recently been studying the works of Jung. We were agreed that by Jungian definitions he was an extravert and I an introvert. Consequently he saw fit to use the word 'introvert' as a term of abuse.

I knew perfectly well that it was unrealistic. The real point was that I had said 'propriety' because I was too ashamed to say 'caution'. I did not let Myrtle live with me in the cottage for the same reason that I did not call regularly upon her family – in fact I never went near them. Caution.

I did not reply to Tom.

'It would not do for me,' he said. He smiled reminiscently, like a great lover. 'I like my Saturday nights.'

'So you may!' I said, and laughed aloud. 'You don't live in the shadow of a girl wanting you to marry her!'

Tom replied amiably: 'My dear man, I live in the shadow of something else.'

I saw the truth of this remark. The reason Tom did not live in the shadow of a girl wanting him to marry her was that when it was his week-end to occupy the cottage he took out a boy.

I nodded sagely.

'Ah,' said Tom, with a sigh. 'The shadows one has lived under! It makes one feel very, very old.'

One of Tom's women loves had been absurd enough to tell him that she thought he was an 'old soul'. Tom had taken it very seriously, and for months afterwards had gone about feeling older in soul than anyone we knew. It was only quite gradually that his oldness of soul had worn off, and it still cropped up on occasion.

I did not take him up because he had previously proved conclusively that I was a young soul.

I poured out some tea, while Tom began eating a chocolate éclair. We were sitting beside the window, looking out on to the tops of the market-stalls. The ridges of those at right angles to the last rays of sun gleamed with a golden light. In the air hung faint blue fumes from the coffee-roaster below. There seemed to be a lot of people wandering about, carrying baskets and bunches of bright yellow daffodils.

'You probably ought to have Myrtle out on Saturday nights, anyway,' Tom said.

'Why?'

'You know where she spends them when you won't have her.'

'Yes.' I did know. Often it was with a young man named Haxby.

'Well, if you know . . .' Tom's voice trailed off doubtfully. I could see that he was thinking again 'You introverts'.

I considered the matter. Tom was not the only person who thought my behaviour towards Myrtle was strange. To me it seemed perfectly understandable. I loved Myrtle but I did not want to marry her – because I did not want to marry anybody. That was the point, and I was puzzled that everybody else found it so difficult to comprehend. Having had to put up with so much opprobrium, I was rather on the defensive about it. Many a man before me had not wanted to be married, I argued. It might be called abnormal, but nobody could pretend it was unusual. My argument made not the slightest impression. Nor did other people's arguments make any impression on me. I did not want to be married, and that is all there is to it.

And yet I have to admit there was something more – such is the contradictory nature of the heart. I hated the idea of Myrtle marrying anyone else.

'Now,' said Tom, 'I want to talk to you seriously.'

Our main conversation was to be about his week-end in Oxford. The friend of ours with whom Tom had been staying was Dean of the small college at which I had been educated. His name was Robert, and he was a few years older than us. He was clever, gifted and wise; and he had a great personal influence on us. We had appointed him arbiter on all our actions, and anything he cared to say we really accepted as the word of God. We spent most of the time talking about the state of the world.

I listened. Tom and I talked a good deal about politics – so did we all, Myrtle and her friends, the masters in the staff-room, even the boys. Unfortunately it is very difficult to write about politics in a novel. For some reason or other political sentiment does not seem to be a suitable subject for literary art. If you doubt it you have only to read a few pages of any novel by a high-minded Marxist.

However I am writing a novel about events in the year 1939, and the political state of the world cannot very well be left out. The only thing I can think of is to put it in now and get it over.

Robert, Tom and I could be called radicals: we were made for a period thirty years earlier, when we could happily have voted liberal. The essence was that we thought life for us would be insupportable in a totalitarian state. We did not argue very much: it went without saying. It may have been because we thought of ourselves as artists: it may not – we might have been just the same if we had not been artists. Though we were three very different men, we had in common a strong element of the rootless and the unconforming, especially the unconforming. We had not the slightest doubt that were some form of authoritarian regime to come to our country we should sooner or later end up in a concentration camp.

So much for our political sentiments, if that is what they should be called. They led us to be deeply pessimistic about the state of the world. We were completely serious about it, and we became more serious even as our actions became more absurd.

When Tom said he was going to tell me what conclusions Robert had drawn, my spirits sank. Our spirits had been low ever since we came to the conclusion that the government of our country was not disposed to challenge National Socialism, though never so low as on the night the Prime Minister returned from Munich. I always recalled buying an evening newspaper: Tom was with me and we spread it out between us to read it together. And a great wave of despair overwhelmed us, the deeper and the blacker because in some inexplicable way we felt caught up in responsibility. We had still not recovered from it in the spring of 1939. Our sense of shame had induced a mood in which we became certain that the same thing would happen again. And the second time would be the last.

'The old boy says that if there isn't a war by August we shall be refugees by October.'

I stared at Tom, thinking 'March, April, May . . .'

'We ought to be thinking about moving,' said Tom, 'while there's a reasonable amount of time at our disposal.'

The idea had made fleeting appearances in our talk during the last few months. Tom's big, greenish eyes bulged unblinkingly.

'He's beginning to bestir himself.'

I felt there was nothing for me to say. I glanced through the window. The sun had disappeared from the market-place and naphthalene flares were flickering out brightly from the stalls.

Tom went on: 'He's decided America's the best place. He proposes I should go first.'

This proposal was obvious because Tom was Jewish while Robert and I were not. I thought it was hard luck on Tom; because his attitude would have been just the same if he were not Jewish, and because of the three of us he probably had the greatest share of physical courage – certainly he was the most rash.

Tom began to outline his plans. We thought we were men of more than average intelligence and gifts and we were not particularly alarmed at the prospect of having to make our way in another country – certainly we were not alarmed at all so long as the project remained in the air.

My spirits rose a little. I could not help seeing our gesture in a romantic light. We were proposing to leave our country for the sake of Freedom. I have to confess that I sometimes saw us as Pilgrim Fathers, though admittedly of a rather different type from the originals. And in moments of honesty I realized that there was a distinct attraction in the idea of leaving everything, and – more detestable still and never to be admitted to Tom – even in the idea of leaving everybody.

I thoughtfully inscribed a pattern on the tablecloth with the haft of my knife.

'I advise you to start considering what you're going to do about Myrtle,' said Tom.

I blushed. 'What do you mean?' I said, as if I had not the slightest idea what he was talking about.

'You presumably aren't thinking of taking her with you to America, are you?'

'I hadn't thought about it,' I said.

'Really!' said Tom, with a mixture of incredulity and indignation. It was clearly, 'You introverts' again.

'There's no hurry, is there?' I said amiably. 'I shall finish the year out at the school.' I was thinking of the delight with which I should hand in my notice in July.

'I should have thought it was hardly fair to Myrtle,' said Tom. 'You do intend to tell her, of course, don't you?'

'Of course,' I said, with the mental reservation that it was to be in gentler terms. 'Actually we've discussed it already. She knows that it's a possibility.' I knew that Myrtle, though I truly had discussed it with her, did not think for a moment that it would ever happen.

'If it were me,' said Tom, 'I should probably begin breaking it off now.'

Immediately my memory took me back to a previous occasion. I had been in love with a married woman whose husband earned £5000 a year against my £350. 'If it were me,' Tom had counselled, 'I should break up the marriage.' Happily it was not Tom.

Tom said: 'You don't consider her feelings as I should. It could be done understandingly and subtly.'

I thought there was a contradiction somewhere, as there was in most of Tom's counsels, but I could not put my finger on it before he went on.

'I think I should lead her to feel that it was' – he waved his hand elegantly – 'best for both of us.'

'In that case you don't know Myrtle!'

Tom shrugged his shoulders.

We abandoned the topic, and went on planning how to earn a living in America. I was troubled all the same. Tom was capable of infecting me with doubts. I was in a vulnerable position, because

I knew I was behaving like a cad. I intended to go to America. I did not want to marry Myrtle.

But was it essential that Myrtle should be left behind? I wondered. I did not want to make up my mind. Tom was probably right on psychological grounds. The point that Tom, with his penchant for violent ridiculous upsets, did not see but which occurred to me only too readily was this: outside psychological grounds, breaking it off with Myrtle had for me a very obvious drawback. I drew the generalization that one's friends find nothing easier than advising a course of action which involves ceasing to go to bed with one's young woman.

I did not tell Tom what I intended to do.

2

A Day in the Country

After Sunday lunch at the Dog and Duck, Myrtle and I strolled back over the fields to my cottage. It was a regular thing – I saw to that.

On Sunday mornings she came out on her bicycle, looking fresh and elegant and lively. Sometimes she found me washing up my breakfast pots in the scullery, where I had been keeping an eye open for the flash of her handlebars coming up the lane; sometimes she found me having a bath under the pump, which provoked a blushing, sidelong glance and the remark: 'Darling, I don't know how you can stand that cold water'; and sometimes she found me just ready for a bit of high-toned conversation about reviews in the Sunday newspapers.

'Darling, I've brought you this.'

It might be anything that had caught her fancy, a tin of liver *pâté*, or a book of poems by T. S. Eliot. This time it was a bunch of freesias. I should have received a tin of liver *pâté* much more warmly, a book of poems by T. S. Eliot much less.

Then we set out for the Dog and Duck. The cottage was two miles from the nearest public-house; but over the fields, choosing gaps in the hedges and jumping narrow brooks, we could get to the Dog and Duck in twenty minutes. Neither of us had any inclination to exhaust ourselves in the labour of cooking lunch.

The stroll back was singularly pleasurable. It did not take too long. Also it gave our lunches time to digest, and brought to our notice the beauties of nature.

As we had been his regular customers for over a year, the pub-keeper shared his lunch with us; and his wife, to please either him or us, cooked it superbly. Myrtle and I drank two or three pints of beer apiece while waiting for it: Myrtle would have drunk more, but I thought it would not be good for her. Then we sat down to slices of roast beef, red and succulent in the middle and faintly charred at the edges; apple pie with fresh cream liquid enough to pour all over it; and cheese, the unequalled, solid, homely cheese of the county.

We walked very slowly at first, for we both took a pleasure in digestion. We patted our stomachs and sighed at the prospect of the first hill. The country rolled gently, and there was a second hill to climb before we came in sight of the cottage. If I happened to belch, Myrtle gave me a ladylike look of reproach and I begged her pardon. I took her by the hand.

At the top of the first hill we looked around. It was a heavenly afternoon. The sun was shining. It was only the end of February and we could feel its warmth. The rime on the naked hedgerows had melted, and drops of water glittered like the purest glass on twigs and thorns. The sky was covered in a single haze of milky whiteness; and the tussocks of grass, wilted and brown and borne down with water, caught heavily at our feet.

'How I long for the spring,' said Myrtle in a far-away tone. Her voice was lightly modulated and given to melancholy.

It was on the tip of my tongue to say: 'Yes, and when it's spring you'll be pining for summer.' It was true: she had a passion for hot weather. But had I said it she would have looked hurt. Instead of speaking, I glanced at her. What I saw was entirely pleasing. The sooner we reached the cottage the better.

Myrtle was modestly tall and very slender. She was wearing grey slacks and a cerise woollen sweater. Her breasts and buttocks were quite small, though her hips were not narrow. She was light-boned, smooth and soft. There was nothing energetic or muscular about her. She walked with a languid, easy grace – I walked with a vigorous, over-long stride and perpetually had the impression that she was trailing along behind me.

Myrtle felt me looking at her, and turned her face to me. It was

16

oval and bright with colour. She had round hazel eyes, a long nose, and a wide mouth with full red lips: her hair was dark, her cheeks glowed. She smiled. Then she turned her head away again. I had no idea what she was thinking. I was thinking of one thing only, but Myrtle might easily have been thinking about El Greco – equally she might have been thinking about the same thing as me.

Whatever she was thinking about, whatever she was doing, Myrtle preserved a demeanour that was meek and innocent – especially meek. Sometimes I could have shaken her for it, but on the whole I was fascinated by it.

With a demeanour that was meek and innocent, Myrtle had two characteristic facial expressions. The first was of resigned reproachful sadness; the other was quite different, and only to be described as of sly smirking lubricity. As her face was both mobile and relaxed, she could slip like a flash from one expression to the other, naturally, spontaneously and without the slightest awareness of what she was doing.

We walked down the first hill, and this seemed to me an opportunity for moving a little faster. I was not as relaxed as Myrtle. However, she comfortably took her time, making a detour to cross the brook by a plank. Two horses, their coats shaggy with moisture, raised their heads to look at us. The brook was high with spring water, and the weeds waved in it sinuously. I put my hand on Myrtle's waist.

As we climbed the opposite hill Myrtle called to the horses, but they sided with me and paid no attention.

At the top of the hill we always paused and sat on a gate for a few minutes. It was a sort of ritual, and to me it seemed a thoroughly silly sort of ritual. Below us we could see the cottage. No sooner had I settled on the top bar than I was ready to leap off again. But Myrtle always took her time, and as she went by atmosphere I could never tell how long it was going to be. It was at such moments that I sensed the great gulf between our temperaments: Myrtle went by atmosphere and I went by plan.

My plan was lucid and short. There, shining in its cream-coloured wash, small, intimate, isolated from everything, was the cottage. I felt as if my skin were tightening. No doubt I had a hot fixed look on my face.

Suddenly Myrtle slid down from the gate and quietly made off beside the hedgerow.

'What on earth?' I began, jumping down.

She stooped, and I saw that she was picking some celandines she had spied on the brink of a ditch. She held them up, glistening in the sunshine.

'What are you going to do with those?'

Myrtle's face promptly took on a distant unconcerned look, as if she were going to start whistling. I laughed aloud at her, and grasped her to me.

'Darling!' I cried. I kissed her cheeks: they had a soft bloomy feel.

I slipped my hands down from her waist. She struggled away from me.

'We're in the middle of a field, darling,' she said.

It was my turn now. I am too direct to look lubricious. I took her firmly by the hand. 'Come on, then,' I said. And down the hill we went, in the plainest of plain sailing.

Whatever she was doing, Myrtle preserved a demeanour that was meek and innocent. She preserved it to perfection as I finally turned back the sheets for her. Yet, meek and innocent though her demeanour was, virginal and ladylike, anything else you may be pleased to call a nice girl, it was more than Myrtle could do, not to take a furtive sideways glance at me. I caught her.

I have said that Myrtle had two characteristic facial expressions. As a result of her furtive glance she managed to wear both of them, resigned, reproachful, sad, sly, smirking and lubricious, all at once.

Some time later we were just finishing a short rest. Idle thoughts floated vaguely through my mind. A spider was spinning down slowly from the corner of the room. Nameless odours stirred under my nose. A crow's wings flapped past the window. I was sweating profusely, because Myrtle insisted on having a lot of bedclothes. It occurred to me that there is a great division of human bodies, into those which feel the cold and those which do not. Myrtle and I belonged one to each class. How many marriages, I meditated, had been ruined by such incompatibility? Marriage – my thoughts floated hastily on to some other topic.

Myrtle was wide awake. I thought she was probably thinking how a cup of tea would refresh her. Suddenly I heard the sound of a car coming up the lane. We never expected to hear any traffic go by the cottage. It was approaching at a moderate speed, and I thought I recognized the sound of the engine. I jumped out of bed and ran to the window.

I was just too late to see it pass, so I flung down the sash and put my head out. Again I was just too late.

'Who was it?' said Myrtle.

'It sounded like Tom's car.'

'What was he doing here?'

I shrugged my shoulders. I had my idea. There was a pause.

'Don't you think you ought to come away from the window, darling?'

'Why?'

'You've got nothing on.'

'All the better . . .' Out of respect for her delicacy I closed the window with a bang that drowned the end of my remark.

She was smiling at me. I went over and stood beside her. She looked appealing, resting on one elbow, with her dark hair sweeping over her smooth naked shoulder. I looked down on the top of her head.

Suddenly she blew.

'Wonderful Albert,' she said.

I may say that my name is not Albert. It is Joe. Joe Lunn.

Myrtle looked up at me in sly inquiry.

I suppose I grinned.

After a while she paused.

'Men *are* lucky,' she said, in a deep thoughtful tone. I said nothing: I thought it was no time for philosophical observations. I stared at the wall opposite.

Finally she stopped.

'Well?' I looked down just in time to catch her subsiding with a shocked expression on her face.

'Now,' I said, 'you'll have to wait again for your tea.'

'Ah . . .' Myrtle gave a heavy, complacent sigh. Her eyes were closed.

In due course we had our tea. Myrtle felt the cold too much to get out of bed, so I made it. She sat up and put on a little woollen jacket: it was pretty shell pink to match the colour of her cheeks. Her eyes seemed to have changed from hazel to golden. We held an interesting conversation about literature.

I felt a slight check on me when I held literary conversations with Myrtle, because her taste was greatly superior to mine. I wrote novels, and when she brought to light the fact that I had no use for long dramas in blank verse, I felt coarse and caddish, as if lust had led me to violate a creature of sensibilities more delicate than I could comprehend. Secretly I thought she was invariably taken in by the spurious and the pretentious, but this I put down to her youth. She was only twenty-two.

It grew dusky outside while we finished our tea. As we settled down again, the firelight began to glow on the ceiling. A wind was rising in the branches of the elm trees across the road, furiously rattling the bare twigs against each other. 'If only we could stay here,' was what we were both thinking from time to time; and at first sight it was not obvious what prevented us. Certainly it was not obvious to Myrtle at all. It was with difficulty that in the end I persuaded her to get up.

'Come along, darling,' I said. I was thinking how necessary it was for us to get back to the town, she to her parents' home, I to my lodgings. Atmosphere did not indicate to Myrtle that this was the case.

'It's so cold outside, I shall die,' she said, hopelessly.

I bent down and kissed her: she put her arms round my neck. I could not resist it.

At last we were dressed and ready to go. I drank the remainder of the milk.

'I know you need it, darling,' Myrtle said in a subtle tone that I could not quite place.

A final glance round the living-room, at the dying fire and the empty flower-vases, and we went out into the darkness. There was a moment of nostalgia, as I turned the key in the door. We felt impelled to say something foolishly sentimental, like 'Goodbye, little home'.

On the journey back our spirits rose again. We pedalled cheerfully against the wind, our lamps flashing a wavering patch on the road ahead. We had good bicycles, with dynamos to light the lamps. Myrtle said she was tired, and sometimes I tried to tow her, but it was too difficult an operation mechanically.

The lights of the town came into view, looking particularly bright in the cold, wintry air. In the distance lighted trams passed each other slowly. The roads on the outskirts were lined with trees, and there were big houses far back from the road: this was the way into the town which did not lead through the slums. Big lamps swayed over the tramlines: in their light I could see Myrtle's eyes glowing. I put my hand on her shoulder.

At a cross-roads we parted. It was our convention that it would be indiscreet to go to each other's house. With our bicycles leaning against the small of our backs we embraced fervently. At this time on Sunday night there were few people about, especially when the wind was icy.

'When shall I see you again, darling?'

Myrtle shivered, and looked woebegone.

This was always an apprehensive moment for me. It sometimes happened that I already had an evening booked in advance: Myrtle was certain to light upon it. There was nothing wrong about it, but she made it only too plain that she was wounded. I could never think how to explain and reassure. She had all my love: I wanted no one else: she had no cause to feel a moment's jealousy. Yet she was wounded if I disclosed that there was one evening when I was not free. And somehow I wanted that evening to myself, that evening and possibly one or two more. It was the moment when I sensed another great gulf between our temperaments.

On this particular occasion, I had arranged to go out for supper on Tuesday evening – Myrtle and I lived in the social stratum where the midday meal is often called lunch instead of dinner, but where the evening meal cannot properly be called dinner and so goes by the name of supper.

'When shall I see you again, darling?' I waited with my fingers crossed.

'Not tomorrow, of course.' Then in a melancholy tone: 'And I've promised to go to the dressmaker's on Tuesday . . .' Her voice trailed off, and returned with surprising briskness. 'Wednesday.'

I kissed her. Relief multiplied my fervour by about fifty per cent. Myrtle looked sad. We arranged to telephone each other, and parted.

As I cycled fast down my own road, I felt as if I were borne on a stream of the purest, most powerful emotion. It almost seemed to lift the bicycle off the ground. Everything seemed entrancing, permeated by the atmosphere of joy – the prospect of a hearty supper that my landlady would have waiting for me, of a hot bath that I needed, and of the blessed sheets of my own bed. Myrtle, Myrtle. The sting of cold air on my forehead, the strange brilliance of the streetlamps, the bare trees waving in the shadows.

I put away my bicycle and slammed the garage door. I was thinking of Myrtle, and I looked up at the sky. There were stars, sparkling. I was feeling happy and I had left Myrtle looking sad. Why, oh why? I am an honest man: one of my genuine troubles with Myrtle was that I could never tell whether she was looking unhappy because I would not marry her or because she was feeling cold.

3
A Morning at School

Next morning I had to get up and go to school. It was going to be a bright day. The balls of my feet felt springy as I ran downstairs, and as I jumped on to my bicycle the saddle felt springy. Hoorah! for Myrtle, I thought; there is nothing makes a man feel so wonderful as a wonderful girl. Flying downhill past the cemetery I skidded violently in the tramlines and gave myself a fright: a wonderful girl does not fill a man with courage to face death – quite the reverse.

The school was a big grammar school for boys, in the centre of the town. The building was Victorian, dark, ugly, ill-planned, dirty and smelly.

Instead of going to morning prayers I went down to the laboratory. My task in the school was to teach physics, and for the whole of the morning I was due to take the senior sixth form in practical work. I felt more inclined to prepare the apparatus for their experiments than to take part in communal devotions.

Every so often the headmaster sent round a chit, asking all masters to attend morning prayers, but it produced not the slightest effect. One half of the masters claimed more important matters of preparation, and the other just did not go: I fluctuated between the two. The headmaster was zealous and high-minded, but he had not a scrap of natural authority. He ought to have been a local preacher, on a circuit with very small congregations.

This school was the first at which I had ever taught, so I had no other to compare it with. And I found that like many other men I had no objective recollections of my own school, or of half the things I did there – this appears to be nature's way of avoiding embarrassment all round.

I could not help feeling this school was something out of the ordinary. On my very first day there I overheard a small boy, apparently also on his very first day, say to another small boy in the crowded corridor: 'It's like Bedlam, isn't it?' After six years I still could not improve on this innocent description.

The small room used as a laboratory by the sixth form was on the ground floor at the end of the building. I could only get to it by going through the main laboratory, which was empty. Though both rooms were empty neither was quiet. Traffic roared past a few feet from the windows, while upstairs the school was singing its head off with 'Awake, my soul!'

There were four boys aged eighteen or nineteen in the senior sixth form, and they did experiments in pairs. I was at work, with all the cupboard doors open, when one of them came in. He was mature in appearance, and greeted me in a friendly fashion.

''Ello, Joe,' he said. 'I'n't it a luvly day!'

The local dialect was characterized by a snarling, whining inton-ation: Fred spoke it in the soppy, drawling, baby-talk of the slum areas.

The school did not have number one social standing in the town, and the pupils all came from the lower middle class and upper proletariat. Fred came from the proletariat. He was strong and stocky, with a sallow, greyish skin. His hair was covered with brilliantine and his hands were always dirty – I thought it was the grease off his head which made his hands pick up the dirt so readily.

Like Fred, most of the older boys called me by my Christian name, outside the lessons if not inside. I had wanted to get on free-and-easy terms with the boys – how else could I find out all about them? – and I had achieved the feat with little trouble, chiefly through letting them say anything they liked.

To an outsider the manners of my pupils must have been surprising. It happened that I was not given to being surprised; which very soon made the manners of my pupils more surprising still. The boys, when they discovered there was nothing they could say that would shock me, relapsed into the happy state they appeared to be in when I was not there.

At one period the upper forms had devoted a few days of their attention to choosing theme songs for members of the staff. I was told that mine was 'Anything Goes': it seemed to me fair. Unfortunately my free-and-easy attitude was strongly disapproved of by my senior master. He wanted to have me sacked, and frequently expressed his point of view to the headmaster.

It was absolutely necessary, if I wanted to become a novelist – and that was the only thing I wanted do – that I should keep my job. Nevertheless I found it unbearably tedious to pretend to be surprised when I was not, to be shocked when I was not, to be ignorant when I knew all about it, and to be morally censorious when I did not care a damn. To be frank, I found it impossible.

Fred was mooning about, so I told him to get out the travelling-microscope. At this point a boy called Frank came in.

Frank was the eldest and the cleverest of the four. He was captain of the school rugby football team, more because he had an eager, pleasing personality than because he carried a lot of weight. He had wavy hair, high cheek-bones, and a rather long nose that, to his secret sorrow, turned up at the end. Had it not been for his nose he would have been very handsome. He was an old friend of Tom's.

'Have a good week-end?' he said.

'Very.'

He glanced at me briefly. I suspected he had found out from Tom where I had spent it, though the cottage was supposed to be a secret. All the boys showed powerful curiosity and imagination about the private lives of the masters.

'It's time you and Trevor tried to find Newton's rings,' I said. It was a difficult experiment, appropriate as Frank had won a scholarship to Oxford.

It may not have occurred to everybody that most schoolmasters are preoccupied not with pedagogy but with keeping the pupils quiet. There are numerous methods of achieving this, ranging

from giving them high-class instruction to knocking them unconscious.

Frank began to search for his experiment in the index of a textbook. Fred interrupted him.

'Fred,' I said, 'you and Benny can do Kater's pendulum.'

This was where my guile came in. The experiment necessitated
one of them counting the oscillations of a pendulum and the other
watching a clock, so precluding all foolish conversation.

Suddenly there began a distant roar as the school came out of
prayers. They thundered down the staircases out of the hall, stamp-
ing their feet and raising their voices. It was no longer possible to
hear the traffic outside the windows.

The last two boys, Trevor and Benny, came into the laboratory.
Benny was big and ugly and heavy, with the comic-pathetic expression of a film-comedian. He generated a superabundance of
emotion and physical energy, and he was not clever.

Trevor was quite different, unusually small, fair, pale and delicately formed. He had beautiful silky golden hair that he was always
combing. He was languid, petulant, sarcastic, quick-tempered and
horrid to anyone who gave him an opening. I was quite fond of him
because he was intelligent and inclined to be original. He wanted
to be an artist, and he had failed badly in the Oxford scholarship
examination. I was worried about his future, and afraid that we
might have trouble with him one day.

'What are we going to do, sir?' said Benny, standing too close
to me and hopping about from one big foot to the other. Trevor
went and combed his hair in front of a glass cupboard door.

I paused for a moment. A form was assembling in the main
laboratory next door and the wooden wall between was resound-
ing like a huge baffle. There was a loud hallooing shout from a
master, and the noise subsided. I explained to my pupils what they
had to do. Then I sat down in my chair to meditate.

One of the boys asked a question. 'Do as you like,' I said. I
addressed the form as a whole. 'It's important that you should all
learn to be resourceful.'

Trevor turned his small sharp face and laughed nastily.

'It saves you a lot of trouble.'

I did not speak to any of them.

'Come on, Trev,' said Frank, and ran his fingers through Trevor's hair.

Benny dropped a couple of metre sticks on the floor. On picking them up he discovered he could make a clacking noise by shaking them together. In a few moments this pleasure palled and they were all settling down to work.

I began to think about Myrtle.

The brightness of the day was beginning to be manifest. A pale ray of sunlight cut across the little room and glimmered on the green-painted wall. Trevor was drying out a piece of asbestos soaked in brine over a bunsen flame, and it made spluttering yellow flashes. Sounds of all kinds kept the room echoing. It was another day in which you could feel the air cleared and sharpened by dormant spring. My thoughts drifted into fantasies as they do when I listen to music.

There was another hallooing shout in the room next door. Then silence.

'It's Roley,' said Frank. Roley was the boys' name for my senior master, Roland Bolshaw.

There was a crash against the wall: it was the unmistakable sound of a boy being knocked down.

'The sod!' said Trevor, in a superior accent.

'Oo-ya bugger!' said Fred, in the language of the town.

We listened, but nothing else happened.

Frank went on polishing a lens with his handkerchief.

'You haven't got anything to do,' he said. 'Haven't you brought a novel to read?'

I shook my head. He had reminded me of the fact that I did not read much nowadays. I was faced with an inescapable truth: you cannot have a mistress and read. Sometimes my illiteracy made me ashamed: at other times I thought, 'Bah! Who wants to *read*?'

From his pile of text-books Trevor produced a copy of *Eyeless in Gaza*. I had read it once and found it too unpleasant to read again.

'If I go to my locker I shall have to stop and talk to Bolshaw on the way,' I said thoughtfully.

Immediately Benny was standing beside me. 'Let me go and fetch you something, sir!'

I refused, and that committed me to going through Bolshaw's room.

The headmaster of the school was regarded by staff and pupils alike as ineffective. The result of this diagnosis, right or wrong, was that there was little discipline among the boys, and a high degree of eccentricity, laziness and insubordination among the staff. The manners of the staff were no less surprising than those of the boys. By my simple standards of common sense, about one-third of them not only qualified for dismissal from this school but would never hold a job in any other. To say they habitually cut lessons, or spent lunch-time in a public-house, or held hilarious sessions of beating, was putting it mildly.

There were of course a number of masters, another third, who were ordinary decent men. The sort of men we all remember as the schoolmasters of our youth – a little less clever, shrewd, ambitious and successful than ourselves, but firm, honest and hard-working. Unfortunately these were not the men who made much impression at the time upon any of the boys I had a chance of observing.

My senior master fell into a third category. He was immediately recognizable as a schoolmaster, while at the same time he was impressive. I think he was most impressive because in the staff-room, the class-room, or any other gathering, he had the power of confidently assuming he was the most important person there.

Bolshaw was built on a big scale. He had a large heavy body, with thinnish arms and legs, and a slight stoop. He was fair-haired and blue-eyed, but that is not to say he was an example of nordic beauty. He was in his fifties, and his hair was thinning everywhere except on his upper lip, where it grew in a tough, straggling, fair moustache. He had to blow the whiskers of his moustache away from his mouth in order to speak. His eyes were sharp and clever, and he wore steel-framed spectacles. And he had one of the loudest booming voices I have ever heard.

It was the way his head came up out of his collar, and the way his moustache fell back from his greenish, ill-fitting, false teeth, that gave him the vigorous tusky look of a sealion. I could imagine such a head emerging from the surface of icy waters to blow and boom at other sealions.

By temperament Bolshaw looked solid and conventional. He was arrogant, lazy, more or less goodnatured, statesman-like, and given to confident disapproval of others. Bolshaw disapproved of me, with enormous confidence: he disapproved of the headmaster with equal confidence. The headmaster was conventional but possessed not a scrap of natural authority. I was solid enough but wilfully showed no signs of decorum.

On the whole, Bolshaw and I did not dislike each other. Had we not been members of the same profession I doubt if we should have quarrelled at all. Bolshaw merely wanted me to behave like a schoolmaster. He wanted me to conform. You may ask, who was he to demand conformity? The answer is, Bolshaw.

Bolshaw had natural authority and he exerted it. He entered the class-room in a solemn, dignified, lordly manner. He was, I repeat, a solid and conventional schoolmaster. On the other hand I am forced to record that he never taught the boys anything.

I bore Bolshaw very little ill-will. I was always interested in his devices for avoiding work, and enthralled by the tone of high moral confidence in which he referred to them. Also I appreciated his sense of humour: he made harsh, booming jokes. It was a pity he was trying to have me sacked.

As I passed through Bolshaw's room I tried to evade him, though nothing pleased him more, when he was supposed to be teaching a form, than to gossip with me. On this occasion I failed. He had adopted the schoolmaster's legal standby for keeping the pupils occupied – a test. He looked up at me as I passed, with his steel spectacles gleaming and his yellow moustache revealing a tusky grin.

I glanced at his list of questions on the blackboard, and then at the form, which was composed of louts. Bolshaw strolled across my path.

'I always think,' he began – it was one of his favourite beginnings, especially for a statement of egregious arrogance – in a loud, confident undertone that carried to the other end of the laboratory, 'that I'm the only person who knows the answers to my own questions.'

There was a pause.

'Have you heard this morning's news?' Bolshaw said.

I was a little surprised. At first I thought he must mean Hitler's latest move, but as we disagreed over politics we did not pretend to discuss such things. Bolshaw approved of Hitler in so much as he approved the principle of the Führer's function while feeling that he could fulfil it better himself.

'Simms is away again.'

I looked at him with interest. Simms was the senior master of all the science departments; physics, chemistry, mathematics and biology: as such he was paid more money. Bolshaw, though he spoke as if he were headmaster of the school, was only senior physics master. Simms was a kindly, sensitive, unaggressive old man who suffered from asthma. Bolshaw was waiting for him to retire.

'I told the headmaster only last week,' said Bolshaw, 'that Simms is a sick man.'

I smiled to myself at the phrase. If your friend is ill, you say, 'So-and-so's down with asthma.' 'So-and-so's a sick man' is the phrase reserved for someone you hope will be eliminated to the material improvement of your own prospects: it has a lofty, disinterested sound.

Bolshaw was a power-loving man. Getting Simms's job meant a great deal to him. It meant something to me too; since I argued that if he got Simms's it would be difficult to prevent me getting his,

30

Bolshaw's, job – which also carried more pay. This was only the beginning of my argument. Bolshaw was not only strong: he was wily and circuitous. And he was in a position to make the running. Up to date I had held my own, by at least keeping my job – but this, I reflected, might not be due as much to my own moral strength and manœuvring power as to the headmaster's utter supineness.

'My wife and I went out to see him yesterday. I thought he was a very sick man.' He spoke with the solemn grandeur of his knowledge. 'I'm afraid he doesn't believe in his own recovery.'

I said I thought Simms would recover. 'Asthma's really a defensive complaint. The poor old man's asthma keeps him out of the hurly-burly for a while. It may be . . .'

'I always think,' interrupted Bolshaw, raising his voice by several decibels, 'the most important thing is that a man should believe in himself. It encourages the others.'

I had heard enough. 'Do you believe in that boy over there?' I said, pointing to a boy who was blatantly copying from his textbook.

The form heard what I said, and there was a sudden stillness. As Bolshaw turned to look, I made for the door.

In a few minutes I returned, and to my surprise Bolshaw did not attempt to waylay me again. I was suspicious.

I sat down in my own room and said:

'What's Bolshaw been up to?'

Frank said: 'He came in to see if he could catch us playing the fool. He threatened Benny.'

'What was Benny doing?' Benny was always playing the fool.

'Nothing, sir!' Benny put on a look of ludicrous innocence.

'Benny wasn't,' said Frank. 'Roley only said he was so as to criticize you.'

'Nonsense,' said Trevor malevolently. 'Roley enjoys threatening.' He giggled.

I began to read.

After an hour or so I noticed that the sun was shining quite brightly. I stood up and stretched my limbs. I thought how much less cramped I should feel if I were sauntering over the fields with Myrtle. I threw my book down on the bench and leaned against the wall. Fred and Benny were counting with concentration; Frank was looking down the travelling-microscope; Trevor was filing his nails. A neighbouring church clock began to chime. Something inside me was chafing, and I said aloud:

'*Que je m'ennuie!*'

There was a pause.

'Why don't you go out?' said Trevor.

'Go and have a cup of coffee,' said Frank. 'We shall be all right.'

''E can telephone somebody,' said Fred suggestively.

I shook my head. 'It means another encounter with Bolshaw.'

'Go through the window,' said Benny. 'Roley won't know you've gone.'

One of the panes of the window at the end of the room could be opened. If I climbed over the bench I could just squeeze through and drop into the street. I had tried it before.

Benny had already climbed on to the bench and was eagerly holding the window for me.

'We'll promise to help you in again,' he said.

I did not trust him not to play tricks that would bring in Bolshaw and reveal my absence. It was tempting fate; but I decided to risk it.

A moment later I was walking outside in the cold sparkling sunshine. It made a pleasant relief to a morning in school.

4

Two Provincial Ménages

Tom's boy was named Steve, and he was aged seventeen. I suggest that anyone who is in the act of picking up a stone to cast at Tom, should change his target and cast at Steve instead. Many a man, were the truth but known, would find himself in as weak a moral position as Tom: on the other hand any man whatsoever might count on being in a stronger moral position than Steve. Steve had practically no moral position at all.

Steve was tall and gauche and precocious. He was pleasant-looking, with a shock of soft dark hair that kept falling over his eyes, and a wide red-lipped mouth. There was nothing particularly effeminate about him. He hunched his shoulders shrinkingly and wore a faintly rueful smile, as indications of his delicate nature: there was not the slightest need for either, since physically he was well-formed and temperamentally as self-centred as anyone I have ever known.

As with Tom, it was Steve's idea of himself that guided his actions. He saw himself as hyper-sensitive and artistic, in need of protection, help and support. Much happiness and satisfaction was created by Tom's seeing him in the same way. It was Tom's role to give Steve protection, help and support. Their relationship was that of patron and protégé.

I liked Steve. He wrote some poems that showed talent. As I felt that writing poems was a very proper occupation for the young I encouraged him. I subscribed to Somerset Maugham's theory, that creating variegated minor works of art is part of juvenile play: it seemed to me that the young might play at much worse things, such as rugby football which left them tired out with nothing to show for their pains.

Most of all I enjoyed Steve's company. Like most people of weak moral fibre he was thoroughly engaging. It is a sad reflection that everybody admires persons of strong moral fibre but nobody shows any inclination to stay with them for more than five minutes. We all agreed that it was fun to be with Steve for any length of time.

Though the relation between Tom and Steve was that of patron and protégé, I thought their behaviour was more like that of corporal and private. Tom was energetic and bustling: Steve was incorrigibly lazy. Much of their time together was spent in Tom's giving loud commands: 'Now Steve, do that!' and Steve's putting up, as befitted his station, a token show of obedience.

Steve appreciated readily the advisability of a protégé's retaining his patron; but where his token show of obedience required physical action he was usually careless and inept to say the least of it. This promptly led Tom to give him suitable instruction, to which Steve submitted uncomplainingly – far too uncomplainingly, in my opinion, as much of the information Tom saw fit to impart was grossly inaccurate. Fortunately Tom was satisfied by the act of imparting, and Steve neither knew nor cared about inaccuracy.

Tom was very serious about his devotion to Steve. It was Myrtle and I who had conceived the idea of renting a country cottage, and Myrtle who had found it: it did not take Tom long to see that Steve's devotion to him would be increased if he were able to entertain him over the weekends in the country.

Furthermore Steve sighed with relief when Tom bought a car. Steve did not own a bicycle, and when Tom offered to lend him one there was some doubt about whether Steve could ride it without falling off every few yards. In the end Steve got more than he bargained for, because Tom was a wild and impulsive driver – he had excellent eyesight but he did not appear to use it. Steve, like all the rest of us, was terrified. 'It does him good to be thoroughly frightened now and then,' Tom confided to me, with a meaningful smile. Tom's devotion was very great, but it did not entirely eclipse his shrewdness.

When Tom was arranging to entertain Steve for a weekend at the cottage, it was his habit to indicate that he, like Myrtle and unlike me, went by atmosphere. There is a very simple difference between going by atmosphere and going by plan. If you go by atmosphere you spend week-ends at a cottage when you feel like it – which is every week-end. When I insisted on taking my turn Tom denounced me as cold, methodical and machine-like.

There were additional complications. Tom did not mind my being present when he was entertaining Steve; the last thing I wanted was his presence when I was entertaining Myrtle. And more troublesome still was the fact that I was supposed to conceal Steve's visits from Myrtle – looking back on it, I cannot for the life of me see why. Myrtle would certainly not have been shocked or disapproving. Women take such matters much less seriously than men: they sometimes express passing displeasure at the thought of two men being out of commission as far as they are concerned, but that is all there is to it. I did not think: I acted with cold, methodical, machine-like loyalty to Tom. The result was farce.

The existences of Tom and Steve were enlivened by frequent scenes of passion and high emotion. Mostly it was beyond my powers to fathom what they were about. I really thought Tom invented them. He reproached me with not having scenes with Myrtle.

'I must say I find it slightly . . .' he paused, 'surprising.'

'Indeed,' I said, crossly.

Tom gave a distant, knowing smile, as truths about passion crossed his mind that were beyond my comprehension. I could see that he thought scenes were absent from my life with Myrtle because of serious deficiencies in my temperament, if not actually in my powers as a lover.

Anyway, scenes were constantly present between Tom and Steve, and since Steve was too lazy and conceited to initiate anything they must have originated with Tom. There was one in progress, goodness knows why, over Steve's career.

Steve had left school the previous summer and had been articled to Tom's firm of accountants. It was in the office that they first met. By the spring Steve's helpless and sensitive nature had found its fulfilment in Tom's masterful capacity for support. Steve decided he was not cut out to be an accountant. Trouble promptly broke forth.

Steve's parents had very modest resources, and had been forced to borrow money to pay his premium. Tom, partly because he wanted Steve to be kept in his office, and partly out of sheer common sense, told Steve he would have to stay where he was. Steve began to suffer.

'Think of it, Joe,' Steve said to me. 'Five years as an articled clerk!' His pleasant face contorted with an expression of agony. 'It will be like prison.' He paused, as a worse thought struck him. 'Only *duller.*'

I could not help smiling.

Steve's expression of agony deepened. 'You don't understand, Joe. I can't do *arithmetic.*'

I shook my head.

'I never could,' he said. 'Think of becoming an accountant if you can't do arithmetic.' He glanced at me sharply, to enjoy my amusement. Suddenly the agonized look disappeared, his narrow grey eyes sparkled with hard realism, and his tone altered completely. 'I can tell you it's terribly hard work, too.'

When Steve dropped his nonsense and came out with the truth he was at his most engaging.

I thought it was time to bait him a little. I said: 'Tom will teach you arithmetic. He likes teaching.'

'I don't want to learn arithmetic.'

'What do you want to learn, Steve?'

'I want to learn about love, Joe. Everyone does.'

'I should have thought you were doing quite nicely.'

'I'm not, Joe,' Steve said with force. 'I'm not!'

I shrugged my shoulders. 'You'll be a poet some day.'

'I'll never be an accountant. I never wanted to be. It's my parents' fault.' Steve looked at me. 'They chose accountancy because it's *respectable.*'

'In that case they made a singular choice,' I observed.

Steve grinned with satisfaction.

I surmised that Tom's conversations with Steve on the same theme had a different tone and went on much longer. Tom took Steve seriously, for one thing, and was easily roused to rage, for another. They had passionate quarrels over whether Steve could do arithmetic.

The upsurge of a quarrel led to an atmosphere of emergency in which previous arrangements about who should go to the cottage were swept aside, that is, if it were my turn. Tom rang me up early on Saturday morning, just as I was about to leave my lodgings.

'Are you having Myrtle out tomorrow?'

I said I was.

'In that case I think we'll come out today. Naturally we'll leave before Myrtle arrives tomorrow.' Tom paused diffidently. 'Steve wants us to come.'

I was annoyed. The only thing Steve wanted was physical comfort and unlimited admiration. On the other hand Tom had special claims because it was only a matter of months before he went to America.

A few minutes later Myrtle rang up.

'Darling, can I come out to see you this afternoon?'

Nothing would have pleased me more, but it was too late to stop Tom. I could not let Myrtle come, because I had told her I was going to be alone, writing.

'I was going to come into town to see you, darling,' I said, resourcefully. 'I thought we might go to a cinema.'

'But darling! . . .' Myrtle's voice broke off in surprise – as well it might, since the day was exquisitely sunny, I was in excellent health, and none of the cinemas sported a film that anybody in his right mind could want to see. I decided to banish Tom and Steve from the cottage immediately after lunch.

At lunch Tom displayed irritation that I had not put Myrtle off.

'What time will she be leaving tonight?'

'About ten o'clock.'

We ate our lunch in a state of tension, which increased on my part as Tom showed no signs of hurrying when the time approached for Myrtle to appear. Tom and Steve were quarrelling because Steve had surreptitiously eaten an apple before lunch and would not admit it.

'There were eight in the bowl before lunch and now there are only seven!' Tom was saying furiously. 'Neither Joe nor I ate it.'

Steve looked sulky and tortured. He was still growing quite fast and he was always hungry. Nobody objected to his eating anything, but he did it secretly and denied it afterwards. Food was always disappearing mysteriously when Steve was about.

'Myrtle will be here any moment,' I said, on tenterhooks.

I should like to point out that I thought none of this scene was in the least funny.

Tom looked at me, disgusted with my incapacity for understanding the overwhelming importance of conflict.

A bicycle bell rang joyously in the lane, and in came Myrtle.

Tom swept forward and greeted her effusively. He presented Steve to her. And then he said:

'How nice you're looking, Myrtle.'

She did look nice. She gave Tom a bright-eyed, smirking look. The smell of her scent caught in my nostrils. I could readily have taken a carving-knife to both Tom and Steve.

'Now what Myrtle would like,' said Tom, 'is a nice cup of tea.'

'I'm dying for one,' said Myrtle, in an expiring voice.

'Of course you are, my dear.' He paused. 'I understand these things.'

Myrtle played up to him shamelessly. 'I know, Tom.'

Tom's face wreathed itself in a silky smile.

Tom's stock method of making an impression on anyone was to indicate that he understood them perfectly. In this strain he was setting to work on Myrtle.

'Now Steve,' he said, 'put the kettle on!'

Steve shambled into the scullery, and reappeared in a moment looking tragic.

'The primus is broken.'

I pushed him out of the way. The primus was not broken: he had never tried. When I returned with the tea Tom and Myrtle were in full flood of the most inane conversation I could imagine.

'I love dogs,' Myrtle was saying, in a soulful tone.

'So do I,' said Tom, copying it ridiculously.

'I wish I had three.'

'One can't have too many.'

'Red setters,' said Myrtle. 'Don't you love red setters?'

'Wonderful,' said Tom.

'And their eyes!' said Myrtle.

'So sad!' said Tom.

'I know.'

'Just like us, Myrtle.' He gave her a long look.

Myrtle sighed.

Steve and I caught each other's eye, and I signalled him to help me hand round the cups. There was no place for us in the conversation.

At last Tom decided to take himself off. He made signs at me behind Myrtle's back. 'Ten o'clock!'

Myrtle and I stood in the doorway and watched his car disappear round the bend in the road. Big white clouds went floating across the sun. The hedgerows were leafless and glistening – I watched a twittering troop of little birds which every so often took it into their heads to move on a few yards. I did not speak to Myrtle.

'What's the matter, darling?' Myrtle said, innocently.

'Nothing.'

'Is anything wrong?'

'Nothing at all.'

She put her arm round me, but I would not speak. Her body leaned softly against mine. She began to caress me: I decided to sulk a bit longer. I tried harder and harder to go on sulking. Suddenly I turned to her. She looked beautiful.

'I love you,' I whispered into her ear, and bit the lobe of it.

'Darling!' She struggled away from me.

39

We looked into each other's eyes.

'You didn't mean this afternoon as well, did you, darling?' she said, in a shocked reproachful tone.

'You know perfectly well, I did,' I said, and bit her again.

Instantly Myrtle looked away, and I knew that I had made a mistake. I was being found lacking in romance. I held her close to me. 'Poor Myrtle,' I thought; 'and poor me as well'. I went on holding her close to me till I ceased to be found lacking in romance.

Saturday afternoon passed like a dream – in fact much more satisfactorily than any dream I have ever had. Men can say what they like about dreams. Better awake, is my motto.

We were happy, we were harmonious, we were ravenously hungry. The dusk fell and we cooked a meal. By daylight you could see that the cottage was filled with everybody's cast-off pieces of furniture. At night, by the light of candles and the fire, it was transformed. We lingered over our eating: we lingered over each other. And the clock moved round to ten.

Myrtle showed no signs of going. I ceased to linger over her: she did not cease to linger over me. I had promised to get her away by ten, and it was useless to pretend I had not. Myrtle began to look at me reproachfully. I now suspected her of planning to stay the night; and realized that in a simple way she had broken me down to the idea. She put her arms round my neck. We were one: I would have given anything for her to stay the night with me, sleeping peacefully together. Like husband and wife.

Tom's car drove up, and Tom came in. He saw Myrtle. His face was distorted with anger and passion.

'What, Myrtle!' he said. 'Are you still here?'

Myrtle, not unnaturally, looked surprised and hurt. His tone was very different from that in which he had unctuously explored their identity of tastes earlier on.

'We were just going,' I said.

'That's right.' Tom relaxed a little, and smiled at Myrtle. 'And take Joe with you!'

I stood on my dignity. 'I always take her as far as the main road.'

Myrtle and I stepped out into the night, and picked up our bicycles. There was no sign of Steve in the car. Tom must have left him under a hedge.

We cycled down the lane. It was calm and starless.

'What was the matter with Tom?' She sounded miserable.

'I don't know.'

'He seemed strange.'

I did not speak. This was unfortunate as it enabled Myrtle to hear Tom start up his car and drive away in the opposite direction.

'Where's Tom gone?' she asked.

'Goodness knows,' I said.

I felt furious. Suddenly I felt cold as well. I had forgotten to put on a top coat. There was nothing to do but go back for it. I told Myrtle to wait where she was and pedalled hastily away.

I returned to meet Myrtle wheeling her bicycle towards me, with no light showing.

'The dynamo's broken,' she said, with deep pathos.

I think she thought she was going back for the night now that Tom had gone.

'You must take my spare lamp,' I said. 'You must!' We were nearly at the cottage again.

We heard Tom's car coming back.

'Tom's car's coming back,' said Myrtle, in a voice that had reached its peak of astonishment and could go no further.

I waved my lamp wildly to warn Tom.

The car drew up. Only Tom got out. I presumed that Steve must now be under the seat.

Tom rudely persuaded Myrtle to take my lamp, and we set off again.

We did not speak very much until we came to the main road. There we paused and embraced. Myrtle leaned against me passively, and I tried to revive her.

'Darling,' I said.

There was a long silence.

'You want to get rid of me.'

It was too much for me. I wished Tom were in America and I was not far from wishing he were removed from this world altogether. We stood in the middle of the road, our bicycles ledged in the small of our backs, weeping on each other's cheeks.

'Darling, I do love you,' I said, wondering why on earth we were not married to each other.

I held her face between my hands: it was so dark that I could barely see it.

'Please come to me tomorrow afternoon.'

Myrtle did not speak. A tear rolled on to my thumb.

'Promise, promise!'

Myrtle nodded her head.

I resolved that Tom should be got rid of next morning, if it meant dissolving our friendship for ever. When she came in the afternoon everything should be as if this night had never happened.

I took out my handkerchief and dried her face. In a little while we parted. Then I rode slowly through the empty lanes.

You may wonder why I put up with all this nonsense, why I did not break my word to Tom and tell Myrtle what was going on. There were two reasons. The first I am so ashamed of that I can barely bring myself to write it, but I shall have to write it in order to explain some of the later events: it is this – realizing that I was not a good man, I was trying to behave like one; and to me that meant being patient, forbearing and trustworthy to the last degree.

The second reason is this – frankly, I had no sense.

A Party of Refugees

I advised Tom to emigrate to America as soon as possible. International events gave me a strong explicit foundation for my advice. From time to time we met for tea in the café and counted the growing roll of disasters.

'A fortnight since Hitler took Memel, and the British Government has done *nothing*!' said Tom.

'Nothing,' I echoed.

Alternately we received gloomy letters from Robert, which we read to each other. 'If there isn't a war by September we shall be refugees by November.' I noticed the date had slipped on a month, but did not point it out to Tom. I thought there was every reason why he should move without delay.

As the afternoons lengthened, we were leaving the window before the lights came on in the market-place. Easter was approaching: blue fumes of coffee mingled with the spring dust that circulated in the wind. The twilight glimmered on hosts of flowers, on waxen Dutch tulips in exquisite shades. Some of the shoppers had discarded their top coats. The weeks were passing: we could feel it, with nostalgia for the summer and apprehension for our fate.

Tom had a newspaper spread before him.

'Chamberlain Pledges Defence of Poland,' he read aloud. 'Balderdash! Poppycock!' Excepting the glare of his greenish eyes, his head began to look red all over. 'We shall give Poland away just like the rest. We shall see Chamberlain fly to Berlin in a golden aeroplane, accompanied by Peace in the shape of a dove.'

I smiled faintly and Tom blinked.

'Why is it always a dove?' he asked me. 'The *horse* of peace would be better. Doves are stupid, back-biting creatures, but horses are noble and intelligent.' He thumped his fist on the table. 'I can't stomach doves!'

The atmosphere lightened momentarily. Tom had the power of being able to hearten me. There was a good robust sense of life in him that made one's troubles seem smaller – one's own troubles, that is: it made his seem larger, absurdly larger.

We began to talk about writing. Tom was not working on a new novel, because of the prospect of his being uprooted. He declared that he was too busy, making preparations, to write: I agreed from observation that he was too busy – he was too busy pursuing Steve. I, on the other hand, had been brought to a stand-still by Miss X.Y. She had still not written to me.

'I think you ought to write to her,' said Tom, always counselling action.

I shook my head. I already had some experience of reading unpublished manuscripts, and knew how maddening it was to be prodded by an impatient potential novelist.

Tom shrugged his shoulders, and then began to console me.

'She's bound to like it,' he said. 'She liked your first, and this is so very much better.' He spoke with great authority. His tone reminded me of Robert, whom we both copied when we spoke with author-ity. 'You're one of the most gifted writers of our generation.'

I did not reply. I was making a feeble effort to discount some of Tom's exaggeration – about five per cent of it.

'She may have sent it to her own publisher,' Tom said. 'I would, in her place.'

I believed him. When he was not in the grip of one of his passions, Tom could be most sympathetic. He was capable of unconsidered acts of kindness. He could be momentarily free from envy and jealousy. It was for this that I valued his friendship. It is characteristic of our own egoism, that we value others for their selflessness.

'It's a remarkable novel.'

I did not speak. I found myself contrasting Tom's attitude with

Myrtle's. Whenever we met, Tom asked me first of all if I had heard from Miss X.Y. Whenever I met Myrtle she failed to speak of it unless I raised the subject myself. I had given her the manuscript to read, and I strongly suspected that she had not read it all – my fourth novel, a class better than the other three, forty thousand words longer and nowhere near as funny. For Myrtle not to have read it all seemed to me next door to perfidy.

'How,' I asked myself, 'can Myrtle love me and not want to read my books? How can a woman separate the artist from the man?'

The answer came pat. Women not only can: they do. And they have a simple old-fashioned way of selecting the bit they prefer. At the same time I have to admit that if Myrtle had made the other choice I should have accused her of not loving me for myself. Men want it both ways and I am surprised that women do not make a little more pretence of giving it – especially when they want to marry the men in question.

'What are you thinking about?' said Tom.

'Meditating on incompatibility. On the utter incompatibility of two people who want different things and can't accept compromise.'

Tom's mouth curved knowingly. 'Have you made up your mind if you want Myrtle to go with you to America or not?'

I stared at him. I had not, of course. And I did not like the question.

Tom began to smile. He made a smooth gesture with his hands. He said: 'My dear Joe, there's no need . . .'

'If she likes to go under her own steam,' I said, 'I see no reason why she shouldn't.' I paused. 'She can support herself.'

I made the latter remark with emphasis. Tom had been getting at me: this was my way of getting at him. I meant that our party should not include Steve.

Tom said equably: 'It sounds perfectly sensible.'

'I'm a sensible man,' said I.

'Have you told her definitely that you're going?'

'Not in so many words.' I liked this question even less than the earlier one.

Tom shrugged his shoulders. He began to read the newspaper.

I began to think what I was going to do about Myrtle, which brings me to the point where I must complete my description of her.

Myrtle was very feminine, and I have described up to date those of her traits which everyone recognizes as essentially feminine. She was modest, she was submissive, she was sly; she was earthy in its most beautiful sense.

In addition to all this, Myrtle was shrewd, she was persistent, and she was determined. At the time I thought she was too young to know what she wanted. Looking back on it I can only reel at the thought of my own absence of insight and capacity for self-deception. She knew what she wanted all right: it is just possible that she was too young to know exactly how to get it.

Myrtle was a commercial artist, employed by a prosperous advertising agency in the town. In my opinion, based on her salary, she was doing well. This much at least I could see. At a hint of the intellectual Myrtle's eyes opened in wonderment, at a hint of the salacious she blushed; and at a hint of business she was thoroughly on the alert.

Myrtle had been trained at the local School of Art. She had talent of a modest order – that is, it was greater than she pretended. Her drawings were quick, lively, observant without being reflective, pretty and quite perceptibly original. I, with her talent, would have been trying to paint like Dufy or somebody: not so, Myrtle. There was no masculine aspiring about her. Trying to paint like Dufy with her talent I should have been a masculine failure. Myrtle with feminine modesty and innocence took to commercial art.

Myrtle's talent was not of the primary creative order that sometimes alarms the public: it was the secondary talent for giving a piquant twist to what is already accepted. She was made for the world of advertising. And she accepted her station in life as an artist as readily as she accepted her salary. My efforts to encourage her to rise above this station, which would have brought her little but misery, fortunately made no impression upon her whatsoever.

In her business dealings Myrtle showed the same flair. It was one of her gifts to accept quite readily men's weaknesses. She was tolerant and down-to-earth about them: she fought against them much less than many a man does.

Myrtle's employer was a middle-aged man who had introduced his mistress into a comparatively important position in the firm – to the envy and disapprobation of everyone but Myrtle. Myrtle accepted that such things were likely to happen, made the best of it, and showed good-natured interest in the other girl. In due course Myrtle found, to her genuine surprise, that the boss began to show much greater appreciation of her work.

So you see that Myrtle was by no means a poor, helpless girl who had fallen into the clutches of an unscrupulous, lust-ridden man. I may say that I saw it, plainly, while I sat in the café with Tom reading his doom-struck newspaper. I was behaving like a cad – admitted. But anyone who thinks behaving like a cad was easy is wrong.

As a result of Tom's pressing me I made a definite plan. It was to include Myrtle in our party of refugees without marrying her.

I was convinced that Myrtle could earn a living in America. If only I could convince *her*! If only I could persuade her to *act* on the conviction! Then there was no reason why our relationship should not go on just as it was.

That was how I came to my plan. It was only too easy for Tom to say afterwards that I never intended to carry it out, that if Myrtle had agreed I should have been something between alarmed and appalled. I at least half-believed it. As a love affair declines one can still go on making plans for a future that does not exist. And that is what I was doing. For, alas! make no mistake, our relationship really was declining.

There is a kind of inevitability about the course of growing love: so there is about its decay. It comes from time flowing along. You can shut your eyes and pretend that you are staying still – and all the while you are just being carried along with your eyes shut. You can make plans – but if they do not fit in with the flow of time,

47

you might just as well save yourself the trouble. So with Myrtle and me. Wanting something different and being unable in our hearts to compromise we were being carried along towards final separation. We appeared to be doing things of our own volition: we had our breaks and our reconciliations. Round and round we went, spinning together like planets round the sun. May I remind you that even the solar system is running down?

To begin with I thought I had had a stroke of luck. Myrtle rang me up to tell me that she had been promoted to a better job in the firm. In the evening she came round to my lodgings for us to drink a bottle of beer to her success. 'Now,' I said to myself, 'now is the time!'

My landlady was clearing away the remains of my supper, when Myrtle sauntered into the room with an alluring whiff of cosmetics. The landlady retired promptly. Myrtle stared at me with a meek smirk of triumph. I kissed her. I wanted to know exactly what difference promotion made to her salary.

When questioned on matters of money, Myrtle always became quite unusually vague and elusive. I asked my questions, and somehow found myself listening to an elaborate account of intrigues in the firm, and adventures of Myrtle's employer and his mistress.

When the turn ended I quietly returned to my aim. Myrtle's face was still lit up with the pleasure of entertaining me. Instead of asking my questions all over again crudely, I led up to them by another spell of enthusiastic congratulation.

Something happened. Myrtle looked at me suddenly with a different expression.

Insensitively I forged ahead.

'It really is wonderful!' I said.

After remaining silent, Myrtle spoke in a hollow voice. Into her words she put sadness and reproach.

'It isn't *really*.'

'But it is!' I insisted. 'It proves you'll be able to get a job anywhere.'

Myrtle said nothing. She stood up and walked slowly across to the window. She stared out.

I was disturbed, but determination had got the better of me. I followed her, and stood beside her. I lived in the back room of a small semi-detached house. We were looking through a french window at a narrow strip of garden that sloped down to the garden of another semi-detached house in the next road. It was dusk.

I patted her. 'The more money you earn, my girl, the better.'

'Why?'

'Because you're an artist,' I said encouragingly. 'And Art must pay.' I kissed her cheek. 'We're two artists,' I said.

Myrtle did not speak. Being two artists is one thing; being husband and wife another, quite different. Then suddenly she turned on me and said with force:

'You *know* that I don't care.'

I looked down. Sad words, they were, falling upon my ear. When a woman tells a man she does not care about her career he ought to make for the door. It means one thing – the end of liberty for him.

I did not make for the door. I was overwhelmed by tenderness and I embraced her. It was no use making for the door because I still had to broach the subject of her taking a job in America.

I broached it. And it was a failure.

I suppose I was being singularly insensitive and obtuse, but I do not know what else I was to do. I thought: 'How strange – she doesn't realize that if she sticks to her career she can follow me to America.' And I will not swear that I did not think: 'And in America she might even succeed in marrying me.'

Alas! the flow of time asserted itself. I made matters worse.

'The world's going to be in a chaotic state,' I said. 'We shall all do best if we can fend for ourselves.'

Myrtle showed no sign of following me. The last thing she wanted to do was to think of fending for herself in a chaotic world. She was powerless to stand outside her personal affairs of the moment.

'I'm sure you could get a job in America.'

'Whatever for?'

'If we all decide to go.'

'Oh, that!' Myrtle moved away from me, as if the idea were tedious and repugnant and unreal.

I realized that I had not the courage to tell her that we were definitely going to America. I thought: 'I must tell her. I must!' And I said:

'I'm sure you'd be a great success in America.'

Myrtle tilted her head back to look at me. Her eyes were round and golden and unbearably appealing. I took her into my arms. You can see that I am both obtuse and a failure as a man.

The conversation went on a little further. I could hardly have been more inept, so I will not record it. I was direct, and for anyone as evasive and suggestible as Myrtle, directness was positively painful. My efforts to discover whether Myrtle's firm had American customers led us nowhere. She replied to my questions in an abstracted tone. I was tormenting her, and that was literally all. We were both completely trapped in our own worlds, quite separate, quite cut off.

At last the conversation dwindled into nothing. I thought Myrtle suffered from a low vitality of interest. I suggested that we should go to the cinema.

Immediately Myrtle perked up. Low vitality of interest, laziness, instinctive self-preservation – which was it? I do not know. We went to the cinema.

That was what became of part one in my plan. I moved to part two. Robert was coming to visit his friends in the town. I asked him to lunch at the cottage on Sunday and invited Myrtle. Tom was out of the way: he was supposed to be taking Steve up to London to see *The Seagull*. I hoped that when Robert saw Myrtle without any distraction, he would deem her worthy to join our party of refugees.

I was anxious. Up to the present Robert had deemed Myrtle distinctly unworthy. On having her presented to him he had commented that his remarks appeared to bounce off her forehead. I was willing to admit that Myrtle had an uncogitating, unreflective air; but Robert's comment seemed to me both unkind and untrue. Being Robert's comment, it had to be accepted all the same. I was hurt. Myrtle and I may have been quite separate, quite cut off, and all the rest of it: but when Robert said his remarks bounced off her forehead, she was my mistress, my love, my choice and part of me.

I had difficulty in persuading Myrtle to come to the cottage at all while Robert was there.

'You won't want me,' she said. I think she would rather I assumed she was jealous of my friendship for Robert than that she was frightened of him.

Myrtle was abashed by the idea of Robert's being an Oxford don, which she associated, wrongly, not with intellectual but with social superiority. In the society of people she considered her social superiors, Myrtle was thoroughly ill at ease: she was only really completely free with her social inferiors. Robert saw her at her worst.

'Of course I want you, darling,' I said. And encouragingly: 'Robert will want to see you.'

Myrtle stared at me in disbelief. And I thought fate had been hard on me in sending a woman who could not meet my friends.

Nevertheless Myrtle arrived at the cottage bright and smiling on Sunday morning.

'I passed Robert. He's walking.' She glanced at me slyly. 'I told him I couldn't stop because you were waiting for me.'

I felt more cheerful. Robert came. We walked over to the Dog and Duck and had a most enjoyable lunch. Robert and I talked about literature. Myrtle was impressed. She drank an unduly large quantity of beer. Robert was impressed.

We walked home in good spirits, to find Tom in the cottage. He had driven back from London that morning. Robert greeted him affectionately, and so did Myrtle. I did not.

'I have a letter I wanted you and Joe to see.' Tom pulled the document out of his pocket and passed it round.

The letter was from one of the American professional associations of chartered accountants. Tom had been writing about jobs. I did not look at Myrtle. I had warned Robert not to tell Myrtle that our plans were already far advanced, but I had never dreamed that Tom would appear. He and Robert sat down and began openly to discuss our project.

If it had been possible for Myrtle to doubt our intention in the beginning, the possibility must have entirely disappeared in five minutes. I was too alarmed to say anything.

Tom had completed his five years of professional practice as an associate of the Institute of Chartered Accountants, and attached importance to being elected to fellowship. There had been a hitch because he had seen fit to quarrel with the senior partner of his firm; but he computed that the formalities would be complete by June. He proposed to leave England immediately afterwards.

The plan for me was to follow as soon as the summer school term ended. Robert had ordered himself to come last. Tom argued with Robert about cutting it fine. I watched Myrtle. I was more than surprised that Tom and Robert did not see the effect they were having on her. She was taking no part in the conversation, and it was plain that she was too wretched even to follow it properly.

They went on to argue about how Robert and I should earn our living, by writing or by teaching. Neither of us wanted to teach. Tom was slightly huffed and pointed out a paragraph in the *Sunday Times*, which we had already seen, about a slump in the book trade. 'One bookseller this week reports no sales whatever.'

Robert suggested that he and I might have to live on Tom to begin with: the whole talk had been high-spirited instead of grave, and now Robert induced an air of mischief and nonchalance. Myrtle looked as if she was going to burst into tears. She got up and went into the scullery.

I followed her, expecting to find her weeping. She was taking down cups and saucers.

'I thought I should like some tea,' she said, in a flat voice.

I stroked her hair. Suddenly she looked at me and I was accused of heartlessness and treachery. I turned away without speaking and went back to the others.

After tea Tom drove Robert away. Myrtle and I were left alone. I did not know how to look her in the face. There was nothing I could say. The damage was done. We cycled back into town without discussing it.

This was our last meeting before the Easter holidays. I arranged to ring up Myrtle as soon as I returned to the town. I told myself she might have got over the damage in the meantime. I was apprehensive.

Part Two

Up at the Games Field

During the holiday I received no letter from Myrtle. And when I returned to the town she had gone away. I telephoned each day till she came back: it was a Friday, and she agreed to meet me on the following afternoon. I was down for duty at the school games field, so she said she would join me there. It did not seem a good arrangement to me, but before I could persuade her to do something else, she rang off. Whatever had gone wrong was not repaired.

Saturday afternoon came; and with it, for the opening of the school cricket season, a spell of cold drizzly weather. Usually I enjoyed my tour of duty. The boys played cricket in a comparatively orderly fashion, and those who were watching the match came and talked to me in a tone designed to shock less than usual. The field was attractive. At the gates there was a nicely planned tram-terminus and modern public lavatory, but neither was visible from inside. On the left of the pitch there was a line of poplars and on the right of sycamores and oaks; and straight ahead the ground fell away to a view of the town, with gasometers shimmering through the smoky haze of middle distance.

I stood in my overcoat pitying the boys in their blazers and white flannels. In a feeble effort to compensate for deficiency of social *cachet*, the headmaster insisted on the boys wearing white flannels whenever they went to the field in the summer term. It was about the only rule they kept, and they looked surprisingly presentable as a consequence.

On a summer evening, with golden light slanting through the trees on active little white-clad figures, it was easy to catch again the romantic air of boyhood – that air which every man delights to remember, whether he has ever breathed it or not. There was everything present: the heart-touching mixture of repose and vigour, the small sounds of the game, the occasional voice, the clapping of a few hands, the calm and movement, the green glow of the ground. On a cold drizzly Saturday afternoon they were present, but, it seemed, to a lesser degree.

Keeping my eye open for Myrtle, I shook off boys who were inclined to come and converse, and stood alone near the sightboards.

'Ello, Joe!' My interest in the match was cut short by Fred who had sidled up without my noticing.

Fred's white flannels were spotless. The green of his blazer was echoed in the greyish colour of his skin. His hair was dripping with brilliantine.

'You're looking very spruce, Fred.'

Fred grinned foolishly. 'Mr Chamberlain's got me!'

For a moment I could not think what he meant. He was referring to the prospect of conscription. The crisis had reached the boys. It came to me as a shock.

'He's got us all,' said Fred.

'He's welcome to you,' said I.

Fred stood still. It seemed as if my remark made its impression gradually. In the end he sighed and drifted away.

I sat down on the sub-structure of the sightboards. For me the match might not have been going on: Myrtle was late.

The sky began to cloud over a little more, but the drizzle ceased. The first innings ended unexpectedly, and I noticed Frank coming round the boundary towards me.

'Do you mind if I come and talk to you?'

I glanced up at him without enthusiasm.

'I'm sorry to bother you.' He paused: there was something the matter.

As he had seen me often enough with Myrtle, I told him I was waiting for her.

Frank sat down beside me. 'I'll go away as soon as she comes.'

We were both silent.

Frank said: 'It's about Trevor.' He was apparently watching the match.

'Oh?'

'I wish you could use your influence over him a bit.'

'What for?'

'To make him pull himself together.'

'What's the matter with him?'

'He isn't doing any work, for one thing.'

'He never did do much.'

'He's doing none, now.'

'I suppose he'll go in for art.' I glanced at Frank, slightly amused.

'He's not doing any work at that, either.'

My interest began to stir. 'What *is* he doing?' I stopped looking across the pitch and looked steadily at Frank.

'He's going to stupid parties, night after night, and getting drunk.' Frank's voice grew louder. 'He's doing himself no good.'

I did not care very much whether Trevor was doing himself good or ill; nor was I seriously troubled by Frank's alarm. I do not know why I persisted with the conversation. Somehow I was drawn on.

'What parties?' I said.

Frank muttered something about the School of Art. Immediately I knew why I had been drawn on.

'Who goes to them?'

Frank suddenly glanced at me. 'I've only been to one . . .'

'But you must know. Hasn't Trevor told you?'

'I don't think you'd know them. They're not the sort of people you'd know.'

'Not any of them?' I could not make my voice sound unconcerned.

'I think Myrtle goes, as a matter of fact.'

Frank looked at me, diffidently. I said nothing. I remembered Tom's solemn warnings about what Myrtle did when I would not have her.

'Does Tom go to these parties?' I said.

'No. But I think that friend of his called Steve does.'

I have to admit that I felt a gleam of satisfaction.

'They're very bohemian parties,' said Frank.

'What does that mean?'

'They drink a lot of beer and lie on the floor.'

I said nothing.

Frank said: 'I hope you don't think I'm a prude. I suppose it's all rather silly.'

I said: 'Who invites Myrtle?'

'A journalist on one of the evening papers. Called Haxby, or something. They say he's in love with her.' Frank's voice warmed to me. 'I know he doesn't stand a chance.'

I turned a little. 'Look, Frank,' I said. 'I'll have a word with Trevor.' I felt that everyone was the worse for going to such parties. I would have liked to stop them all, forthwith.

'It won't be easy. He's very flattered at being invited.'

'I'm surprised he's so popular. I thought you and I were the only people who liked him.'

'He's allowed to take the family car and drive people home afterwards.'

'Don't worry, Frank.' I tried to make the remark sound conclusive. I wanted to get rid of him. I felt uneasy and alarmed. Bohemian parties. Haxby. Vistas opened before me, thoroughly unpleasing vistas. I was not thinking for a moment about Trevor.

Neither of us spoke. There was a cry from the field as the bowler and his mates appealed for l.b.w. It was disallowed. Frank glanced at his watch, and then gave his collar a stylish look by pulling the points against his chin.

I was too proud to look at my own watch. I glanced at the sky, which was brightening.

'I think this is the cue for my exit,' said Frank.

Myrtle had just come through the gates at the far end of the field. I went to meet her.

'What a dreadful day!' Myrtle's first remark seemed to set the tone for us completely. Her voice sounded hollow and distant. I kissed her on the cheek.

'Not as bad as all that. I'm glad to see you, darling.'

Myrtle glanced at me, and then looked away. Some woe appeared to be weighing her down, though she was clearly making a gallant effort to bear up. I noticed that she was wearing a new coat. It was made of black Persian lamb and suited her well. I commented upon it, and she drew it closely round her.

'I'm so cold.'

I suggested that we should stroll a little. After all, what better way is there of getting warm than exercise? Myrtle gave me a look to indicate that my imagination was inconceivably earth-bound. We strolled, all the same.

I was disturbed. A month of separation had elapsed, but we were just in the same state as before. Our first meeting for a month – how I had been looking forward to it! Myrtle was displeased with me. Absence had not lived up to its reputation.

Myrtle's presence beside me raised my spirits a little. In spite of her displeasure, her cheeks glowed prettily and her eyes were bright. I began to try and raise her spirits, too. I began to think about plans for the evening.

Myrtle gave me a sudden flickering look. This time I sensed not so much reproach as will. She intended to do something.

'What's the matter?' I asked.

'Nothing.' Myrtle turned away.

I suppose I might have pressed her. Instead I glanced idly across the field. I saw Bolshaw coming towards us.

I was surprised. Bolshaw rarely showed any sign of being interested in doing games duty when it was his own turn, let alone mine.

'Do you want to meet Bolshaw?' I asked Myrtle.

'If you like.'

She was looking so elegant and attractive that I would have liked. It would have given me innocent pleasure to show her to Bolshaw. His wife was bossy rather than pretty.

Myrtle was undecided, I wavered, and Bolshaw went past us. Myrtle, in spite of herself, glanced at him with furtive interest.

'You'd be amused by him,' I said.

'Would I?' She now glanced at me with furtive interest.

Encouraged, I began to tell her about Bolshaw's most recent activities in the staff-room. I do not profess to be a mimic, but I did my best, saving my greatest efforts for a remark that had caught my fancy.

'When I look round me at my colleagues,' Bolshaw had said, 'I can always tell the married men.' Pause, while he looked round at his colleagues, most of whom actually were married. 'They have that *tamed* look!'

I can only repeat that the remark had caught my fancy. It did not catch Myrtle's. She did not say anything: she did not need to. In common language, the fat was in the fire.

I tried feebly to carry it off. I doubt if I should have redeemed myself if I had managed to achieve levitation. I did not achieve levitation.

Myrtle looked at her watch. She paused; and then she broke the news to me that she was not going to spend the evening with me.

I was astonished. I had sensed that she intended to do something, but not this.

'You didn't give me a chance to tell you,' she said.

'What are you going to do?'

'I've been invited to a party.'

I did not go on. I stared at Myrtle. Suddenly tears came into her eyes and disappeared again. I looked away, embarrassed and touched. I should have liked to put my arms round her. It was the moment to do it. But we were standing in the middle of the field with scores of boys watching.

Having broken the news to me, Myrtle seemed as if she could not bring herself to leave. I was certain that she did not really want to go to the party.

'Oh dear!' I sighed.

'What's the matter?' Myrtle was genuinely concerned.

'You've got to go.'

'Yes.' She dropped her head, and pulled her coat closely round her again.

Quietly I walked her to the gates. She hesitated.

'There's your tram,' I said.

Myrtle held out her hand and I took her fingers in mine. And then she went towards the tram. I watched it move clatteringly away. 'There goes sweetness and sadness,' I thought.

I speculated about the people, other than Haxby, who would be at the party. Saturday night – I did not doubt that it was one of the parties Trevor and Steve had started to go to. Frank had observed that they were not given by the sort of people I knew. That was true. Unhappily for me, the people who went to them got to know each other. Yet although I was jealous, I intended not to follow suit. I had several circles of friends in the town. This was a circle that I meant to keep out of. It was not my style.

Perhaps I ought to remind you that I had several circles of friends that were not necessarily shared by Myrtle and Tom. I had a circle of artistic friends made through my interest in writing: I had a circle of bourgeois friends made by letters of introduction from Robert: I had a couple of friends on the staff of the school: and in another town I had my family circle to which I was devoted. For the sake of describing myself completely, I should have to explore the lot. Let me give prompt assurance that I do not intend to do so.

Trollope discourses somewhere upon the difficulty that arises in novel-writing of disentangling men and women from their surroundings in order to isolate them as literary characters. A novel cannot contain everything. This novel is the story of Tom, Steve, Myrtle and me. In between us and the circles of friends I propose to leave out altogether, there are two people who played a part in our story whom I propose to leave half-in and half-out. Robert and Haxby.

Robert was a man of remarkable stature; to do him justice I should be inclined to give him the novel to himself, and that would make you feel he played a more important part than he actually did. On the other hand I never knew Haxby, so I cannot write about him: not being the kind of man who is impelled to establish intimate relations with his rival, I never tried to meet him. If you want to know more about Robert, ask me to write another novel: if you want to know more about Haxby, ask someone else.

Pondering on how little we can share of the sum of someone else's life, through not being present at the parties she goes to, for instance, I returned to my duty. I found Bolshaw walking in front of me again. This time he beckoned me.

'Come and have a chat with me,' he said.

We walked back to the pavilion. Bolshaw dislodged a row of small boys who were sitting on a bench in front of it. He ordered one of them to bring his attaché case out of the pavilion. I waited: I did not know what we were to talk about.

The afternoon had brightened a little. The cold breeze had dropped: the clouds had thinned and there was a glowing patch where the sun was. Many of the boys had gone home, and those who still played on moved in a tired, desolate fashion. Yet the growing light brought the green of the grass and trees to life again. The air was warmer.

Bolshaw opened his attaché case and pulled out a notebook and a sheaf of papers. He handed them to me.

'It's my research,' he said.

I was astonished. I had heard him mention his research, but I did not really believe in its existence. I had imagined him much too lazy.

I recovered from my astonishment while Bolshaw was explaining to me his problem. It was a piece of theoretical research in astrophysics. I can tell you that it was of practical importance to anyone interested in certain of the spiral nebulae.

'Of course, I don't expect you to understand it,' Bolshaw said.

I suppressed the desire to say: 'Then why are you showing it me?' Bolshaw was making a friendly gesture. I thought of his job. Even if I was leaving the school at the end of the term I wanted to be offered his job. Since the headmaster was likely to do what Bolshaw recommended, Bolshaw's friendly gesture had extraordinary, almost spiritual significance for me. 'What's the next move?' I asked myself.

'I can simplify it for you,' he went on.

I listened. He did simplify it. Whatever his failings, he had considerable intellectual power and acuity. He drew the skeleton of his work beautifully.

'And now,' he said, 'this is how I'm attacking it.'

I listened again. I did not understand it, of course. It was not in my line – a long way from it. Yet the principle of his attack was ingenious, and I grasped it just well enough to see that if it came off he could make an elegant coup. I admired. But listening and admiring were all very well – I did not know what he was leading up to.

'Now,' said Bolshaw, pointing with his pencil at the sheet of paper on which he had been writing down headings as he went along: 'Now, I may run into a bit of trouble here.'

'Trouble?' I looked closely at the paper, though I do not know how that could have helped me. 'A bit of trouble?' I said rashly. 'You mean a bit of hard work!'

Bolshaw's expression did not change by a flicker. 'Do you think so? Do you think you could see your way through it?'

I had been neatly trapped. I had meant what I said. He needed somebody to try out a number of tedious calculations. I could do nothing but nod my head.

'That's interesting.' Bolshaw spoke with weight, and then looked at me suddenly. 'Would you like to join me in this work?'

I could have kicked myself. 'I'd be delighted,' I said, and mumbled, 'Honoured.'

Bolshaw then said: 'Would you care to take the papers with you now?'

'Oh!' I stared at him with a pained expression, largely at the thought of having to do the work. 'I'm afraid I'm not free at the moment.' I saw what seemed a clever way of getting out of it. 'I'm just completing the manuscript of a book.'

Bolshaw looked at me.

'I've just received some extremely interesting suggestions from a distinguished critic,' I said, lying for the sake of verisimilitude. Of course Miss X.Y. had not returned the manuscript.

Bolshaw nodded his head understandingly. I wondered if I had done right.

Bolshaw put his papers away with equanimity. I felt a slight exhilaration.

I changed the subject. 'By the way,' I said, 'what's the news of Simms?'

'He's very sensibly taking my advice,' said Bolshaw. 'He's putting in his resignation.'

Instead of saying, 'You'll be getting his job; what about me?' I kept my glance firmly fixed on the case containing the work he wanted me to do, and said in a solemn tone:

'I think it's the wisest course. For everyone.'

Bolshaw suddenly said:

'I intend to think about your position.'

It sounded like a remark from one of God's first conversations with Adam. I looked forward to the consequences just as hopefully. I went home, pondering them.

And then I rang up Myrtle again. I was told that she had gone out to a party. I felt gloomy and spent the evening alone.

2

Not as Good as a Play

I bore Myrtle's new tactics with patience. The next time we spent an evening together there was no quarrel. To avoid it I took Myrtle to a cinema. We did not mention Haxby. On the other hand it was impossible to pretend that either of us was light-hearted. Myrtle's expression of unhappiness was deepening. Day by day I watched her sink into a bout of despair, and I concluded that it was my fault – had I not concluded that it was my fault, the looks Myrtle gave me would have rapidly concluded it for me.

The topic of conversation we avoided above all others was the project of going to America. Even a casual reference to Robert made Myrtle shy desperately. I cursed the tactlessness of Robert and Tom. I felt aggrieved, as one does after doing wrong and being discovered. I did not know what to do.

When you go to the theatre you see a number of characters caught in a dramatic situation. What happens next? They have a scene. From the scene springs action, such as somebody popping off a revolver. And then everything is changed.

My life is different. Sometimes observant friends point out to me that I am actually in a dramatic situation. What happens next? I do not have a scene; or if I do, it is small and discouragingly un-dramatic. Practically no action arises. And nothing whatsoever is changed. My life is not as good as a play. Nothing like it.

All I did with my present situation was try and tide it over. I quail at the thought of tiding-over as a dramatic activity. Anybody could have done better than me. You, no doubt, could have offered me a dozen suggestions, all of them, as they were designed for someone else to follow, setting a high moral standard.

When Myrtle emerged from the deepest blackness of despair – after all, nobody could remain there indefinitely – I tried to comfort her. I gradually unfolded all my plans, including those for her. It produced no effect. She began to drink more. She began to go to parties very frequently. It was very soon clear that she had decided to see less of me.

I did not blame Myrtle. Had I been in her place I would have tried to do the same thing. Being in my own place I tried to prevent her. I knew what sort of parties she was going to: they were parties at which Haxby was present.

We now began to wrangle over going out with each other. She was never free at the times I suggested. Sometimes, usually on a Saturday night, she first arranged to meet me and then changed her mind: I called that rubbing it in a little too far. Here is a specimen of our conversation upon such an occasion, beginning with an irascible contribution by me.

'Where *are* you going?'

'Nowhere, darling.'

'Then why can't you meet me?'

'Because I've got to stay at home.'

'What *for?*'

'Some people are coming round to listen to gramophone records.'

'Gramophone records!' I knew what that meant. Haxby and his friends listened to gramophone records for hours on end.

'It was the only night they could. I'm sorry, darling.' Myrtle paused, and then said in half-hearted reassurance: 'I *am* going to see you tomorrow.'

'But what am I going to do tonight?' Saturday night.

Myrtle reminded me that my circle of bourgeois friends had invited me to a dance. She advised me to go.

'I said I wouldn't go because you wouldn't go with me.' Myrtle did not dance.

'They don't like me.' Myrtle's voice came over the telephone like that of a soul in purgatory.

'You don't try with them,' I said, thinking, 'Why on earth can't she get on with my friends?'

There was a pause.

'You can come round to my place if you like.' Her voice trailed off.

'To listen to gramophone records!'

We had reached an impasse.

I decided to follow Myrtle's advice. As a matter of fact I greatly enjoyed dancing. I also enjoyed listening to gramophone records.

Myrtle's behaviour, I repeat, was perfectly sensible. By seeing less of me she stood a chance of finding somebody else, or of making me jealous, or of both. Either way she could not lose.

The impasse being reached, my behaviour became perfectly odious.

Myrtle said: 'I've just bought some records of the Emperor.'

'Good heavens! Where did you get the money from?'

'I earned it, darling.'

'I shouldn't have thought you could afford it.'

'I shall be broke for weeks.'

'What a prospect!' Some vestigial restraint prevented me from saying that I should have to pay for all her entertainments, which would have been quite false.

'Hadn't you got a record of the Emperor?'

'Yes, but this is a better one. I shall sell the old one.'

'Who to?'

'Somebody will buy it. A girl at the office.'

'Oh.'

I paused, seeking new fields for odiousness.

'What else are you going to play in the cause of culture?'

'I haven't thought.'

'Beethoven followed by Duke Ellington?' This was a hit at Haxby's friends who followed the high-brow cult of respectfully admiring jazz. Myrtle had told me.

'What's wrong with that, darling? I thought you liked the Duke?'

I said with rage: 'The Duke, indeed!'

Myrtle did not say anything. I had started off feeling righteous. Now my righteousness took control of me.

'I suppose,' I said, 'you've had to buy lashings of drink?'

'What makes you think that?'

'You don't appear to be able to take your culture without it.'

Myrtle actually laughed, or at least it sounded like it on the telephone. And it could only have been me she was laughing at.

'If you want to make yourself ill, I suppose you can,' I went on.

'I shan't drink it all, darling.'

'Other people will!'

'But if they drink it, I can't, darling.'

'I meant they'll make themselves ill.' My voice rose. 'At your expense!' I cannot think which appalled me more, the drunkenness or the cost of it.

'You're wrong,' said Myrtle.

'I'm not. After the last of these parties you looked like death, yourself.'

There was a long pause. Out of the silence I heard Myrtle simply say:

'I feel like death now.'

My righteousness was removed in a single twitch. I saw myself without it. I had nothing to say. The fact of the matter is that my righteousness and my odiousness were the same thing, and they were both something else. Plain jealousy.

On the following afternoon the weather had changed to something more nearly like what is expected of April. The sun was shining. I lay on the sofa in my lodgings, reading the *Observer* and wishing I were at the cottage. From where I was lying I could see some lilacs in the next-door garden: the buds were unopened, and they rocked gently in the breeze. I closed my eyes – it was after lunch and I was waiting for Myrtle.

I forgot that Sir Nevile Henderson had been to Berlin to explain British plans before Parliament heard them: I forgot that Myrtle had probably been drinking herself silly with Haxby and others till two in the morning. I imagined piles of chestnut flowers, some of them tinged with pinky-brown now the leaves were unfolded; and ash trees in the lane, rustling with handsful of silver-green feathers. Red campions in the ditches: white and yellow stars all over the meadows: the hedges and the animals and the birds.

I was awakened by the landlady's niece showing in Myrtle. I rolled back lazily. Myrtle looked ravishing. Her cheeks were lightly coloured and her eyes bright golden brown: from where I lay her long nose looked shorter. Over the back of the sofa I took hold of her hand, and drew her down to look into her face. She smiled at me with gaiety and innocence. Her despair had vanished. There was no sign round her eyes of a drunken debauch. Her breath was clean and fresh. I could hardly believe it. I rose to the occasion like a shot.

'Kiss me, sweet,' I said, and she did.

'You lazy old thing, you were asleep!'

'I was dreaming about being at the cottage, darling.'

'You would!' Her look indicated what she thought I had been dreaming about – thus showing that a girl who is earthy in its most beautiful sense can be totally wrong about a man.

'I was dreaming about flowers,' I said.

Myrtle shook her head, smirking at the thought of how I could lie. She came and sat beside me on the sofa.

I caressed her. In this mood I did not intend to mention Haxby. As I touched the bloom of her skin and felt the warmth of her flesh, my jealousy disappeared. She smiled at me encouragingly. I knew and she knew – she was almost telling me – that Haxby was nowhere.

'Darling,' I whispered into her ear.

This went on for a little while. There were sounds outside the door and Myrtle sat up attentively.

Anyone who has ever lived in lodgings, especially respectable lodgings in a semi-detached house on the outskirts of a provincial town, will know the obstacles to enjoying illicit love therein.

We both listened.

'It's all right,' I said.

Myrtle was much too indirect to nod, but somehow I knew she concurred. We had heard sounds that we recognized.

By a stroke of good fortune the obstacles in our case removed themselves on Sunday afternoon. It was good and rather peculiar fortune, such as is not commonly associated with a semi-detached house in a provincial town. I can only describe it truthfully. Every Sunday afternoon, at precisely two-thirty, the landlady's niece was visited by a very respectable-looking middle-aged man, who lived higher up the street. The landlady was sent out for a two-hour walk with the dog, no matter what the weather; whereupon the niece and the respectable-looking middle-aged man promptly went upstairs.

'He's as regular as clockwork,' Myrtle whispered.

She was right. It was a singular performance and it fascinated us constantly. The explanation that had come first to our minds was that he was a married man. Not at all. I had drawn the landlady into conversation about him, and had discovered that he was a bachelor living quietly with his mother and father.

'Why doesn't he marry her?' Myrtle would ask.

'*I* don't know.' I felt that Myrtle was insensitive, putting such a question to me. Nevertheless I felt exactly as she did. One can always have the conventional response about somebody else. Why on earth did not he marry her?

The man was never referred to, by the landlady or her niece, as anything but Mr Chinnock. He was well built and rather handsome, in a solid, meaty way. The suit he wore on Sundays was made of hairy tweed: across the waistcoat was stretched a heavy gold chain with a framed golden sovereign dangling from the middle. In manner he was slow, gentle and more than a little stately.

I supposed Myrtle and I ought to have assumed that the niece and Mr Chinnock went upstairs for a Sunday afternoon nap. Going by the sounds, we should have thought them restless sleepers. I am afraid we judged their conduct by our own – in fact, we used to speculate on how far their conduct differed from ours. Myrtle imagined the niece called him Mr Chinnock in all circumstances. 'Now *then*, Mr Chinnock!' Or '*That's* it, Mr Chinnock!' I was beguiled by such invention, though Myrtle pretended to have no idea what it was about. She smirked at the ceiling. The thought of somebody else, in the room above, on a Sunday afternoon – the mystery of it! What man can honestly say he does not know what I mean?

The Sunday afternoon I began describing passed rapidly and delightfully. Myrtle and I stood beside the french window, arms round each other's waist, looking down the garden at the grass and budding plants and the smoke rising from chimneys of little houses like our own.

At exactly four-thirty we heard the niece and Mr Chinnock come downstairs. They went into the scullery.

'*I'll be loving you, always,*' sang the niece in a quavering soprano.

'*With a love that's true, always,*' sang Mr Chinnock in a full baritone.

'Phon and antiphon,' said I to Myrtle.

'Mr Chinnock's putting on the kettle,' said Myrtle to me.

All was right with the world.

It may seem strange that Myrtle and I could feel that all was right with our particular world. We ought not to have done. There was a dramatic situation; but nothing had happened. Myrtle had introduced Haxby into the situation. I was jealous of him. Still nothing had happened. Instead we were mysteriously enjoying an interlude in the same old way.

Only by strenuously searching my memory can I recall a novel incident. That night I broke my custom and visited Myrtle's home.

There was no one in the house and she took me up to her room. It was a pretty room, decorated by herself. With humility she had hung no drawings of her own on the walls. The colour scheme was warm and rosy. There were leopard-skin rugs, deep red curtains and looped muslin over the windows. A little vulgar? I suppose it was. Myrtle was a little vulgar, and I must say that I liked it. The room was evidence that she could let herself go, and that was what I liked. People who cannot let themselves go on occasion will not do for me.

I sat down on the bed. Myrtle sat beside me. I put my arm round her. The minutes passed.

Suddenly it felt as if she softly collapsed against me. I was utterly seduced. It felt as if she had melted into the marrow of my bones – my woman, my wife, my squaw. And then –

'That *tamed* look!'

'By Heaven!' I thought. 'What am I doing with a woman, a wife, a squaw?' I sprang off the bed. Tamed!

Myrtle looked up at me, startled. Our eyes met. There was a fleeting moment of clairvoyance. She read my thoughts.

'My foot's gone to sleep,' I said, and stamped it on the ground.

Myrtle did not say anything. She knew, I was certain she knew, that I had in some way recoiled from her. I sensed the shock to her as clearly as I sensed the other shock to myself.

I stretched out my hand and stroked her hair. Myrtle remained still, with her head bent. She began making small pleats in the bed-cover.

'Is it getting better?' she said, lightly.

'Yes, I think so.'

I looked down at her. I wondered what had happened. She was apparently paying no attention to me. The air was warm and scented; the light glowed on her hair; she was breathing softly, all on her own. Suddenly I felt in touch with something inexplicable, far beyond the place where our thoughts revolved and our wills told us what to do. I felt in touch with something like instinct. And I knew how little, how hopelessly little our thoughts and wills affected us. At the root of everything we did was . . . the unknowable.

'No wonder,' I thought, as I remembered to give my foot a last shake, 'we go on doing such damned unknowable things.'

3

Two Dramatic Turns

The mysterious interlude with Myrtle lasted. There were no more incidents of recoil, no more intimations of anguish to come. Three weeks later I was spending Saturday at the cottage, happily looking forward to Myrtle's visit next day. From time to time I wondered where she was spending the night. I was not seriously worried: Haxby was nowhere, I thought.

It was a beautiful May afternoon. Our private lives were drifting inexorably towards dissolution, like the whole of Europe towards catastrophe: the weather was perfect. The sun was shining; cloud shadows passed slowly over the grass, dousing the glow of daisies and buttercups. I roamed over the meadows, half intending to pick some flowers to decorate the house, but really passing the time in aimless thought. I was wondering what to do about Miss X. Y. and my manuscript.

It was the time of year when the whole countryside seemed to be bursting into bloom. The hawthorn was not yet fully out, but the air was strong with the sweet light perfume of wild flowers. Under the hedges were campions and dead-nettles and bird's-eye, turning their petals to the sun: beside the brook there were some big late mayflowers: sprinkled over the slopes were a few cowslips, looking dusty and etiolated beside the brilliant buttercups. I picked a bunch of wild forget-me-nots and greeny-gold wild mignonette. I thought it really was time Miss X. Y. did something about it. I was going to America.

I sat on top of a gate, filled with the poignance of leaving such a lovely country. Where could America show anything to compare with this for delicate, sweet-smelling lushness? Where else could the sky be so luminous and yet so gentle, the flowers so bright and yet so freshly perfumed? Where else could I feel was home? The beauty of it shone over everything, like a shimmering haze – one could stretch out one's hand and seem to touch it with one's finger-tips. Where else, except over English meadows, does beauty leap so nearly to the verge of being palpable? Do not ask me. I do not know.

Idly I watched some lambs cropping the grass. They had grown to look more like sheep; but every now and then one of them reverted to earlier lambhood, tried to take a pull of mother's-milk, and got buffeted in the ribs for its pains. I wondered where their fathers were – over the hills and far away. Only the human male is tied to its female and its young, tied and tamed. Oh! to be a ram, I thought, and then be over the hills and far away: till it occurred to me that rams cannot write books or get drunk with their friends – and in fact only feel rammish for deplorably limited periods.

I climbed down from the gate. I had decided to write to Miss X.Y. If it irritated her, so much the worse. If she did not want to read my book the lapse of more weeks would not bring her round to it. I walked down to the cottage and wrote her a polite letter immediately: the letter could not be posted for another twenty-four hours, but I felt much better for having written it. I made myself some tea and lay in my armchair dreaming of Myrtle.

The door of the cottage was open, and a bluebottle buzzed in. Suddenly I realized that summer had come. The end of summer is signalized by the last rose: the beginning by the first bluebottle. My last summer in England, and here it was. I was roused from my dream. The beginning of the summer: the end of an epoch. The bluebottle buzzed round the room, and I felt very solitary. Restlessly I went and stood in the doorway.

To my surprise I saw Steve coming up the road, alone and on foot. He appeared to be swinging along steadily, judging by the way his dark head bobbed up and down above the hedgerows. When he came into the last stretch, and saw me watching, he began to drag his feet.

'I hope you don't mind me coming to see you, Joe.' He looked diffident and awkward. 'I came on a bus to the village. I won't stay long.'

'You're just in time for tea.'

'Good.' The diffident expression changed immediately to one of simple anticipation. Steve came into the cottage. 'I'll get the cup and saucer myself,' he mumbled. 'Please don't bother about me, Joe.'

I sat down. I did not intend to bother about him. 'Look after yourself,' I said in a tough, hearty tone.

Steve glanced at me, and then poured himself some tea. Then he helped himself to a single chocolate biscuit – a very unusual performance. I waited to see what he had come for. I felt sure from his manner that he was eluding Tom for the afternoon.

Steve drew a deep breath, and then said:

'Joe, I've just done something terrible.'

'Oh, what?'

'I suppose everybody will say it's terrible . . .' He glanced down.

'Come on – out with it, Steve.'

Steve looked at me with a solemn, tragic expression. He said: 'I've volunteered for the Merchant Navy.'

'Good Lord!'

Though I did not exactly burst into laughter, I was not far from it. I said: 'Say it again!'

The reason I asked him to repeat it was that I did not for a moment believe him. By nature I am a credulous man, but with Steve I had been forced to see that credulity, admirable though it may be, rarely offers the best means of arriving at the truth.

'I've volunteered for the Merchant Navy.'

Steve's tone deferentially indicated that he thought it was rather captious of me to make him repeat a remark I must have already heard.

'You can't have,' I said. I supposed it was a cold, unfeeling way of receiving such a dramatic piece of news, such a solemn, tragic, false, dramatic piece of news.

'But I really have, Joe.' Steve put down his cup and saucer, and looked at me with an anxious, imploring expression. Although Steve was given to egregious lying, he never took umbrage at being accused of it.

I knew nothing about the normal age of entry to the Merchant Navy, but I recollected reading parliamentary discussions about the age at which young men might be called up for compulsory military training.

'You're too young,' I said, on the off chance of defeating him.

'I'm not, Joe. Not for the Merchant Navy.' Steve was too tactful to make any such remark as 'You don't seem to believe me.'

'Have you actually signed on?' I said.

'Of course.'

'When?'

'This morning.'

'Is the office open on Saturdays?'

'Yes. How could I have signed on if it weren't?'

Steve sometimes broke down if you asked him enough questions. This time I saw that he was patiently going to prove that he had done it. I paused. During the pause Steve helped himself to another chocolate biscuit. He munched it. Then he poured out another cup of tea. Naturally I had not varied a hair's breadth from my original disbelief. I was inclined to think he had *thought of* volunteering: there were some handsome recruiting posters plastered about the town. In fact I thought he might have visited the recruiting office and made some inquiries. I took another biscuit myself. I said:

'What made you decide on this powerful step?'

'I've got to do something.'

'Going to sea is a bit drastic, isn't it?'

'It's the only way of escaping, Joe.'

'Escaping from what?'

'Tom, I suppose.'

'Good Lord!'

Steve glanced at me seriously. I turned to face him.

'Do you really want to escape from Tom?' I said, in the shrewd, penetrating manner of a psychologist.

'I don't want to be an accountant!'

'Is the Merchant Navy the only alternative to accountancy?'

'You don't understand, Joe.'

'What?'

Steve looked at me. 'Imagine what it's like to be in my place.'

'For once, Steve, my imagination boggles.'

Steve had been on the point of assuming his suffering look, but a smile supervened.

'I've always wondered,' I said, 'exactly what caused technical boggling of the imagination. Now I know.'

'It's nothing to laugh about. It's terrible.' Steve stood up. He walked across to the doorway, picking up another biscuit as he went.

'I'm sorry, Steve,' I followed him, pushing the plate of biscuits out of sight as I passed.

'Anyway, I've taken the step now, haven't I?'

'*You* know that, Steve.'

'You don't blame me, do you?'

'Blame you, Steve? Of course not.'

'Other people will.'

'Blaming is one of the favourite human occupations. People blame you whatever you do.'

'You are the first person I've told. I daren't tell my mother and father.'

'I think,' I said, 'you can expect Tom to do that.'

'Joe!'

We strolled across the road and leaned against a gate, looking idly at the cottage.

'I had to do it, Joe. I can't go on being an accountant.' Steve looked at me. 'It's the arithmetic. It's torment. And Tom wants me to go round to his house for a lesson three evenings a week.' His voice rose. 'Three evenings a week!'

'That certainly is torment,' I agreed, disloyally to Tom.

Steve paused. 'Anyway, it will be over now.' He pondered. 'I won't have to do any arithmetic in the Merchant Navy, will I?'

'Not much.' I grinned. 'I guess you've already received enough training for the Merchant Navy in arithmetic. As in certain other basic subjects, too.'

An amused flicker appeared in Steve's eye, in spite of his agonized expression: it was merely momentary. He said:

'You don't understand, Joe.'

'What?'

Steve suddenly spoke with force. 'I want to sleep with women.'

'You get that as well in the Merchant Navy. While you're in port.'

'I mean it seriously.'

I looked away. 'I did realize that.' There was a long silence broken only by the occasional chirping and flutter of birds in the hedge. Steve stirred – I imagined he must be turning to look at me more closely as he spoke.

'Do you think it's silly of me? I mean, I'm only seventeen.'

'I don't think it's silly at all, Steve. No more than the things we all do are silly.'

'I want to get to know some girls.'

I nodded my head.

'I suppose you think I'm being stupid and conventional, Joe.'

I could not help smiling. 'No, Steve.'

'Sometimes I want to be just ordinary, Joe. Terribly ordinary.'

'I think you'll find it terribly tame.'

'I suppose I would. That's the trouble.'

'Don't let that put you off, Steve!'

'It doesn't. I want to start going out with girls, even if it is tame.'

This was not what I meant, but I did not propose to argue.

'I wish Tom would realize this,' Steve said.

It seemed to me that if Tom was trying to make Steve go round to his house three evenings a week he must have a pretty shrewd idea.

'I don't seem to be able to talk to him about it, Joe.'

I foresaw the day when he would, but held my tongue.

Steve turned and leaned his chest against the gate, looking up the field. The movement attracted the attention of some bullocks, who began to advance under the impression that we were going to feed them. Steve picked up a boulder and rolled it towards them.

'It's a relief to have told someone about it.'

I did not know whether he meant the relief of having told me about his signing-on for the Merchant Navy, which was fantasy, or of having told me about his adolescent woes, which were real. It is possible to get a deep relief from confessing something that is untrue: Steve got it frequently.

I said: 'These things work themselves out, you know.' I did not know what it meant, but I had learnt that meaningless remarks of this kind give a bit of comfort.

Steve said: 'I suppose I ought to be going back. Is there a bus?' He gave me a helpless look.

'There's a timetable on the desk. You know where it is.'

Steve slouched across the road and disappeared into the cottage. I began to meditate, on Steve and Tom, on Myrtle and me; and on the difficulty, the transience, the poignance of all human relationships.

I was roused from my meditation by the arrival of Tom's car. As an arrival it was sudden, noisy, unexpected and menacing.

'Have you seen Steve?'

'Yes. He's here.'

'Where?'

'In the cottage.'

Tom got out of the car. I did not move from where I was leaning against the gate. There were signs of passion in his face, a slight goggling of the eyes.

'I thought I'd find him here.'

I was puzzled. The cottage seemed an odd place for Tom to look for Steve – I began to wonder if it might have been pre-arranged.

Tom came and stood beside me, making an effort to look unconcerned. He straightened his tie, which was wine-coloured – a mistake, in my opinion, since it enhanced the contrast between the gingery redness of his hair and the purplish redness of his face.

'It's been a beautiful day.' Tom glanced at the sky, which was melting into the tender shades of twilight; at the hedgerows, leafily stirring in the evening breeze. Glanced is the word for it: before I could expatiate on the charms of the flora, Tom said:

'Shall we go indoors?'

As if to convince me that he was not making a beeline for indoors to discover what Steve was doing, Tom said in a weighty, pompous tone:

'I have an announcement to make.'

We went into the cottage. Tom stared at Steve. Steve fluttered the pages of the bus timetable furtively.

Tom sat down. We all sat down.

'I have some news for both of you,' said Tom. 'I've had a most satisfactory talk with our senior partner this lunchtime, about my fellowship of the I.C.A. That's all settled –'

'Good,' I interrupted, thinking this was the announcement.

'Consequently,' Tom went on, 'I've decided my date of departure for the U.S.A. I've just ordered my tickets. I leave this country on June 15th.'

Steve and I were completely silent, I with surprise and Steve with shock. Tom had his eyes fixed on Steve.

It was useless to pretend the news had not induced a high state of tension, but I said, 'Well, well,' in a light easy tone, hoping to reduce it thereby.

Steve had his eyes fixed on the ground. Tom looked strong and determined.

'It means a break,' Tom said, 'but it's got to be done. Thank God we shall do it in time!' He looked at me. 'Robert says we must decide when you're to go.'

I nodded. I must say that I felt a pang. I thought Tom's tone was bullying. It is all very well to agree on the analysis of a situation; but to act upon it does not follow so readily for every man. Tom sensed my failing enthusiasm.

'It would be most unwise to delay it any longer.'

'I agree.'

My failing enthusiasm sprang from reluctance to leave England, not from lack of faith in our historical prophecy. I had great faith in our historical prophecy, based as it was on the word of Robert.

Tom and I exchanged our interpretations of the latest European events. I will not record them because they will make you think us feebler prophets than we really were – this may be called omission of true facts in the cause of art. Anyway, I think our motives were far from contemptible. Sympathy, I beg, for those who were wrong before the event instead of right after it.

The exchange of interpretations was brief, because Tom's interest was focused entirely on Steve's reaction. I felt embarrassed. It seemed to me the odds were now at least ten to one on Steve's producing his story about the Merchant Navy. There was a peculiar silence. I said:

'Would you like some sherry?'

Tom accepted, with a strained over-polite smile. Steve shrugged his shoulders. While I was taking the bottle out of the cupboard, Tom looked at my letters; that is, he examined the envelopes on my desk, in the cause of not flinching from the attempt to understand human nature. I had taken the precaution of sealing them.

'I see you've written to Miss X.Y.' He paused. 'Of course, if it had been me I should have gone up to London and seen her, weeks ago.'

I poured out the glasses of sherry, and we raised them to our lips. Tom and I drank ours. Steve, instead of drinking, said:

'Tom, I've volunteered for the Merchant Navy.'

The result was devastating. Either from the sherry going down the wrong way or from pure rage, Tom's face turned purple.

'What!' he shouted, in a great splutter.

He stood up. 'You silly little fool!' He went across to Steve, and Steve looked frightened as if he thought Tom were going to beat him. Steve was the taller but Tom easily the stronger. 'Tell me exactly what you've done!'

'I've volunteered for the Merchant Navy.'

'The details! I want the details!' shouted Tom.

I say that Steve looked frightened: he did – and yet I got a distinct impression that at the same time he was enjoying himself.

'When? Where?' Tom was asking him.

And Steve was replying, in spite of his supposed fright, in an easy, provocative manner. His small eyes were lazy and bright. Suddenly I felt sorry for Tom, who was beside himself with passion. I should have felt sorrier still for Tom if I had thought there was a word of truth in what Steve was saying.

'It's got to be stopped, immediately,' Tom said.

'It can't, Tom,' said Steve.

'I'll *buy* you out!' shouted Tom.

Steve was taken aback. His signing-on had now become so real to him, from the inflating power of Tom's belief in it, that he was taking Tom as seriously as Tom was taking him.

'You're under age,' Tom repeated. 'I'll buy you out!'

'But the money?' said Steve, in a tone of anguish.

Tom looked round him. 'If we go straight away and withdraw your signature it may not be too late.'

I could see that he knew no more about the legal side of it than I did. He took hold of Steve's arm.

'Now?' said Steve incredulously.

'Of course.'

'But I don't want to.'

'Don't you see what it means, you little fool!' Tom glared at him, and explained slowly, like a corporal explaining slowly to a private. 'If there isn't a war I shall go to America. And if there is a war you'll be at sea. In either case we shall be separated for ever!'

Steve displayed a mixture of superficial discomfort and basic equanimity.

'For ever!' Tom shouted.

I thought, 'Poor old Tom.' I saw this scene going on for a long time: Steve was lying back in his chair, and Tom was tireless.

They paused, so I intervened in a reasonable tone.

'It probably could be stopped if you acted rapidly.' Tom could never resist action, and I saw it as a means of getting them out of the house and back to the town.

'Exactly,' said Tom, seizing Steve's arm, and hauling him up.

'Not now, Tom,' said Steve. 'It's too late tonight. The office will be closed. We can't go now. I don't want to.'

'Come on!'

Steve had been pulled out of his chair. 'Let me drink my sherry first,' he cried.

Tom paid no heed. Steve was torn away from his sherry. I thought 'You worthless boy, that serves you right.' Tom dragged him into the car, and pressed the self-starter.

There was a mysterious clanking noise under the car and then silence.

The car would not start.

Tom tried again and again. He got out and lifted up the bonnet. Then he got back in again. There were a few more sporadic noises, and then silence of striking permanence. Steve sat, hunched up and silent, inside the car. Tom, powerful and purple, engaged in action such as cranking the engine and stalking to and fro. I did nothing: I have occasionally felt like a professional scientist but never like a motor mechanic.

Tom muttered some kind of explanation. 'She won't start.'

And then the same thought struck both of us. 'We shall have to stay the night,' Tom said, in a masterful tone.

I was about to say there was another bus, and then remembered the wretched man had only till June 15th – I never doubted that Tom would leave for ever on June 15th. 'Who am I,' I asked myself, 'to stop him getting the most out of his last month, however singular that most may be?' I was not expecting Myrtle till the following afternoon.

'All right,' I said. 'I was going over to the pub later on.'

Tom nodded. 'We'll go for a stroll in the meantime.' He turned to the car: 'Now, Steve, you'd better get your coat.'

Reluctantly Steve got out of the car, went into the cottage, and emerged with his coat. Tom's eyes followed him. Then Tom and he walked away up the lane. I heard Tom's voice rising in power as it moved into the distance. The scene was going on.

I went indoors, and poured myself another glass of sherry. And I noticed that Steve's glass was empty – in the few seconds he had spent fetching his coat Steve had swigged off his sherry. I could not help smiling.

4

Night on the Park

I was invited to have supper with Bolshaw and his wife at their house. I had taken care to meet Myrtle first of all. The interlude was over. Our situation had sprung up again: this time it was worse.

Myrtle lived in a street that debouched on the park. I was just entering it – I was a little late – when I met her, apparently already on her way to wherever she was seeing fit to go.

It was a light evening, and I could see from a long way off that she was in a state of abysmal depression. She had begun to look sadder and sadder during the last days. I suppose I was unfeeling and detached: I thought of it as her 'I'll-never-smile-again' expression. Really, she overdid it. I felt genuinely upset and, such was the weakness of my nature, faintly irritated by remorse. I kissed her warmly on the cheek.

'I'm sorry I'm late, darling.' I had a perfectly satisfactory excuse.

'It's all right,' she said, in a distant tone.

'Where are you going?'

Myrtle put her hand to her forehead. 'My dressmaker's.'

'Oh,' I said helpfully, 'that's nice.'

Myrtle looked at me. I knew it was not nice at all. I put my arm round her waist – when anyone looks woebegone I cannot help trying to cheer them up.

'I'm sorry you're feeling so low, darling.'

I suppose Myrtle thought the remark became me ill when my conduct was at the root of her depression.

'Have you been sleeping badly?'

Myrtle nodded her head.

'Nightmares?'

Myrtle nodded again. She roused herself sufficiently to make a tragic revelation. 'I dream that I'm *two people.*'

Satan entered into me. 'Two?' I said. 'There's no cause for alarm till it gets to ten.'

Cheering people up may be good-natured: it appears that making jokes is sadistic. All I can say is that if somebody had said it to me I should have been amused.

We were at the top of the street. Tramcars passed between us and the park. Beyond the railings we could see couples lying under the trees, and little boys playing cricket. I observed two youths from the school approaching us on bicycles: I recognized them by their blazers. They turned out to be Benny and his younger brother. They took off their caps very politely; and rode on without staring, though they missed no detail of Myrtle's appearance.

I may say that despite Myrtle's obvious misery she was beautifully dressed. I gave her great credit for that. She was wearing a new summer frock, made of material prettily printed in a pattern of greens and bright yellow and covered all over with handwriting. Her shoes were American. Her hair was dressed in the latest style.

'That's Benny,' I said encouragingly. 'I've told you about him. Do you remember?'

'I didn't know he was so old.'

I had frequently told her he was nineteen.

'He looks quite well-behaved,' she went on, apparently remembering at least that I had told her definitely that he was not well-behaved.

'He's a menace,' I said, with conviction. 'Some day one of Benny's tricks will get him thrown out. And me too, probably. I shall heave a great sigh of relief when he leaves.'

Myrtle had ceased to listen: it made me feel as if I were babbling.

I touched the material of her dress. 'Where did this come from?' She told me without interest.

I kept my finger inside her sleeve, so that it touched her flesh. 'Darling,' I said, looking at her face.

Myrtle looked back at me. For a moment I thought she was going to weep.

'Darling,' I said, 'I do wish I could think of something to say.'

Myrtle made a perceptible effort to smile, but failed.

I wanted to take her into my arms and comfort her. The trouble was that I could only have comforted her by taking her into a registry office.

I realized that I was now late for my next appointment. Myrtle showed no signs of moving. More trams passed with a cheerful clang: I ought to have been on one of them. At last I said: 'I must go now, darling.'

Myrtle looked down. I took hold of her hand, and held on to it tenderly. There was something else I had to say before I could go.

'Are you coming out to the cottage this week-end?'

Myrtle did not reply.

I felt embarrassed, ashamed, apprehensive and determined.

'Are you, darling?'

Myrtle looked at me, absolutely blank-faced: 'Do you want me to?'

'Of course.' There was a pause. 'Will you?' I held her fingers tighter.

Myrtle made the faintest possible gesture that could be recognized as assent.

I kissed her and we parted. I took a tram down to the station and there changed to a bus. Throughout the journey my thoughts turned round and round. Why? how? and why? again. I knew by experience that she suffered this mysterious ebb and flow of mood, but I felt slightly reassured if I could link it with some external event. I had told her that Tom was due to leave England on June 15th. No event seemed too irrelevant for me to strive fatuously to make it relevant. I had not told her about Steve's signing-on for the Merchant Navy, because he never had signed-on: Tom found that out by a dramatic visit to the recruiting office. I tried to think what precisely I had said or done.

My efforts led me nowhere, and I joined the evening's entertainment in a mildly abstracted fashion.

Just as I was about to leave Bolshaw's house there was a tele-phone call for me. I knew what it was going to be. Myrtle wanted me to meet her again, on my way home.

Myrtle met me at the station. It was after eleven o'clock. She was already standing there, waiting, when I arrived. She had been home for a coat to put over her summer frock.

'What is it, darling?' I said.

By the light of the street lamps I could see faint signs of anima-tion in her face.

'I wanted to see you again.'

I stared at her anxiously. Somehow I had wanted to see her as well. It felt inevitable, as if we had been drawn together. I did not speak.

We stood on the edge of the pavement, facing each other. Myrtle said:

'I wanted to say I was sorry for being rude to you earlier this evening.'

I felt a sudden stab of pain as I recognized the words – apology of one who is in love to one who is loved. How well I recognized it! You apologize to the one who ought to apologize to you – to such straits does love reduce dignity and common sense.

The one who is loved invariably behaves badly, and I was no exception. I thought, 'Oh God! She's in love with me.'

'That's all right, darling,' I said. Fortunately I did not utter the most cruel remark the loved one can utter in these circumstances – 'Forget it!' The result was more or less the same.

Myrtle drew away from me. It was not all right.

I put my arm round her waist, and began to lead her along the road.

'I realized you weren't feeling well, darling,' I said.

'Well?'

'It's a sort of malaise you're having. Being touchy is part of it.'

'Is it?' There was a faint edge to her voice.

I said comfortably: 'I wasn't perturbed.'

'Then you ought to have been!'

I was alarmed. Purposely I pretended not to have caught on. 'It wouldn't do for us both to be touchy at the same time, or else . . .'

'Yes,' Myrtle breathed. 'Or else? . . .'

'It just wouldn't,' I said. 'Clearly.'

We were silent for a while.

Myrtle was walking slowly. I suppose she must have felt me tending to go faster: I found it hard to get along at Myrtle's pace.

'Do you want to go home?' she said.

'No. What makes you think that?'

'It's getting late.' A tram lumbered past us, dimly lit and filled with people who had been to the cinemas. 'You mustn't miss your last tram.'

I said I was going to take her home before I left her.

Myrtle said: 'I suppose they were angry when I rang you up tonight.'

'Angry,' I said, in astonishment. 'Why should they be? I think Bolshaw thought you must be slightly eccentric, that's all.'

'Were you angry?'

'Not at all. I'm glad you rang.'

'Why?'

'I don't know. I think I wanted to see you again, because . . .'

'Because of what?'

'I don't know, darling.' I felt embarrassed. 'Because of the way we parted.'

'What was wrong with that? I thought you seemed satisfied.'

'Really!'

I stopped. Myrtle stopped and we stared at each other. We were quite near the end of her street, but there was no street lamp and we could not see each other very well.

'What's the matter?' said Myrtle.

'You say I seemed satisfied. You can't have any idea, darling. How could I have been satisfied?'

'I said I would see you at the week-end.'

'I thought you didn't want to come.'

Myrtle burst out with great emotion:

'It didn't seem to matter to you if I didn't!'

'Of course it does.'

'I seem to see less and less of you!'

I did not know what to say. She had seen me at the cottage just as often.

'Oh, I don't know,' Myrtle went on, passionately. 'Here we are now . . . Why is it like this, darling? You go out to see your friends and I spend the evening with my dressmaker.' She looked at me. 'I spend hours and hours with people I don't really want to be with!'

People she did not want to be with – Haxby, she must be including Haxby.

'Darling . . .' I began.

'It's true. You're always somewhere else.'

'It isn't true. I have to go and see other people sometimes.' I was on the point of saying 'You could always come with me if you would' but it seemed cruel: also it was not quite true. Even had she felt at ease with all my friends, I should have wanted to see them alone sometimes.

We then began a futile argument about how often I ought to spend evenings with different friends and acquaintances. Myrtle was facing the road, and as a tram swayed past the light crossed her face. I was relieved to see no tears.

'Since Easter I seem to have seen absolutely nothing of you.'

I enumerated meetings missed through accidents chiefly on her part. I brought up the Saturday afternoon at the games field when she had dropped me. My list was impressive – impressive as a list of facts, but not as the truth.

'And it doesn't seem to matter to you,' Myrtle said, as if she had not heard.

There was a pause. We were still standing in the same place. People were passing us. I said:

'Let's go on the park!'

I knew that it was a useless thing to say, that the scene could only go on and produce no result.

We walked through the gates, and turned off along a narrow path beside some shrubbery, disturbing a boy and girl who were locked in each other's arms against the railings. They seemed curiously remote from us, as if love-making were of no interest.

We resumed our argument about how I should dispose of my evenings.

At last we came to a seat. Arid though the argument was, we could not leave it. Anyone who has ever been involved in this kind of scene will recall the peculiar boredom of it, the peculiar boredom that ties both of you together, like twine round a parcel.

There were long periods between each remark, enormously long. For me they were often spent in reframing my next remark, trying to take off the edge of my words, trying to transmute them into something of whose hardness I should be less ashamed afterwards – I could not forget that Myrtle was a tender girl and so very young. On the other hand some of the periods were spent in thinking how late it was; and others in watching car headlamps moving along the main road – something obscured the lower part of them, a palisading, possibly. It is hard to keep one's concentration up to concert pitch in this sort of scene.

As a minor counter-attack I put forward the proposition that I never seemed to go anywhere myself nowadays. If I was not seeing Myrtle it was not because I was seeing someone else. Naturally this did not please: second only to my offence of seeing other friends was my offence of spending evenings alone.

At last, in desperation, I gave the argument a heave which overturned it on to a deeper plane. I said gently:

'Aren't we getting into this mess because I'm going to America and we shall be separated?'

Myrtle softened a little. 'Well, it is really . . .'

'What can we do, darling? I shall have to go.'

Myrtle's emotion broke out again. 'You don't seem to mind! You want to go!'

'I don't want to go.'

'You said you did.'

'There are some things I want to do most. To do them I shall have to get out.'

'But that needn't mean being separated. That's what I don't see. You never mention me going!'

I was astounded. After all the time I had spent persuading her to think about taking a job in America, it seemed incredible. She had never listened to me. Her going to America meant only one thing – being married to me. She was unable to listen if I talked of anything else.

Hastily I began to invent reasons why she could not go to America in a state of dependence on me. I should have no money, no job.

'I don't see that it matters,' said Myrtle. 'If you were fond of somebody you'd want them to be there all the time.'

'But not in those circumstances!'

'Why not?' said Myrtle, inexorably, there being a good deal in what she said. 'I should have thought it meant assured happiness.'

'Assured happiness!'

'And you could *work*!'

Heaven help me! I thought. By work she must mean school-teaching. I realized what I had always suspected – that not for a moment did she take my writing seriously. Assured happiness!

'You'd be settled,' said Myrtle, in a tone that was not the tone of a tender girl or a very young one either.

'Tamed!' said I, in an anguished voice. I saw myself settled, with someone I was fond of there all the time. There all the time, mark you! How could I write books about people? How could I go out and discover what they were like? How could I support my curiosity about them? How could I watch what they were doing, have long intimate talks with them – and, if it came to that, get into bed with some of them? How indeed?

'What's wrong with being settled?' Myrtle ignored my interjection. 'Everybody else is.'

I fell straight into the trap.

'I'm not like everybody else!'

94

'But you could be!' Myrtle went on. 'If only you'd – if only you'd . . .' She gave the sentence up, but not the meaning. The latter was only too clear to me.

Myrtle could not utter the word 'marry'. In the whole conversation neither of us had used it. I could not bring myself to utter it, as a child will not utter the name of something it does not want to happen. And I seemed to have hypnotized Myrtle into doing the same thing.

Myrtle was not entirely wrong about me: that was the trouble. Somewhere she touched in me a vestigial romantic belief that if I were abandonedly in love I should want her to be there all the time. For a moment I sensed what her idea of permanence could mean, what it could mean to me if I were somebody else.

'We can't go on talking like this, darling.' I shook my head. 'There is something deeper than these tedious mechanical reasons. I just can't have anyone about me. Somehow I do know that I want –' I searched for a phrase – 'I want to go on alone.'

It was an unusual phrase, that must have made it sound as if I were aiming at the North Pole. Myrtle said nothing.

'I've always felt like that, darling,' I said.

'Yes,' said Myrtle. 'You were careful to tell me that at the beginning.'

'Didn't you think I meant it?'

'Yes. Then.'

'Why not now?'

'It was different. We weren't so fond of each other then.'

'That doesn't alter it. Darling,' I said, 'my personality's stuck. It can't be changed.'

Myrtle had stopped listening, and I said under my breath, 'Even under the regenerating influence of a woman!'

We were silent. I felt cold. It was a dark night, with a clouded sky – no wind, yet coldish. It must have been the first time I had ever noticed the cold before Myrtle did. I took hold of her hand, and helped her up from the seat. We began to walk. Myrtle began to walk away from the direction of her home, but I gradually steered her round.

'What are we to do?'

Myrtle's voice was soft and melancholy, and she looked at the sky. Yet there was a reasonable note in it, as if she were facing the problem realistically. Still looking away, she repeated it. We were sufficiently in tune for me to know that she was raising the question of whether we should part.

I shrank from it.

'What do you think we ought to do?' I asked.

I heard her draw in her breath sharply. She knew it was not really a question.

I said: 'Darling, do you think I ought – do you think it would be better if I started keeping out of the way?'

'We couldn't not see each other!' Her voice was louder and more passionate. I thought this affair would have to end.

'I ought not to have let this happen,' I said.

'I don't see that we *shall* have to!' said Myrtle, cutting into my maunderings.

'But what else?' I began a long speech. We were standing at a cross-roads, and a tram-repair lorry came up, with a violent clatter of loose tools and implements. We were in the middle of the night.

Myrtle said something.

'What did you say?'

'Only more protestations.'

We were both silent, worn out. Aimlessly we watched two young policemen in mackintoshes shut themselves up in their little police telephone-box: a small red light flashed on the top of it.

'I think you'll have to think of it like that,' I said.

'Well, I can't . . . And I don't suppose I ever shall!'

We moved to go home. Nothing was decided. We stopped and looked at each other. When were we to meet again? I could not bring myself to ask her.

'Do you want me to come on Sunday?' Myrtle asked gently.

'Yes. But darling, I can't ask you like that. Not now . . .'

We were holding each other's fingers.

At last I mumbled: 'I shall be there . . .'

'Then of course I shall come.'

We whispered good night.

I walked home by the road along which I had been used to cycle so joyously on Sunday nights. I felt utterly empty. I wondered what Myrtle thought was the outcome of our scene. I asked myself how much good it had done. I thought I saw now that an end of it all was appointed for us. I could have wept.

5

In Disgrace

At this point I began to look forward much less equivocally to my departure for the U.S.A.

For the time being I looked secure in my pedagogue's niche. Ever since our talk at the games field, Bolshaw and I had been on good terms; so I judged the headmaster was hearing less about my irresponsibility, laziness and other forms of moral delinquency. All the same, I thought with unrestrained pleasure about giving in my notice at the end of the term. It would be a real coup to walk out when I was obviously in no danger of being pushed out.

One fine Monday morning I sat in the playground, counting the accumulation of worries that rose from my enforced vocation. There was a row of ancient lime trees growing up through the asphalt, and I used to let the sixth form boys sit under them to work during the summer term. It was pleasant: the sun shone down; girls in summer frocks walked briskly past the railings; scarlet buses ran to and fro.

While waiting for Frank and the others to come from prayers I was making a list of physics questions likely to be set in the coming Higher School Certificate examination. I was very adept at what the boys called 'spotting'. My skill was widely recognized, and the boys had suggested, with the intention of helping me on my way, that instead of dispensing my information free to a whole form I should sell it to them individually.

Suddenly I stared at my divining-chart. 'Why am I working on this? Why am I not writing a masterpiece?' The answer was that I had written a masterpiece; but my letter to Miss X.Y. had produced only the information that she was touring in the Balkans. 'Why am I working on this chart?' No answer, except that it fell within the scope of duties I had to perform in order to buy myself food and lodging.

From the building came the sound of the boys at their devotions. The organ chimed out and they began to sing 'Blest are the pure in heart'. Strangely enough, in spite of all they did, many of them managed to remain pure in heart. From plain observation I decided that superficially innocent they were not: yet it was quite easy to see them as surprisingly free from contamination. Pureness of heart is an odd thing, rarely comprehended by the righteous. I could write a lot more about it.

Frank came out to me, with a firm, graceful tread.

'I wanted to see you before the others come.' I saw him looking diffidently along his nose. 'Have you heard what happened on Saturday night? Trevor was run in for dangerous driving.'

Now you see the sort of worries that rose from my enforced vocation.

Frank shook his head lugubriously. 'It's a sod, isn't it?'

'What'll happen to him?'

'He'll probably get his licence endorsed.'

'The rows there'll be!'

Frank and I stared at each other.

'Hello!' Trevor had quietly joined us. The sun lit up his golden hair. Sometimes his small pale face looked debauched, sometimes angelic. This morning, when it would have been helpful to look angelic, it looked irritatingly debauched. 'I suppose you've heard?' he said, spinning out the last words with a nasal emphasis.

'Were you drunk?' I said.

'I wish I had been. I didn't do anything wrong. I think the cop was just bored. He said I jumped the traffic-light at the corner of Park Road.'

'Were there any witnesses?'

'Yes. Another cop coming off the park. One of those officious cops that goes round preventing people from copulating on the grass.'

'For Pete's sake!' Frank seized him by the back of the neck to shake him.

'Were you alone?'

'No. I'd got a girl.' Trevor languidly pushed back the hair that had fallen when Frank shook him, but there was an unmistakable look of bravado and provocative triumph in his face.

I had always known we should have trouble with Trevor.

'I didn't even jump the traffic-light.'

Frank interrupted. 'Look out! Here comes Benny and Fred.'

With their faces shining like the bright sky, the other pair joined us. Fred was soppily singing, to the tune of 'Blest are the pure in heart', some words he was making up as he went along. 'I do not want to work . . . pom, pom . . . I'd rather sit and dream . . .' He stopped singing: 'About luv . . .'

Benny jumped behind my chair. 'What are you doing, sir? Making us a list of questions?' He breathed heavily down the back of my neck.

'I'm goin' to make a list,' said Fred, 'of questions we *won't* get. And then I won't 'ave to learn them.'

I ought to say they had all passed the examination the previous year and pretended they were going to fail it this.

Frank and Trevor had taken out their pocket-combs and were combing their hair. Benny and Fred made some show of composing themselves, since they were on view to the public. I began to collect the written work they had done over the week-end.

Out of the corner of my eye I saw Bolshaw crossing the yard. He beckoned to me. I had to go.

I followed Bolshaw into the laboratory. His form of silent oafs looked up and then down again. Bolshaw's forms spent the whole of the summer term in silent revision for the examinations.

From Bolshaw's serious statesman-like expression I deduced that he had some project in hand. I was afraid he might be going to try and lure me into his research again. He sat down at his desk with a heavy shambling movement. It occurred to me that he was looking older; his eyes looked faintly bleary, and his false teeth a trifle greener – though why false teeth turning green should be a sign of age I did not know.

'I've been working!' Bolshaw blew through his whiskers. 'I enjoy it.'

I concealed my astonishment.

Bolshaw opened his case and pulled out the folder containing some of his research papers. 'I should like you to have a look at this.'

I realized that nothing could stop him. He repeated his earlier proposition. He held up his hand as if he were going to give me his blessing.

'I think the time has come,' he said.

The time had indeed come. Simms could not delay his retirement beyond the end of the term. In our present stable condition of amity, Bolshaw was bound to nominate me as his own successor.

My heart sank at the prospect of having to do his computations for him. Till suddenly it occurred to me that I could take away the papers, so satisfying him, and not do the computations, so satisfying myself.

My inspiration was not, of course, an original one. Miss X.Y. had had it long before me, and hosts of people before her. I could have kicked myself for not having accepted in the first instance. To give the maximum satisfaction one should always accept people's papers, whether one ever intends to read them or not.

As I assented I gave Bolshaw a look of restrained enthusiasm. He was too shrewd for me to risk anything really effusive.

Bolshaw appeared to be satisfied. 'I always admire a man,' he said, with characteristic impartiality, 'who recognizes when the time has come.'

I did not feel called upon to reply.

'I wish our headmaster,' he went on, 'gave me cause for this type of admiration.' Every word echoed down the room.

'It's a pity,' said Bolshaw, 'that I'm not the headmaster. A genuine pity.' He blew through his whiskers again. 'What?'

It was more than I could do to keep any trace of glimmer out of my eye. As he noticed it an answering glimmer came into his eye as well. I would not have thought him capable of it. I suddenly saw a clever, sensitive man behind this ludicrous facade. There was a moment of *rapport*. I thought 'Bolshaw's not a bad chap,' and I thought he was thinking the same about me.

I went back to my pupils. I found Trevor calculating quietly, like an angel-child, with his slide-rule; and Benny absorbed in tracing out a simple wireless circuit. Perhaps I was wrong to let other people's doings oppress me. It was highly satisfactory to be secure in my job. After all, I had got to consider the eventuality of my trip to America not coming off.

A few days later I was teaching a form of junior boys in the laboratory. I had them at the end of the afternoon for two consecutive periods, in which they were supposed to do experiments. They were tired. So was I. In the last two periods of the afternoon everybody was slack, and on this occasion the weather was warm and humid and oppressive. Across the playground I could see shapeless grey clouds, apparently hanging round the tops of the lime trees: I felt as if they were hanging round the top of my head as well.

I decided to ease my state by taking a leaf out of Bolshaw's book. Instead of trying to teach them anything, I commanded the boys to open their note-books and do silent revision for the examinations. Then I slumped down into my chair.

For a while I was occupied with reflections on my private affairs. The room was silent. I thought about Myrtle and America – a cloud of claustrophobic reflections hung like a veil between me and the light of happiness. There were clouds everywhere. The boys began to whisper to each other: silent revision had begun to pall.

I walked round the room, threading my way methodically between the benches. Sweat glistened on the boys' foreheads. Their hair was slightly matted and their collars soiled. Some of those who had really been revising, and so had no cause to feel guilty, looked up at me reproachfully. With a blank expression I moved on. There were toffee-papers on the floor. I inspected a boy's note-book at random, and brought to light a drawing that must have been on its way round the class. The drawing was quite unconnected with the subject the boys were revising. I tore it up and left the bits on the bench. Then I sat down again.

I began to think about the drawing. 'Why,' I asked myself, 'were they passing that round instead of studying a diagram of the earth's magnetic field?' 'Because,' I answered myself, 'it was much, much more interesting.' The subject of the drawing had fascinated the human race since the beginning of time. The earth's magnetic field had not. The boys' heads were bent silently again over their notebooks. Poor little devils!

A bell rang for the end of the first period. The boys looked up. In a mood of compassion, I suddenly said:

'Who'd like to go for a walk round the yard?'

I could not have said anything sillier in the circumstances. Any schoolmaster will tell you, even I can tell you, that you should always let sleeping boys lie. I deliberately woke mine up. The idea was reasonable enough, and certainly it was kindly: not two minutes had elapsed before I regretted it.

There were cries of delighted surprise. It was the first time such a thing had ever happened. The rest of the school was bathed in a droning silence. I specified one circuit of the playground and immediate return to the class-room.

The boys rushed out. Through the window I watched them happily make their circuit. And then they embarked on a second circuit. They did not return. And the noise they made echoed wildly back to the building.

I strode out into the playground. 'Come back!' I shouted furiously.

The boys stopped. They looked up at me. I glanced up at the windows of the school. From every class-room stared the face of a master: from the headmaster's window stared the face of the headmaster. Instantly I thought: 'There's going to be a row about this!'

The boys went back into the class-room and spent the rest of the afternoon in apprehensive, agitated silence. I did the same.

They were afraid I was going to punish them. I was much too preoccupied to bother. I was expecting a visit from the headmaster. The only way I could have punished them was by keeping them in after school, and I had every intention of making myself scarce the moment the last bell sounded.

I escaped, that afternoon. I received a letter from the headmaster next morning. It began:

Dear Mr Lunn: I really think I must ask you to reconsider your choice of vocation as a teacher. After . . .

That is enough. I was not exactly sacked; I was not exactly anything. Yet in no sense was it possible to interpret the letter as favourable to my career in pedagogy. I viewed it with alarm. 'One more letter like this,' I thought, 'and things will be serious!'

I could not blame Bolshaw for not intervening, because he was away ill. It was entirely my own fault. And yet, it seemed to me that my crime was not great. In the past I had committed greater. Why had the headmaster seen fit to act on this one?

From questioning the headmaster's actions, I went on to question my own. I was soon immersed in serious philosophical doubts. Perhaps the headmaster was right. It might well be that a schoolmaster really ought to behave like a schoolmaster. If I could not behave like a schoolmaster, perhaps I ought not to be one.

This left me faced with the most alarming question of all.

'What *can* I behave like?'

Part Three

I

False Alarm

The next few times we met, Myrtle and I were chiefly concerned with talking about the headmaster's letter. I am afraid we were taking an opportunity of not talking about ourselves. A week-end at the cottage had restored us, and our night on the park was not mentioned again. Nothing had been resolved: our fate still hung over us, but in tacit agreement we were ignoring it. I asked myself why we should not go on ignoring it. I was willing to ask anyone else – except Tom.

'You're behaving like ostriches,' he said.

'And what's wrong with the ostrich?' I asked. 'It's despised very unjustly. I've a great fellow-feeling for the ostrich. An ostrich doesn't look things in the face.'

Tom made an indecent rejoinder.

'I can see that looking things in the face is a moral exercise,' I said. 'But does it do the slightest good? Sometimes it does not. Some things are much better not looked in the face. You ought to know that.' I paused. 'Anyone with a grain of tact and kindliness knows it.'

Tom was silenced. I considered that I had won a small victory. I was willing to call a small victory anything which prolonged my pleasant relations with Myrtle.

In the meantime I responded with perverse anger to the prospect of being asked to resign. Out of pride mingled with political ineptitude I refused to go and see the headmaster.

Myrtle, with commendable common sense, advised me to placate the headmaster: she did not want me to move to a job somewhere else. Tom strongly advised me to go and denounce him. Neither of them understood or sympathized with my passivity. To me it seemed the way of the world. Nobody could know as well as I, who, whatever else I might be, was not a prig, the roll of my manifold offences against society.

'Darling, you didn't do anything wrong!' Myrtle said, one evening as we sat in a public-house. Outside it was raining.

'I know,' I said obtusely, 'but that doesn't have anything to do with it. As you see, my sweet.' I shaped a small pool of beer on the table into a pattern. 'You talk,' I said, getting the argument on to a really abstract footing, 'as if there were a connection between crime and punishment. I can see practically none.'

Poor Myrtle had no idea what I was talking about. She could break social conventions without a qualm; but that did not stop her feeling they were right and pretending she had not broken them.

'Darling,' she said, 'sometimes I really don't know what to make of you.' She was reproachful and cross.

'All right,' I said, relenting. I smiled. 'I'll do something about it.'

Myrtle was right. The headmaster, out of weakness and exasperation, had allowed himself to be provoked beyond the limits other people would admit.

Myrtle took a small sip of beer thoughtfully.

'What will you do, darling?' she said, looking at me. Reflection was over for her, if not for me. We were on common ground again.

I decided to consult Bolshaw.

'I thought Bolshaw wanted the headmaster to get rid of you, darling.'

I explained to Myrtle about my part in Bolshaw's research. She listened with interest. I could see that she now saw much stronger reasons why Bolshaw might want me to stay. I cannot say she looked shrewd or calculating – she was too young for that. Yet her soft pink cheeks had a brighter tinge, and her brown eyes shone with a more hopeful light.

The landlord switched on the wireless, and the din made it hard for us to converse. Outside, it was still raining. We sat quietly holding each other's hand.

Next morning I saw Bolshaw. For once I had done the right thing. It happened to be Bolshaw's first morning at school after being away ill. He did not know about the headmaster's letter to me. It was a surprise to him. Bolshaw was always surprised if anyone did anything without having previously been advised to do so by him.

'Fancy him writing you a letter!' said Bolshaw, in a grand, slow manner, as if it were scarcely credible that the headmaster's hand was strong enough to hold a pen.

I showed him the letter. Bolshaw read it carefully. He was sitting in the staff-room at the time. He lifted his head, and the light gleamed on the steel frames of his spectacles. He kept his head lifted: I thought he was not going to bring it down again.

'What is it supposed to mean?' he asked.

I shrugged my shoulders, and looked at him with the nearest I could muster to a solemn, repentant expression. I described the occasion which had provoked the letter. I have to admit that I did not describe it to Bolshaw as I have described it to you. I doubt if you would recognize the description I gave Bolshaw.

On the other hand Bolshaw was not a fool. He knew me well enough. I tried to maintain my solemn, repentant expression for the sake of keeping up the appearances to which he attached so much importance, but I did not for a moment assess them at more than a marginal value in the balance he was weighing up. How much did he want me to be sacked? How much did he need me to assist in his research? How much did he deplore independent action on the part of the headmaster? I do not know. I stood waiting while he swept across some kind of balance-sheet that was beyond my comprehension. All I cared for was to know whether the total for me was printed in black or red. It came out black.

Bolshaw handed me back the letter. 'A silly letter,' he said. 'A silly letter.'

I put it in my pocket.

'Let me give you some advice, Lunn!'

I knew I was safe. I nodded meekly.

Bolshaw threw back his blond head again. His voice resounded like that of a mythical god.

'Keep your nose to the grindstone!'

Later in the morning I rang up Myrtle. I repeated the conversation verbatim.

'Then it's all right, darling?'

'Bolshaw's going to see the headmaster today.'

I went back again into the school. In a sense it was all right. At least I was going to escape being asked to resign.

Though Myrtle and I were going together again, she did not give up Haxby. He existed as a perpetual reminder to me that all was not well – and I was damnably jealous of him.

I never knew Haxby, but I can tell you what he looked like. He was tall, dark and skinny; and he had a friend who was slightly less tall, dark and skinny. They had intense black eyes and jerky movements. I thought their appearance was mildly degraded, and I called them the Crows. I could see that Myrtle was wounded. I called them the Crows in a careless, natural, confident tone, as if it would never occur to anybody to call them anything else.

You may think I was being cruel to Myrtle: I can only say that Myrtle was deliberately tormenting me.

Myrtle frequently made it clear that she preferred the Crows' company to mine. They were always available; and they were young, inexperienced, never likely to give her good advice, ready to lead her into things she really liked – such as playing inane games at parties, listening to gramophone records, showing devotion to culture by long pretentious discussions, and staying up half the night.

Myrtle knew that I disliked her preference thoroughly. It was not in my style. It went further than that. It was a powerful affront to some of my deepest feelings. At this time my deepest feelings circulated round two activities – one was writing books, the other making love to Myrtle. I thought she made it only too clear that she did not care at all for the first. I would gladly have thrashed her for it. Unfortunately, thrashing your young woman does not make her admire you more as a novelist. I felt frustrated, angry and hurt. When I thought of marrying Myrtle – yes, there were many, many moments when I did think of marrying her – this angry hurt recurred. I could not get over it. It stuck, as they say, in my craw. And my *cri-de-cœur* was one of such anguish that it must be recorded.

'She doesn't believe in me as a writer!'

And so I ask you not to be too hard on me for condemning the Crows. But a veil over *cris-de-cœur*! They are embarrassing.

'How are the Crows?' I would say lightly.

'All right,' Myrtle would reply in a distant unhappy voice, indicating that she was too far borne down to argue with me.

And she would look at me with a soft, appealing, reproachful expression, as much as to say she would never go near them if she could be with me all the time. It was the soft, appealing, reproachful expression of blackmail.

One Sunday morning Myrtle arrived at the cottage with a hangover, after an evening with the Crows.

'Bohemianism!' I cried, in a righteous tone to which print can never do justice.

You may think I had no room to express moral indignation. No more I had. No more have you, I suspect, half the time you express moral indignation – but does that stop you any more than it stopped me?

'Bohemianism!' I repeated, as if once were not enough.

Myrtle was appropriately flabbergasted.

I took Myrtle, figuratively speaking, by the scruff of the neck. I took her to the Dog and Duck for lunch, and back again in double-quick time.

The same night I asked Myrtle if she would like to go to Oxford with me the following week-end to see Robert. Myrtle was pleased with the idea. I thought if she was in Oxford she could not be with

Haxby. I was pleased with the idea myself. And then I noticed an unmistakable smile of satisfaction on Myrtle's face. I had been led into doing just what she wanted. So much for the soft, appealing, reproachful looks given you by beautiful, ill-used girls!

Yet when the next week-end came near, Myrtle's enthusiasm vanished. She was afraid of meeting Robert; and she feared more discussion of our plans for going to America.

However, Myrtle did not flinch. When we met at the railway station on Saturday afternoon she was showing a brave front. She was dressed elegantly and a trifle theatrically. She had a very pretty dress and a new hat, with which she had seen fit to wear an Edwardian veil. Anyone could see the veil was becoming, but the effect was eccentric. I smiled to myself, thinking that girls of twenty-two can never help overdoing it. I was touched, and kissed her, through the veil, with great feeling.

And as I kissed Myrtle I noticed that her breath smelt odd. I looked at her closely. Her cheeks were highly coloured, and her eyes looked bright and strained. Her breath smelt of gin.

'What's the matter?' I asked.

Myrtle looked at me. 'Darling,' she said, *you* know.'

My knees knocked together. 'Oh!' I cried. I knew exactly what she meant.

We were standing in the station entrance. The sun was shining brightly through the glass roof. A taxi drew up beside us, and a porter pushed us out of the way. I took hold of Myrtle's arm to hold her up. What a way to begin a week-end!

I led Myrtle towards the ticket office. I questioned her, but I did not doubt that she was speaking the truth. In spite of all I might have said or thought about her, I really trusted her completely. We were passing a glass case containing a model locomotive, brilliantly illuminated. The Flying Scotsman.

As usual on such occasions, I assumed a knowing, matter-of-fact expression.

Myrtle's expression was less knowing, less matter-of-fact.

I said: 'It's happened before, you know.' My voice sounded clear and firm. It was the only thing about me that was clear and firm. 'There's no need to worry.'

I bought the tickets.

'Perhaps I ought not to go,' said Myrtle, looking up at me in great anxiety. 'You go by yourself.'

I glanced at her in surprise and refused to go without her.

She took hold of my arm. 'You won't tell Robert, will you, darling?'

'Of course not.' I thought I should have to tell Robert quickly enough if it turned out not to be a false alarm. He would have to lend me money.

Myrtle sat opposite to me in the railway carriage, looking meek and distracted, inside an Edwardian veil.

At Bletchley, when we changed trains, I bought Myrtle a glass of gin.

When we reached Oxford we went straight to our hotel. Myrtle stood in the middle of the stuffy little bedroom, which smelt as if people had been sleeping in it for years.

'Could you buy me a bottle of Kuyper's, darling?'

'Of course.' I did not know why I had so much faith in the efficacy of gin. I suppose the less idea you have of what to do the more readily you take over someone else's faith.

I made off to my old wine merchant's with an energetic, resourceful stride. How can men who do not know what they are about walk with an energetic, resourceful stride? They do, shams that they are.

The weather had changed. The sun had disappeared, leaving a grey, drizzly afternoon. I stood on the street corner, waiting for a stream of bicycles to pass, and I was poignantly beset by nostalgia for my undergraduate days.

I turned into Broad Street, and ran into Tom.

I was astonished. Tom was supposed to be enjoying his turn at the cottage.

'What are you doing here?'

'I got a letter this morning from the American Institute of

Chartered Accountants,' Tom said, with a bland, pompous gesture. 'I thought it wise to consult Robert immediately.'

I thought, 'Liar – you knew Myrtle and I were here and didn't want to miss anything.'

'We won't interfere with any of your plans,' Tom went on, in the tone of a psychiatrist reassuring a lunatic. Then he glanced at me suspiciously: 'By the way, where is Myrtle?'

'In the hotel. She isn't well.'

I could see that Tom did not believe me. He obviously thought there was a domestic quarrel brewing. He looked more suspicious when I shook him off in order to do my shopping. He bustled away down the Broad, to report the news directly to Robert.

I felt depressed and anxious and worried. 'If only I can get out of it just this once,' I kept thinking. And I kept telling myself it was a false alarm – possibly brought on, I was inspired to diagnose, by being afraid to meet Robert. One inspired diagnosis led to another: for once I found the psychology of the unconscious useful and consoling. The one diagnosis I did not face was that it might have been brought on by a desire for holy matrimony.

My consolation did not last long: if it were not a false alarm there was no need for the psychology of the unconscious at all.

On my return I found Myrtle sitting in an armchair quietly reading *Vogue*. Her apparent anxiety had entirely disappeared. I did not know whether to be pleased or alarmed. She measured out a very healthy dose of gin in the single tooth glass provided by the hotel, and proceeded to drink it with signs of enjoyment.

'You have some, darling,' she said, holding out the glass.

'I don't need it.'

Myrtle smiled. 'Have some instead of tea.' She giggled.

We sat on the edge of the bed, and passed the glass to and fro. I could not help noticing that Myrtle was becoming high-spirited.

'That can only lead to trouble,' I said.

Myrtle looked at me with a wide-eyed, furtive glance, and drank some more gin.

I too drank some more gin. I had begun to feel the situation slipping outside the bounds of my comprehension. I was, quite frankly, beginning to feel amorous.

'Will you take me to see the statue of Shelley?' Myrtle said. What she was thinking about was written all over her face.

'If you want to gaze at a man with no clothes,' I said, 'there's no need to go chasing down to Univ.'

Myrtle looked deeply shocked. 'He was a poet,' she said. 'I love poetry.' She began to finger the buttons on my shirt. I could smell the warm air near to her.

'Give me some more liquor!'

'You've had quite enough, darling.'

'Then you have some.' I paused. 'How about me posing as Shelley?'

'Darling!' Myrtle pushed me away.

'Then you pose as Shelley!'

'Really, darling!'

'Then,' I said, triumphantly getting the better of my shame altogether, 'we'll both pose as Shelley!'

Myrtle stopped fingering the buttons on my shirt. As if she were thinking of something quite different, she put down her glass on the bedside-table. Her eyes looked smaller with excitement. I pushed her back on to the pillows. She made a feeble resistive movement. I was deciding I might as well be hung for a sheep as a lamb – when there was a knock on the door.

It was a chambermaid telling me I was wanted on the telephone.

Robert wanted to know if he should cancel our dinner-party. With badly concealed impatience I told him not to cancel it.

In surprise he asked if Myrtle was better.

'Yes,' I said, and rang off.

When I got back to the room Myrtle's high spirits had disappeared. She was now depressed, standing beside the window and looking out over the dreary back of the hotel. The drizzle had thickened into rain.

I was suddenly overwhelmed by the seriousness of our predicament. I put my arm round her, to comfort her. Neither of us spoke for a long time.

'Would you rather not dine with Robert?' I said.

Myrtle looked at me reproachfully. 'We must.'

I felt apprehensive. I felt the dinner-party was going to be disastrous.

'I think I'll change my dress,' said Myrtle.

'You look perfect as you are.'

Myrtle was not listening.

I sat down beside the dressing-table. Myrtle had brought with her a copy of a book by a successful American humorist. She sometimes read me passages which she found exceptionally funny, presumably to show me how it ought to be done. I now picked up the book and began masochistically to read it myself.

Myrtle remained in low spirits, but the dinner-party went off well, and next day her behaviour was normal.

I watched her anxiously, more anxiously, I think, than she watched herself. I did not tell Robert what was the matter, and I felt still less inclined to tell Tom. I knew that Tom, with his down-to-earth understanding, would tell me that Myrtle was trying to force me to marry her.

We returned to the town, with no sign of relief, and I spent a sleepless night.

I spent two sleepless nights – and ought to have spent three, but I was too tired for even the deepest anxiety to keep me awake.

Then Myrtle rang me up to tell me that all was well. I ought to have felt overcome with relief. I ought to have gone out and celebrated.

I was relieved, of course; and yet I felt no desire to celebrate. Myrtle's voice came to me through the telephone as if she were speaking from a long way off.

'I'm glad,' I said.

Yet I knew that I felt as if something had been lost. These things are very strange.

2

Beside the Swimming-Pool

There was a short spell of hot weather and we began to frequent
the local swimming-pool when we came out of work. It was an
agreeable place, with a high entrance fee imposed to keep out the
lower orders. Young men with rich fathers in the boot-and-shoe
trade brought their girls in M.G. sports cars: we came on our bicycles. There were half a dozen showy young divers, and at least a
couple of young men who could swim more than two lengths in
very fast free style. The girls wore bathing-costumes made of what
they called the latest thing in two-way stretch. You could not have
wished for more in the way of provincial chic.

I usually arrived first, having a greater passion than the others
for swimming and lying in the sun. On the evening when the
course of our lives perceptibly took a new turn I had arranged to
be joined by Myrtle and Tom. While I sat waiting for them I enjoyed the scene.

The owners of the pool had clearly had in view, when choosing
their design, something colourful. They had got what they wanted.
The bath, through which constantly flowed heavily chlorinated
water, was lined with glittering cobalt-blue tiles, which gave the
water a quite unearthly look. The white surface of new concrete
changing-sheds glared brilliantly in the afternoon sunlight, and
against it were lined deckchairs made with orange and green
striped canvas. There were two plots of grass, from the centres of
which sprang fountains of pink rambler roses.

Against this background, to my surprise, appeared Steve. When
he was stripped Steve looked much more bony and boyish than
when he was dressed: he hunched his shoulders and walked

flat-footedly. He tended to hang about on the edge of the bath, though he was a fair swimmer, with his arms crossed over his chest, apparently shivering. He saw me, and came and sat on the grass beside me.

'Where's Tom?' I asked.

'I don't know.'

There was a peculiar silence, to which my contribution was more surprise.

'I suppose you know he's coming, Steve?'

'Is he?' Steve turned quickly in agitation. 'Honestly, Joe, I didn't know. What shall I do?' Steve's face assumed an expression of frantic alarm. 'What shall I do? I've arranged to meet a *girl* here!'

'Really!' I said, not committing myself immediately to unqualified belief.

'What shall I do?'

'I don't know, Steve.' Then I said helpfully: 'Perhaps love will find a way.'

'It couldn't get past Tom!' Steve hunched his shoulders. 'Honestly, Joe, it wouldn't stand a chance.'

'Oh!'

'This is terrible, Joe. Honestly, you don't understand.'

'Are you sure you didn't know Tom was coming?' Somehow I could not help feeling that in spite of his frantic alarm Steve was looking forward to a scene with Tom.

'Of course not. He'll go mad when he finds out.'

'He'll get over it.'

Steve gave me a look that was cold and cross. 'What will happen to me in the meantime?' he asked.

That question I was unable to answer. I suggested that we should go and swim, but Steve shook his head.

'I want to think,' he said. So he thought for a while. 'I want to talk.'

'What about?'

Steve turned to look at me. 'I really did like it, Joe . . .'

'What?' I had no idea what he meant.

'Taking this girl out, of course. I took her to the pictures last night. You may think it sounds silly, Joe, but it wasn't! I liked it. It made me feel I was doing something that was real and true. It made me feel like other boys. Other boys take their girls to the pictures.'

'What film did you see?'

Steve's air of passionate sincerity vanished: he looked nettled.

'We went to the Odeon. It was a terrible film, I know. But she wanted to see it.'

'That's nothing, in the course of love, Steve. You must be prepared for greater sacrifices than that.'

'But it really was terrible. It was excruciating. All about a *sheep-dog*.'

'As you grow older, Steve, you'll realize that love is inseparable from suffering,' I said. 'Myrtle once made me go to Stratford-on-Avon to see *A Comedy of Errors*.'

'No!'

'If girls aren't ignorant, they're cultured,' I said. 'You can't avoid suffering.'

Steve spread out his towel over the grass and lay down on his stomach.

'Tell me about your girl,' I said.

'There's not very much to tell. I met her here last week. She's only a schoolgirl. Quite pretty, though. A bit silly, but I don't mind that. It makes me feel older than her, and I like that.'

'How old is she?'

'Fifteen. Nearly sixteen.'

'That's a bit young.'

'That's what I want, Joe. It's innocent, and I want to keep it innocent.'

'If she's only fifteen you're likely to succeed for a good many years.'

'Years!' said Steve, obviously presented with a new concept. He pondered it with chagrin. 'Won't it be terribly monotonous?'

'Not exactly,' I said. 'But it won't have the ups and downs of the other state.'

Steve was silent for a while.

'I did try to kiss her on the way home,' he said. 'Actually I didn't particularly want to. But I thought she'd expect it. One has to be conventional.'

'That seemed to be the aim.'

Steve turned his head up to see how I was taking it. 'She let me kiss her on the cheek.'

I maintained a serious expression. 'And then?'

A glint came into the corners of his eyes. 'She said: "Aren't I pretty!" and touched her hair.'

'But Steve!' I burst out: 'That wouldn't do for you at all!' I knew Tom constantly told him he was Adonis and this was not a whit too much or too often.

'It made a change,' said Steve, grinning, 'but not a nice one.'

Some people who were camped a little way off turned to listen to us. We stopped talking. Steve laid his face on the ground. I looked at the crowd – and saw Tom coming, bearing down like a battleship on Steve.

I greeted Tom, who spread out his towel and sat down beside us. Steve kept his face on the turf, and Tom glared at him. Steve was deliberately behaving badly. Thinking of Myrtle I asked Tom what time it was. He looked at his watch and told me. Immediately Steve heard the time he roused himself and stood up. He must have been due for his rendezvous.

'Steve, where are you going?'

'To get a handkerchief out of my locker.'

'What for?'

'I need it.'

'I've got a spare one.'

'I want my own.'

With bulging eyes Tom was watching Steve, whose errand sounded most improbable. Steve was furtively looking round at the crowd.

Tom shrugged his shoulders, and Steve shambled away, clearly searching for his schoolgirl. I glanced at Tom. It was the signal for him to plunge immediately into intimate conversation about Steve.

In a moment he was asking me questions – Where was Steve going? What was he doing? How long had he been there? Had he been with me all the time? What had we been talking about?

I answered the questions as truthfully as I could without making matters worse. My heart sank as I followed the boring routine of jealousy in someone else.

'I don't know, Tom,' I found myself saying. 'How can I know?' I paused. 'And even if I did know it wouldn't make you any more satisfied if I told you.'

'I should want to know all the same,' Tom said, rebuking me.

I shrugged my shoulders. I knew he was in no mood for seeing Steve's latest manœuvres in their true ridiculous light.

'You forget that I'm in love,' said Tom.

'At least you're jealous,' said I.

'The two things don't necessarily mean the same thing,' said Tom, 'as you ought to know, Joe.' Tom could never resist the satisfaction of teaching his grandmother to suck eggs.

'One can be jealous without being in love,' he went on; 'but one can't be in love without being jealous.'

He gave me a sidelong glance, so I presumed he was referring to me. I had been too ashamed of my own jealousy to confide in him: consequently he found my display of that emotion suspiciously inadequate.

We were silent for a while.

Then Tom said, with great feeling: 'I'm afraid this is beginning to get me down, Joe.'

My sympathy quickened. 'Can't you begin to – I don't know – pull out?'

'Of course not.'

I felt inclined to shrug my shoulders. However, I simply said: 'I'm sorry.'

'I've never been able to withdraw,' said Tom, with some truth. 'I have to go on.' He paused. 'I'm afraid this time it may drive me mad.'

'That appears to be what Steve's aiming at.'

'Not at all, Joe. He can't help it,' said Tom.

'Oh.'

'That's what makes it so moving. That's why he needs me.'

Thinking of cash I said: 'He certainly needs you, Tom.'

'I don't know what he would do without me.'

'He'd lead a life of vastly restricted enterprise.'

Tom indicated that my remark showed lack of understanding.

'I think he's devoted to me.'

'He is, Tom.'

'If only I could feel sure of him.' Tom shook his head. 'That's the trouble with love, Joe. If only one could feel sure . . . If only I could be sure this was going to last even another year.'

For the moment I forgot, just as Tom did, that he was supposed to be leaving the country in another three weeks. He was speaking from his heart, and I was moved. I believed the kind of love he felt for Steve could rouse as deep feeling, could cause as sudden happiness and as sharp anguish, as any other kind. But I had no faith in its lasting: I could no more believe it would last than I could believe water would flow uphill.

'But it may last six months,' said Tom, and I swear that his tone was that of a man who is announcing a not unsatisfactory compromise.

Tom was a powerful swimmer: he had a good layer of fat which kept him afloat, and strong muscles well-suited for propulsion. We dived into the bright blue waves, and came up blinking chlorinated water out of our eyes. Tom followed his usual practice of setting out to swim many consecutive lengths at a slow, steady pace. I swam beside him for a while and then changed my mind. I climbed out of the bath and looked round.

I was not the only person who knew Tom's usual practice. Steve, confident that Tom's head would be under water for most of the next fifteen minutes, was standing in full view of everybody present conversing gaily with two schoolgirls.

I did not know what to do. Intervention of any kind seemed to me fatal. I could only stand watching, while drops of water trickled down from my hair on to my shoulders, hoping for the best.

Now hoping for the best is one of the most feeble of human activities, and I ought to have known better: especially as I knew that one of the most obvious characteristics of showy divers is entire disregard for the comfort of swimmers. I glanced back and forth, from Steve and his lively, leggy, young girls to Tom's carroty head thrusting steadfastly across the bath. And I was just in time to see two boys in a double dive enter the water a yard ahead of Tom. He was immediately brought to a standstill bouncing angrily in the wash. He spat water from his mouth, and rubbed it out of his eyes; and looked all round. The first thing he saw was Steve.

In half a dozen strokes Tom was at the side of the bath, climbing out, and marching up to Steve. I saw the startled look on Steve's face as Tom tapped him on the shoulder. There was a brief exchange of words, and then they both came away together, leaving the young girls looking at each other speechlessly. Tom strode in front with the sunlight glistening in the fuzz of red hair on his chest: Steve reluctantly brought up the rear.

I went to collect my towel, and we all fetched up simultaneously at the same spot. Tom's eyes looked startling, the irises greener with rage and the whites bloodshot with chlorine.

'You're driving me mad, Steve!' he said, hurriedly wiping his face. His passionate tone was somewhat muffled by the towel.

Steve said nothing, and began ineffectually to dry the inside of his leg, where the water was dripping from his trunks.

'Do you hear?' said Tom. 'You're driving me mad.'

'What?' said Steve. 'I can't hear because of your towel.'

'You're driving me mad!'

Steve said sulkily: 'I wasn't doing anything wrong. Don't be silly, Tom.'

I thought it was time to remove myself, although I knew that Tom had no objection to my presence during his domestic rows – in fact I suspected that he rather liked me to be there, adding to the drama.

I turned away and began to dry myself. I heard Steve say:

'Here's Myrtle.'

It was a great relief. I saw Myrtle sauntering towards us, looking fresh and bright.

'You do look funny, all standing like that, drying yourselves. Like a picture by Duncan Grant.' She smiled to herself. 'Only his young men weren't wearing...' Her voice faded out, suggestively.

'Myrtle, you've not changed your dress,' said Tom, peremptorily. 'Aren't you going to bathe?'

I thought he was trying to get rid of her.

'No, I don't think I will,' said Myrtle and sat down on the grass. I sat down beside her. She did not often swim: I thought she was shy of appearing in a bathing-costume because she was so slender and small-breasted. And of course she always felt cold. 'I don't think I can.'

I glanced at her. She looked at me with round, apologetic eyes: 'I'm sorry, darling. I can't stay and go home with you. I want to go somewhere later. Do you mind?'

It was my turn to be alarmed and irritated. 'Not at all,' I said.

There was a pause. Myrtle was watching Tom and Steve. I was thinking. It reminded me of other occasions when she had behaved like this. My mind went back over many events during the past year, and suddenly I saw their pattern. Provocation, leading to an outburst, leading to reconciliation – and then the cycle all over again. We were just entering the first round once more.

'You sound cross,' she said.

'I'm not cross at all.'

Tom sat down on his towel beside her, with his back to Steve. He glanced at me, and said to Myrtle:

'Joe, saying he's not cross, has a wonderfully unconvincing sound.'

'I know.' Myrtle smoothed her dress over her knees. 'He's always cross. He's always cross with me.'

Tom's anger with Steve had faded or else he was concealing it well. He smirked warmly at Myrtle.

'These introverts,' he said to her.

Myrtle shook her head. 'I suppose I must be an extravert.'

'You are, my dear,' said Tom.

Myrtle gave him a sad-eyed, appealing look.

'You're like me.' Tom returned her look. 'That's why we understand each other so well.'

Myrtle did not reply.

'That's why you'd find me so much easier to live with.' He now turned all his attention upon her, as if neither Steve nor I were there. 'You like to feel relaxed, don't you? You like to do things when you want to do them – when you *feel* like it. When the *spirit* moves you, my dear. Not when Joe does . . .'

Myrtle looked thoughtful. I cannot say I was pleased. I felt like saying: 'That's a bit thick', or 'Come off it, Tom'.

'We're easy persons to live with,' Tom went on. 'In fact I think we above all are the easiest. We go' – he paused, before shamelessly introducing my own phrase for it – 'by atmosphere.' And he waved his hand gracefully through the air.

Myrtle put on the expression of a young girl listening to revelations. I may say that there was nothing false about it. Both she and Tom were in a sense carried away by what they were saying to each other. I may say also that I was not carried away, and what is more my high resolve to be patient and forbearing had wilted disastrously. The only thing that stopped me intervening now was a feeling that Tom might make a fool of himself. I was waiting.

Myrtle nodded her head.

'Ah, Myrtle!' Tom put his hand on hers. 'There isn't anything you couldn't tell me, is there?' He looked into her eyes.

Myrtle blinked. I could have sworn Tom had gone a step too far. I think she must have moved her hand, because Tom took his away.

There was a pause. Myrtle said, in a friendly tone of observation: 'You're getting fat, Tom.'

This was not at all what Tom wanted her to tell him. Tom looked down at his chest, with the tufts of red hair that I personally found repellent, and inflated it.

'I like getting fat,' he said.

'Joe's always exercising,' Myrtle said. 'So boring.'

'It has its rewards,' I said, in a cross, meaningful tone.

Tom shook his head at Myrtle. 'He doesn't understand us, does he?' He stroked his diaphragm. 'If you and I settled down together, Myrtle, you'd fall into my easy ways, just like that' – he snapped his finger and thumb together – 'and you'd get fat as well.'

This was not at all what Myrtle wanted Tom to tell her. I was pleased.

'I couldn't, Tom,' she said, faintly despairing.

'You would, my dear. And you'd love it. You wouldn't feel so cold.'

I watched Myrtle's expression with acute interest and pleasure. Naturally in the past I had not failed to tell her that she always felt cold because she had too thin a layer of subcutaneous fat. This explanation she regarded as mechanical and soulless in the highest degree. Myrtle knew that her feeling cold arose from distress of the heart. Tom had missed it. She sighed painfully.

Tom apparently did not notice. After all it must have been slightly distracting for him to have my eye fixed on him while he was making up to Myrtle, and to have Steve sulkily listening to him behind his back.

'I shall always feel cold,' Myrtle said.

'Not if I were looking after you, my dear. I should know exactly how you were feeling all the time.'

Myrtle looked distinctly worried at this prospect. I sympathized with her.

'And I should know' – Tom gave a clever, shrewd glance at me – 'how to give you good advice.'

It was one of Tom's theses that I did not know how to handle Myrtle, particularly in the way of giving her good advice. He appeared not to know that Myrtle hated advice of all kinds, good, bad and indifferent.

'Would you?' she said, looking at him with a soft lack of enthusiasm.

Tom was silent. He stared at her with his confident, understanding expression. He appeared to be judging, out of love and sympathy, her present state of health.

'You're tired, my dear,' he said, presumably finding shadows round her eyes.

'I am.'

Tom glanced at me again, as much as to say: 'This is how it ought to be done.' He leaned towards her, and said:

'You should go to bed earlier.'

If there was one thing Myrtle hated it was to be told she ought to go to bed earlier: in one simple move it negated her love of life, her profundity of soul and, more important still, her determination to do as she pleased.

Myrtle did not speak. She was feeling much too sad.

There is a dazzling reward for allowing your best friend to make advances to your young woman in your presence – the dazzling reward of seeing him put his foot in it.

In my opinion Tom had put his foot in it up to the knee, up to the hip.

At the same time I was a little surprised: my faith in extraverts was very strong. It did not occur to me that it was in very bad taste for Tom to talk to Myrtle in this way: I was concerned that he had not made a better job of it. I concluded that he must really be distracted by thoughts of the impression it must be making on Steve.

I glanced at Steve: it was impossible to tell what he was thinking. His dark hair had dried in a soft mop that was falling over his eyes. He appeared to have lost interest in the schoolgirls. I think he was simply bored.

The sun was beginning to go down. Myrtle stirred uneasily, and Tom began to study the people round about.

'Joe, look over there!'

I looked. Tom was pointing towards the bathing-sheds. Myrtle and Steve roused themselves.

It was Trevor and a girl. I have already remarked that Trevor was unusually small, that he was small-boned and altogether made on miniature lines. I now have to remark that Trevor's girl was unusually big.

We were startled. They came forward together, Trevor stepping firmly and delicately, and his girl walking with powerful tread. He was talking animatedly, and smiling up at her. She was listening in a big, proprietorial way. She was wearing a perfectly plain, light green bathing-dress, and a white rubber cap concealed her hair: nothing for one instant distracted one's attention from her physical form. It was a form not to be despised – far, far from it.

'She looks like Genesis,' said Tom, laughing.

'My dear Tom, you don't know anything about Genesis,' said Myrtle; and then suddenly blushed.

'The bulges!' said Tom. 'It's stupendous.'

We watched them, fascinated, as they strolled away and ensconced themselves privately in the furthest corner of the compound.

'After that,' I said, 'I think it's time for us to go.'

Tom and Steve went indoors to dress, and I bade goodbye to Myrtle. I thought she must be going to see Haxby but I refused to ask her. She held out her cheek and I kissed it lightly. As she walked lazily away I felt sad and irritated.

I found Steve standing in the doorway of a cubicle, rubbing himself perfunctorily with a towel. I stood in the doorway of mine, next to him. Tom was having a shower.

'Is that Trevor's regular girl-friend?' I said.

'I think so.'

'Was that the one he had in his car the night he was run in for jumping the traffic-lights?'

'I don't know.' He sounded uninterested.

There was a pause.

'Joe!' Steve called.

There was an odd tone in his voice. I stepped out into the aisle to look at him. His face had a curiously worried expression. He stopped rubbing himself.

'What's the matter, Steve?'

'Has Myrtle gone?'

'Yes.' I was puzzled by the question.

'Of course, she's gone. That's silly of me . . . Listen, Joe, you know why Tom was making those advances to her? . . .' His speech came in staccato bursts. 'I know you won't believe me, when I tell you this . . . Do you know Tom's latest idea? He's planning to marry Myrtle!'

I was astounded. I stared at Steve.

'Incredible! He can't! It's ludicrous!'

It was the most incredible story Steve had ever told me, and for the first time I had not accused him of lying.

'You're not supposed to know, Joe.'

'I should think not.'

'He talked to Robert about it last week-end. That's why he was in Oxford.'

It may seem absurd, but I was believing him.

Somebody came out of an adjacent cubicle, and we had to stop talking while he pushed past me. Looking down the aisle I saw Tom, with a towel round his waist, combing his hair in front of a mirror.

'Please don't tell him I told you, Joe.'

'Don't be ridiculous, Steve.'

'But you mustn't, Joe! Please don't let him know you even suspect until he tells you. Otherwise I shall have terrible scenes.'

'Look, Steve, you'd better –'

'He's coming! I can't tell you any more.' Steve backed into the cubicle and hastily flung his shirt over his head. His elbow stuck in the sleeve.

Tom came along.

'Now Steve, hurry up!' He glanced at Steve. 'If you put on your shirt the way I showed you, Steve, you'd find it would slip straight on.'

I retired to my cubicle.

And after we parted I went to my house. I had something new to think about.

I was utterly astounded. Apparently nothing was too ridiculous for Tom to do. First of all he professed to be wrapped up in Steve; secondly he knew Myrtle was in love with me; thirdly he was due to leave the country in less than three weeks anyway. I could not make sense of it; but I knew only too well that a situation was not less likely to arise because I was unable to make sense of it. Few situations, especially those precipitated by Tom, made sense.

'Steve must be lying,' I said to myself that night when I went to bed.

3

Two Scenes of Crisis

It was early in the morning, and I was sitting in the school play-ground, waiting for Frank and company to join me. I was not preparing a lesson: I was not preparing anything. I was thinking. It seemed to me that my affairs had become desperately complicated. In fact I said to myself that they were in a hell of a mess. It was the morning after Steve had confided Tom's latest idea. I had a headache and felt curiously tense.

The sky was clouded over, and during the night there must have been some rain. Every now and then drops of water fell from the leaves of the lime tree under which I was sitting: the ground was damp, and the atmosphere carried a warm, pervasive smell of dust. Birds fluttered to and fro between the trees. Everything seemed unusually quiet.

My morning newspaper lay folded in my lap, and I noticed part of the headline. I had already read it. The fate of Europe was rolling on, but I had begun to lose any accurate sense of what it was rolling towards. I was aware to my shame that I had become less interested.

Sometimes I tried to link the disintegration of our private lives with the disintegration of affairs in the world. I saw us all being carried along into some nameless chaos. Yet it rang false. In spite of what the headlines told me every morning, in spite of what I reasoned must happen to the world, I was really preoccupied most deeply with what was going on between me and Myrtle and be-tween Tom and Steve. People can concentrate on their private lives, I thought, in the middle of anything.

I had written to the American Consulate in London about a visa for myself. My slackness in *Weltanschauung* had not robbed me entirely of the capacity for action.

I had made a beginning with Bolshaw's computation. I had to do something. There was no reply from Miss X.Y., and I needed to know the fate of my last book before I could begin a new one. Suppose she never came back from the Balkans, suppose I were kept waiting a lifetime! My anxiety had become completely unreasonable. Small wonder I took to computation.

The idea that my true love was being pursued by my best friend did not cause me an entirely sleepless night. It was far too ridiculous. And as it had been conveyed to me by a notable liar, I reserved my right to make a scene. However, Tom's new gambit had brought me to one important conclusion; namely, that if I did not intend to marry Myrtle myself I ought not to stop anyone else marrying her.

This conclusion was important to me, and it was only afterwards that I learnt it was incomprehensible to everyone else. I must make it clear now that I not only came to the conclusion: I stuck to it. To understand it entails harking back to a revelation I made earlier on, that, feeling myself not to have been born a good man, I often sought to try and behave like one. Alas! I accepted that all was fair in love and war as far as primary things went; but if I could show a bit of decency in secondary ones, so much the better, I thought.

That was my aim. Nobody understood it. And I might have known that the result, if it was anything like the result of my previous attempts in this direction, was likely to be farcical. With my usual optimism, determination or crassness, I did not foresee it. I sat alone under the lime trees fascinated by the general concept rather than practical results. And of course I had a headache.

The boys came out and drew up their chairs beside me. I noticed that Trevor was missing and asked Frank where he was. Frank did not know.

'I saw him last night,' I said.

I thought Frank gave me an odd look.

'With 'is girl?' said Fred, getting down immediately to his favourite topic of conversation.

I did not reply.

'Wish I'd got a girl,' said Fred. 'I've been reading Freud. It's bad not to 'ave a girl.'

Had Trevor been present he would have lured Fred into an innocent, half-baked disquisition on psychoanalysis. As it was, Fred was ignored. He sighed and began to work.

A little while later a boy came out to me with a chit from the headmaster. It forbade the holding of lessons in the playground.

I was amazed. 'Look at this,' I said to Frank and passed it to him. Fred and Benny read it over his shoulder.

'What a sod!' said Frank.

'Oo-ya bugger,' said Fred.

The messenger, who had read it himself, sniggered cheerfully. I handed back the slip of paper and sent him on his way.

'What are you going to do, sir?' said Benny. It was a trivial annoyance. The practice of holding lessons in the yard was of long standing. The senior boys regarded it as one of their privileges.

'I don't propose to move now.'

I happened to look up, and saw the face of the headmaster peeping at me through his window.

Then I made a silly mistake. I decided to go and talk to Bolshaw. I thought he would be only too ready to gossip about the latest *démarche* of the headmaster. I walked into the school, and found him sitting in his room with the door open. He came out into the corridor to talk to me.

There was no excuse for me. I knew well enough that Bolshaw was unpredictable. His having recently been my ally did not make him approve of me any the more. To imagine that he would agree with me was walking into danger in the most imbecile fashion. Into it I walked, and a moment later found myself in the midst of a violent quarrel.

'I've just come out of the yard,' I said.

'Free period?'

'No. Teaching the sixth. I got the headmaster's note.'

'Have you taken them into the small lab?'

'Not on your life.'

'What do you mean, Lunn?'

'I don't propose to do anything about it.'

'Why not?'

'It's too silly.'

Bolshaw stood peering at me in the semi-darkness of the corridor, with his heavy shoulders rounded and his hands in his pockets.

'Why have you come to me?'

I ought to have known there was something wrong. To me the incident was trivial, and I was blind to his view of it. I replied:

'To see what we can do about it.'

Bolshaw raised his voice. 'Surprising as it may seem, I agree with the head for once. It's time this unconventional behaviour stopped. Look here, my good fellow, I told you that you'd got to put your nose to the grindstone. That meant this kind of thing has got to stop.'

I was furious. It crossed my mind that he had put the headmaster up to it.

'It's becoming increasingly clear to me,' Bolshaw said, 'that there's no room on this staff for people who flout the conventions.'

'What the hell's it got to do with you?'

I had been trapped into losing my temper.

'Everything. I know what the conventions are.'

'Do you indeed? Do you know that I and other masters have been taking lessons in the playground for the last seven years? When everybody does a thing – then it is conventional!'

Bolshaw snorted.

'That's what being conventional means!' I said. 'It's got nothing to do with whether they're good, bad, moral, wicked, useful or just damned lazy!'

'Listen to me, my good fellow! I don't propose to argue with you about what it means to be conventional. I *know*! And I can tell you this. Sooner or later the members of this staff who flout the conventions are going to find themselves' – he paused – 'outside!' He took a blustering breath. 'It may interest you to know that it was I who decided the chit should be circulated. The headmaster agreed with me, that more persons than one have got to put their noses to the grindstone!'

It was too much for me. I shouted angrily. 'What about yourself?'

And Bolshaw clearly had not the slightest idea what I meant.

'My function is to see that the noses, having been put to the grindstone, are kept there.' He gave a braying, self-satisfied laugh. 'The proper place for them!'

'It's the proper place for yours,' I said. 'You may appoint yourself to be keeper of the conventions, but I notice you don't appoint yourself to do any teaching.'

'I do more teaching than anyone else in this school.'

'You certainly teach fewer periods.'

'That's because I have the power of imparting knowledge more rapidly than others.'

'I don't know how you manage it from the staff-room. Do you teach by telepathy?'

Bolshaw looked away in a dignified fashion.

'It's a pity that you find it necessary to quarrel with me, Lunn. It's most unwise.'

I was alarmed. I knew that he was speaking the truth. Unfortunately he had spoken it too late. I had already done myself damage.

'I don't want,' he said, 'to have our collaboration disturbed.' He paused to allow the effect to sink in.

I could have cried out with rage. I had been thinking this quarrel would mean my labours in his research coming to an end. Now I saw that he was going to use it to force me to go on. I had played into his hands.

I was silent. Nothing could be unsaid.

Bolshaw rattled the change in his pockets, and glanced into the class-room. Then he turned back to me.

'I think it's a very good rule,' he said, 'never to quarrel with one's superior in authority.' He paused. 'I'm happy to say I've always kept to that rule. Except, of course, on rare occasions when I deemed it wiser to break it.'

There was nothing for me to say.

Immediately school was over on that afternoon I went to the café to meet Tom. I felt unusually agitated, and hardly noticed when I splashed through puddles of water lying in the cobbled market-place. I was thinking the sooner I was in America the better.

Tom was not there. I sat in our customary place, watching for him through the window. I suppose the sky was still grey and damp, but I do not recall it. There must have been delphiniums and lilies on the stalls. What I do remember, and strangely enough the recollection is vivid to this day, is that the waitresses were wearing a new uniform. They had previously worn black with white aprons: now they were in brown with aprons the colour of pale *café-au-lait*. Our waitress had blonde hair, and the new colours made her look very pretty.

Tom came in.

'You're looking worried,' he said. 'Have you had bad news from Miss X.Y.?'

I shook my head. Tom ordered tea. The ritual of ordering a meal was very important, whatever else was going on.

I described my quarrel with Bolshaw.

Tom listened with patience and sympathy. I was just coming to the end of it when the waitress brought the tea. We paused.

Tom poured out some tea and gave it to me, saying: 'It probably won't be serious.'

'It's maddening. There was no need for it whatsoever. I just took leave of my senses.'

Tom smiled. Instead of saying. 'You introverts,' he said:

'I do it frequently.' He looked at me with concentrated interest. 'If you lost your temper as frequently as I do, Joe, you wouldn't be so upset by it. You don't seem to realize how often other people do lose their tempers.'

'Bolshaw didn't really lose his.'

'No. He was satisfied with you losing yours. Are you under the impression there's no emotion flying about between you and Bolshaw? The two of you aren't counters in a complicated puzzle.

136

You're both human. At this moment Bolshaw's probably feeling a glow of satisfaction, instead of feeling frustrated irritation.' Tom called the waitress: 'I should like another meringue, please.'

I confess to being comforted by this revelation of truth. Tom was speaking precisely in the tone he copied from Robert.

The next thing he said was, 'I think you'll find it cleared the air.' It might have been Robert speaking, had the remark not been so absurd.

'Cleared the air!' I cried. 'It's probably cleared me out of my job!'

Tom shrugged his shoulders.

There was a pause, and I said: 'I think the sooner I'm in America the better.'

'Yes.'

Something made me glance at Tom – he met my glance with patent evasion.

'I've been thinking about my own plans,' he said.

'Yes?' I should hope he had.

Tom adopted his weightiest manner. 'I may possibly postpone my departure.' He spread out his hands. 'Just by a fortnight.'

I was brought up sharply. 'Why?' I said.

'Certain affairs at the office are running behind time.'

I did not believe him. 'Is it Steve or Myrtle?' I asked myself. I was just framing an oblique question, when we were interrupted. There was a stir beside us, and I looked up to see Frank.

I was startled. I had not asked him to come. Occasionally we invited him to have a drink with us in a public-house, but neither he nor any of the other boys was supposed to join us without being asked. Tom looked surprised.

'I thought I should find you here.' Frank looked very embarrassed. He had naturally pleasant manners.

'Sit down,' said Tom.

Frank drew up another chair to our table. He sat down and nervously straightened his tie, which was already tied to perfection.

'I know I'm intruding,' he said, 'but I had to come.' He addressed himself to Tom. 'I hope Joe won't mind.' He pointed his nose diffidently towards me.

I shook my head.

Frank said: 'It's about Trevor.' He glanced round. 'I suppose you know he's been having an affair with a girl? Well, he's . . . you know . . . got her into trouble.'

I exclaimed in surprise.

Tom said: 'He'll have to marry her.'

At this moment the waitress came up to ask if Frank wanted anything. 'Bring some more tea,' Tom said to her commandingly.

I was silent. I was seeing us all ruined by a scandal.

'He'll have to marry her,' Tom repeated.

'That's out of the question,' said Frank.

'Nonsense. How old is he?'

'Nineteen.'

'Then why can't he marry her?'

'*She* doesn't want to marry *him*!' Frank replied, with great seriousness.

'Good gracious!' said Tom, and added: 'I can't say that I blame her.'

'That isn't the point,' said Frank.

'Why doesn't she want to marry him?'

'She wants to be a sculptor.' It appeared that all parties concerned thought sculpture and wedlock were mutually exclusive.

Tom laughed. 'She looks as if she's sculpted herself!'

I said: 'Is it that big woman we saw him with last night?'

'That's right,' said Frank. 'She's huge.'

Tom said: 'He's proved his manhood, anyway.' He smiled flickeringly: 'I suppose he thought the bigger the woman he took on the surer the proof.'

Frank laughed ruefully. 'Poor little Trev!' Tom gave him a knowing glance.

Frank's expression changed suddenly. 'But what are we to do, Tom?'

'What's Trevor doing?'

'Nothing. He's terrified. He doesn't get on with his family. He nearly got chucked out after the trouble over the car. If they hear about this . . .'

'Is it quite certain?' I asked – a question appropriate to me.

Frank looked at me. 'It's quite certain. This is the third month.'

'The little fool!' said Tom.

I said: 'It's no use taking that attitude.'

'I feel it,' said Tom. 'I feel healthy rage, Joe.'

The waitress brought us a fresh pot of tea, and a cup and saucer for Frank. Tom poured the tea.

Frank said to me: 'I'm sorry I came to you, Joe. We couldn't think of anyone else.'

'That's all right.'

Tom said: 'We must make some plans.' He paused. 'First of all we'd better get the situation clear.' He paused again. 'They ought to get married.'

'They can't,' said Frank.

'If she doesn't want to marry him, then she ought to have the child without.'

'There'd be a terrific scandal. It would ruin Trev's career.'

Tom pursed his lips. 'Then there's only one solution.'

'Trev says she's willing . . .'

In alarm I pushed my chair away from the table.

'Look!' I cried. 'I can't possibly be mixed up in this!'

'There's no need!' With a grandiose gesture Tom swept me aside. 'I'll handle it.'

His voice was full and resonant. He meant what he said. It was just the generous, disinterested action of which he was capable: he would plunge in without counting the risk – and also, as a matter of fact, he would enjoy himself. I forgot his bustling absurdity and felt great affection for his good heart.

'I'm afraid in my position at the school . . .' I began, feeling ashamed.

Tom interrupted. 'You'd better keep out of this.'

I nodded my head, thinking of the trouble I was in already at the school. I said: 'I think it would be best if I'd heard nothing about it.'

Frank looked worried. 'I won't say that I've told you.'

I smiled at him. 'It isn't your fault, Frank.'

Frank smiled back, readily restored.

I prepared to leave them. First of all I took out my wallet, and counted the pound notes in it. I handed them all to Tom, thinking it was rather handsome of me.

'You'll probably need these,' I said, in a solemn tone.

Tom accepted them, clearly thinking there were not enough. I was ruffled. I felt in my pockets for small change and found insufficient to pay for my tea.

'You'll have to let me have one of them back again,' I said.

'I'll lend you half a crown,' said Tom, not intending to part.

I walked away through the market-place. I realized that I had lost my resilience. I felt as touchy and cross as Myrtle accused me of being. I was inclined to ask myself rhetorical questions, such as: 'Why do I get involved with people?' and 'Why don't I leave them all?' It seemed to be that in some distant way Trevor was responsible for my having quarrelled with Bolshaw.

America, I thought, was the place for me. Land of liberty, where my pupils would not get their girls in trouble. Or would they? Exactly what sort of liberty was it? My speculations were suddenly interrupted by recalling that Tom had postponed his setting sail for the land of liberty.

My speculations changed to suspicions. 'What,' I asked myself, in a question that was far from rhetorical, 'is Tom up to now?'

4

Conclusion in a Public-House

It was evening and I was waiting apprehensively for Myrtle to come. We had just had a strange conversation over the telephone. For the last few days I had seen nothing of her; things were going wrong again. She had rung up to tell me she was going to a midnight matinée.

'Midnight matinée!' I had cried, in surprise. 'What on earth of?'

'Of a film.'

'You didn't tell me, darling.'

'I didn't think you'd be interested.' Her voice sounded desolate and reproachful.

As she did not tell me the name of the film I gathered it must be 'Turksib' or 'Earth'. I said: 'Who are you going with? The Crows?'

Myrtle did not reply. I thought: 'So much for that!' and began a gossipy conversation to divert her.

'I've got an excellent story about Tom,' I said. 'He told me he'd postponed going to America so I sent a postcard to Robert, asking if it was true. And got a postcard back from Tom himself.'

'How queer,' said Myrtle.

'Not queer at all. He was in Oxford, and must have been in Robert's rooms, reading through his correspondence while he was out – saw my postcard, and just replied to it.' I thought the story was funny. 'What could be simpler?'

'How queer,' Myrtle said again, rather as if she had not been listening.

I tried another tack. I said:

'I'm feeling slightly more cheerful about school. There's a bit of intrigue going on in the staff-room against Bolshaw. I'm not taking part because it won't succeed. Shall I tell you about it? It's interesting because I could reasonably support Bolshaw for once.'

'How queer.'

It was the third time. Her voice sounded distant and lifeless, as if it were repeating the phrase from some worn-out groove.

'What is the matter, darling?' I said. 'You keep on saying "How queer" in an extraordinary way.'

'Do I?'

'You do.'

'I don't know . . .'

'In that case, I might just as well have been talking about the weather.'

'I suppose it's because I'm so empty-headed!'

'Myrtle, what *is* the matter?'

'I often wonder how I compare with Robert and Tom!'

I gave up. I had a sudden vision of her desperate unhappiness.

'I want to see you,' I said. 'Will you meet me, darling?'

'I'm going to a film! . . .' Her voice trailed off in pain.

'Let's have a drink before you go. Will you? Please, darling!'

At last Myrtle agreed, though her tone remained lifeless.

And so it came about that I was waiting apprehensively for her to come and join me in a public-house near my lodgings.

I sat in the public bar, which I had chosen instead of the saloon because it was always empty. The floors were made of uncovered boards, and the table-tops were not scrubbed very often. The wall-paper had been given a coat of shiny brown varnish: over the fireplace there was a dusty mirror with a knot of red Flanders poppies twisted into one corner of the frame: on the opposite wall was an oilcloth chart showing the town Association football team's fixtures of three years ago, surrounded by advertisements for hair-dressing, sausages and furniture removals.

On the mantelshelf stood a fortune-telling machine shaped like a miniature wireless set. You put in a penny and selected a button to press, whereupon a coloured light flickered, and the machine delivered a pasteboard card with your fortune inscribed upon it.

I put in a penny. The card said:

YOU ARE SUNNY AND GOOD-NATURED.
BEWARE THE INFLUENCE OF OTHERS.

'Dammit!' I said aloud. I took the card between my first and second fingers and flicked it, as I used to flick cigarette cards when I was a boy, into the empty fireplace.

The door opened and Tom's red head looked in. I was astonished.

'Ah! I thought I might find you here.' Tom came towards me. 'I've just called at your house.' The latter sentence was uttered in a vaguely apologetic tone.

'Did you know I was meeting Myrtle?'

'Are you?'

I looked at him. Tom had a remarkable talent for turning up at rendezvous I had made with someone else. His instinct for not missing anything amounted to second sight. I said:

'Yes. You can push off when she comes.'

'Of course,' said Tom, as if I had offended his taste for old-world courtesy.

'Did you want to see me about anything special?'

'No.' Tom stood on his dignity for a moment. Then he went across to the service hatch, where he bought a pint of beer for himself and another one for me.

'How is Myrtle?' he asked.

I told him. I was so worried about her that I paid no attention to my suspicions of him. I confided my fears and my self-reproaches.

Tom reassured me.

'It wouldn't make the slightest difference if you married her,' he said. 'It's the ebb and flow of her nature.' He spoke with great authority, though not necessarily with great truth. 'If you married her she'd still have those bouts of accidie. It's the ebb and flow you know.' He was pleased with the phrase and illustrated it with his hands.

It seemed to me that we had too much ebb and not enough flow. 'Poor Myrtle,' I said, with a deep stir of sympathy for her. She had a lightly balanced emotional nature – that was what made her so attractive to me – but for some reason or other, alas! it tipped over too readily in the downward direction.

'I shouldn't take it very seriously,' said Tom. 'It really is her temperament, and fundamentally, you know, she's accommodated to it.' He smiled at me. 'I understand these things, Joe.'

I knew perfectly well that when he was alone with her instead of with me he approached the problem in a very different tone.

'I'm much nearer to her in this way than you are,' he said.

This remark, on the other hand, Myrtle must have had addressed to her very frequently in their *tête-à-tête*.

'Much nearer, you know,' Tom repeated.

I did not mention any steps he might be proposing to take on the basis of this peculiar nearness – time would display them soon enough.

And then I said, honestly: 'You give me great comfort, Tom.'

'That's what one's friends are for,' said Tom.

'God knows, I'm in need of it.'

Tom shook his head. 'It's time this affair was over,' he said, in the tone of great wisdom that he used when he spoke from the depths of his soul – you remember, the very old soul. I recalled Bolshaw saying: 'The time has come.' I wondered how on earth everybody but me recognized the time with such certainty. I decided it was because they lacked the capacity for recognizing anything else.

Tom drank off about a third of a pint, and sighed with satisfaction. I noticed the barman had appeared at the service-hatch: he was polishing glasses which he placed on a shelf out of sight.

Suddenly the door opened. I thought it was Myrtle and my heart jumped. It was a seedy-looking man wearing a peaked cap and a muffler. He glanced at Tom and me, apparently did not care for the look of us, and went out again. We heard him go into the saloon.

We were silent. It was a warm evening, and an invisible fly buzzed round the ceiling. 'Have some more beer?' said Tom.

'It's my round.'

Suddenly I remembered Trevor's crisis. I asked Tom what had happened.

Tom smiled blandly. 'I think everything will be . . . managed,' he said. 'Apparently we have to wait. The timing is important, you know.' He stopped. 'I think it would be wise for you to be ignorant of it.'

'Will you need more money?'

Tom shrugged his shoulders. I stood up to buy the next round of drinks. Myrtle came in.

Myrtle saw me first and made no effort to raise the light of recognition. Then she saw Tom, and smiled tremulously.

'Ah, Myrtle,' said Tom, in an effusively sympathetic tone.

'Tom was just going,' I said to Myrtle, malevolently recalling the times Tom had got rid of me or of her.

Tom shrugged his shoulders, and smiled at Myrtle. 'Joe behaving as usual.'

The remark unaccountably plunged Myrtle into despair. She made it very plain and Tom was not at all pleased.

'I think I'll go,' he said.

I watched him leave while Myrtle settled herself beside me. I was suddenly overwhelmed by apprehension. I thought, 'This is going to be the worst scene.'

Myrtle and I looked into each other's eyes. It was a light evening, but the room was dark and we were sitting with our backs to the window.

I saw written in Myrtle's face all the things I wished not to see. Fear and shame suddenly rose up in me, mingled with a deep poignant sympathy. Myrtle did not speak. She sat there, just letting me look at her. Not a word had been passed between us, not a touch, and yet I felt as if the whole scene were already over. 'This is the end.'

'How are you feeling now, darling?' I could not help myself from speaking as if she were in the grip of an illness from which she might already be recovering.

'I don't know.'

I looked at her closely. Her eyes looked bigger, and the bright patches of colour in her cheeks had spread out more widely. Under her eyes there were brown stains. She seemed to be breathing with a deeper movement of her heart.

'Darling.' I took hold of her hand. She let it lie in mine.

'This can't go on,' she said.

I said nothing. I felt as if I had been struck.

There was a long pause. 'Can it?' she said, and looked at me.

I did not possess the courage to say 'no'. I said, nearly inaudibly: 'I don't know. If you don't think . . .'

There was a movement and the barman appeared in the hatch to see if we wanted anything.

Myrtle asked for a double whisky.

Out of surprise I bought her one, and I thought I had better have one myself. I set the two glasses on the wooden table in front of us.

We each drank a little. Neither of us said anything. We drank some more. The minutes passed by us, like the flies buzzing across the room. The flies congregated at the mirror.

'How *can* it go on?' Myrtle spoke without looking at me now.

'I don't know.'

We were silent again. I drank some more whisky. I could not tell what I was feeling or thinking. I was overwhelmed by recollections of the past.

I noticed her gulp down her drink. The expression on her face remained exactly the same. She said:

'I think about nothing else, nowadays.'

I said: 'Nor I.'

There was a pause. And I said: 'Do you want it to end?'

'How could I?' Faint life came into her voice.

'Then how? . . .'

'I love you.' She suddenly looked at me.

146

'Oh God!'

Myrtle drew in her breath sharply. She was holding the glass quite close to her lips, looking into it.

'What's the matter?'

'You don't want to marry me!' No sooner had she uttered the words than she burst into tears.

I was faced with the truth, with the core of my own obstinacy. I could have stretched out my hand and whispered, 'I'll marry you.' She was so near to me. It was so little to say.

I shook my head. 'No.'

Myrtle sobbed quietly. I watched her. I finished my glass of whisky. Do not think I was not caught in the throes of self-reproach and remorse. I was. I was confronted with the core of my own obstinacy, and it was a hateful thing. Yet I neither could nor would break it. Not for a moment did I see that she had a core of obstinacy too. Everything that was causing her pain was my fault. I tortured myself – because I would not give in.

We sat for a long time thus, concerned, each of us, with ourselves: and the bonds between us were snapping. We had reached the final question and the final answer – what seemed the final question and answer to us – and there was nowhere further to go.

Myrtle took out a handkerchief and tried to wipe her eyes. She glanced at the stains on it of mascara. Quietly I went and fetched us another double whisky apiece. I dropped too much water into Myrtle's. She picked it up and absent-mindedly began to drink it as if it were lemonade. I stared at my own glass. We could not speak.

In the saloon bar someone switched on a wireless set, and I heard a voice inexorably reading out cricket scores. Myrtle appeared not to hear it. We were still entirely alone in the bar. At last she looked up.

'I must go away,' she said.

'Don't go yet, darling.'

'I must . . .'

It seemed unbearable to let her go. I put my arm round her, as if to comfort her.

'My own darling!' I cried, hiding my face against her neck. I felt as if I possessed her completely, and it touched me so that I could have burst into tears. I felt another living creature, closer to me than I had ever felt anyone before, now, at the moment when we were going to part.

Myrtle uttered a great sigh. I picked up her glass, and held it for her to drink out of it. Then I had a drink.

'I'm late already,' Myrtle said.

'Never mind.'

'But I've got an appointment.'

'Are you going with Haxby?'

'Yes.'

'He can wait.'

Myrtle freed herself from my arm in order to turn to me. 'Don't you care about anybody?'

'I don't understand what you mean.'

'Of course, you don't.' She began to show signs of life. 'You don't care if he waits. You don't care if I go.'

'That's all you know about it.'

'How can I tell? You never say anything. Other people do, but you never do. *You* never say anything one way or the other. You talk about Haxby as if he didn't matter.' She rounded upon me with impressive force. 'Do you know he wants to shoot you?'

'Good gracious!' I exclaimed.

'He's jealous!' said Myrtle.

'I suppose he must be.'

'There you go! You just put yourself in *his* place!'

'How can I be a writer if I don't?'

'I don't know *how* you can do it. You don't care about me.'

'If you mean that I don't know what it is to be jealous, then you're . . .'

'Do you? Do you?' Myrtle faced me. 'Then why didn't you tell me?'

'Because I don't tell anybody. Because jealousy's hateful!' I cried. 'I hate being jealous of Haxby. I wish I'd never heard of him!'

'There's a way out, isn't there?' She meant by marrying her.

I stood up. 'No!' I cried. 'I won't take it.'

Myrtle watched me. 'No, I realize that now. Tom made that pretty clear to me.'

'Tom?' I said. 'You've been talking to Tom about this.'

'Of course. Who am I to talk to? I haven't got any friends. And Tom understands you.'

'Says he does.'

'He understands you better than you think.'

'There's no truer word than that!'

'How horrible you are!'

I sat down again.

We were silent for a while.

'Does Tom think he understands you?' I said.

Myrtle did not reply.

I said: 'I'm sorry, darling.'

Myrtle looked at me, this time gently. 'You don't understand how I have no one to turn to. Tom is being kind to me, that's all. He's wonderfully sympathetic.'

I wondered if she had any inkling of Tom's motive in being wonderfully sympathetic, and decided not. It was not for me to enlighten her – anyway I was not sure myself.

I put my arm round her again, in a friendly way. My anger was subsiding and so was hers.

'Please, don't let's quarrel, darling.'

Myrtle was suddenly silent. It must have crossed both our minds simultaneously that I meant 'Don't let's quarrel before we part.'

'Don't say that!' she cried.

There was a pause. I finished my drink. Myrtle left hers. She sat looking at it, as if she wanted never to go any further with it, so as never to move from where she was now sitting with my arm round her.

The room was in twilight, and the barman unexpectedly switched on the light. We hid our faces.

Myrtle stood up, and I did the same.

'I must go,' she said.

We looked into each other's eyes. 'What is it to be?' Neither of us could utter the question.

'I'll put you on the bus,' I said.

Myrtle nodded, and we went into the street. It was less dusky than we had imagined. The air was warm on our cheeks. The street was wide, and lined with trees. We strolled to the bus-stop and waited.

I stood beside Myrtle for a while and suddenly looked at her. I saw that her expression had changed completely. Even though I was determined not to take the lead, I could not let the moment pass again without asking her:

'What do you want me to do?'

Her voice sounded hollow and distant as she said: 'I suppose we ought to stop seeing each other?'

I made no pretence of not accepting it.

'I'm terribly sorry,' I murmured, finding words feeble and hopeless. Myrtle appeared not to hear.

We saw a bus approaching.

'Goodbye, darling.'

Suddenly we were in each other's arms. I kissed her and she clung to me.

The bus passed us without stopping. We were at a request stop and had failed to hold up our hands.

'You'll have to wait for the next.'

Myrtle drew away from me. She was crying. 'Goodbye darling.'

'I'll wait with you.'

'No, don't; please don't! Go now!'

'I can't leave you.'

'I beg you to go!' She spoke with force and anguish.

I took hold of her hands for a moment, and then turned away.

I walked along the road, which sloped upwards and curved away to the right. As I reached the bend, I looked back. I saw Myrtle standing alone. Tears welled up into my eyes, so that I could not see where I was going. But I went on.

I went back to my house. The landlady and her niece were out, and the place was completely empty. I switched on the light in my room, and my glance fell on the telephone. I felt unutterably lonely.

I sat down in my chair, and began to think. The break had come at last. Yet there was something strange about it. Myrtle had said: 'I suppose we ought to stop seeing each other'; but she had framed it as a question, so as to leave it open for me to say, 'No, no!' I felt very confused. Had we parted or not? It seemed like it, yet somehow I felt sure that Myrtle had not. It takes two to make even a parting.

Gradually I became calmer. My mood changed. I went over the scene again and again; and I found it beginning to strike me differently. My confusion was disappearing and something definite was being revealed to me. I received the revelation with a bitter kind of resistance, because it made me feel cold and heartless.

I knew now that whatever Myrtle did in the future, for me the affair was irrevocably over.

Vertiginous Developments

Each time the telephone rang during the next few days I thought it would be Myrtle. It was not. I kept away from places where I might meet her and arranged to go and spend the week-end in Oxford. I felt uneasy and miserable, and at the same time convinced that something was going to happen.

I diverted myself with tedious business-like activities. The American Consulate in London had told me it was necessary to go to the Consulate in Birmingham to obtain my visa, so I arranged to collect it on Friday afternoon, when the school had a half-holiday. And I wrote again to Miss X.Y. about my manuscript.

On the day after my ambiguous parting with Myrtle Tom rang up, aiming to discover what had happened. I made him come round to my lodgings to find out.

I was sitting in my room, beside the open french window, eating tinned-salmon sandwiches for tea, when Tom arrived.

'I see you haven't lost your appetite,' he observed.

I thought the remark was in bad taste. 'I'll ask the landlady to make some more for you.' He was very fond of salmon sandwiches. 'I hope she hasn't run out of salmon,' I added, to frighten him.

Tom greedily ate a couple of mine, just in case. He glanced over the cake-stand. 'Very nice cakes she makes you. She's very devoted to you.'

'The niece makes them.'

'Ah! She made them for Mr Chinnock, of course.' He wagged his head sagely, at the thought of more devotion in a different guise.

I took the last sandwich, and went to order more. I met the landlady bringing them of her own accord. Tom saluted her in a flowery fashion, which clearly pleased her. She was a lean, middle-aged woman, with a pale, indrawn face and narrow, dark eyes. Tom made a gleam appear in her eyes. When she had gone out of the room Tom said:

'Now she'll be more devoted to you than ever.'

As there had been numerous quarrels over Myrtle visiting me late at night, I thought a little more devotion would do me no harm. Up to date I had seen no signs of it. Possessiveness, yes: devotion, no.

Tom said: 'I hear that Myrtle was looking dreadfully unhappy at the film show last night.'

'Who told you?'

'Steve went to it. He saw her. She was with Haxby.'

I did not say anything.

'What happened after I'd left you?' Tom asked. 'Did you break if off?'

'Break it off!' I exclaimed. 'It's not a stick of toffee. You don't break things off just like that.'

Tom's disapproval was evident. In my place he would have broken it off. However he said amiably: 'Then it's still on?'

'Not exactly,' I replied. 'That's the trouble.'

'Poor girl!'

'You told me yesterday she wasn't such a poor girl.'

'Is that how you left it?'

'Well, yes.'

Tom shook his head. 'I don't understand how you can leave it neither one way nor the other. I couldn't. I should have forced a decision.'

I was feeling in no mood to be amused. 'In a sense I did. I forced one from myself – afterwards. It's over as far as I'm concerned.'

'That's better. You'll feel much better for it.'

'I don't. I feel worse.'

'Purely transient,' said Tom.

There was a pause. Tom helped himself to the last of the fresh batch of salmon sandwiches.

I decided to tell him what had happened as honestly as I could. I repeated most of the conversation verbatim. I described Myrtle's tears and our last embrace at the bus-stop.

'My dear Joe,' said Tom, 'how you make the poor girl suffer!'

I said: 'How she makes me suffer, if it comes to that!'

'She probably thinks you don't intend to see her again.'

'That's just what you advised me to do.'

'It's positively brutal!' said Tom, paying no attention whatsoever. 'How you make her suffer!' His voice rose with anger. 'You treat her appallingly!'

You may find Tom's behaviour mildly contradictory: that is nothing to what I found it. In my own behaviour I aimed at some sort of consistency, and until I knew Tom I was under the impression that other people did the same. Not a bit of it! Tom was a revelation to me, and through him others were revealed. Only through observing Tom, I decided, could one understand the human race.

Tom denounced me for several minutes. After counselling me to break off the affair, he now abused me passionately for doing it – and at the same time managed to convey additional contempt for my pusillanimity in not making the break sharper. His face got redder and his eyes began to glare. He was carried away by his sympathy for Myrtle.

'You've ruined her life!' he cried.

I said nothing. Tom let the torrent carry him on. He turned his attention to my failings. While he ate my cakes he denounced my self-centredness, my coldness of heart, my unawareness of the feelings of others, my lack of passion – my complete unsatisfactoriness as man, thinker and lover. A few years earlier I should have lost my temper and argued furiously.

'What are you going to do next?' Tom demanded to know.

'Nothing,' I muttered.

'That's just like you.'

I did have a faint sensation of not knowing whether I was on my head or my heels. However, I pulled myself together and said ingeniously:

'What are *you* going to do next?'

Tom was brought momentarily to a standstill.

'I shall have to consider that,' he said.

I thought: 'That's unusual.'

'Myrtle has suffered terribly,' he said, more quietly. 'I think I'm the only person who understands exactly what it must have meant to her.'

'She told me you understood.'

'She said that, did she?' Tom suddenly looked at me quite naively.

I nodded my head.

'We've both suffered,' said Tom.

I nodded again. It seemed the only appropriate gesture to such monumental nonsense.

'I've been thinking about Myrtle for some time, Joe.'

'Oh?' I pricked up my ears.

Tom looked at me with a changed, unidentifiable expression. 'I've been thinking,' he said, 'that if you don't marry her, it might be a good idea for me to.'

I received the suggestion without a tremor. I was proud of having identified his expression – it was that of a man who is confident that he has introduced a delicate topic with unequalled tact and dexterity.

I made a non-commital murmuring noise. I think Tom had expected more. He was clearly puzzled that I showed no surprise, let alone passion. He said:

'What do you think?'

I said: 'I've been thinking about it, from a different point of view, of course, for some time.' I paused. 'The trouble about finding a husband for one's mistress, is that no other man seems quite good enough.'

Tom was extremely cross. He laughed, but a purple flush suddenly passed over his face, making his hair look yellower and his eyes greener.

'Witty as usual,' he said.

Whenever anyone says I am something or other 'as usual', it means he is disapproving of me.

'Perhaps,' he went on, 'we ought to talk just a little more seriously.'

'Would you like some more tea?' I said.

'Thank you.'

A stately air had now come over the proceedings. Tom accepted a cup of tea, and then said with great politeness and consideration:

'I take it that you would have no objection?'

'To your marrying Myrtle? I'm in no position to object.' I changed my tone to one of seriousness. 'I resolved some time ago that if I wasn't going to marry her myself I ought not to stop anyone else marrying her. Of course I don't want to let anyone else – or anything like it. But I shall make myself do it.'

'I see. It seems quite incomprehensible to me, of course.'

I bowed.

Tom said: 'This makes matters a little easier than I'd expected.'

'Easier?' I exclaimed. Perhaps I ought to interpolate that, even after having been prepared for it by Steve, I still thought I had never heard such a silly idea in my life as Tom's proposition. Also I thought Myrtle would see it in exactly the same light.

Tom pursed his lips and smiled.

The telephone rang. Tom and I glanced at each other, each thinking it was Myrtle. I closed the french window and took off the receiver. Tom waited to see if I wanted him to leave the room. I heard the voice of Steve.

'Joe, is Tom there?' He sounded worried.

'Yes.' I handed the receiver to Tom.

They conversed for a few moments, making arrangements to meet in half an hour. Tom put down the receiver, and turned to me with a self-satisfied smile.

'How are you getting on with Steve?' I asked.

'Perfectly well, Joe.' There was an amused glint in his eye, as much as to say: 'If you understood us you would not be alarmed.'

I called the landlady to clear away the tea.

'How's he getting on with his schoolgirls?' I said.

'I don't know. I don't really ask him.' Tom had now taken to setting me an example.

Recalling the scene at the swimming-pool, I said: 'That's wise of you.'

Tom sat in his chair again. 'He's growing up, of course. I realize that he's bound to grow away from me. It's very natural.' Tom paused. 'I encourage him. I don't want him to feel tied.'

I could not help being interested by this crescendo of lies, which, seemingly, we were only half-way through, as he said next: 'The important thing is to avoid scenes, Joe.'

'Don't you have any?' I could hardly believe my ears.

'No, Joe.'

We were interrupted by the landlady. Tom lit a cigarette. When she had gone he leaned forward confidently, and said:

'Of course, Steve doesn't know anything about my intentions towards Myrtle.'

'No,' I said. 'No.' I accepted this last, most glorious lie, with a recrudescence of the head-or-heels sensation.

'I hope you won't mention it to him.'

'If Steve doesn't know,' I said, 'you can rely upon me not to tell him, Tom.'

'I know you're one of the discreetest of men, Joe.'

Tom rose to go away, and on this happy, fraudulent note our conversation ended.

Tom had only left the house a minute or two when the telephone rang once more.

'It's Steve again. Has Tom gone? I wanted to speak to you, not him, when I rang before.' Steve's voice was agitated. 'I want to see you, Joe.'

'What for, Steve?'

'I can't tell you now. There isn't time. Tom will be here any moment. I want to see you, Joe.'

I had taken care to have all my time booked up until I went to Oxford. Steve was insistent, and at last I agreed that we might meet in the station refreshment room while I waited for my train. He rang off promptly.

I was mystified.

On Saturday morning I received a letter in unfamiliar handwriting. It was from Miss X.Y. and she said:

> Dear Mr Lunn: I do not know how to begin this letter, as I feel I am at a terrible disadvantage. I quite understand your anxiety about your manuscript, and of course I forgive you for writing a third time. I am afraid I have to ask *you* to forgive *me*, because the manuscript has unfortunately been mislaid. The reason I have delayed so long in writing to you is because I hoped it might turn up. Of course I was looking forward immensely to reading it . . .

I burst into a shout of mingled laughter and rage. Miss X.Y. had wasted five months of my time at a most critical point in my career; I was exactly where I started. The letter ended with an offer to read the novel, if I would send another copy, within a week.

At first I was too annoyed to accept, but in due course common sense supervened. I remained convinced, however, that should disasters of any magnitude be possible they would certainly befall me. In this mood I went off to meet Steve.

I hurried down to the platform and into the refreshment room. Steve was nowhere to be seen. I bought a bottle of beer and a cheese roll, and began to eat, keeping my eyes fixed on the door. I finished the cheese roll and I finished the beer. Still no sign of Steve. Suddenly it occurred to me that Steve was in a refreshment room on the wrong platform. I ran across the bridge, and searched for him on the other side. I found him. He was quietly reading a volume of poems by Baudelaire.

'Come out, Steve!' I said impatiently. 'You're in the wrong refreshment room.'

Steve looked injured. 'But I'm not, Joe! This is the right platform.'

'The right platform for somebody else's train, but not mine,' I said, taking him by the elbow and dragging him out. He stuck to his argument. There were two alternative routes to Oxford: he had chosen the platform for a train that left three hours later. I realized to my horror that I was behaving rather like Tom. I decided that Tom had great provocation.

'Do you want a bottle of beer?' I said, when I had safely installed him in the right place.

'Yes, please.' Steve wore the expression of a saint on the eve of martyrdom. This expression did not prevent him putting down half a Bass in one breath. 'I got very thirsty, waiting for you,' he said.

'Now, what do you want to tell me?'

We were leaning against the marble-topped counter, looking outwards at the platform. Behind us were two glass domes, containing buns, which served as a screen between us and the waitress. Steve glanced at his glass, and restrained himself out of politeness from drinking the rest of the beer before beginning his story.

'I found out that Tom's postponed his trip to America.'

'I know that.'

'I mean *again*, Joe. He's not going till the end of July now.'

This was news to me.

Steve said nothing. With a mixture of injured dignity and triumph he now finished his beer.

I was lost for a moment in alarm.

'What's his excuse now?' I asked.

'The job we're doing in the office.'

'I don't believe it.'

'That's what he's going to tell you anyway,' said Steve.

'What's his real reason? Do you know?'

'How should I know? He tells me so many things.'

'Repeat some of them.'

'I wasn't supposed to tell you.'

'Repeat them all the same.'

'He doesn't want to arrive ahead of you and Robert. He says you intend to send him first to do all the work.'

'But we're tied till the end of July.'

'You told him you were going to make him support you.'

'That's absurd – it was a joke,' I said. 'Robert said we were going to settle on him like Russian relations.' I smiled at the thought of it. 'And then treat him badly, as if he were a servant.'

'He took it seriously.'

'He's got some other reason, I'll be bound.'

'You mean it's part of his plan for marrying Myrtle?'

'Nonsense! He can't marry Myrtle. It's idiotic!'

'He's trying to make me believe it,' said Steve. 'And he's made himself believe it.'

'That's as may be. It does seem to me that his principal obstacle is making Myrtle believe it.'

Steve looked at me with shrewd grey eyes. 'She's seeing him a lot more than you think.'

I was slightly taken aback. 'Really,' I said.

There was a pause. I sipped a little beer. Steve eyed his empty glass, having no money to buy any more.

'And where do you come into this, Steve? Is Tom's devotion to you correspondingly weaker?'

'Weaker?' said Steve. 'Did you say weaker, Joe? It's stronger. Honestly, it's terrible! I can't get away from it for a moment. He tells me I'm growing away from him, and he doesn't want me to feel I'm tied to him – and then he refuses to let me out of his sight! Last night I wanted to stay at home. To work on my poetry. Honestly, I didn't want to go out with anyone else. I just wanted to stay at home. But he came round to the house. He stood in the middle of the room and said: "I want to know. Are you coming or aren't you?" In front of my father and mother!'

I imagined the scene well, with Tom glaring across the room. 'What did you say?'

Steve shrugged his shoulders. 'I had to go with him.'

'Extraordinary,' I said.

'He's terrified of me being unfaithful.'

I could not help laughing, though it hurt Steve's feelings. 'What about when he goes to America?'

'He expects me to join him in two or three years.'

This was more news to me. 'Indeed!'

'Yes,' said Steve. 'As far as I can see, he intends to marry Myrtle and take her to America; and me to stay here and be faithful to him. For three years!'

I was speechless from the staggering imbecility of it.

'Think of it, Joe!' Steve said, in tones of anguish.

'I'm thinking of what's supposed to happen at the end of three years, Steve, when you join the happy couple in America.'

Steve said: 'I don't think he's got as far as that.'

'It seems a very arbitrary place to draw the line.' I glanced at him, and just at that moment he happened to glance at me. We caught each other's eye, and burst into helpless laughter. All the other people in the refreshment room turned and stared at us.

I glanced at the clock, and realized that the train which was drawing in was the one I had to catch.

'You need another drink, Steve,' I said. 'Goodbye!'

I threw down some money on the counter to pay for a bottle of beer, and left him to drink it.

I reported Tom's latest manœuvres to Robert, who was alarmed. I could see quite clearly that he thought Tom would never go to America on his own: I think he really doubted whether Tom would ever go at all. We decided to concentrate on our own plans. I now had my visa, and Robert had applied for his. Escaping from the atmosphere of the town for a few hours enabled me to see our affairs in some sort of perspective. I became aware of how events were rolling on. It was June.

We dined in the college, and afterwards went back to Robert's rooms feeling a little more relaxed. We talked about our books, and Robert laughed somewhat unkindly over Miss X.Y.'s letter. As the evening passed I confided more freely my emotions about Myrtle.

'In ten years' time I shall wish I'd married her,' I said, bitterly.

Robert made no comment.

I had begun to feel tired and I launched a boring tirade about remorse, the gist of it being that after doing what you wanted to do it was hypocritical to express remorse.

I noticed Robert looking at the clock. It was after eleven.

The telephone rang.

Robert crossed the room to answer it. I picked up something to read. It was a trunk call for me.

I was frightened: I took over the receiver, certain that I was going to hear of some tragedy.

I heard the distant voice of Myrtle.

'Is that Joe?'

'Yes.'

'It's me, Myrtle.'

'Oh.'

'Darling, I've got a dog!'

'What!'

'I've got a dog, darling. A *dog*!' Her voice sounded excited. Either her depression had been dissipated or she had been drinking.

'Isn't it wonderful?'

'Yes.' First of all I had found it impossible to believe she was saying it was a dog she had got: now I found it impossible to understand what was going on at all.

'I said, "Isn't it wonderful?"'

'I said, "Yes."'

Myrtle's voice came to me with reproach. 'You don't sound very enthusiastic!'

There is only one phrase for expressing what I felt. It was a bit much.

'I'm sorry,' I muttered.

Were it possible to hear anyone's spirits fall, I should have heard Myrtle's fall with an echoing 'woomph!'

'I'm glad,' I said, with as much enthusiasm as I could summon – very little, as a matter of fact.

'It's a red setter.'

'Good,' I said.

162

'It answers to the name of Brian.'

'What?'

'Brian, B-r-i-a-n.'

'Good heavens!'

'I can't hear you.'

'I said, "How are you?"'

'All right. I'm feeling wonderful. Brian and I went for a walk in the park this afternoon. We had a wonderful time.'

I could think of nothing to say. I just listened to her voice, which expressed pure happiness.

'You must come and see him.' She paused. 'When do you come back?'

I was suspicious. I said:

'Tomorrow evening.'

'Will you come and see Brian and me?'

'If you'd really like me to . . .' My spirits now fell.

'I'll expect you tomorrow night. Goodbye, darling.'

'Goodbye.'

I glanced at Robert, who had been standing by the fireplace listening.

There was a short silence. Then I said:

'Are we all going off our heads?'

I really meant it.

Part Four

I

In an Interlude

I sat in the open doorway of my cottage, listening to the noise of the rain on the leaves. The hedgerows and trees had come to their full summer thickness. The may was all gone, and green berries were already showing, standing up instead of hanging down; and the ash trees had put out tufts of seeds with beautiful little wings on them. It was nearly the end of June. The first date of Tom's departure had passed, and we were soon to pass the second. In spite of the rain, yellowhammers were diving like chaser-planes from the tree immediately opposite, and magpies strutted in the field. It was Saturday morning and I was expecting Myrtle.

Yes, incredible though it may seem, Myrtle was coming to spend the afternoon, and apparently she was coming to spend it in the highest of spirits. Ever since the arrival of her dog she had shown no signs other than those of happiness. Tom spoke with enormous portentous knowledge about ebb and flow. I doubted him. Through her gaiety sounded a faintly crazed note that reminded me of hysteria. I thought this kind of happiness must be unstable – just as suddenly as it had come it would collapse and plunge her into deeper despair. Tom thought I was making too much of it.

'You take your responsibilities too heavily,' he said.

I thought it over and decided that perhaps I did. I studied Myrtle, and half-reassured myself. Our meetings were sunny and light-hearted, and apparently quite casual. Of course I asked myself what Myrtle thought she was doing. Nobody could accuse me of not asking myself innumerable, internal questions. But you are more interested in the answer? I have to confess that I expressed my answer in a most undesirable form, the form of a business phrase. Myrtle was continuing our relationship on a day-to-day basis. I presume that a man who is about to go bankrupt still continues to visit his office, use the telephone, and enjoy the creative act of composing business letters. So, Myrtle, before bankrupt love.

On a day-to-day basis, Myrtle was delightful company. Having done justice to my conscience, I began to do justice to myself as a whole again. It was Myrtle's choice. 'Remember that!' I kept saying to myself: 'It's her choice.' I got a consolation from the concept of Myrtle's choice.

The rain ceased and I went out into the lane to pick some flowers. In the hedges there were two kinds of dog-roses, white and pink, and the pink ones had deep carmine buds. Though I knew it was useless I picked a bud, and it unfolded, like a living creature, immediately. I was looking for honeysuckle. In the ditch the campions and cow-parsley had gone. At last I found some honeysuckle that was nearly in bloom: it was growing up a big tree; the stem was old and twined like bast. In the warmth of the bedroom the flowers would open. Ah! Myrtle, I thought.

I returned slowly to the cottage, kicking a loose stone along the road.

I began to think about Tom. During the week there had been a crisis with Steve. As yet I had heard only Tom's side of it, but that was enough to trouble me.

Tom and I had met by chance in the central lending library. It was a large hall with a gallery running round it. The floor was highly polished, and the room always smelt of beeswax and turpentine. Bookshelves were built out from the walls at regular intervals dividing the space into a number of alcoves. These alcoves were used by serious-minded people for silent reading, and by the young for whispered flirtation. I found the mingled amorous-cum-literary tone of the place most estimable, since it encouraged the serious-minded to flirt and the flirtatious to read.

I had a suspicion that Tom was trying to avoid me. However in the course of moving round the shelves we met face to face.

Caught unawares he had an unusual expression. His features looked set, and his skin showed a greyish tinge.

'What's the matter?' I asked.

'I'm a little disturbed. That's all.'

'What about?'

Tom did not reply. I followed him as he went to have his book stamped, and we left together. In the street he paused uncertainly.

'I'll walk along with you,' I said. It was about half-past six and the streets were empty: everyone was having an evening meal. The air was luminous and cool, and our reflections flashed by in the shop-windows.

'What's Steve been doing?' I asked.

'How did you know it was Steve?'

I did not imagine it was Myrtle because I believed his feeling for her to be thoroughly bogus. 'I guessed.'

Tom said: 'He told me last night that he was going on holiday with his father and mother.'

I was puzzled. 'What does that matter to you?'

'It matters to me because I was going to take him away myself.'

'But you're going to America, Tom.'

'Before I go to America.'

I was silent for a moment, distracted by confirmation of our suspicions that he did not intend to go. I remembered what Steve had told me in the refreshment room.

'When *are* you going?'

'Later.' He waved his hand impatiently. 'Later . . . my dear Joe, don't let your anxiety run away with you.'

'I see,' I said. 'Where were you taking him?'

'To France. He wants to improve his accent.'

Often I had seen the comic side of the patron–protégé relationship. I now saw the reverse. When Tom said Steve wanted to improve his French accent he was speaking with heart-felt seriousness. A vivid picture sprang up in my mind of Steve lounging in a Parisian bistro, probably drinking Pernod and trying to get himself seduced by the woman behind the cash-desk – improving his French accent.

'I promised to take him,' said Tom. And added: 'He promised he'd go' – thus giving the show away completely.

'Poor old Tom!' I said.

Tom glanced at me, but did not understand why I was smiling. I was thinking of the lectures I had received from him, Tom, the worldly wise, on how little importance one should attach to people's promises.

'Of course, I could insist,' said Tom. 'His parents would back me up.'

'Good gracious!'

'They're ambitious for his future,' said Tom, reprovingly.

I thought: 'As if Steve hadn't got his eye on the main chance!' I said:

'Where are they going?'

'Grimsby,' said Tom, with distaste.

I said: 'I suppose he'll have to make his own choice.'

'Exactly. It would be disastrous for him to feel tied to me.'

It must have been the tenth time I had heard this phrase, from one or the other of them. Why, I wondered, did nobody point out that Steve had never been tied to anyone but himself, nor was ever likely to be? I contented myself with saying:

'Won't he feel tied to his parents?'

'Certainly! It's very foolish of him.'

It had occurred to me, as no doubt it had to Steve, that escaping from his father and mother in Grimsby would be child's play compared with escaping from his patron in Paris.

'I'm afraid,' said Tom, 'he's going off the rails.'

'Alas! he's not the only one,' said I.

We had come to a crossing of the main streets, and we stopped. In day-time the crossing was the busiest in the town: now it was deserted. In the centre, where the policeman stood on point duty, there remained his pedestal with nobody on it. We were silent. Tom suddenly lowered his head, and I saw a look of misery on his face.

'I'm awfully sorry, Tom.'

'It's my last chance. It means more to me than anything has

ever done.' He looked up at me with strained eyes. 'Do you think I ought to buy a new car?'

It was a totally unexpected question. I saw quickly enough what he meant. He had so far lost control that he could envisage trying to bribe Steve with a new car. I wanted to cry 'no'. I said:

'I doubt if it would really help.'

Tom's voice suddenly went dead. 'I didn't think it would. I'm not a fool.'

We both knew the conversation had ended, and we went away immediately in different directions. Something made me look back, and I saw Tom walking with a changed gait. Instead of propelling himself along with his diaphragm thrust out and his shoulders swinging to and fro, he was walking with the slow, stiff movements of an automaton. I had never before realized he was capable of the change. I was shocked and touched.

This sight continued to haunt me in recollection. It came back to me while I was kicking the loose stone along the road up to the cottage. I thought of Tom's predicament, and of all the other people who had found themselves in it. 'Ought I to buy a new car?' Other people; other vehicles – such as steam yachts.

'Ought I to buy him a steam yacht?'

Bearing Steve in mind, I felt the answer was almost certainly 'yes'. Amusement led me to wonder if I was taking Tom's responsibilities too heavily. Indoors, I laid down the bunch of honeysuckle.

My reflections were cut short by the sound of a bicycle bell.

'Darling!' shouted Myrtle's voice from the roadway. 'Come and see who I've brought!'

'Who?' I cried, in mixed incredulity, disappointment and anger. I went outside to see.

'Doesn't he look beautiful!' In the basket on the front of Myrtle's bicycle sat the dog.

'Well!' I exclaimed, in unmixed relief.

Myrtle's face was alight with pleasure. I kissed her. She was wearing a new kind of scent. I kissed her again, and slid my hand warmly over her back.

She made me hold the bicycle, while she set down the animal.

'Brian! Brian!' she called, without the slightest appearance of noticing the inappositeness of its name.

The animal bounded and fussed around. It was a pretty red colour, and it had a charmingly silly, affectionate expression. It kept leaving a little watery trail behind it. I led Myrtle indoors.

Myrtle stirred beside me.

'I thought you were asleep,' I murmured.

'I thought you were!'

We were quiet. The smell of honeysuckle had begun to fill the room.

'Can you hear something?' said Myrtle.

I could. It was the animal whining downstairs.

'Brian wants to come up,' said Myrtle.

'Well, he can't,' said I.

'Oh darling, why not?'

I did not want to get out of bed to open the door. 'You don't have to have dogs in the bedroom.'

'But he's crying. He's only a puppy.'

'All the more reason,' I said. 'We should make him feel shy.'

Myrtle took hold of me gently. 'Please go and fetch him, darling.'

I did as she asked me.

With a flustering patter the animal ran upstairs. Myrtle was delighted. We persuaded it to lie down on one of the mats while I got back into bed.

Myrtle began to chatter happily. She told me about the latest events in her firm. She was doing well. One of her ideas had got the firm a valuable contract from a new client in London. Her employer had promised a rise as well as commission.

I listened with entirely unselfish pleasure, hearing the voice not of hysteria but of clear-headedness and resource.

After outlining her idea with undisguised competence, Myrtle suddenly felt it was time to retrench behind her true maidenly modesty. 'Of course, it's all luck,' she said. 'I think the people in London just wanted to be nice to me.'

I took hold of her.

Myrtle fluttered her eyelids. 'Don't be silly, darling.'

I began to feel rather more attentive. 'How's your boss getting on with his mistress?' I said, leaning over her.

Myrtle frowned. 'About the same.'

'And how are you getting on with her?'

Myrtle's frown changed to a look of sadness. 'Not very well. I don't think she likes me getting on in the firm.'

'Oh dear.'

Myrtle said with absurd innocence: 'What does it matter to her if I make an extra £5 a week? She can have another £5 any time she likes, without doing any *extra* work . . .'

'Don't you see,' I said, 'she knows everyone says she's planted there because she's the boss's mistress? She probably takes her position in the firm very seriously.'

'Do you really think so, darling?' Myrtle pondered this new idea. 'She did try to prevent him taking this contract – because it would mean too much reorganization for her! . . . He didn't give in, but he forbade me to go to London again and went himself.'

I laughed quietly.

Myrtle settled herself comfortably against me. 'Ah well,' she said, with a modest smirk, 'I'll find some way of getting round him.'

We were on the verge of beginning to make plans, but something stopped us.

And it turned out that this was her most sensible stretch of conversation. My feeling that the crazed note had disappeared from her gaiety was soon dispelled. A little while later she was talking about cars.

'. . . like the one I shall have next year.'

'Myrtle!' I said. 'Are you going to have a car?'

'Next year.' She paused. 'I'm not going to have the money and not have a car.'

'Why do you want one?'

'For getting about.'

I let her run on. The next time I listened she was saying:

'My gun's come.'

'Your what?' I was constantly finding it impossible to believe my ears.

'My gun. Didn't I tell you I was getting a gun? It came yesterday.'

I felt dizzy – a dog, and a car, and now a gun. I thought she must be going mad. A gun! I suddenly connected, with emotion not far from terror. It may seem very unsoldierly of me. When girls get guns I am convinced it is time for me to go.

'What ever do you want a gun for?'

Myrtle looked thoughtfully at the ceiling. 'To shoot with.'

'Shoot what?'

'Rabbits and things.'

'But where?'

'Oh, in the fields . . . woods . . .'

I laughed. 'Good heavens! I didn't know you could shoot. Have you learnt?'

'Not yet.'

'Then how on earth? . . .'

Myrtle sounded dignified and reproachful. 'The husband of a girl down at the printer's is going to teach me.'

'And then?'

'Then,' said Myrtle in a reasonable tone, 'if I see a rabbit, I shall take a pot at it.'

My fear that she was suffering from hysteria came back in a single bounce. Also, I must add, a certain fear that her gun might fall into the hands of Haxby.

'I rather look forward to potting at rabbits,' she said.

No, I decided: if I had to choose between her potting at rabbits and Haxby potting at me, I should probably be safer to choose the latter.

'There's a warren, or whatever it is, just before we get to the Dog and Duck.'

I suddenly realized what she was thinking.

Myrtle went on, with a giggle: 'I've ordered some tweeds for the autumn.'

I thought: 'You won't be coming here.' It was quite simple. I had no doubt of it.

Even while she was lying beside me I did not doubt the affair was over. This afternoon, for the first time for months, we had been easy and harmonious together. I had felt simple, kind, ready to please; I had said nothing to torment her – because my mind was no longer divided. I felt no temptation to jump out of bed for fear of being tamed. There was no question of my trying to live the rest of my life with someone who did not believe in me as a writer. No *cris-de-cœur*! The struggle was over. I was in the clear.

Myrtle appeared to notice nothing. She prattled on. At last she said gaily: 'Now I'll have to leave you, darling. I'm going to a party, tonight.'

I laughed, as if it were really a joke. 'With the Crows?'

'Given by them!' said Myrtle. 'And Tom's going to be there too.'

'Tut-tut,' I said, lightly smacking her.

'And Brian as well,' said Myrtle. 'Can you imagine it!' She began to play with the dog. 'Come on, Brian! . . .'

In the end she persuaded the animal to sit in the basket, and prepared to leave. I noticed that in the excitement we did not arrange to meet again. We kissed and she rode off, down the lane.

As she disappeared round the corner, I could hear her talking animatedly. 'Look! Brian. Are we going to see some rabbits? Brian? . . .'

I went indoors. I began to read. I failed. I found it was impossible to concentrate. I kept thinking of Myrtle, and thinking: 'It won't do.'

My spirits switched over completely. I had not relaxed when it was time to go to bed, and I found myself unable to sleep. It was light very late, and there was one of the loveliest of sunsets. The trees were quite still and the sky was glowing. I kept getting out of bed to look. Each time the rising moon was a little brighter. The flowers began to smell in the hedgerow opposite, and the birds to be quiet. It was exquisite.

Suddenly, through the open doorway, I noticed a vague patch of moonlight on the wall. I fancied it was a girl, standing soft and naked. When I looked it was nothing like it, of course. I smiled at myself. And from the window came a gust of air, blowing over my body. My imagination stirred violently, and a new thought burst in like a shooting-star.

'I must look for someone else.'

2

Sports Day

The school sports had been postponed because of bad weather. Nobody wanted them now. Sports day was the sort of climax you could not approach twice and the headmaster's second choice of date lighted on the coldest day of summer. After morning prayers he called attention to the temperature – as if the boys were not shivering already.

'Now don't let me see any boy this afternoon without his overcoat!'

The boys listened in a docile fashion.

'Now don't let me see any boy . . .' His particular form of injunction always sounded less like an order to obey than an invitation to deceive. He descended from the rostrum, clutching his gown tightly round him. Daily he was embarrassed by little boys who waylaid him.

'Well, what is it?' This morning he had to stop because there was a long queue of them. I sauntered by. Each little boy appeared to be asking the same question.

'Please sir, will a mackintosh do?'

I moved away. I was concerned with the part I had to play in the sports. The arrangements were in the hands of Bolshaw, and in the previous year I had found myself down on his list as telegraph-steward. This meant that I was on duty beside the cricket scoreboard, thirty yards in front of the distinguished spectators' row of chairs, for the whole of the afternoon. I thought telegraph-steward was an intolerable rôle, suited only to someone who felt a pathological desire to be in the public eye. I aspired to be the prize-steward, since this appeared to involve no duties at all. I told Bolshaw that

I thought if I were only given a chance I could make an exceptionally good prize-steward. I tried to convey that I could care for the prizes as if they were my own children.

I went to the field early in the afternoon. Bolshaw had failed to circulate his list in the morning, and I was hopeful. I decided to install myself as prize-steward before he arrived. The games master was already there. Bolshaw did the organizing: the games master did the work. The weather was wretched and I was wearing an overcoat. There was a wind blowing, no blustering winter wind, but a summer one that insinuated its iciness. The games master came out of the pavilion, wearing a high-necked sweater and a pair of gym shoes.

'Come on, Joe!' he said. 'Come an' 'elp me with the prizes, before the nobs come.'

The games master was a friend of mine. He was a middle-aged family man, an ex-sergeant-major, unlettered, cheerful and fond of boys. I helped him unpack the prizes. The wind rustled the pieces of tissue paper out of our fingers.

'Brr,' said the games master, jumping springily from one foot to the other. 'The ruddy Lord Mayor'll 'ave to be set up like a brass monkey for this. 'E'll need 'is gold chain to tie 'em on with.'

We surveyed the table, and the desired objects for which, like children of my own, I was to care. There were electroplated cups of different sizes, accompanied by a collection of teaspoons, cruets, rose-bowls with wire across the top and jam-pots with electroplated lids.

''Ere, what's this?' said the games master. 'Not something useful?' It was a safety-razor: I read the card, on which was written:

JUNIOR 100 YARDS

'Good God!' I said, and rapidly went through the other cards. Someone had playfully exchanged them all. A handsome case of silver teaspoons was going to the winner of the junior egg-and-spoon race, while the victor ludorum was going to get a plastic serviette-ring for his efforts.

We began a hasty redistribution. The Lord Mayor arrived. He was going to give away the prizes. He was a short, vigorous, red-faced man, with a bay-window and a powerful glare. He looked as if he had high blood pressure. He also looked as if he thought the games master and I were trying to steal the prizes. He stationed himself very close to the table and glared at us. We retired to the pavilion, which was filled with boys in different stages of undress, chattering at the top of their voices.

The games master pushed his way in.

'Now then! Listen to me! You all know what a cold afternoon it is. Well, we're going to get it over at the double. I'm not going to 'ave you all standing there, doing sweet fanny adams and catching your death. Understand this, now! Any boy who isn't ready for 'is race loses 'is chance!' There was a hush. 'What's more, I'll run 'im round the gym tomorrow morning with the slipper be'ind 'im.' The hush turned to laughter. 'Who's not brought 'is overcoat or 'is mac?' The laughter turned back into a hush. 'All right!'

We were about to begin what promised to be the fastest sports meeting in the history of athletics.

Many of the boys were excellent untrained athletes, and the school games record was highly creditable. But the Greek spirit burned with the lowest possible flame in the staff. Those given official duties walked about with their collars turned up and a look of hard-boiled irritation: as prize-steward, I was sorry for them.

As I walked across the field I met Bolshaw.

'Lunn,' he said, 'Lunn!'

'Yes.'

Bolshaw stared at me, with his shoulders hunched inside an old-fashioned overcoat. His hat was pulled down to his spectacles.

'Lunn,' he said, 'I've rearranged the duties. I've got a different one for you.'

'What?'

'Telegraph-steward.'

I thought: 'It's not different at all!' I said: 'But the prizes,

Bolshaw. Who's to look after the prizes?' At that moment I felt devoted to the prizes.

'I've thought of that,' said Bolshaw. 'I'll keep an eye on the prizes myself.'

'Myself.' I could not argue. I turned up the collar of my overcoat and made for the telegraph-post.

At the post I found Trevor and Benny waiting to assist me. I looked at Benny. 'What are you doing here?' I said loudly.

Benny's face took on a grossly pathetic expression.

Trevor said: 'He's a menace. Send him away!' He disliked Benny.

This made me feel inclined to let Benny stay. Like a dog Benny sensed it.

'Don't listen to him, sir.'

I hesitated. Benny's expression was poised on the edge of a ludicrous, grateful smile. There was a loud bang. The first race had begun. It occurred to me that if I sent Benny away I should have to take a hand in the work myself. That settled it.

Soon I was delighted by the way things were going. I normally found sports meetings tedious: today's performance began at the pace of a smart revue – it was perfect.

As usual, perfection did not last. Bolshaw had instructed the starter not to wait for boys who were late for the start. Naturally it was not long before a wretched little boy ran up as the gun went off. The starter shouted at him. The boy jumped like a rabbit and started to run down the track. The effect was dramatic. The spectators immediately came to life.

'Go it, the little 'un!' they shouted. He did not catch up but they cheered him loudly as he walked off the field.

Races followed each other at a pace more suited to Americans than Greeks. And then the weather took a hand. The clouds had been lowering, the wind dropped, and now there came a shower of icy rain. Immediately the spectators made for the lines of thick leafy trees on each side of the field.

The boys in the middle ran towards the pavilion. On the way

they surged past the distinguished spectators, and saw the head-master beside himself with alarm because rain-drops were falling on the prizes.

'Look after the prizes!' he was crying. He stripped off his over-coat and laid it over them. 'Give me some more coats! You there, boy! Give me your overcoat. Boy! Boy!'

The Lord Mayor was struggling to undo his chain. The boys swarmed round, and in a few seconds the table was covered with a mountain of clothes.

'That's enough!' cried the headmaster. 'Enough! Enough! Don't be silly!' He furtively cuffed a boy who was taking no notice and the Lord Mayor pretended not to see.

The rain fell.

Under the trees it was dry. Several masters sat in their cars: the remainder, together with the boys and their parents, walked up and down to keep warm. It looked like a German theatre audience on the *Bummel*.

I was walking gaily with the games master. As we came to one of the turns in our promenade I glanced idly at the cars. Somebody inside one of them waved to me. The windscreen was steamed up, so I went closer. To my astonishment I saw it was our senior science master, Simms. He beckoned to me, and opened the door of his car.

Bolshaw had led me to believe he was at death's door. Simms shook my hand with a light, firm grasp, and I found myself looking into a pair of clear, healthy, blue eyes.

'I haven't risen from the dead,' he observed.

I was too embarrassed to reply.

'I expect I shall in due course,' he went on. He spoke slowly. 'But I haven't yet passed through those preliminary formalities that cause us so much concern.'

'I'm delighted,' I stammered.

I was very fond of Simms. I liked his face. He had a broad head, bald with a fringe of grey hair, and narrow, delicate jaw. His skin was pink, and his face showed his passing shades of emotion. It was the face of a man who had always gone his own way, and had thus arrived at a state of lively self-satisfaction. He was now old and frail, but it was probable that he had always looked frail. He was gentle and unaggressive – the opposite of Bolshaw. Yet had I been asked to say which of the two had done fewer things he did not want to do, I should have said Simms. The question would have been particularly relevant at this juncture, when the subject was Simms's resignation.

'Are you quite better?' I asked.

'My asthma still distresses me frequently.'

'I mean, well enough to come back to school?'

'Had you heard to the contrary?' He glanced at me. 'I'm very curious, my dear fellow,' he said, his hand on my arm. 'People come and give me advice, good and disinterested advice. And shortly afterwards I hear, to my astonishment, that I've taken it! Can you explain that to me?'

I shook my head.

'I'm very gratified that anyone should think I have the sense to take good and disinterested advice. One is. You would be, I'm sure.'

'When are you coming back?'

'Oh, quite soon, you know. This term. There's the matter of salary during the summer vacation to be considered.' He smiled slyly to himself.

I looked out of the window, amused.

The rain had stopped. I told him I must return to my telegraph-board.

'It has been nice to see you,' he said. 'I shall be seeing you again shortly. Next Monday.'

I stared at him. He was going to give up his job to nobody; and he had every intention of teasing Bolshaw and me for as long as he could spin out his time.

The weather was now colder. The headmaster and the Lord Mayor returned to their places of honour, but several of the other distinguished spectators and parents had quietly deserted. Before the headmaster sat down he called the boys to remove their over-coats from the prize table. They cheerfully obeyed, and after jostling and fighting they went away again, leaving the array of cups and cruets to shine sullenly in the grey light.

Fred joined me to watch one of the field events. His bare arms and legs looked greyer than ever. He said:

'I saw your girl-friend, Joe.'

I was surprised, because Myrtle ought to have been at work.

'While you was talking to old Simms in 'is car. She just came in to shelter and went out again.'

'Are you sure?' I said.

'It's quite true,' put in Trevor. He laughed with nasal contempt as he said: 'She was with that awful man, Haxby.'

I said nothing, and the boys were diffidently silent. Fred was upset. ''Ave I said the wrong thing?'

I shrugged my shoulders.

Myrtle's action must have been deliberate. It could only mean the interlude was now over. More than anything else I felt irritation. If the interlude was over the whole thing had to end once and for all.

It had taken me a long time, far too long a time, to steel myself to do it. Now I was ready at last. It seemed a curious off-hand occasion on which to decide, but that is how it was.

My duties at the board came to an end. The only remaining event was the senior mile, and I decided to watch it from near the winning-post. It was one of the events in which Frank was hoping to shine, since he was in the running for victor ludorum.

While I was standing in the crowd of boys, I overheard a strange remark. 'Where's the victor ludorum's prize?' I turned round but I was too late to see who had spoken. I knew the answer, because I had labelled it myself: it was the case of a dozen silver teaspoons, right at the front of the table.

Frank won the race. There was cheering, and all the boys gathered round the Lord Mayor to hear him speak before giving the prizes.

The Lord Mayor spoke for a long time. He clearly had great stamina. His was the most Greek performance of all. I thought he would never stop.

At last the boys filed up to him for their prizes. He shook hands vigorously. The boys blushed and grinned and walked away with cruets, toast-racks, jam-pots and so on. The safety-razor was very properly won by a bearded boy in the fifth form.

We came to the victor ludorum. The contest had been won by Frank. He came up, with a mackintosh thrown over his athletic rig, looking pale and handsome and unusually shy. The Lord Mayor gave Frank his warmest handshake and his most powerful glare: then he prepared to give Frank his prize. The victor ludorum's prize was not there.

A sudden hush fell on the crowd of boys.

'Where is it?' came the headmaster's nattering voice. 'Where is it?' I thought if there was one question not worth asking, that was it.

'Where is it? What is it? What was the prize, I say?'

'Some silver spoons,' came the voice of his secretary, from below the horizon.

'They're not here now!'

'It's no use blaming me.'

'I'm not blaming anybody! I only want to know where they are!' Pause. 'Who was responsible for the prizes?'

I thought of the prizes, my prizes.

'Mr Bolshaw,' said the secretary.

I looked round. There was no sign of Bolshaw: he had gone home.

'I thought it was Mr Lunn,' said the headmaster.

I trembled.

'No, Mr Bolshaw.'

Truth had prevailed. I could hardly believe it.

Meanwhile, the Lord Mayor was filling in time by giving Frank's hand more jolly shakes.

Murmurs ran through the crowd. 'They can't find the victor ludorum's prize. Someone's swiped it.'

'Be quiet there! Do be quiet!' cried the headmaster.

Undismayed, the Lord Mayor shook Frank's hand again. The headmaster whispered furiously into his ear. 'Send the boy away! Tell him we will give him his prize later!'

I wondered what would happen to Bolshaw.

The house-captains filed up for their shields, but the crowd now paid the scantiest attention to the proceedings. Where were the teaspoons? Who was the lucky boy?

It was quite obvious what had happened. While the boys had been clustered round the table, struggling with their overcoats, one of them had smartly caught up the silver teaspoons. The games master and I could swear to the case's having found its way safely to the table. It was up to the headmaster to find out where it had gone next.

The headmaster did not find out, nor did any of the other masters. I can tell you now that nobody ever did find out. And was Bolshaw held responsible for it all? Was he asked to resign, for lacking sense of responsibility and discipline? Does justice prevail on this earth?

I went away from the field thinking about Bolshaw. I arrived home thinking about Myrtle.

The more I thought about Myrtle's appearance with Haxby, the more I felt venomous. My forbearance, my detachment, all those qualities to which I aspired, vanished. And I can only say that to the very depths of my soul I was fed up with her.

3
Scenes of Domesticity

The newspapers were filled with international crises. They were beginning to have a mesmerizing effect. But I was not completely mesmerized: I had decided to see Myrtle as little as possible until the term ended; and then, whether I was going to America or not, to quit the town without leaving an address.

It takes two to make a parting, and it takes two to avoid a meeting if they live not much more than a mile apart. Never before had I been so intensely aware of playing out time. Sometimes I felt like a powerful man in control of his own destiny: sometimes I felt I was being hunted by Hitler and Myrtle in conjunction.

One evening I was sitting peacefully outside the french windows of my lodgings marking examination papers. At the bottom of the garden the landlady's niece and Mr Chinnock were working. It was one of what Myrtle and I had been used to call their 'off-nights', and they were spending it in weeding the vegetable plot.

Occasionally one or the other of us would stop to cough. This was because smoke was blowing over us from a bonfire of weeds in a neighbouring garden. It was always the same. There were so many gardens and the neighbours were such indefatigable incendiarists, that one could never hope to sit in one's garden for an hour or so without somebody lighting a bonfire. The breeze appeared to blow in a circular direction.

I was just completing my estimation of the mathematical powers of a junior form, when I heard the landlady showing someone into my room. I looked round, and saw Steve. He stepped out of the window.

'I'm sorry to bother you,' he said, and sat down on the step near my chair. He waited till I put down the last paper, and then pulled out of his pocket a poem that he had written.

'You see, Joe!' he said. 'When I can get away from Tom for a week-end I really do do some work.'

I read the poem. I have observed earlier that Steve's poems showed talent. This poem showed quite as much talent as usual and somewhat greater length. I congratulated him.

The trouble I find with a poem is that when you have read it, and congratulated the author, there is nothing else to say. It is not like a novel, where you can sit down to a really good purging burst of moral indignation at the flatness of his jokes, the shapelessness of his plot, and the immorality of his characters.

A silence fell upon Steve and me. 'Britons, never, never, ne-ever shall be slaves!' whistled Mr Chinnock.

'Tom isn't going to America,' said Steve.

'Why not? How do you know?'

Steve shrugged his shoulders. 'He says there's going to be a war.'

'Oh.'

'Don't you think there is?'

'What?'

'Going to be a war.'

'Possibly.' I paused, and said with shameful lack of conviction: 'I hope so.' The fact is that I did not want to give up the idea of going to America.

Steve glanced at me. 'By the way, you know Myrtle's going about saying that you intend to go to America if there *is* a war.'

'The devil!' I was very angry.

'That's what she's saying, anyway.'

'Who told you?'

'I heard it myself.'

Though my own conduct may not have been above reproach, I was infuriated by Myrtle's perfidy. I began to question Steve for more circumstantial evidence. He was speaking the truth, and he was in a position to know what Myrtle was saying to other people, since he was now going regularly to the parties she frequented with Haxby.

In my anger, I thought: 'That's one more thing against her!'

'Surely Tom's furious?' I said.

Steve said: 'I think he thought she was saying it to provoke you.'

'Well, it has!'

Steve laughed good-naturedly.

'What else has she been saying about me?'

'I don't think I ought to repeat this scandal, Joe,' he said with embarrassment.

'You can't put me off now, Steve.'

'She told Tom,' Steve began slowly, 'that she was never in love with you.'

'For what reason does she think she? . . .'

'I know, I know. She admits that you have a curious attractive power. You're now spoken of as if you were a sort of Svengali. It's ridiculous, of course. Anybody can see that you're not like Svengali.'

'Hell!'

'I think we ought to be a little quieter, Joe.' Steve motioned towards the landlady's niece and Mr Chinnock, who were easily within earshot.

With an effort I simmered down.

'Anything else?' I asked.

Steve did not reply.

'I bet Tom put that idea into her head.'

'If you're going to break it off, it's not a bad idea, is it, Joe?'

'That wasn't why he did it. He'll next prove that she's always been in love with him. And he with her.'

'Heavens!' said Steve, not having thought of this before.

'That's his plan, mark my words. It leads to a proposal of marriage.'

Steve looked distinctly crestfallen.

'Though what her plan is, I don't know,' I went on. 'No doubt it will do her more harm than good.'

'I'm sorry,' said Steve.

I was regaining my detachment. There was much in what Steve observed about Myrtle saying she had never been in love with me. It was a face-saving device. It was the first sign of her beginning to protect herself. I suddenly thought: 'She's pulling out.'

Steve broke into my reflections.

'I suppose you know Trevor's safe.'

I felt as much shock that he knew about it as relief that a disaster had been avoided. I said: 'Oh!' in a sharp, off-hand tone.

We relapsed into silence again. Steve stepped indoors and brought a cushion to sit on.

'It's very bad to sit on anything cold,' he said.

'Nonsense.'

Steve paused, and began to smile at me. 'I know what you haven't heard about. I've been learning First Aid.' He saw my look of disbelief. 'Honestly, I have Joe. If there's a war and I'm conscripted and I've got my certificates perhaps I'll be able to get into the Medical Corps.'

I had no idea whether he was speaking the truth, but I could see his aim was to soothe my feelings, so I let him go on.

'I've taken an exam in it,' he said. There was a glint in his eye. 'I doubt if I've passed.'

I said: 'Was it hard?'

'It wasn't hard,' said Steve, 'but it was terribly repulsive.'

Steve recounted his incompetent performance in the practical tests, and in spite of my woes I began to smile.

Steve played up.

'The theoretical was terrifying. They asked me what I'd do with a baby in a convulsion. Fancy asking *me*, Joe! I wouldn't know what to do with a baby if it was *not* in a convulsion.'

'What was the answer?'

'Put it in a bath!' Steve paused triumphantly. Neither of us heard my landlady show in somebody else. There was a bustling noise beside us, and there stood Tom. His face was like thunder.

'I have something to say to you. Would you mind coming indoors?'

Steve picked up his cushion and I my examination papers, and we trailed into my room. Tom closed the french windows behind us.

'It's as well to keep these matters private,' he said, with an air that was both polite and reproving.

I did not reply. I had no idea what Tom had come to say. Our laughter had disappeared, as if he had made us feel ashamed of it. Steve, on the grounds that nothing Tom would say was likely to make life easier for him, was already looking apprehensive.

I sat down. Steve sat down. Tom remained standing. By great effort he was keeping his features composed. I refused to open the conversation.

'I came to tell you that I've bought a new car.'

To be quite frank, the speech for me was something of an anti-climax, and also mildly funny. In my imagination Tom's new car had become mixed up with a steam yacht.

Steve had apparently not been previously informed of the manœuvre. He was not unnaturally surprised. Foolishly he said:

'What for, Tom?'

Tom turned his attention to him. 'Aren't you interested to know what kind it is?'

'Of course,' said Steve. 'But I wondered what you'd bought it for?'

'Don't you know?' Tom was looking at him fixedly. His tone of voice was level enough; but there was a look in his eye, a bursting, concentrated look.

'No,' said Steve, trying to look at me, but finding the hypnotic effect of Tom's gaze too powerful.

'Can't you guess?' Tom smiled at him.

There was silence, in which I thought of saying: 'Tom, for Pete's sake stop it!' and rejected the idea.

Steve looked down, shaking his head.

'I should have thought you would have realized,' Tom said, with ominous silkiness, 'it was to make our trip to Paris more comfortable.'

Steve looked at him. Nothing was said.

I shifted in my chair. I was irritated that Tom had not given me a chance to get out of the room if he intended to make a scene. On the other hand I was faintly hypnotized, myself.

'I said I couldn't go, Tom,' said Steve.

'Don't be silly, Steve. Of course you can.'

'I can't, Tom. You know my people want me to go away with them.'

'They want you to come with me.'

'That isn't true.'

'Yes, it is.' Tom glared at him now. 'I have it in writing!'

'Look!' said Tom, pulling out an envelope from his pocket. 'This letter's from your mother, saying she agrees to your coming with me. Now we have it in black and white!' He handed it to Steve. 'Read it!'

Steve refused to read it.

'All right,' said Tom, angrily. 'If you haven't the manners to read it . . .'

'I'm *not* coming!' Steve interrupted him.

'What's your excuse?'

'I don't need an excuse, Tom.'

Tom waved the letter in front of his face. 'What are you going to say to this?' He waved it again, with a sweep of greater amplitude. 'I've got it in writing!'

I thought he must be going slightly mad. The whole of his face, though composed, now looked somehow inflamed.

'It's in black and white.' He deliberately lowered his voice again.

Suddenly Steve leaned forward, snatched the letter from his hand, and threw it in the fireplace. There was no fire.

Tom stared at it, and pursed his lips in a smile. Then he glanced at me. I felt embarrassed.

Steve said: 'This is intolerable. Why do you make these scenes, Tom?'

'Because I want you to go with me to France.'

'But I don't want to go.' Steve was looking miserable.

'I think you do really.'

'I've told you, I don't. I can't say more than that. I want to feel free.'

'I *want* you to feel free, Steve.'

'Then why don't you give me a chance to be it?'

'You can be perfectly free with me.' Tom moved nearer to him. 'You're perfectly free now.' He made a gesture. 'There's the door. You're free to go out through it, this very moment.'

Steve did not move.

'At least go out and have a look at the car.'

'I don't want to see it. And I don't want to go in it!'

'Do you mean to say I've wasted my money?'

At the mention of money, I thought Steve looked startled.

'Are you going to let me waste my money, without even looking at it?' Tom's voice was becoming angry again.

I thought that as he must have bought the car on the hire-purchase system the waste was not permanent.

'Heaven knows!' Tom now burst out, 'I've spent enough already. And what have I got for it? I've spent pounds and pounds!'

'I didn't ask you to.'

'Pounds and pounds!' Tom shouted.

'I don't want the car.'

'Then at least *see* it!'

'I'm not going to see it.'

'You're *going* to see it!' Tom had been getting nearer, and now he pounced on Steve.

There had been so much argument about the car that certainly I wanted to see it. Steve was determined not to. He resisted.

'Come and see it!' shouted Tom, and dragged him off his chair. He rolled towards the fireplace and upset the fire-irons with a deafening clatter. Outside, in the hall, the landlady's dog began to bark.

'Pipe down!' I said.

They desisted. Steve picked himself up, and Tom stood glowering. Looking sulky and furious, Steve straightened his tie.

'I've had enough of this!' said Tom, in a powerful whisper.

'I'm sorry, Tom.'

'I've had enough of this! Are you going to come and see the car or aren't you?'

No reply from Steve.

'It's the last chance.'

No reply.

Tom was now oblivious of my presence. He thrust his face close to Steve's. Steve wilted.

'Are you going to come to France or not? I must have the answer now.'

No answer.

'If you don't answer now, I shall never give you another chance. I have my plans.'

Steve glanced at him.

'It may interest you to know that if you don't go' – Tom paused for dramatic effect – 'I shall take Myrtle!'

'Don't be ridiculous, Tom!' At last Steve spoke. He glanced at me for support.

Tom was furious. 'It's not ridiculous! Who told you it's ridiculous? Joe?' He glanced at me. 'You may think it's ridiculous, but Myrtle doesn't! I know Myrtle. You may not think I'm wonderful, but Myrtle does! She needs me. It's only my responsibility for you that's kept me from going to her. She needs me, and I need her! We need each other.' His voice, though kept low, had tremendous power. 'I want your answer now. Is it to end or isn't it? If you don't speak I shall go straight to Myrtle – she's waiting for me now – and ask her to marry me!' He choked. 'Is it to end or isn't it? I shall go straight to Myrtle!'

Steve did not speak.

Tom waited.

Steve still did not speak.

I saw nothing for it but for Tom to go.

Suddenly he let out an indistinguishable cry.

Steve and I looked at him in alarm.

Tom opened his mouth to speak again and failed. He had to go.

Steve looked down at the carpet.

Tom picked up the letter from the hearth.

I thought: 'Come on, you've got to go!'

In a last dramatic move Tom tore up the letter and threw down the pieces. Then he turned. I made to open the door for him, but he pushed me out of the way. You may think it strange that I opened the door for him to go out and propose marriage to my mistress. The fact is that I was determined to see the car. I followed Tom across the hall and prevented him from slamming the door, so that I could peep out. I saw it as Tom drove away. And I concluded that Tom was not as mad as he seemed. In my opinion it was a car that would melt the heart of any boy.

I went back to Steve, who was sitting in his chair, shivering and almost on the verge of tears.

I said: 'You'd better have a drink, my lad.'

Steve waited helplessly while I mixed some gin and vermouth in a tumbler. He drank it.

I had nothing more to say, so I picked up another bundle of examination papers and resumed my marking.

After a while, when he had drained the glass, Steve stood up. I looked at him questioningly.

In a jaded voice he said: 'I suppose I'd better go after him.'

4

Round the Clock-Tower

To relieve my feelings I wrote a letter to Robert. It will save writing anything fresh if I quote a piece of it. Here it is:

> My sympathy for Tom is quite exhausted. And so is my patience. He said that Steve caused him a lot of pain, and I took it quite seriously. Sometimes the man was obviously in a state of abject misery and it would have taken a heart of stone not to be concerned for him. But his latest efforts are the limit. At one and the same time he's trying to get Steve to go away with him and proposing marriage to Myrtle! What he thinks he's doing, I cannot imagine. But it's me who's the biggest fool for being taken in by him. I thought he was heading for a tragedy. Instead of which it's quite clear it's nothing but a harlequinade. If clowns come in with red hot pokers and policemen with strings of sausages I shan't be surprised. Anything they can do has already been eclipsed by Tom's own clowning. As for his proposing marriage to Myrtle, it's laughable. What a proposal! Goodness knows how she'll take it. Faint with surprise – unless she simply concludes that he's gone off his head. It's time he went to America – only I doubt if he'll ever go. I really think he is a lunatic.

I wrote a good deal more in the same strain. After completing it I felt a certain satisfaction at having stated my position. To state one's position is a firm manly thing to do: it is right that it should give satisfaction.

There followed a few days of unexpected respite. I neither saw nor heard anything of Tom, Steve or Myrtle. I was very busy at school, because the end of the term was near. The days passed and I counted them as eagerly as my pupils counted them for not dissimilar reasons. They were days that separated me from freedom.

However I was doomed not to escape so easily. Myrtle began to ring me up again, wanting to see me. I tried to put her off.

'Surely you can spare me a few moments?' she said.

I felt bitterly cruel, but I kept to my resolve. Was I doing it for her sake? I do not know. But I do know that in the end it is harder to go on loving someone you do not see than someone you do.

When I refused to meet Myrtle I had not considered the possibility of our seeing each other by chance. Though the town was large, one was always running into people one knew. In the early days of my falling in love with Myrtle, when I did not know her well enough to ask her to meet me, I had spent many hours glancing into the windows of shops where I did not intend to buy anything. I used to have a superstition that if I circulated round the clock-tower long enough she would be sure to come.

I will not describe our clock-tower in detail, because I feel that if you were able to identify our town my novel would lose some of its universal air. Fortunately I can indicate its outstanding quality, since this does not distinguish it from the clock-towers in most other provincial towns. It was wondrously ugly.

Our clock-tower really did provoke wonder. Its ugliness set fire to the imagination, but that was only the beginning of wonderment. In the first place I always used to wonder why anybody had ever put it there. For displaying the time of day it was totally unnecessary: the surrounding shop-fronts were plastered with an assortment of clocks which offered the public the widest choice in times they could possibly have wished for. Could it be, I wondered as I stared at its majestic erectness, our contribution to the psychopathology of everyday life? And who had designed it? Was such a monument designed by an architect who specialized for life on clock-towers; or was it thrown off by some greater man in his hour of ease? Surely the latter! Small wonder, then, that the citizens of our town were proud of the clock-tower. It had its place in our hearts. 'It's ugly,' we thought, 'but it's home!'

Now my desire to avoid meeting Myrtle was not so frantic that I broke the routine of my movements round the town. If I happened to be circling the clock-tower, that was that. And one morning at lunch-time I happened to be circling it, on my way to lunch. It was not Myrtle I ran into; it was Steve.

Steve was walking alone, with his shoulders hunched and his face expressing misery. I caught him by the elbow, as it looked as if he were going to pass me without seeing me. He pushed the hair out of his eyes and tried to smile at me.

'I haven't seen you for a long time,' I said.

'No, Joe.' He looked down at the ground.

For some reason or other I noticed that he was taller than he had been six months ago.

'Have you been busy?'

'No. Just jogging along.' He glanced at me furtively. 'I couldn't face you after that scene Tom made in your house.'

I said: 'You shouldn't worry about that.' I paused. 'You're looking under the weather. Is Tom still playing hell?'

'I don't know.'

'What do you mean, Steve? You must know.'

'I don't, Joe. I haven't spoken to Tom since he left your house.'

I was astounded. I drew Steve out of the stream of men and women going to their lunch, so that I could go on talking to him. We leaned against some rails of steel tubing that had been erected to prevent people stepping off the pavement underneath buses.

'Where is he?' I asked.

'He's in Oxford today, but he was here before that.'

'And you didn't see him?' I continued incredulously.

'I've seen him in the office, of course.' He stopped. 'But he won't speak to me.'

'What a change for you!'

Steve did not smile. He looked extremely glum. 'It's a change for the worse.'

I had been tactless.

'He's been spending a lot of time with Myrtle, as far as I can gather. He won't spend any with me.'

I did not know what to say. I was trying to frame some appropriate remark when Steve burst out:

'It's really over!'

'Surely, it can't be.'

'You never took this business with Myrtle seriously enough!'

'I should think not. It's ridiculous.'

Steve shrugged his shoulders. He was completely downcast. He said: 'I feel absolutely lost without him.'

He must have noticed a look of alarm in my face. He moved away, saying: 'We can't go on talking about this here.'

We moved a few yards further along, and then we stopped again, frequently being wedged against the railing by the passing crowds. Traffic swept by.

'Did you see his new car?' said Steve.

'Yes.'

'He's gone to Oxford in it.'

I thought this conversation was getting us nowhere. I said: 'I'd no idea you'd take it like this, Steve. I'm awfully sorry.'

'I'd no idea, either,' said Steve. 'It's come to me as a terrible shock.' For an instant I fancied I heard a dramatic note that rang false; and then it occurred to me that people often are dramatic when deeply moved. 'I suppose I shall get used to it in time,' Steve said, rather as if his mother and father had suddenly died. 'I was a fool!' he cried, and tears came into his eyes.

'This is beyond me,' I said.

'You don't understand, Joe!' Steve spoke with force: his voice was trembling. 'I feel terrible. I feel lost, Joe. There's no point in anything! . . . You can't imagine what it's like to feel that all your plans for the future have broken down. You don't know what it's like, when you've had somebody who flatters your self-esteem all the while and makes you feel you're somebody – and then he stops, suddenly! I feel like a man in a ship that's sunk.' He was trembling with anguish. 'I feel,' he cried, 'like a banker who's lost his bank!'

At that moment a bus passed so close that I could not be expected to reply. A banker who had lost his bank – never had I imagined a remark could contain so much accuracy, penetration and truth.

Steve was waiting for me to say something.

'Poor old Steve,' I said. 'You'll find another.'

The following morning I received three letters. They were from Tom, Myrtle and Miss X.Y. I looked at the envelopes. I was sitting in my lodgings, just about to begin my breakfast. I was alone in the room.

'Dammit!' I said aloud. 'Art comes first, and I'm damned if I'll pretend it doesn't!'

And I opened Miss X.Y.'s letter first. It was short and to the point, and my spirits rose incredibly. She praised my book. I felt as if my hands were trembling. She suggested some revisions and some cuts: instantly I saw how they could be done. 'I'm safe!' I cried. 'I'm safe!' I did not quite know what it meant, but I knew it was true. I was ready to begin work on the manuscript immediately: I could hardly wait. The world might be falling about my ears but something went on telling me – to be correct, I went on telling myself – I was safe.

In this mood I opened Myrtle's letter. It said:

I must see you. Please. M.

And then I opened Tom's letter. It began thus:

Dear Joe: I challenge what you say about me in the letter you have just written to Robert.

I was flabbergasted. I already knew that when Robert left his room Tom took the opportunity of reading his private letters, but this was the first time he had ever taken the opportunity of replying to them. I knew that Robert could never have shown him my letter. I remembered Tom's having read one of my postcards on a question of fact – namely, the date of his departure for America. He had replied with fact – namely, a date that subsequently turned out to be false. But this was quite different, and so was the nature of Tom's reply.

Tom's letter began with a challenge, moved on to a denunciation, passed through a reproach, and ended up with a rebuke. Was there any sign of his being ashamed of having read someone else's private correspondence? No. Was there any sign of his being aware of a weak moral position? No. Was there any sign of self-consciousness whatsoever? Not a vestige.

I glowered. 'I stand by every word of it!' I said aloud.

Had I known where he was I would have written to him on the spot. I threw down his letter, and picked up Myrtle's. My glowering died away. I realized that I must see her again. I went to the telephone.

Having made up my mind to see her I wanted to behave with some show of decency, but it was not easy. I wanted the meeting to be as short as possible. I pretended I was exceedingly busy; Myrtle said she was, too. After an awkward discussion we arranged to meet in the town immediately we came out of work that afternoon. Our routes home crossed at the clock-tower, and it was there that we fixed our rendezvous. I thought of Steve. I promised myself that after I met Myrtle at the clock-tower I would go nowhere near it for months.

It was an airless, golden evening. Early in the morning the clouds had drawn away from the sky, leaving a pale brilliant dome of pure blue, from which the sun shone all day upon the roofs and streets. I arrived at the clock-tower first. There was a big chemist's shop, and I leaned against the railings in front of it. From time to time I caught its characteristic smell, though there was no breeze. Trams halted and moved on at different points in the circle. Buses passed to and fro leaving a trail of petrol fumes. The sun went on shining. Myrtle was late.

I looked at the clocks. They all showed different times. Myrtle was late and I wanted to go away. Whatever the clocks said, I had to remain.

At last Myrtle came. It was quite a long time since I had seen her, and my first thought was that she was feverish. Her face looked heavily coloured, and her eyes seemed smaller. When closer I saw that she had been crying.

'Thank you for seeing me,' she said.

I could not answer. I meant to ask her where she would like to go, for us to talk in peace, but every thought left my head. She must have thought I intended us to go on talking at the clock-tower, for she said nothing about moving on, and so we simply remained.

Myrtle spoke in a distant voice, yet she was quite firm.

'I wanted to ask your advice,' she said. 'I expect you know Tom's asked me to marry him? Do you think I should?'

I could not speak, this time for entirely different reasons. 'It's laughable. What a proposal!' My words came back to mock me. Never had I made such a stupid mistake. 'Faint with surprise – or think he's gone off his head!' Nothing of the kind. I can laugh at myself now. I know now that no girl faints with surprise at any proposal of marriage, and never, never does she think the proposer has gone off his head. But when I turned to look at Myrtle, as we stood in the sunshine, the chemist's shop behind us and the clock-tower in front, she must have seen written on my face nothing less than mixed astonishment and chagrin.

'You look strange,' Myrtle said. 'Is there something the matter?'

'No,' I muttered. 'Just emotion, I suppose.'

'Unusual for you.'

I did not comment: she must have learnt it from Tom.

Myrtle was staring at me. In her eyes I saw the faintest shade of bitter detachment.

'I can't advise you,' I said.

Myrtle said: 'Why not?'

'I don't know. I can't.' I stumbled for words. 'I'm not in a position to. You must know why.'

At that instant Myrtle's gaze faltered, and her detachment vanished never to return. She looked down and clasped her hands together. I noticed the mole on her forearm, just where it came out of her sleeve.

'Then I suppose it was no good our meeting . . .'

Immediately, I drew back. I could see her expression beginning to change.

She said: 'What have you been doing? I haven't seen you for ages.'

I told her about my letter from Miss X.Y. Even as I spoke to her I could not help feeling my own interest quicken – and I saw hers fade. Her silence bore me down and my explanation petered out.

She went on clasping her fingers between each other. Suddenly she looked me full in the face for a moment.

'I suppose this is the end.'

The end. I looked at her. And I knew with certainty that she was there at last. I did not know the reason. I supposed that something I had said or done during the last few days must have been the last straw. I do not even now know what it was, and if I did I should not believe in it as she did. To most of us the movements of the soul are so mysterious that we seize upon events to make them explicable. Myrtle and I had come to the end because of movements of the soul. They had ebbed and flowed – we had swayed closer together and further apart. Events and actions. What were events and actions? Something I had said or done, or, if it came to that, more probably something Tom had said or done, must have seemed to her the last straw.

I said: 'Yes.'

Myrtle burst into tears.

I cannot well remember what we said after that. Some of her phrases echo still. 'After this last year I don't know how you can do it!' And, 'I only wish you were feeling half of what I'm feeling now.' But I will not go on. A love affair cannot end without heartbreak. And as I have already told so much, I think the time has come for me to draw a veil.

At last we parted. The trams were still halting and moving on.

The buses were still passing to and fro. The clock-tower was bathed in golden light. There were sounds and smells, and many people going by. Myrtle lingered. Then suddenly among the traffic she saw a taxi. I did not notice her stop it. I only saw her get into it, and unexpectedly drive off.

I remained where I was. Now that I no longer needed to stay there I felt no compulsion to move away.

I do not know how long I remained there. The next thing I noticed was the glint of bright red hair in the sunshine, and a familiar vigorous swaying walk. Tom came to me.

'Ah, there you are!' he said. 'I heard that you were going to meet Myrtle . . . I didn't expect to find you still here.'

I did not speak.

Then Tom said gently: 'Come and have some tea.'

Neither of us spoke as I let him steer me to the café. Outside the shop the smell of roasting coffee was stifling. We went upstairs, and sat down at our usual table. It was long after tea-time, and we were the only people in the room. The waitress brought our tea rapidly because she was waiting for it to be time to close.

Tom said: 'Is it all over?'

I nodded my head.

There was a pause.

Tom handled his tea-cup with a nervous gesture. 'She said she couldn't marry me, of course.'

'When?'

'Several days ago.'

It was my turn to pause. I drank some tea. I said:

'What are you going to do?'

Tom said easily: 'Oh, I've just come away from having a talk with Steve. While you were seeing Myrtle, actually. He's changed his mind, of course.' He smiled with self-satisfaction. 'He's coming to France with me next week. I think it wiser for us to go almost immediately.'

At the time I was in no state to comment, so I let it pass without comment now.

Tom went on talking, and, much as I deplore having to admit it, he restored my spirits a little. It was not the moment for bickering over his letter. He was in a pleasing, philosophical mood. His confidence had come back. He could see that he was restoring me, and could not resist the old temptation to try and impress. He was an affectionate and generous man, and he was devoting himself whole-heartedly to consolation; but he was as susceptible to human weakness as anyone else. He wanted to speak of Myrtle: he wanted to ease my heart and my conscience: and he could not resist giving me a lesson in psychological observation.

'I think the trouble arose from the grave mistake you, Joe, made about her,' he said.

'What?' I asked humourlessly.

Tom spoke with warm, enveloping authority. He moved his face a little closer to mine.

'Myrtle,' he said, in a low voice, 'didn't want marriage: she wanted passion.'

I looked at him. As an absurdity it was so colossal that it took on the air of a great truth. To it, as such, I bowed my head in silence.

5
Provincial Life-Histories

That is the end of my story.

A few days later the school term ended, the holidays began, and I left the town for six weeks. When I returned the Second World War had broken out.

The awkwardness about finishing a novel lies in thinking the fact that though the story is ended the characters are still alive. I have chosen to end my story at this incident, because it was the last I saw of Myrtle; because the war broke out and we were all dispersed. But we all went on living. It seems to me that if you have been sufficiently interested to read as far as this you can hardly help wondering what we did after the end of the story.

I can tell you what we did. I could call a roll, indicating the fate that befell each of us. If only print could speak, you would hear my voice ring out sonorously:

Myrtle: married,
Myrtle's dress-maker: married,
Tom: married,
Steve: married,
Robert: married,
Haxby: married,
The other Crow: married,
My landlady: married,
Frank: married,
Benny: married,
Fred: married,
Trevor: married – twice!

This is all very well. It will doubtless be of interest to the race, but not, I fear, to the individual reader. So I will stop playing and get down to business. I will push on with my story just a little way, and then sum up what happened to each of the main characters.

I completed the term at school without being asked to resign. I thought I was doing rather well. Bolshaw told me my retention was dependent on his patronage. I thought the headmaster had forgotten his threatening letter to me in his agitation over not being able to trace the teaspoons. Bolshaw ceased his practice of denigrating my character in the explosion of rage he experienced when he heard Simms was coming back.

The boys of the senior sixth form left, and in the fresh term I felt lost without them. However it was not very long before I was called up for military service, and I shook the dust of the school off my shoes for ever.

Shortly after leaving for ever I had to go back for some books, and I heard that Simms had died suddenly.

'Of course it was a happy release,' Bolshaw said, in what I thought was a very ambiguous tone. He blew through his whiskers and stared at me. Certainly it had been a happy release for Bolshaw. 'I'm glad to say the headmaster has listened to reason over the reorganization. He asked me to take over both jobs. I'm now senior science master *and* senior physics master. It will mean I shall have less time for teaching.' He gave me a grandiose smile, in which his moustache drew back from his tusks.

I left without calling on the headmaster, and I never saw him again.

My landlady must have had enough of schoolmasters. In my place she took an insurance agent twenty years older than me. Her choice could hardly have been wiser, because he married her and was kind to her dog. On the other hand, her niece has still had nothing like enough of Mr Chinnock, who calls on her at two-thirty every Sunday, like clockwork.

★

The friends of mine who were killed in the war are not any of those who appear in this story. Trevor, Benny, Frank and Fred all escaped.

Trevor dabbled in what he called art until he was called up, when he got into the Intelligence Corps. He remained a sergeant till the end of the war, and then he married the big girl over whom we had had all the fuss. Tom was furious when he heard about it, and proposed that Trevor should start paying back our money. After marrying her, he divorced her and married another big girl.

Frank had a year at Oxford doing science and then he became a radio officer in the Navy. He had a creditable career, he looked very handsome in uniform, and he married a thoroughly nice girl. Somehow he feels he has missed something.

Fred got a job in the corporation electricity department, did his military service, and returned to it. If you happen to be near the clock-tower and go into the electricity department's showroom, the stocky man with brilliantined hair and a good-natured soppy voice, who is trying to interest you in an immersion heater, is Fred. He has begotten a large family.

Benny worked his way into the Royal Army Medical Corps. After congratulating himself on his apparent safety, he found to his consternation that he could not be commissioned without being a doctor. Towards the end of the war the regulations were changed and he became a 2nd Lieutenant. On the basis of this medical career, he set up in a room above one of the shops in the market-place as a radiologist. He now has three rooms, an assistant, a nurse, a lot of ponderable equipment and the minimum qualifications. He has offered to X-ray me at any time free of charge.

So much for the boys.

And now we come to Steve. It will be no surprise to you that Steve did not free himself from his patron. They continued to enjoy scenes of violent emotion both with and without motor cars. Steve's French accent was improved by a holiday in France, and Tom did not go to America.

On the other hand, in the following year, the war removed Tom from the town, and his devoted interest in his protégé seemed inexplicably to wane. Steve found his freedom returning at an embarrassing pace; and soon there was literally nothing to stop him becoming as ordinary as he pleased. When he was called up Steve finally showed his independence: he volunteered to become a pilot in the Royal Air Force.

Steve actually reached the stage of flying an aeroplane – he flew it with skill, but he was unable to land it. With all his gifts, Steve had been born without the knack of bringing an aeroplane down intact. Everybody recognized it; some of us, including Steve, with relief. The Air Force tried to make him a navigator, but Steve's arithmetic let him down. They tried to make him a wireless operator and he mysteriously developed sporadic bouts of deafness. Steve was unglamorously kept to the ground. However, one thing Steve had mastered from life with his patron was the art of bearing up. Indeed he must have had a talent for it. His gesture had failed, but he was more than content from merely having made it. He bore up remarkably well. He soon began to look round.

What Steve saw was the daughter of the junior partner in his old firm of accountants. She was an attractive, strong-minded girl, and she had fallen in love with Steve. Steve wanted to be married: he wanted to be a father. And in the end he accommodated himself to the idea of becoming an accountant. This, too, cost him some suffering, but his fortitude saved him. He was just the sort of man the firm wanted back; a young Air Force officer, clever, charming, well-bred, conventional and right-minded. He married the girl.

And there in the town Steve remains. He is unostentatiously successful as an accountant. He and his wife live in style. He is very proud of his children. As the years pass he deplores other people's divagations with decreasing self-consciousness. Steve has become respectable.

There is something peculiarly edifying about Steve's life-history. Steve is now respected by others. I should like to call him a pillar of society. Yes, I will call Steve a pillar of society: it is fitting.

★

I said that Tom did not go to America. That is not true. He did not go to America as a prospective political refugee in August 1939. None of us went. Tom delayed and delayed, and Robert exerted no pressure to make him leave. 'There's going to be a war,' Tom said, first of all because he did not want to go, and then because there was going to be a war.

Before he was due to be called up Tom was offered a job in the Ministry of Aircraft Production. He took it, and before long he had become successful in it. He went to work in Headquarters, in London, and was unexpectedly promoted by Lord Beaverbrook. It was reported that he was promoted because the Minister left his brief-case in the lift and Tom chased after him with it. I do not think the report is true.

With the changes of regime in his ministry Tom moved up and down the scale; till finally he quarrelled with one of his superiors and was sent on a mission to Washington. So he went to the U.S.A. after all.

Now you ought to know Tom well enough to answer in one go the simple question: 'What did Tom do in America?'

Tom became an American.

In America Tom found a limitless field for his bustling bombinations, spiritual, emotional and geographical. Suggestibly he began to speak with an American accent. Rashly he proposed marriage to an American girl, who accepted and made him marry her. He was offered an attractive job if he would take out first papers. The war ended, he stayed on, and there he is.

Some time ago I was in America, and I stayed with Tom and his family. I found his appearance had changed a little: his red hair is still as thick and curly as ever, but his physique is showing signs of portliness. He has not become as portly as he would have become in England, but the signs are there. Otherwise he had not changed.

On my second evening he sent his wife to bed early, brought out a bottle of whisky, and began to talk about old times.

He asked about Steve, who no longer writes to him, and Myrtle, who no longer writes to either of us. Talking of Myrtle threw him into his pleasing philosophical mood. In the intervening years he had learnt more of the secrets of the heart, so he informed me. The thought of Myrtle stirred him.

'Ah, Myrtle,' he said, pursing his lips and smiling.

'Ah, Myrtle,' I said, myself, and drank some whisky.

'You made a grave mistake over her, Joe.'

'What?'

'Myrtle,' he said, in a low, authoritative voice, 'didn't want passion. She wanted marriage.'

I might have been listening to him in the café.

It all came back to me. The low tone of voice was exactly the same: only the words were exactly the opposite.

Tom smiled with self-satisfaction. You see that he had not changed at all.

At last, Myrtle. Myrtle married Haxby.

During the months I lived in the town after the summer holidays, I saw her only twice by chance in the street. We did not stop to speak to each other. I supposed that she must be hearing scraps of information about me as I was about her. Her bohemian parties were still in full swing, attended by Trevor and Steve. Her rejection of Tom's proposal of marriage appeared to cause neither of them any embarrassment. I think Myrtle liked him the more for it. Tom went to her parties and told me the news about her.

The first subject of gossip was my resemblance to Svengali. This wilted as a love-match with Haxby came into view. I did not pretend to try and keep up with it. At this point I left the town for good, and they had been married for some time before I heard.

Myrtle became a success in the advertising business. She remained a success. When you see the advertisements for a well-known brand of nylon stockings, sleek, attractive advertisements that at first glance look perfectly innocent and at second perhaps not, you are looking at the work of Myrtle – and she is being paid a lot of money for it.

Myrtle is happy. She looks sad and her voice sounds melancholy. Only Tom's insight could pierce to the depths of her heart: I would say she was happy. She still looks meek, and she still smiles slyly. When hard-natured businessmen offer her contracts she gives a fluttering downward glance, as much as to say she knows they are only doing it to be nice to her. And often they, poor creatures, grin foolishly in return.

Myself. I knew, as soon as I started telling the life-histories of the others, that I should be left with the embarrassing prospect of telling my own. It is one thing to give away what belongs to somebody else, quite another to part with what belongs to oneself. I think of the string of delights and disasters that have come my way since 1939. And then I think of all the novels I can make out of them – ah, novels, novels, Art, Art, pounds sterling!

My own life-history. The past years suddenly spring up, delightful and disastrous, warm, painful and farcical. I reach for a clean new note-book. I pick up my pen.

Scenes from Married Life

THIS BOOK IS DEDICATED TO MY WIFE

Part One

I

On a No. 14 Bus

'P.S.A.,' said Sybil, in a tone of amiable comment. She was looking through the window of the bus and I had my arm round her.

Startled, I followed her glance. The bus was going along Piccadilly – I was on my way to seeing her off at Euston – and I judged that her glance was directed towards one of those huge-windowed shops which in London appear to be indispensable for selling motor-cars, though there is no evidence that fewer motor-cars are sold per financially eligible head of population in say Aberdeen without them. P.S.A.? Or was it B.S.A.? That rang a bell – it was the make of bicycle I had ridden when I was a schoolmaster before the war. A ridiculous idea. There could be no B.S.A.s among Hillmans and Austins and Bentleys, in fact there was no connexion between them other than in my imagination, where, when a provincial schoolmaster astride a B.S.A., I had imagined myself writing a novel which could sell enough copies to buy me a Bentley, or for that matter an Austin, even just a small Austin.

I could see no letters P.S.A., nor B.S.A. In fact I could see no three-letter group anywhere on anything.

'What on earth does P.S.A. stand for?' I asked.

Sybil half-turned to me and said: 'Pleasant Sunday Afternoon, of course.'

I burst into laughter. It was appreciative laughter. Just before getting on to this bus, Sybil and I had been in bed together. My appreciation was enormous.

Sybil was an unusually pretty girl. She looked remarkably like Marlene Dietrich – Marlene Dietrich when young, though Sybil was now about thirty-two. Sybil was aware of the resemblance and plucked her eyebrows accordingly. Above her wide-open blue eyes, they rose in two hyperfine arches, which, when she was talking to you, wiggled in a remarkable manner. I was fascinated by them: I could never understand why they did it.

'I thought you must have seen the letters on a shop-front,' I said. 'I was looking for them everywhere.'

At this Sybil turned away thoughtfully. The fact which I might have remembered, thereby saving myself some trouble, was that Sybil was so short-sighted she could scarcely see the shops. There was a pause while we went round Piccadilly Circus, and then she turned back on me and, with her eyebrows wiggling, said:

'Joe, do you think I ought to wear contact lenses?'

Like a fool, I replied: 'I should have thought a pair of specs would have done just as well.' Having bits of glass against one's eyeballs seemed to me creepy.

Sybil's expression was not a hurt one: it was an uncomprehending one. Contact lenses were something she could envisage: spectacles were not. I realized why not, by reference to a concept which originated from a friend of mine named Robert, who knew Sybil well. Robert was convinced that in her inveterate perusal of women's magazines Sybil had succumbed to the propaganda that any woman can be beautiful by following certain rules of make-up – 'Glamour Tips' was what Robert was convinced they were called, and he believed that there was a fixed apocalyptic number, actually forty-four, of them. Robert, I realized, would have understood at once why Sybil looked uncomprehending – not that he did not understand everything at once, being that sort of man: I revered him for it. Robert would have understood that contact lenses were numbered among Sybil's Forty-four Glamour Tips, whereas spectacles were not.

'Perhaps you ought to have contact lenses,' I said, to get on the rails again.

'Yes,' said Sybil. 'I can't see very much when I'm out.'

'How much can you see?' I said, thinking of her when she was in.

Sybil looked through the window again. She read out the name of the play that was then on at the Globe Theatre, *The Lady Is Not For Burning* – the year was 1949. As the letters were a foot high and only a pavement's width away, I said:

'If you look at the people on the other side of the road, can you tell which sex they are?'

Without hesitation, and with what seemed to me a touch of characteristic complacency, Sybil said:

'If it's fairly clearly marked.'

I laughed, and then something, perhaps actually looking at the people on the other side of the road, made me speculate on how the world looked to Sybil. Very, very different from how it looked to me. The difference visually was obvious – whatever my moral defects were, I had pretty good eyesight – but that was only the beginning. Not only did Sybil see the world differently from me with the outer eye: the truth was that after knowing her for years I had no idea *what* she saw with the inner one.

I had known Sybil off and on for fifteen years. She worked as a librarian in the provincial town that I came from. I repeat, as a librarian. Sybil looked so like Marlene Dietrich that you might have thought she would never have had a book in her hand, that nobody would ever even have shown her one. Not a bit of it. Once during a lull when we were in bed she recited the whole of one of Hamlet's soliloquies – and not the '*To be or not to be*' one either. I was amazed.

Sybil was a mystery to me. After knowing her for fifteen years I had to confess that I had not the faintest idea what moved her immortal soul, what made her tick. Nor had Robert. We used to discuss it with persistence and chagrin. You may think I was in a better position to solve the mystery because she had slept with me and not with Robert. Well, no, you are wrong there, I think.

Anyway, the generalization that you will penetrate the mysteries of somebody's nature if she sleeps with you is a shaky one at the best of times, and in the case of Sybil it was simply non-operative. There she lay, for example, happily reciting one of Hamlet's soliloquies. Amazing, but not exegetical.

'What does Sybil want out of life?' Robert would ask me. When propounding a question to which neither he nor I knew the answer, Robert always safeguarded his own self-esteem by aiming the question at me.

I told him I had heard her say she would like to be a film star.

Because it was out of the question for her to become a film star, Robert looked at me as if he thought I were reporting her untruthfully. It was not possible for Robert to believe that aspiration could exist so independently of action: in Sybil they existed together without the slightest mutual influence – they appeared not to cause each other a scrap of bother. Sybil went on her way imperturbably. Sometimes I thought conceitedness might have been the source of her imperturbability, but she never seemed particularly conceited.

Then Robert and I argued about whether Sybil wanted to be married again. Robert wanted to know if she wanted to marry me, and when I said I saw no signs of it, that between Sybil and me marriage somehow did not come into it, he looked neither satisfied with my reply nor dissatisfied. He said: 'H'm.'

Sybil and I were friends who had slept together off and on for years, the off spells corresponding on my side to the times when I was in love with someone, and on her side to the spell when she was married. The latter, alas, was short. In 1943 she married a willowy, dashing young man in the Parachute Regiment, and he was killed at Arnhem. After that she went on working in her library, helping to support her mother. There were always men about the place who wanted to marry her, and no one was more in need of a guiding hand, literally, than Sybil. Sybil standing on the pavement looking for a bus-stop was a sight so heart-rending that any man who saw her longed to drive up in an expensive car and carry her away. Yet she did not marry.

Marriage and widowhood had made no difference in Sybil's attitude to me: failure to marry and confirmation in bachelordom had obviously made no difference in my attitude to her. Sitting in the No. 14 bus that November Sunday evening, we might just as well have been sitting in a provincial tram soon after we first met.

Oddly self-possessed yet diffident, in some ways ineffably remote
– not to mention others in which she was deliciously contiguous
– with beautiful eyes picking up next to nothing and eyebrows
wiggling like antennae, she gave me no clue whatsoever to what
made her tick. She never had. She never would.

That Sunday evening was almost the last time I ever saw Sybil,
so that I have had ten years to recollect her in tranquillity. Still no
clue.

The bus fetched up at Euston and we went into the station.
Euston is dark at the best of times and, on this particular evening,
night had come early, coldly and wintrily, wafting into our nostrils
fog flavoured with sulphur dioxide. We were in no hurry. We
went through the classical entrance into the forecourt, where the
lights were burning without seeming to make the slightest difference to the degree of illumination. A faint shadow had crossed
both our minds, for a glance at the clock had reminded us that
although time was passing it was still too early to get a drink.

How often I had entered this station, just before seven o'clock
of a Sunday evening! *Autres temps, autres femmes*, I reminded myself
in a sprightly way – that suddenly fell flat . . . I was reminded of
autres temps, some years back, when I had thought I was all set to
get married.

'Damn this station!' I must have said it aloud, because Sybil said:
'Yes. It isn't as nice as Paddington.'

We went on to the platform and found that the train was in. It
was always in. I put Sybil's case on a seat and then we strolled
down the platform. The faint fishy, appley smell was too poignant
to be borne, I thought. I really wished I might never be seeing
anybody off from this station, from this particular platform, ever
again. I said to Sybil all the same:

'How soon can you come and see me again?'

'Not till after Christmas, more's the pity!'

A porter beginning to slam the doors at the top end of the train
took us by surprise. It was time for Sybil to get into the carriage.

When the train had gone out I made for the bar, which was

now open, and ordered a large whisky. It may sound as if I had fallen into a bout of *tristezza* consequent on the pleasures of the afternoon, but to my mind it was consequent on something of much longer duration, and not pleasurable either. To ward it off I drank the whisky quickly and ordered another. I paused. And then inspiration suddenly hit me in the way a large whisky does.

There was something wrong with my life, and my predicament at this moment expressed it perfectly. Having just seen off Sybil, what had I got to go home to? An empty flat. At my age – I was thirty-nine – what had all other men got to go home to? A cosy house with a wife in it and some kiddies. What a corny dream-picture! I thought, and yet what an attractive one! (For the moment I disregarded the fact that if there had been a wife and some kiddies in my flat I should have been lucky to get out for a solitary whisky, let alone to see off at Euston, *con tristezza* or *con allegria*, some such girl as Sybil.)

A romantic bitterness about my fate temporarily overcame me, in the deserted bar. When I was young I had not wanted to get married. And now! At that question my spirits slipped a notch lower. I began my second whisky.

As my colleagues in the Civil Service would have put it, I 'reviewed the situation'. What a situation! And what an awful review! For fifteen years I had slept with someone whom I comprehended so little that somehow marriage just never came into it. Like ships that pass in the night, Sybil and I, for all the passing and re-passing which practically amounted to a regular service, were still a couple of ships, lone in the night. I was still lone in the night. Was it, could it possibly be, that there was something wrong not with my life but with *me*? When I thought that, I felt something deep in my psyche like the fall of ice-cream on teeth that have just been scaled.

'Joe,' I said to myself as I drank some more of the whisky, 'it's bad, very bad.' I meant the prognosis was bad.

Mine was indeed a predicament – in Robert's idiom, a predicament and a half.

Remembering Robert made me decide to explain my latest view of my predicament to him. Of course he knew all about it, as he knew about everything else. The trouble with our predicaments, especially when they are painful, incapable of resolution, even tragic, is that we are just a bit proud of them, just a bit attached to them. Though Robert knew all about mine already, I had every intention of explaining my latest view of it even if I bored the hide off him.

I made my way out of the station and caught a No. 14 bus going in the opposite direction to the one I had come on.

'Terminus,' I said to the conductor heavily, but meaning it literally. I was living at Putney.

Talks with a Fat Man

Harry was one of those active fat men who are really more muscular and less fat than they look, though that is not saying much in
the case of Harry, whose shape came as near as makes no matter
to a globe. And like the terrestrial globe, he seemed to be always
spinning. When he approached you, moving bulkily on light,
strong feet, a whirling gust of air preceded him – it was the outskirts of a vortex at the centre of which you saw Harry, sweating
profusely and fixing you with a beady, eager, inquisitive look.

Harry was a distant cousin of mine. (Exactly how distant was
something that he and I – unlike members of the aristocracy, to
whom, with titles and large sums of money in the offing, such
calculations seem to come like second nature – had never bothered to work out.) Though our families saw little of each other,
Harry and I, between the ages of fifteen and eighteen, when he
was going to a country grammar school and I to a town secondary
school, had been companions for pursuits involving bicycles, box-
cameras, airguns, tents and suchlike; pursuits frequently
commended by parents for promoting healthy adventurous
instincts in boys, and often undertaken by boys chiefly as a means
of getting away from parents.

I still possess a small terracotta Roman bowl, artfully stuck
together with Seccotine, that Harry and I ought to have handed
in to the local museum of antiquities. I also keep an old photograph
of both of us, taken by another boy and somewhat imperfectly
'fixed' by the look of it, in which Harry misleadingly appears as
lithe, broad-chested, and quite unglobelike. Globedom, as in those
dried Japanese flowers which you drop into a glass of water, was

then securely hidden in the comely packet of Harry's particular type of physique – a type which he and I nowadays referred to with professional facetiousness as the Pyknic Practical Joke. The joke was comic enough when played by the Deity on Harry, but was seen by us at its most comic when played on a young man who married a beautiful, lithe, broad-chested girl, in whom was hidden, as in one of those Japanese flowers, etc. etc. etc.

Harry, I may say, was surviving the joke with over-high blood-pressure but admirable grace. I found him more fun now than I had done twenty years ago, not because his nature had changed, but because I suppose I had meanwhile learnt how to find people entertaining. Boys have a dim time of it because they have so far learnt only how to find each other useful. Anyway, I was glad when Harry reappeared in my life.

One day the telephone in my office rang – by this time I had become a Principal in the Civil Service – and it was Harry. Our boyhood companionship had lapsed when I went up to Oxford to read science and Harry went to Manchester to start becoming a doctor. Throughout the last twenty years I do not suppose I had seen him more than half a dozen times. My sense of family was strong but of the passive, non-visiting, non-corresponding kind. It was not activated by a feeling that if I did visit and correspond I should be overwhelmed by moral approval of my goings-on. Harry's and my family was sprinkled with Methodist ministers, my father being one of them.

I felt nothing but pleasure when Harry rang me up that day to say he had got a job in the Medical Research Council and had bought a house in Putney. I was ready to take up our friendship just where we had left off.

But the first time Harry and I met again, I realized that it was pure illusion on my part to think that anything had been left off where he was concerned. There was no lapse, no blank, no absence whatsoever of contact from his side. Harry seemed to have a complete dossier of everything I had done during the last twenty years.

At this point in my story I have to make my chief revelation about Harry's nature. About Sybil I remarked that I had not the faintest idea what moved her immortal soul, what made her tick. There was no such mystery about Harry. His mainspring was visible to everyone. What moved Harry's immortal soul can be named in one word – curiosity. I have never in my life known anyone to come anywhere near Harry's level for being moved so constantly, so powerfully, so magnificently by curiosity. It shone in the beadiness of his bright hazel eyes; it whirled in the warm gust of air that preceded him; curiosity, fat, energetic and insatiable.

'Good gracious!' I exclaimed when I first saw him come into the room – we met at my club – not having expected him to be anything like so globular. His waist measurement must be his biggest, I thought with stupefaction.

Harry looked at me shrewdly for a moment, and said in his quick, fluent, high-pitched voice:

'You're greyer than your photographs show, aren't you, Joe?'

I could not think where he had seen a photograph of me. As for being grey – it is very hard to realize how much older one is looking. Whenever I was at the barber's and a wad of hair fell in my lap, I always had a job not to exclaim: 'Is that *mine*?'

Harry, I observed, had not much hair at all now. He had a globe-shaped head, over the top of which his fine-textured, straight, mouse-coloured hair could scarcely be said to hide the pink of his scalp. He had a shining, intelligent face, in the middle of which sat a snub nose. With the years' accretion of flesh round them, his eyes looked smaller than they used to, not quite puffy, not quite baggy, but somewhere in between the two. He took out a handkerchief and wiped a few drops of sweat off his forehead before he sat down.

'I suppose,' he said, when he had sat down, 'getting turned down in marriage, that last time, must have taken a lot out of you?'

'How in God's name do you know all about that?' I said. After all, I had hardly told my parents anything about it, and I presumed our family was his source of intelligence.

Harry said: 'Oh, I pieced it together . . .' His tone might have been thought apologetic as well as explanatory. But his complexion gave him away. I noticed the sudden tinge of a blush. It was a blush of triumph, of pure triumph.

I stared at him.

'I was sorry to hear about your bad luck.' While he was saying this, his eyes seemed to enlarge with sympathy, and he looked at me with intimate concern.

Harry's feeling was not in the least put on for the occasion. His curiosity was linked with unusual empathy. Looking at him now I realized that when we were boys I might have been unaware of what he was like but I had not been mistaken in choosing him for a friend.

'It's the sort of thing that happens to one,' I muttered, looking down.

'I wonder . . .' he said. His tone stayed on its high, honeyed pitch. 'Don't you think you attract that kind of bad luck?'

I looked up pretty quickly at that.

'There's the internal evidence of your novels, you know,' he said. And again he was unable to keep the triumphant look off his face.

'I don't write my novels to provide the likes of you with internal evidence,' I said, trying to hide my huffiness by grinning.

'I think,' he said, without the slightest flicker in his friendly concern, 'they're very good novels. Especially your last one.'

I should like to know what I could say to that.

Anyway, all this happened a year or more before the evening I described when I saw Sybil off at Euston. It is relevant because instead of going home to my empty flat that night, I went round to Harry's house, which was only a quarter of an hour's walk away. It was Harry and his wife, Barbara, who had persuaded me to quit the dilapidated square in Pimlico where my most recent disaster in love had happened to me, and to start life afresh in Putney. Energetically they had found me a flat and supervised my removal. I was grateful to them. I did like the change. Also, I had been constantly troubled by the prospect of my Pimlico landlady giving me notice.

I strolled along the dark, bosky by-roads from the bus-stop, feeling encouraged by the prospect of being offered something to eat at Harry's. I was hungry.

Harry opened the front door to me, silhouetted like a globe against the light from inside the hall. A whirl of air left me standing as his high voice receded down a corridor.

'Come into the kitchen, Joe. Barbara's out, so I'm getting my own supper.'

In the kitchen I could readily see that for myself. There stood Harry, with drops of sweat on his forehead and an apron tied round his equator, preparing an omelette. On the top of the table were a piece of Gruyère cheese from which a teacupful had been grated, a saucerful of chopped chives, and the broken shells of no less than four eggs.

'Are the children still up?' I asked, looking at all this.

'No,' said Harry, taking a cardboard crate of eggs out of the refrigerator. 'Can you eat more than two of these? They're rather small.'

In a moment the smell of hot butter rose from the stove, and the sweat began to run down into Harry's eyes. His movements were deft and quick.

'I'm hungry,' I said.

'I expect you must be,' said Harry, and added lightly, *en passant*: 'Did the train leave on time?'

I could not help laughing, but as he was busy with the omelette he did not notice.

'Platform 17, I suppose,' he said.

'No,' said I, '12.'

Harry spun round, and his astonished look of 'How-could-they-have-changed-the-platform-without-my-knowing?' rewarded me in full. Had the omelette not been sizzling deliciously in the enormous frying-pan that he was holding in front of him, I think he would have whirled off to the telephone instantly to ring up Euston. Suddenly an elephantine glint came into his eye.

'I know why it was!' he said. And he produced on the spot an inordinately convincing explanation of the change.

Having already had my full reward, I considered this was pure bonus. (It had been Platform 17, of course.) I said:

'Let's eat, Harry!'

Harry divided the omelette, and while I took out of the oven a long French loaf that had been warming up, Harry drew two glasses of cold water from the tap over the sink – he drank very little alcohol, under the impression that so doing would keep his blood-pressure down.

We began to eat.

In view of his questions about Sybil's train, you may think Harry's curiosity would have led him to begin quizzing me about the events of the week-end. That would have been a journeyman's method. Harry was a virtuoso. His method was to pick up a detail here, a detail there – the more improbable the quarter the better – to throw in now and then a shrewd guess or a sharp bit of deduction, and then to 'piece them together'. It was only then that professional pride allowed him to ask a direct question, just to prove to himself that he already knew the answer anyway.

Harry did not mention Sybil again that evening. What we began to talk about, while we were eating the omelette, was my job. I have remarked that I was a Principal in the Civil Service. I worked under Robert, who was an Under Secretary, and most of my job was interviewing people. I saw large numbers of them, and, for both human interest as well as professional use, I needed some scheme for classifying them. Nobody can look with detachment at a large number of his fellow human beings without noticing that when two people of approximately the same physical shape turn up they show resemblances to each other in temperament. Some particular kinds of temperament go with some particular kinds of physical shape. Part of the fascination of my job, the claim it had on my imagination, was the search for a generalization, detailed and well-ordered, about these things.

Harry was interested, professionally as a doctor, privately as

Harry – curiosity moved both of us, in this field at least, with the same power. Our discussions lasted us well into the stage of the meal when we were eating delicious cold apple-pie.

However, Harry's curiosity could not be confined indefinitely. I suppose I might admit the discussion had come to an end, but during the following pause I was still thinking about it. Suddenly, sweetly out of the blue, Harry dropped a question. About Robert.

Now my having told you Robert was my boss, my intimate friend of twenty years' standing and my literary comrade-in-arms as novelist – we were fighting to liberate ourselves through Art from the Civil Service, Robert having already half-won the battle and gone on to part-time – has not told you all. It has not made clear how important to me Robert's continued presence in the Civil Service was. Robert was the creator of his own job and of mine. I had reason to believe that if he resigned his job, mine would disappear.

The question Harry dropped, sweetly from the blue while he stood by the stove making our coffee, was:

'Is it true Robert's going to resign from the Civil Service at the beginning of next year?'

Lunch in a Tea-Shop

The effect of sleeping on a troublesome idea is, as every sound man knows, to flatten it a bit. One puts it, like a crumpled pair of trousers, under one's mattress, and oh! the difference when one brings it out next morning. If one is lucky. But then sound men *are* lucky.

Next morning, in the ordinary light of day as contrasted with the dazzling night of Harry's imagination, I saw that Robert simply could not be intending to leave me in the lurch. In my opinion, though not in his, Robert had many faults; but lack of responsibility for his friends was not among them. I had been momentarily swept off my feet by one of Harry's *ballons d'essai* – it suddenly occurred to me that if one ever actually saw a *ballon d'essai*, it would probably look like Harry.

So I got up that Monday morning feeling refreshed by the week-end and looking forward to my work. I did not want my job to disappear. I liked it. I was fascinated by it. Also it kept me from starving.

Robert and I were employed in a department of government that got scientific research done on a big scale. Large numbers of scientists and engineers were involved; and looking after those we had, together with trying to lay our hands on more, was a task and a half. During the war, when anybody who could do a job well got a chance to do it, Robert had taken that task and a half upon himself with great success – and, I should like to add, with my devoted assistance.

If you know the Civil Service only in peace-time you would expect such a task to fall to the lot of the department's establishments division. Though our department had a perfectly competent establishments division, with a brace of perfectly competent Under Secretaries at its head, Robert had got agreement after the war for continuing his job as head of a separate, semi-autonomous directorate. Though his directorate was closely linked with our establishments division, and one of their Under Secretaries was technically Robert's boss, we were, well, not *of* them. Robert, as a novelist, was a creative artist: there was indeed more than a touch of creative art about his Civil Service set-up.

The set-up had obvious advantages for us, but it required hypnosis to make any advantage for our establishments division obvious to that division. Many of them asked themselves how Robert managed it. In the first place he was a man of hypnotic personality. In the second, he had made himself a pretty high reputation and none of his immediate seniors was anxious to take the responsibility of losing him to the Service. Nevertheless, at the end of 1949, when the Service had shaken down to something more like its pre-war regular self – had shaken down far enough for many a regular Under Secretary to have completely forgotten that he was in his present post through irregular entry or promotion during the war – the touch of creative art about our present set-up was becoming over-apparent. And one has to remember that although Mankind has always had Art about the place, there is no evidence that Mankind could not have got on without it. My job of interviewing scientists and engineers and making decisions about their futures was one that quite a few people in our establishments division would have liked. And I have to admit that I had only Robert to hypnotize them into agreeing it were not better so. You see why it was very important indeed to me that Robert should not resign for the time being.

All the same, when I set off for work that Monday morning, Harry's question was not high on my list of things to talk to Robert about at lunch-time. I was thinking mostly – and not unnaturally, if it comes to that – about Sybil. It was a bright November day and I strode down Putney Hill cheerfully singing under my breath.

After all, I had come to Putney to start life afresh. Something brought the tune of 'Sweet Lass of Richmond Hill' into my mind, and I tried to fit in words to denote myself.

'Brave Lad of Putney Hill' commended itself insistently because it was so obvious. Yet its Housemanesque ring, I thought, was so wrong. I was neither young nor bucolic, and offhand I could not recall any occasion that had shown me to be brave. I passed the traffic lights and the Zeeta café, and noticed the usual haze drifting up from the river. The buses flashed a particularly inviting red, while their bile-shaded luminescent posters were more evocative than ever of nausea. Suddenly I caught sight of myself in Marks & Spencer's window, and my unconscious mind got the better of me:

'Smart Chap of Putney Hill!'

Unbidden – I would certainly have turned my back on them had I known they were coming – the words attached themselves to the tune, and the image of a Smart Chap attached itself, horribly, to me. It was not what I thought I was trying to look like at all. 'I don't look like a gentleman,' I thought. 'All well and good, because I'm not a gentleman. But a smart chap! . . . There are all sorts of other things one could look like. But no, not that!'

I passed Marks & Spencer's pretty quickly, I can tell you. And it was with relief that I heard a high-pitched, honeyed voice calling behind me:

'Joe!'

It was Harry, overtaking me. We often met at this time of day and travelled to work together.

'You're looking very dapper this morning,' he said.

I did not reply. I simply did not reply. And on the way to London we discussed neither my appearance nor the question of Robert's plans for getting out of the Civil Service. We read our newspapers. But all the same, he did, merely by his presence, provoke my concern. I decided that I would put the matter higher on my list of things to say to Robert at lunch-time after all.

Robert and I usually had lunch together and we usually went to a tea-shop. Practically all our colleagues went to our canteen, with an air of loyally all keeping together – as if they were not together enough in their offices! – and in the canteen chewed over indiscriminately, but with apparent satisfaction, a mixture of bad cooking and office shop. Robert and I frequented a café where there was not the slightest likelihood of our meeting any of them.

Our behaviour was, of course, completely contrary to the Social Ethic, which tells you to be as other men are. Now in my experience men are more tolerant than they are often made out to be. They do not mind your not being as they are. What they will not tolerate is its *showing*. And here I must point out a great difference between Robert and me. When Robert and I sloped off at 12.45 to our tea-shop, *something showed in me*. There was no doubt about it. But in Robert? Did our colleagues realize that if I had not been there he would guilefully have excused himself from chewing over toad-in-the-hole and shop? They did not. That is the way life is.

I will tell you about me. At the end of the war, when Robert set up his directorate, we had been asked if we would care to be made permanent civil servants. In two minds, but politely, I had filled up a form I was given for the purpose. And in due course I got a reply, Roneo'd on a slip of paper of not specially high quality, measuring about four inches by six, and beginning thus:

MISC/INEL
Dear Sir,
    The Civil Service Commissioners desire me to say that having considered your application for admission, etc . . .

And ending thus:

    They must, therefore, with regret declare you ineligible to compete and cancel your application accordingly.
                                        Yours faithfully,

It was a mistake, of course. Of course it was a mistake. I got an immediate apology from someone higher up the hierarchy than anyone I had had an apology from before. But was it a mistake? Had something *showed* already?

MISC/INEL. Miscellaneous/Ineligible, it stood for. The letter I thought I might, as a literary artist taking on the style of a petty official, have invented. But not MISC/INEL. That was beyond me. That was the invention of an artist in his own right: it had the stamp of uncounterfeitable originality, the characteristic of striking through to a deeper truth than its creator comprehended. MISC/INEL. It could not be a mistake. Through that slip of not very high quality paper, measuring about four inches by six, I saw my epitaph, composed by a delegated member of the company of men and inscribed on everlasting, distinctly expensive marble.

Here lies the body of
JOSEPH LUNN
Who though admittedly
A Great Writer A True Friend
A Perfect Husband and Father
Must in The End be classed
MISC/INEL

Actually the MISC/INEL letter settled my flirtation with permanency. My two minds about becoming a permanent civil servant became one, and that one said No. I asked myself what on earth I had been thinking about. I wanted to be a writer. If it came to that, by God, I was a writer. The battle that I referred to earlier, the battle for the day when I would be nothing else but a writer, was on.

So much for that. Back to the story –

'Give my regards to Robert,' said Harry, as I got out of the bus – and then, never short of a *ballon d'essai*, he loosed off: 'Not forgetting Annette, of course.'

He wanted to know whether Robert was going to marry Annette or not. I said: 'Sure, I will,' in an American accent.

When I got to the office, there was Robert sitting on the edge of my desk, reading a proof-copy of my next novel. He glanced up as I came in and I saw that his face was pink.

'This is very good,' he said, although he must already have read the book five times. He had a characteristic muffled, lofty intonation that gave enormous weight to everything he said, but the pinkness of his complexion gave evidence of something other than weight. Robert was prudish, but that is not to say he was not just the faintest bit lewd. He shut the book, and looked at me with eyes that were sparkling. 'It's very good indeed.'

If that is not the sort of literary comrade-in-arms you want, I would like to know what is. What a friend! And what a book he was reading!

'How was Sybil?' he said.

'Very well.' He glanced away, through the window – not that he could see anything through it, as it faced on a dreary well: modestly Euclidean, I have always felt that an internal circumference, so to speak, would be shorter than an external one; yet our office-architect had contrived to put at least twice as many windows looking inwards as outwards.

Robert said: 'We went to the Zoo,' in a tone which stressed the cultural, rather than the erotic nature of the expedition.

'Oh,' said I, 'we stayed in.' I let it go at that.

There was a pause for reflection, very satisfactory reflection.

Robert, sitting on one haunch, was swinging his foot to and fro. He looked like Franklin D. Roosevelt. I am sorry to have to say, within the space of describing three of my friends, that two of them looked like world-figures, and I will not do it again with any of the others. But it would be absurd for me to let Sybil's resemblance to Marlene Dietrich stop me saying Robert looked like F.D.R., because he did. F.D.R. without the gap teeth. Robert had a massiveness of body and of head that nevertheless gave the impression of a certain lightness. Like the best kind of cake, he was big without being heavy.

It was the same with Robert's temperament. Essentially he was a man of *gravitas*. His temperament was massive and complex, deep-sounding and made for great endurance. From the time when I first got to know him, when he was my Tutor at Oxford, I had sensed his *gravitas*. Yet it was *gravitas* leavened, I am happy to say, by extraordinary wiliness and charm, and by the occasional flash of unpredictable private fun that put you in mind of a waggon-load of monkeys – than which, incidentally, Robert was much cleverer. Much. Robert was as clever as, if not cleverer than, a waggon-load of high civil servants.

It will be apparent to you that I was still in the attitude towards Robert of an undergraduate bowled over by his Tutor, an attitude causing constant irritation to my nearest and dearest, but a source of great satisfaction, not to mention use, to me.

On we go. But not very far. My telephone rang. It was our P.A. (short for personal assistant) saying our Senior Executive Officer wanted to speak to me. While she was putting him through, Robert said:

'Who is it?'

I told him. 'He's got on to me because he wanted to speak to you and you weren't in your room.' I held out the receiver towards him. 'You can speak to him here.'

'He probably wants you in any case.'

I hesitated at this display of extra-sensory perception. He who hesitates sees the other man nip gravely out of the room before he can get another breath.

The day's work had begun. I had some people to interview, and Robert had his usual Monday morning commitment, which was a conference with the Under Secretary, Murray-Hamilton, who was technically his boss, and Murray-Hamilton's Assistant Secretary, Spinks. (Perhaps I ought to explain the titles. In the worlds of commerce and industry, your secretary is your subordinate: in the Civil Service, not on your life. Rating in the hierarchy goes up thus: Assistant Principal, Principal, Assistant Secretary, Under Secretary, Deputy Secretary, *Secretary*!)

I was glad to be in my own shoes and not in Robert's. By a mischance that was tiresome to say the least of it, Murray-Hamilton and Spinks strongly disapproved of me. The last thing I would have proposed for my own good was a morning with those two: I did everything I could to keep out of their way. Yet I say this with some ambivalence of feeling. I disapproved of Spinks – 'Stinker Spinks,' I called him to myself – but there was nothing remarkable about that as he was pretty thoroughly disliked by everybody in the department. On the other hand I approved of, even liked Murray-Hamilton. He was first-rate at his job and furthermore he had – what was unusual among senior civil servants – a brooding, reflective look . . . I had not the faintest idea what he was brooding or reflecting about, but I felt drawn to him by his look.

When I met Robert at lunch-time, he did not show signs of having spent the morning with marked enjoyment. He sauntered along the Strand beside me in an abstracted mood, and at a street corner he bought an *Evening News*, which he began to read as he walked along. The pavement was crowded and he covered the rest of the journey by a sort of 'drunkard's walk', bouncing obliquely off passers-by. The morning sunshine was dimmed by now, and a thin mist, very November-like, seemed to be clinging round the roofs of the tallest buildings. We went into our tea-shop and ordered our usual ladylike snack.

Throughout the meal Robert read his newspaper, so I got no opportunity to refer to any of the topics I had waiting. And when finally he put it down – Robert did not fold up a newspaper when he had finished with it: he just quietly dropped it over the arm of his chair – I saw the heavy, thoughtful look he usually wore when he was irritated or displeased.

'What's the matter?' I asked.

'Nothing of any particular interest.'

I watched him, waiting. His large, light grey eyes appeared to be focused on his cup of coffee and he was frowning. Suddenly he said:

'Actually there is.' And then he looked away from me. 'I'm fed up with being sniped at by these people.'

He meant Murray-Hamilton and Spinks. I said:

'What about?'

He turned to me.

'You.'

There was a pause.

'What have I done now?' I said.

Robert promptly leaned over and picked up his newspaper again.

'Just general,' he muttered in a tight-lipped way that indicated he was not going to say anything else.

He started to read again.

4

Dinner with Two Doctors

Harry's wife, Barbara, was a doctor, too. She was intelligent, good-looking, and well-disposed towards me. In manifestation of the latter she had a way of giving me a look that indicated I-know-you-better-than-you-know-yourself.

I told myself I could have taken it more readily from a man than a woman. After all, I conceded, I actually had taken it from at least one man over a period of twenty years, namely from Robert. Of course you may think there was something wrong with me rather than with Barbara – you certainly may if you happen to be a woman. But that does not alter the fact that I found the look hard to take, above all when Barbara gave it me while declaring:

'*You*'ll never get married.'

You see what I mean?

Harry had married slightly above him, both socially, which may or may not be all to the good, and financially, which is beyond all doubt beneficent. Harry and I were quite simply petty bourgeois: Barbara's father, now dead, had been a provincial lawyer of considerable substance, and a portion of this substance had already come down to Barbara – that was how she and Harry came to have such a large house. Her mother, who stayed with them sometimes, was even slightly grand in her manner: she used to take Barbara to race-meetings, which to me, in spite of seeing the Irish dregs of Shepherd's Bush pour out of trains from Newbury at Paddington, always smacked of the idle rich.

At this particular time Harry and Barbara had been married eleven years and had begotten three children. Barbara was about the same age as Harry – they had first met when they were medical students.

She was a brisk, energetic woman, with the sort of trimness of body that active women often have, though she was now thickening at the middle. She had a longish face, whose length she enhanced by sweeping her hair up at the sides. Her complexion was unusually fine and very fresh in colour, slightly freckled, and her eyes were a clear, light hazel. They were large, clear, knowing eyes.

'Barbara's a strange girl,' Harry used to say to me.

The first time he said it I was amazed. Active, strong-minded, confident and direct was what she seemed to me. Above all, direct. But when he had said it to me on several occasions, I got over my amazement to the extent of being able to note what *his* emotion was. The look in his eyes was not as usual shrewd and inquisitive: it was sentimental, indulgent . . . Barbara seemed strange to him, I realized, because he *wanted* her to seem strange.

The explanation? Harry was, I think, born to be a faithful and devoted husband – I had in my time come across quite a few men who were clearly born to be the reverse and Harry reminded me of none of them. I turned over in my mind the idea that Harry's curiosity played the absorbing part in his life that sexual adventurousness played in theirs. His wife, to Harry, had simply got to be someone around whom his curiosity could play. Whereas to me she looked like a woman destined to be a local councillor and a Justice of the Peace, to Harry she had got to look as mysterious and enigmatic as the Mona Lisa.

'Barbara's a strange girl,' he said. He was always looking away from me when he said it, clearly meditating on goodness knows what subtleties of mind and convolutions of temperament in his loved one.

I nodded my head. The revelation was mad, but oddly appealing to me. I could not help liking him all the more for it.

So there you have Harry and Barbara. Oh yes, I have not told you yet that Barbara, as well as running a house and being a mother, also had a part-time job at a children's clinic on the other side of London. I had a feeling that although she found no difficulty in knowing adults better than they knew themselves, children did present her with certain problems. Whether that made things better or worse for the children was a question upon which I used to speculate.

The occasion when Barbara gave me her I-know-you-better-than-you-know-yourself look and simultaneously said 'You'll never get married' was the first time I went to dinner with her and Harry after I had gone to live at Putney – uprooted from dilapidated Pimlico, mark you, with her exhortation and Harry's assistance, in order to rebuild my dilapidated life. Even if Barbara did know me better than I knew myself, might not she spare me, I wondered, the knowledge of my doom? Might not she and Fate keep it to themselves, as Fate did when operating on its own? Apparently not.

Still, I liked Barbara. And I liked her cooking. I really looked forward to dinner with her and Harry.

The next time I went to dinner at their house, after the night Harry asked me if it was true that Robert was going to resign from the Civil Service, Barbara was going to cook a duck. I was very partial to duck. All previous looks and questions were forgiven and forgotten.

Over dinner Harry and I got down, as usual, to a fine professional discussion about classifications of physiques and temperaments. We were recently completely *épris* – if you can use that word about scientists – by the ideas of an American named Sheldon. He seemed to us a master man, not without reason: he had got over the two hurdles which had previously floored everybody else at the start of their operations in 'typing' physiques, namely how to measure up a physique reliably, and how to cope with the obvious fact that it was not a 'type' anyway but something in between.

Harry and I could scarcely wait to start trying out the ideas for ourselves. You cleared the first hurdle by photographing the physique you were proposing to 'type' in a pre-defined posture from the front, side, and back, and then you made your comparative measurements from the photographs. You cleared the second by regarding this individual physique as a blend, in different proportions, of your

242

chosen 'types' – the rounded fat man, the cubical muscular man, and the linear skinny man. From your comparative measurements you could make a quantitative assessment of the blend. Quantitative! The thing was beginning to look like a science.

But that was only the half of it. The same idea was paralleled on the side of temperament: in the particular temperament you were proposing to type, you made a similar quantitative assessment of the blend of three 'type' temperaments, these 'type' temperaments being the temperaments that characteristically went with the 'type' physiques. The whole thing tied up, was our verdict.

'It's maddening,' said I, 'that we didn't think of it.'

'It's like all the best revolutionary concepts,' said Harry. 'So obvious, so simple!'

You can see how *épris* we were.

At Harry's dinner-table we were concerned not so much with the phon and antiphon of praise as with the prospect of getting down to business on our own. We were agreed that we had got to devise some means of trying out Sheldon's 'somato-typing'.

'If only you could get the M.R.C. to set you up with a research unit!' I said to Harry.

Harry looked at me with baggy bright eyes.

'But surely you,' he said, 'in your job, have all the people we need for it. You've got them all there, simply on tap.'

I looked back at him. And well I might! You see, when one refers to physiques in medical society, one is not thinking of their being clothed. I imagined our engineers and scientists being invited, after I had questioned them on their technical life-stories, to go into an adjoining room to be photographed in the stark – from three view-points!

'Do you want to get me hounded out of the Civil Service al-together?' I said. I was not thinking what would happen if the *Daily Pictorial* got on to it. I only needed to go as far as thinking what would happen if Murray-Hamilton and Spinks heard of it.

For a moment Harry held his large round head on one side. Barbara intervened.

'Couldn't it be combined with a medical examination?' Sometimes Barbara, instead of saying the most peculiar thing, baffled one by saying the most sensible.

'Not in this set-up,' I said firmly.

Barbara gave Harry a glance, but I did not feel inclined to explain to her.

We had finished our dinner and Barbara said: 'Shall we have our coffee in the drawing-room?'

We went into the drawing-room. The house was Edwardian, massive and ugly, but spacious. Harry and Barbara had done it up very agreeably in the first post-war fashion, which was called 'contemporary'. This evening a fire was sparkling in the grate; lamps were glowing in the right places for comfort; and Barbara, wearing a black dress and a big topaz and diamond brooch which set off the colour of her eyes, looked unusually handsome. I said to her:

'That roast duck, Barbara, was simply –' and I made a gesture such as I thought I had seen Italians make in restaurants to indicate that food was delicious.

Barbara laughed. And then she blushed.

I drank my coffee thinking how pleasant life was.

In a desultory way we began to gossip. I scarcely noticed it when Harry first mentioned Sybil. He said he supposed she was coming up to London at Christmas, and I was feeling too relaxed to tell him he was a few days wrong. He was sitting fatly in an armchair whose legs splayed outwards. He was smiling.

'I suppose Robert asks you if you're going to marry her,' he said. I grinned.

Barbara leaned forward and said to him:

'Does Robert really ask that, do you think?'

'I was saying I *supposed* he did,' said Harry. 'After all, Joe's mother asks me every time I see her.' He glanced at me sideways to see how I took this gambit.

I took it with stupefaction: I knew that it would be unlike Harry not to go and see my mother whenever he went to his own home,

244

but that he was on these terms with her was something that I had not even considered.

Harry was quick to see the effect. He went on with a happy smile:

'Only last week she asked me if you were going to marry "your Sybil".'

This instantly conveyed verisimilitude. The prefix 'your' conveyed without a doubt that my mother had said it, since it evoked the particular tone – unintentional, I ought to say – with which my mother always seemed, to my sensitive ears, to refer to any of my young women.

'Did *she* think I would marry Sybil?' I inquired.

Harry shook his big, globe-shaped head. 'I think she's thought for some time now that you've missed the boat.'

'Missed the boat!'

Harry leaned his head against the back of his chair, and said nothing. Barbara said nothing: there was clearly no need for Barbara to say anything.

After a while, Harry said pensively:

'I like Sybil.' He paused. 'I never understand her.'

I said: 'Nor do I, for that matter. I don't really know her even after fifteen years.'

'And that,' said Barbara promptly, 'doesn't affect your relationship with her?'

You will recall my predicament as I saw it on that night of self-revelation in the bar at Euston. I said to Barbara:

'Not an atom!'

Barbara regarded me.

'There's a very definite split, there,' she said, 'between comprehension and function.'

'I see what you mean,' I said. Suddenly I was delighted, as a lewd transformation of her words occurred to me. 'You mean between knowing and doing.'

Barbara looked mystified. 'Perhaps,' she said firmly.

I turned to Harry. I could see that he was thinking about something else. He said:

'I suppose Robert has in mind whether you're thinking of marrying Sybil –'

I interrupted: 'I'm not thinking of marrying Sybil!'

' – because of his plans to marry Annette.'

'*Is* he going to marry Annette?' said I.

Harry looked at me triumphantly and sympathetically. He said, in a high sweet voice:

'Well, *isn't* he?'

I said nothing now. You see, when Harry told me Robert was going to leave the Civil Service, I was disturbed for the practical reasons that I have since explained. When he told me Robert was going to marry Annette, the disturbance was just as serious but much less worthy of a decent man. Robert and I were comrades in the unmarried state, and my first response to Harry's remark was to foresee another kind of desertion.

I picked up my coffee-cup and held it towards Barbara, asking if I could have some more coffee. And I looked at Harry, wondering if he knew exactly what sort of dismay his inquisitiveness caused me. He was a clever man, and I had a strong suspicion that he did know. By nature Harry was generous, kindly, devoted – a good man. Yet I could not help thinking that he was also a devil.

5

A Cocktail Party at Annette's

Annette was a sweet girl. Her father was a high civil servant, a very high civil servant indeed.

At that time, Annette was living in her father's flat. She had just come down from doing a D.Phil. in Oxford. Yes, she was quite young, about twenty-five, I suppose, against Robert's forty-four – he was five years older than me. She was young, pretty and clever. The reason I have said she was sweet was that, granted that there is a strain of the cruel, the uncharitable, and the ill-disposed in all of us, in Annette it was unusually weak. She was charitable, nicely balanced, quickly stirred to sympathy; in a word – sweet. Robert was very fond of her, and that did not surprise me.

Annette was living in her father's flat while she made up her mind what career to go in for. She was taking her time, partly because she was serious about it and partly because – here, alas, I display my own uncharitableness – in my opinion she had fallen in love with Robert. A feminist would say that a woman's falling in love ought not to make her less serious about choosing a career. I say that if it did not make Annette less serious, certainly it made her slower. Annette's choice seemed to me to show distinct signs of hanging fire that were not to be associated with intellectual or moral difficulties over deciding between becoming, say, an Oxford don or a Wapping schoolmistress. It did not worry me, of course. Nor did it appear to worry Annette: she seemed pretty happy.

Robert and I went to a cocktail party at Annette's. (It was called 'drinks at six-thirtyish' – the word 'cocktail' was going out.) Robert seemed pretty happy as well. He had been on another cultural expedition to the Zoo with Annette at the week-end. Though Annette's father retired to his house in Berkshire from Friday to Monday, Annette stayed in London, having the flat to herself.

Robert and I went straight to the party from the office. It was a wretched, sleeting night, and the flat was in an area just north of Hyde Park that was salubrious but inaccessible by bus.

'We'd better have a taxi,' I said. 'I'll pay half.'

'No. Why should you?' said Robert. I told you he was pretty happy.

Annette opened the door to us. Before she had come to live in the flat her father had had a servant, but Annette had insisted on dispensing with her.

'Hello, darling,' said Robert, and gave her a hug of noticeable warmth before taking off his overcoat.

Annette stood back – she was a short, sturdy girl – and looked up at him. Her eyes were shining with amusement and pleasure.

'You can't pretend he isn't spontaneous, in spite of all they say about him,' I said to her.

Annette shook her head. Her hair was straight and cut plainly in a bell-shaped bob: when she shook her head one expected to hear a sweet lucid peal. She took hold of Robert's hand for a moment.

'Come in,' she said.

I thought: 'Well, there you are . . .' and took off my overcoat.

We went into the living-room, which was L-shaped, the walls of the foot of the L being covered with books, and the walls of the stem, which included the windows and the fireplace, being panelled with a light-coloured wood. Annette's father was both a scholar and a traveller, and the objects of decoration in the room were chiefly small pieces of classical statuary. Between the windows there was a statue of a woman, headless and draped, which I should like to have owned.

The party was for Annette's friends, and though Robert and I were the only two civil servants there, also the only two novelists, we were not the only two men who were more than ten years older than Annette. A very satisfactory state of affairs, I thought:

248

the world was all the better a place for the existence of girls like Annette. There were, of course, some young women of Annette's age. I saw a girl I had met there before, a painter from behind the Fulham Road, and one of Annette's Oxford girl-friends who did philosophy too. Still better a place! I recognized some of the men – they were chiefly academic persons, philosophers, some sociologists, and a young scientist whom I had once interviewed for a job. I noted that Harry was not there, or, as I put it to myself, had for once not managed to get in.

Perhaps I ought to have explained before that there was a connexion between Harry and Annette. Harry had discovered that Annette's brother, who was a doctor, had been a house-surgeon at the hospital where Barbara had done her clinical training. Though Harry and Barbara now looked on him with the special contempt they reserved for anybody who had become a gynaecologist, this did not diminish Harry's use for the connexion or his satisfaction with having unearthed it. I may say that for Harry this passed as a strong connexion. When he saw that Annette was a figure in my life and Robert's, he would have found a connexion, even if it was that the housemaid Annette had dispensed with happened to be the illegitimate grandniece of the organist at the church where my father preached his first sermon.

Half an hour later, to make a change from talking to people, I went over to have another look at the statue that fascinated me. I put out my forefinger and drew it lightly, for the sensuous experience, down the folds in the drapery. Then I looked at my forefinger, the receptor of that experience. It was black with dust. There was a good thick layer of dust on the top of the table on which the statue was standing. There was also a pile of books, new books. I picked up the top one and opened it – a review slip fell out and floated down to the floor.

'Are you really going to read that?' It was Annette who spoke. She was standing beside me, laughing.

I retrieved the review slip and put the book back on the pile. It was a philosophical work.

'Is it any good?' I asked.

'I haven't read it yet. I'm going to review it.'

I looked at her with curiosity, as one does at any young person who is going to be entrusted with passing a professional opinion upon a matter of serious import. My interest switched from curiosity to approval. Annette was pretty and her complexion was beyond compare. She never wore any make-up, and there, in all its incomparableness, was her complexion exposed as it might be to one's forefinger. Fine, clear, high-coloured, and glossy with the sheen that comes from heartily washing it with soap. Her lips, without lipstick, were simply red. I did not know why Annette saw fit never to use make-up, but I never felt inclined to question the result. I brought my mind back to her books.

'Have they all seen,' I asked, referring to the authors, 'the great truth that metaphysics is bunk?'

This was my standard joke, for what it was worth, when I was talking to Annette. She belonged to an up-to-date school of philosophers whom I habitually referred to as the 'metaphysics-is-bunk' school, out of what Barbara would have called a distinctly ambivalent attitude. Though I felt that any school of philosophers ought to be treated with irreverence, I was far from sure that I did not think metaphysics was bunk myself.

I had never got over a crucial moment in my young manhood, when, hearing my father proclaim his favourite text, 'God is Love', for the I-don't-know-how-manyth time, I suddenly realized that it did not mean anything to me and I could not see what it could mean. This was a shock. 'God is Love' – I kept thinking and thinking about it, focusing on the word *is*, which now appeared so incredibly between the other two. The only circumstances, I kept thinking pig-headedly, in which God and Love can have *is* between them is not if God is a person and Love is what we all mean by love, but if God and Love are words, merely words.

I had never got over it. Some words were only words: my father's favourite text was a piece of literary algebra. Of course I had been subsequently shown the error of my thought, but it had permanently coloured my approach to metaphysics.

'We don't say metaphysics is bunk,' Annette said. She laughed as if she were amused by my joke, but did not hesitate to correct me just the same. 'We just think there aren't any platonic essences that many of the words we use in metaphysics would have to correspond to – if they were going to have the meaning we've chosen to give them.'

'H'm,' I said, not committing myself to agreeing with her – or understanding her, for that matter. Yet, you can see how, when I was talking to Annette, though I might have been shown the error of my thought I was not entirely convinced by the demonstration.

'Such words as Truth,' I said, doing my best to fall into the swing of things.

'Such words as Truth.' She shook her head, and her bell of hair swung to and fro.

At that, something made me think of my father's second favourite text: 'God is Truth.' Oh dear!

However, I have to say that it was a comfort of sorts to have a young woman like Annette, clever as paint and much admired in academic circles, to assure me that some of the words of which I had never been able to grasp the common use, such as my father's, could with advantage cease to be used in that way.

'Now, what are you two talking about?' Robert interrupted us.

'Scarcely anything,' I said. 'We've only just started.'

Annette looked up at Robert. I could have removed myself to the other end of the room without her noticing. Robert returned her look. I thought they must be intending to get married.

At that moment I noticed Annette's father in the doorway. He glanced round the room as if he were not certain whether to join the party. I heard Robert say:

'Darling, there's your father.'

'Oh yes,' said Annette.

One might have expected that Annette would hasten across to

her father and that Robert would remain with me. On the contrary, it was Robert who lost no time in going across to Annette's father. Annette stayed where she was.

'I hope somebody will give Daddy a drink,' she said.

I laughed at her idea of a hostess's functions. Annette was oddly shy about some things, and entertaining was one of them. She liked having parties and got as far as inviting the guests, but at that point she seemed to get paralysed. I did not understand why, though I felt it might be connected with shyness. And yet, was it? Was it really shyness that made her go without make-up and appear at this kind of party wearing a shapeless woolly jumper and skirt?

'Oughtn't you to go and give him one?' I asked.

'It's all right – Emma's giving him some sherry.' Emma was the painter from behind the Fulham Road. Her name was Margaret, but she was always called Emma. She was a big girl, wearing a sweater and trousers, these, paint-stained, being the current uniform of her set. There was a scruffy-looking man with her in an identical outfit. I had never seen them dressed, at any time of day, in anything different; and pointing to the two of them, I said to Annette:

'Do they take those things off to go to bed?' thinking they looked as if they slept in them.

'Emma doesn't go to bed with *him*,' said Annette. 'I mean, not now. Or at least only now and then.'

'Oh,' I said. 'Oh.'

It was only asking for difficulties, to try and explain now what I had originally wanted to know, so I paused, and then said:

'There seem to be some sociologists here.'

Annette said: 'I don't think I should really like to work with sociologists.' She explained thoughtfully: 'The trouble with all the social sciences is that their laws are reducible to laws of individual psychology. It means they lack the autonomy that the physical sciences have.'

'Oh,' I said. I had been trained in the physical sciences – in physics, to be precise. Her remark sounded favourable to me, so I said 'Oh' again, more enthusiastically.

I looked at her, and found that she was looking at me. Her eyes were a clear bright brown. Her cheeks were glowing.

'Annette,' I said, 'you're a sweet girl.'

She said shyly:

'I do want to marry Robert. Do you think there's any chance?'

6

The Recurring Situation

Did I think there was any chance of Robert marrying her – well might Annette ask! I told her, Yes, of course, but I did not see fit to prolong the conversation by discussing the length of the odds. As Robert had reached the age of forty-four without getting married, it was obvious that he was not the sort of man who takes to matrimony like a duck to water. And though he stood in no danger of being written-off, like me, he did lay himself open, clearly, to the charge of being reluctant. Poor old Robert.

In fact there was more to it than common reluctance, in Robert's case. We had discussed it a good many times. In the past he had fallen so deeply in love as to overcome common reluctance. But on each occasion the girl had been so odd, so eccentric, or even so crazy, that somehow the upshot, partly through her own actions and partly through a final move for self-preservation on Robert's part, had been no marriage.

Suspicious, that! you might say. Why did he not fall in love with someone who was sufficiently ordinary, sufficiently uncrazy – after all, there were lots of pretty girls who came into that category – to be marriageable? The only answer Robert seemed able to find was that they, the ordinary, uncrazy ones, did not seem to him so fascinating.

In the present situation, though, the fact seemed to me that Annette, while eccentric enough to be fascinating, was sufficiently uncrazy as not to be likely to hit him on the head with a bottle of whisky or take an overdose of aspirins – two of the deterrents to matrimony which had come his way in the past. There was definitely a chance for Annette, I thought.

It appeared, the following day, that Robert thought the same thing. He came into my office first thing in the morning, and sat on the corner of my desk.

'That was a very good party, last night,' he said.

I said it was.

He paused, and then said in a different tone:

'I don't know what to do. Ought I to marry Annette?'

I did not reply. Throughout our lives we had often asked each other's advice on matters of this kind. We had never taken it.

I was thinking what to say. We had never taken each other's advice in the exact form in which it was given: what we did was something tangential, something based on what the other advised, but modified by our own impulses, sensible or otherwise.

'She's a sweet girl,' I said.

Robert said: 'Of all the women I've known, she's easily the sweetest.'

'What's holding you back?'

He shrugged his shoulders and did not answer for a long time. I just waited. He said:

'It's hard to say. Some sort of instinct about the future. It's rather hard to place it exactly. Annette's easily the sweetest girl I've ever known, but that doesn't mean that in some ways she's not very' – he tried to find the right word – 'self-concerned. For instance, she attaches much more importance to some of the decisions, in particular the moral decisions, she makes than I ever should.'

'Isn't this part of the current fashion among philosophers?'

'If you mean is it something that has nothing to do with her natural inclinations, I think the answer is No. I think the fashion suits her rather well.'

I thought it over, and said:

'But isn't this all a bit theoretical? I don't see why it should cause any special practical difficulties.'

'Nor can I. And yet something tells me it will.'

'Then don't marry her!' I said, knowing this was the last thing he wanted me to say – his last sentence had ended in 'will'.

Robert laughed and stood up.

'Do you happen to have that file about revised salary scales?' he said in a completely different tone, lofty and rather official. 'It would be a bit of a help if you'd clear it pretty rapidly.'

I was delighted by the change. It was one of Robert's gifts to have at his finger-tips, so to speak, the capacity for chameleon-like transformation.

'Spinks is asking for it,' he went on. 'He seems to think you're holding it up.'

'I'm *not* holding it up!' I said. 'It only came in yesterday.'

Robert shrugged his shoulders and went out of the room.

'Really!' I shouted at the door as he pulled it to behind him.

I began my day's work by dealing immediately with the file about revised salary scales. And, in case you would like to know, I wished Spinks could get sacked.

During the next few days I did not see very much of Robert. It was on the following Sunday afternoon that he turned up unexpectedly at the club to which we both belonged. He knew that I was likely to be there, because on Sundays I usually spent the day at the club to save having to get my own meals at my flat. I lunched with about half a dozen members who enjoyed bachelordom in various degrees of confirmation ranging from that of elderly specimens of my own species to that of middle-aged married men whose wives had left them. Afterwards I took my manuscript to the library to work, and they mostly went into the reading-room to sleep.

At tea-time I had come down to a small central room that was the Piazza San Marco of the club, normally astir with gossipers having tea or drinks but today deserted. It would have been cosy had there not been so many doors always open for people to go through to other rooms. Lights were shining over pictures lent by members of the club, but the chandelier in the middle of the room had not been switched on. I was sitting beside the fire, munching a piece of anchovy toast and reading the novel reviews in the previous Friday's *Times Literary Supplement*. Someone came in and I looked up. It was Robert.

I exclaimed with surprise.

'I thought I'd find you here,' he said, sitting down at the other end of the sofa I was sitting on.

I held up *The Times Literary Supplement* and said:

'You'll observe that I'm keeping up with literature.'

Expecting that, as usual when he found himself having a casual meal with me, he would pick up a newspaper and read, I began, for once, to read myself. A servant brought in a tray with Robert's tea on it and put it on a small table in front of him. Robert poured a cup of tea and then said:

'I'd like you to put that down for a moment, if you will.'

He was looking both solemn and excited. He said:

'I came to see you because I wanted you to be the first person to know that Annette and I are going to get married. We decided last night.'

'That's excellent!' I cried, and shook him by the hand. 'I'm delighted. I hope you'll be as happy, as happy as anybody can be!'

I really was delighted. And I really did feel, suddenly, unutterably wretched. I was devoted to him, I had been whole-heartedly wretched on his behalf when he was having disastrous love affairs – in fact the occasions of the whisky bottle and the overdose of aspirins had been not funny but bitterly serious – but now, when he was going to be happy, I was not whole-heartedly delighted. Envy, the most unpleasing and the most common of emotions, suddenly caught me. In the midst of thinking how glad I was for him, I wished, yes, I wished it were *I* instead of him.

Robert was watching me. I remembered well his once having observed epigrammatically that it was easier to sympathize with one's friends in their defeats than in their victories.

'I thought you would,' I said, meaning 'would marry Annette'.

He laughed. His laughter sounded confident, relieved and faintly rueful. 'There's a difference between thinking one will and actually doing it.' His glance seemed to become more penetrating. 'As you'll discover for yourself.'

Of course he knew I must be wishing it were I. I said:

'Robert, do you think I *shall?*'

'Think you shall what?'

'Do it?'

He did not answer me immediately. Then he said: 'That depends on you. On what you make up your mind to.'

'Make up my mind to?' I said. 'Surely one doesn't make up one's mind to something, just like that . . . It's got to arise from one's nature . . .'

An elderly member with a stick made his way slowly through the room, greeting us as he passed. We smiled at him – in the ordinary way we should have encouraged the poor old man to stop – and then we waited for him to go.

As soon as he was through one of the far doorways, I said to Robert:

'One's behaviour falls into a pattern that arises from one's nature. The reason the pattern gets fixed is because one's nature is pretty fixed, though we don't like to think it is.'

I was referring to a theory Robert and I had of human behaviour, which depended on what we called the Recurring Situation. It was particularly easy to identify in people's sexual lives. Time after time we had seen our friends, not to mention ourselves, embark on a sexual gambit which might superficially look as if it were something new, but which, as time went on, led to a familiar situation – if it were not leading to it in the natural course of events, the instigator of it seemed to force it, himself, into the familiar shape. We got the impression that for many men there was a characteristic situation to which, from whatever point they started, they always tended.

Sitting beside the fire in the club that Sunday afternoon, Robert and I did not discuss all this because we had discussed it at length many a time before. We had accepted our own behaviour as examples of our theory. Certainly Robert had arrived often enough at the situation of being deeply in love with a woman who was – it seemed to him – just that bit too crazy for him to risk marrying her.

In my own case, the recurring situation was twofold: I always found myself either wanting to marry someone who would not marry me or not wanting to marry someone who would. There was no future in my recurring situation, either way.

'I'm not sure it's so completely fixed,' said Robert.

'What?'

'Either the pattern or one's nature. One can be too rigid about these things.'

'Indeed!' I said, rather as if I were in favour of rigidity.

'Yes,' said Robert.

He suddenly gave me a quick, odd glance that made me pull up. I stared at him and then tried to laugh.

'You're not trying to take my recurring situation away from me, are you?' I said.

Robert shrugged his shoulders.

When I was first describing my predicament, I observed how many of us, poor fish that we are, are rather attached to our predicaments, are even a bit proud of them. We also, I might have added, tend to find them something stable in our lives. Take them away – even, as it might appear, for our own good – and we are left faced with . . . we know not what. It is the same with the recurring pattern. We want to get out of it, and yet also we want to stay in it. I do not pretend to be able to explain my own ambivalence – nor the ambivalence of most of the human race, for that matter. Double, double, we are all double . . .

'I have always granted,' said Robert, 'that there is a recurring pattern. But there are times when it's possible to break out of it.'

Even if his reply might be going to take the ground from under my feet, I said:

'How?'

'By an act of will.'

An act of *will*! 'Like all the best revolutionary concepts, so simple, so obvious . . .'

I did not say anything. I knew it was true. An act of will could get me out of my recurring pattern. I felt as if the ground really had been taken from under my feet. And yet at the same moment I was feeling something opposite. It was a thrill of – what? I had not the slightest doubt what it was a thrill of. It was of hope.

Part Two

I

Christmas Eve in the Civil Service

The first and only occasion Spinks set foot in my office – you can imagine I never went out of my way to invite him across just for the sake of his *beaux yeux* – was on the afternoon when we shut down that year for Christmas. Every Christmas Eve Murray-Hamilton and Spinks did the rounds of their own people and then of ours on a visit of goodwill. The members of staff most affected by the prospect of the visit were the messengers, though I could never see why, since the only duty that fell upon their cadre was that two of them should hold the lift doors open while Murray-Hamilton and Spinks got out. But affected they were: their bush telegraph, which in the summer circulated up-to-the-minute Test Match scores, hummed all afternoon with the current movements, from room to room, of the touring party.

It was unusual for Spinks to deliver the goodwill message to me in my own office. At this stage of the Christmas Eve's proceedings, Robert and I were usually at the tea-party which our own people held in the room where most of them worked. This room was referred to by Robert and me as the big room, and by some of its racier inhabitants, I gleaned from passing the time of day with them in the lavatory, as the snake-pit. The room and what went on in it interested me, but my communication with its inhabitants was supposed to be on paper, or if it was a personal matter, through our Senior Executive Officer, who was their boss. At this rate, had it not been for the lavatory, which was small and overcrowded, I should never have identified some of our clerks, let alone – for hygiene is a great leveller – have picked up some of their racier observations.

Perhaps in fairness to the Service, I ought to interpolate that

Spinks's minion responsible for 'accommodation' was shocked when I made him note how small, overcrowded, and dirty our lavatory was, shocked that Robert and I had to use the same one as our clerks.

Anyway, there was the snake-pit having a party and Robert and I sitting in our own offices not invited. And this year it was not a tea-party, far from it. The inhabitants had collected money for drink, and by keeping the collection to themselves had set up a neat basis for excluding outsiders. And why was it, I speculated, as I listened to the sounds of entertainment echo down the corridor, that the inhabitants of the snake-pit wanted to exclude outsiders? There were two possible explanations. The first was that they thought Robert and I were stinkers. The second – this was more than an explanation: it was fact – was that our Senior Executive Officer had got at loggerheads with them.

The chief messenger put his head round the door, which I had left open.

'Mr Murray-Hamilton and Mr Spinks have got separated, sir. Over in Registry. That'll be, Mr Spinks is coming on first. And then Mr Murray-Hamilton sort of after him.'

Thinking of the lift doors, I said: 'Twice as much work for you.'

A burst of riotous noise came from down the corridor. He wagged his head towards it.

'If Mr Murray-Hamilton and Mr Spinks don't get here before long, they'll be dancing down there.'

'Dancing? Will they really?' I said. I was very fond of dancing. Also of drink, too.

'Ar,' he said. Having been leaning a little forward, he now shifted his weight comfortably over his heels. Then he said:

'Have you seen the decorations this year, sir?'

'Yes. I glanced in.'

'Not so good as last year's,' he said.

'Not so necessary,' said I, thinking of last year's tea-party and this year's saturnalia.

'Ar.'

Our conversation went on for a few minutes in this vein, coun-
terpointed by sounds from down the corridor. When he had said
they would be dancing in the big room, he had meant it metaphorically, but in point of fact somebody had brought a portable
gramophone. We heard music.

'Shall I leave the door open, sir?' he said, when he thought it
was time to go back and take his place in the bush telegraph.

'Do. I should like to hear the music.'

I wondered if they really would dance, and what sort of dancing
it would be. When I have referred to saturnalia in the big room, I
may have given the wrong impression about its inhabitants. Every
year, after the Senior Executive Officer had brought in to Robert
their annual reports, Robert said without fail to me in an awed tone:

'You'd be surprised how old some of them are.'

I was not in the least surprised, since the S.E.O. reminded me
of it every time I found something to complain about in the work
of the office. We had what I agreed was a higher proportion than
might be expected of clerks who were past retiring age. In fact I
sometimes thought there was evidence for what the S.E.O. was
always suggesting, that Spinks's side of the organization used our
side as a dumping ground for crocks and misfits in general. We
had our share of them: a walk through the big room confirmed
that. Had we more than our share?

'It's one of the results of full employment, Froggatt,' I said.
(That was the S.E.O.'s name.)

His expression combined deference with disbelief. He argued
that Spinks's side of the organization were dumping crocks and
misfits on us so as to use our resulting inefficiency as a reason for
taking us over themselves – the argument had its points, of course.

So the saturnalia that was going on in the big room, under the
shade of brightly coloured paper chains, tinsel balls, and squares
of cardboard (inscribed with peculiar mottoes) that floated in the
air like mobiles, was not an affair of nymphs and satyrs – not unless
you are prepared to face the fact that some of us stay nymphs and
satyrs till we have one foot in the grave.

'I'd like to get you,' sounded the music,
'On a slow boat to China . . .'

'It would have to be damned slow for some of you,' I thought, having in mind not the aged ones, who were rather nippy, but some of the forty-year-old clock-watchers, who were more bone idle than I could have imagined. Slow! If they had not had all the office-hours in which to do their football pools they would never have got them in in time.

I looked at my watch. Half past five. The sooner Spinks and Murray-Hamilton came in with their Christmas handshake the sooner I could go home. There was no more work to be done – or anything else, for that matter. I wondered whether to go into Robert's room, but thought I had better not as he was doing some rewriting of his next novel. I might have gone into the small room where our P.A. and one or two of her colleagues worked, but I thought they would be busy clearing up the remains of the Christmas tea-party they had loyally given for Robert and me and Froggatt and the H.E.O.s, in default of our being invited to the saturnalia. I had my own next novel to work on, but somehow I was never able to get going in the office, being inhibited either by files coming in or the likelihood of files coming in – remember that unlike Robert, who was part-time, I was full-time.

The chief messenger's head came round the door-cheek.

'Mr Spinks has just left the other side, sir. They say he's got Mr Jacques with him.'

I cannot say the news affected my spirits one way or the other. At that particular moment it did not occur to me that the visit could either have any effect or lead to any action. I did not object to the addition of Jacques, for I liked him. He was the minion I referred to a moment ago as responsible to Spinks for 'accommodation'. It seemed to me that, as a civil servant, his talent for execution was well eclipsed by his talent for sycophancy. He was a tall stringy man with large eyes and a pleasant voice; and like all successful sycophants, he was born with a genuine desire to please:

if I had to choose between that and a genuine desire to kick people in the teeth, I'd choose that. Also I judged that while Jacques sucked up to Spinks with natural abandon, he did not in the least care for him as a man.

'Thank you,' I said to the chief messenger. 'Perhaps you might shut the door now. You know . . . it will give them something to open.'

'Ar,' he said with a non-comprehending grin. I regretted the door's being shut, because from down the corridor came the sound of the gramophone playing, amid delighted shrieks:

'A-hunting we will go! . . .'

'What *can* they be doing to that?' I said to him.

He shook his head. 'I don't know, sir.' He was not interested, other than in the sounds as a manifestation, I thought, of the difference between how the upper and the lower orders behaved.

I was left alone, quiet, in my rather large room. I had switched on only half the lights, so as to enhance the dirtiness of the walls which must once have been painted by the Ministry of Works in a shade known to them, I believed, as primrose. My picture on the far wall was crooked, which puzzled me, since the office-cleaners never touched it. Below it the tablecloth formed a long rectangle of dead navy-blue – it was a piece of felt that had been used during the war for black-out curtains: Robert had got rid of his, leaving his table-top bare, but I kept mine as a souvenir.

I sat swinging around in my chair, waiting for the visit.

Spinks and Jacques came in. They looked hearty and bright, and had clearly been fortified on their way at somebody else's party. They brought in a distinctly Christmassy air, and suddenly we all shook hands in one of those waves of *bonhomie* that sometimes sweep unpredictably through a group of men who hate each other's guts.

'I didn't expect to find you in here,' said Spinks, glancing round my office.

'We had a small sedate tea-party on our own,' I said, and explained

267

that we had not been invited to the non-tea-party down the corridor.

I do not intend to describe Spinks, certainly not in any way which
might lead anyone in the Civil Service to think this is supposed to
be him. I will content myself with saying that he did not look the
detestable man he was. Had you met him you might have presumed
he was a man whose wife and children were probably fond of him:
they were. It would have been a shock to hear that he was the most
detested man in our part of the world: he was.

'This is your office?' he said.

As he was also one of the cleverest men in our part of the world,
I thought he must either be drunk or so little interested that he did
not care what he was saying. He did not look in the least drunk.
Jacques, I was happy to see, did look drunk – he rocked slightly
and said:

'It's dark in here.' He caught my eye. 'We must do something
about it.' His glance moved critically round the walls. 'A coat of
paint . . .'

I knew that he would not get them a coat of paint, but I thought
it was amiable of him to have said it. You see why I liked him.
Spinks was looking at my bookshelf.

'Are these your books?'

'Yes.' They were a very odd collection of throw-outs from my
flat, ranging from a second copy of *The Tale of Genji* to a first copy
of *The Admiralty Handbook of Wireless Telegraphy*.

At this it appeared that the Christmas visit was over. Spinks and
Jacques smiled at each other and then at me. Then we all shook
hands again and said, 'Well, a happy Christmas,' and they went
out of the room. It seemed, as an incident, harmless enough, in
fact positively innocuous. I hung about until they had gone, and
then went and did a similar round of our own people while I waited
for Murray-Hamilton. And that was that.

But was it that? One day in the week after we came back after
Christmas, Robert and I were strolling along to our tea-shop for
lunch, when Robert said:

'By the way, you'd better get one of those trays for your desk, to keep papers in.'

Let me explain. The Civil Service provided a long compartmented tray for the top of one's desk, the compartments usually being labelled In and Out. (The current joke among bosses was to propose four compartments labelled In, Out, Pending, and Too Difficult.) On the grounds that our P.A. always brought in my work in the morning, always took it out when I had done it, and hung on to anything that was pending till the morning when she could bring it in ready for me to do, I had got rid of the tray. A dust-collector, I thought it.

'What on earth for?' I said.

'I know you do a lot of work, but it makes it look as if you don't.' He was not looking at me.

'To whom does it make it look as if I don't?' I asked. For once I thought Robert could put up with having his evasiveness on this kind of topic punctured.

'Just tell me *whom!*' I said.

Robert put his head down. After a pause he said in a muffled, distant voice:

'As it were Spinks.'

I was too enraged to speak. I have to admit that my immediate cause of rage was not so much Spinks's being beastly as his being beastly on Christmas Eve. On Christmas Eve! The fact that Christmas had little significance, either religious or sentimental for me, affected me not at all.

When we got back to the office after lunch I told our P.A. to get me a dust-collector for my desk and then I spent a few minutes considering Spinks.

It seemed to me that the first fact to take into consideration was that Spinks was going to find it hard to get a lot further in the Civil Service than his present mid-grade of Assistant Secretary. Somehow, somewhere among his seniors, a decision had been come to that he was not going to be one of the successes.

This may seem odd. It seemed odd to me. Yet often I felt that the final verdict on a man's career had been pretty well settled, whether

269

he knew it or not, by the time he was forty. A spell in the Cabinet Office, a spell in the Treasury, and the word must have gone round the reaches above him: 'He'll go a lot further,' or 'He won't.' In a way it was not difficult to explain. Firstly, with the Administrative Class being very small compared with the Service as a whole, the number of bosses was small enough for them all to know each other well, and so for the judgement to get around easily. Secondly, the bosses (*a*) were clever men, and (*b*) took to this kind of assessing and judging with enthusiasm. There was nothing to show that they made many mistakes either. Mind you, they were not without the power to help their own prophecies along: the man who was tipped for success got the more exciting jobs, while the man who was tipped for failure was headed towards some backwater of the Service.

If Spinks had not been so beastly to me, I should have been sorry for him. It seemed to me that he must have been tipped for unsuccess and was perceptive enough to have seen it – remember that in this particular sphere, men's perceptions have a notable record of letting them down: it is very hard indeed to perceive that you are tipped for unsuccess.

And what about me? By not becoming a permanent civil servant I had not entered the competition. I wanted to stay where I was, working with Robert, till the day of liberation through the art of letters. I was not to be tipped for going further or for not. As I sat at my desk considering Spinks, I perceived that the two alternatives for which I could be tipped were for being allowed to stay where I was or for being pushed out altogether.

I felt rage again. I recalled Robert's being sniped at about me. Granted that I was by nature MISC/INEL, what, I wanted to know, did I *do* that was wrong? After all, it seemed to me, I was paid my salary for choosing and looking after scientists; not for what I was.

Obviously one of the things I did that was wrong was not having a tray on my desk.

I ask you . . . !

2

Falling in Love

Though Barbara had laid it down as axiomatic that I would not, or could not, get married, she and Harry introduced me from time to time to fresh girls. I was never sure what, if one of them caught my attention, I was supposed to do – I sometimes knew what I wanted to do, but that, of course, was a different matter. I usually met fresh girls when she and Harry gave a party.

Harry and Barbara gave excellent parties. Their drawing-room was big enough to dance in; there was plenty of drink; and the guests covered a wide and entertaining range of society. Their 'party of the year' was on New Year's Eve, when they invited, so they said, everyone they knew, irrespective of social status. Certainly the range in social status of the people who turned up was wide enough to make this explanation seem plausible. There were people from the M.R.C. of rank both some distance above and well below Harry's; there were distinguished doctors and probationer nurses, professors and laboratory assistants; and a smattering of people connected with the arts – a painter or two, two or three writers, and some journalists. Also there was a collection of persons whose profession was not clearly defined, to say the least of it. I used to look forward to New Year's Eve at Harry's.

I had not told Harry and Barbara about my new source of hope. The concept of changing one's fate by an act of will – especially when it referred to my fate not to get married being changed by an act of my will, such as it was – was not likely to impress Barbara. I was not certain how much it impressed me. I felt cautious about it. I contemplated my will, such as it was.

Before I went to the party I had been seeing off Sybil at Euston.

As well as coming to London, for a few days before Christmas, she had managed to fit in a few days after. Barbara had asked me if I would like to bring her to the party.

'She's planned to go home,' I said, hoping to dismiss the idea.

'Surely some plans are made to be broken?' said Barbara.

'They form a small category, compared with that of plans that are meant to be kept.'

Barbara gave me a sidelong penetrating look. 'Very well, then,' she said. 'Come alone!'

As that was what I had always intended to do, I felt I might now relax to the extent of assuming a mournful expression.

'Always alone . . .' I murmured, as if I were speaking to myself and not to her.

And yet, when I sat in the bar at Euston after Sybil had gone, I felt genuinely mournful. The recurring pattern had just recurred.

'A Guinness, please,' I said.

If I stopped the pattern, in its most immediate sense, recurring, I was not going to see Sybil again. Sybil sitting in buses trying to distinguish male passers-by from female; Sybil standing at bus-stops clutching her beaver-lamb coat round her; Sybil lying quietly on her back reciting soliloquies, long soliloquies, from the plays of Shakespeare . . . all over, all gone.

I have to say here and now that it never for one moment occurred to me that, if I did get married, it need not necessarily be all over, all gone. To men who did not take getting married seriously, to men who could get married at the drop of a hat, it might have, it would have, appeared differently. Not so to me. I took getting married very seriously indeed. Few men could have taken it more seriously than I intended to take it.

'And a ham sandwich,' I said, thinking that if I were going to drink a lot at the party it would be well to have food inside me at the start.

'The recurring pattern . . .' I said to myself, lifting the glass of Guinness to my mouth. '*Can* I break it?'

By the time the waitress brought me the ham sandwich I was

shaking my head even more mournfully. I was back again at the contemplation of my will. It's going to take a long time, I was thinking. A long, long time. There was not a soul, probably not even Robert, who believed I could do it. I ate the sandwich.

All the same, however long it was going to take me to break the recurring pattern, I decided to go home before the party and spruce myself up. There was no need to let everybody know that life had got me down. I put on my newest suit, and a bow tie to indicate that I was more of an artist than a civil servant. Then I walked briskly, if not hopefully, from the block of flats where I lived to Harry's Edwardian mansion.

It was a warm and drizzly New Year's Eve that year, and every so often the overhanging ornamental trees in people's front gardens let fall large drops of accumulated rainwater, plop among the specks of drizzle, on my head. Lights were shining from almost every window of Harry's house, and as I walked up the drive I could hear the sound of dance-music. There was a clutter of cars in the roadway and drive, and I noticed some bicycles propped against the large cast-iron dog, a greyhound I think it was, which stood heraldically beside the front door.

The eldest of Harry's children, a boy of nine looking extraordinarily pleased with himself at being allowed up so late, took my coat from me and pointed out to me where his mother was. Already cheered up by the party atmosphere, I kissed Barbara.

'You look very nice,' I said. She had altered the way in which her hair was done. Instead of being severely swept up at the sides it hung softly and loosely over her ears. Her skin glowed with high colour, and the confidence in her clear hazel eyes was masked by excitement. Active, strong-minded, and knowing, Barbara nevertheless had a girlish love of giving parties.

'You do look nice,' I said. Then I felt the rush of air that preceded Harry's whirling up to join us.

'Come along inside!' he said in a high hallooing voice, while mopping his forehead with a handkerchief. 'We've got some pretty girls for you.'

It crossed my mind that, faithful and respectable husband though Harry might be, the pretty girls were perhaps not invited for the delectation of only his guests.

'We want you to dance,' said Barbara. 'We've collected a lot more records for tonight, jivey ones.'

'Why, how did you know? Jive is my second favourite activity.' I thought it was a very old quip.

Barbara gave me a satisfied look. 'I see the connexion!' she said.

I went first of all to the room where they had rigged up a small bar and helped myself to a drink. The room was crowded. Standing just inside the door, where I had missed him when I came in, was Robert, talking to a man who I saw was Harry's M.R.C. boss. I caught Robert's eye and waved to him. Then, having emptied my glass, I had it filled up again and pushed my way through the drinkers to the drawing-room.

Barbara's description of the records was apt enough. As I reached the door I heard a stirring performance of the 'Chicken Reel' coming out of the radiogram. I supposed that although the record happened to have been made a long time ago, it was Barbara's interest in the 'contemporary' that had led her to get it for a party like this. True, in one corner of the room a couple of young men with their hair done in cow-licks – I took them to be lab-assistants – were jiving with their girls: but the rest of the floor was occupied by persons of higher social status indomitably doing the dance they did on all occasions, a sort of walk.

I put down my glass on the nearest ledge and looked round for a partner. Somebody had got to show the flag for persons of higher social status. There was a girl standing quite close to me, watching the dancers while a heavy-jowled man beside her appeared to be advancing the fact that he did not dance as a reason for surreptitiously groping round her waist. I did not blame him. She was dark-haired and comely. Nor did I see why I should not stop him instantly.

'Why don't you dance?' I said to her.

She gave me a surprised half-glance and then laughed.

'Why not?' she said. With a twist she was out of his reach and lifting her hand for me to take hold of. 'I've been wanting to . . .'

She had a pale complexion and she was dressed in a rosy, coral colour. I wondered, somewhat late in the day, if she could dance.

'Let's go over there,' I said, and led her over to where we could congregate with the lab-assistants and their partners.

It was all right – she could dance. A bit too quick on the lead, I thought, but that did not matter: it showed she was anxious to please. I was not looking at her most of the time we danced, because I had been given to understand that in this sort of dance one was supposed to appear abstracted and independent, if not actually schizophrenic. Of course I did glance at her now and then. I was puzzled: she seemed easy-going and relaxed, and yet she was too quick on the lead. How could that be?

The record ended. Before anyone else could forestall him, one of the lab-assistants, both knowing and determined, turned the record over. On the other side was the 'Dark-town Strutters' Ball'.

'Wonderful!' I said to my partner. 'Now we'll really get hep!'

And we did. Her glowing dress spun out this way and that; her short dark hair flopped over her forehead.

'Now!' I cried, flicking her right hand downward behind her waist and catching it on the other side – giving it a spiral tug upwards could send her spinning twice without having to be let go. It *would* have sent her spinning twice without having to be let go, had she not suddenly staggered.

'Oh!' she cried.

She was nearly on the floor before I managed to grasp her. I lifted her. As her head came slowly upwards we looked each other in the face, close to, for the first time. I saw grey eyes, brilliantly sparkling, looking into mine, long red lips twitching up at the corners in chagrined laughter –

I could go on with the description, but I cannot wait to come to the point. We were looking each other in the face, close to, for the first time. I thought:

This one's the right one for me.

Those were the words. I am sorry, but I just did not think

anything else. I can see it was a moment that ought to have brought out the highest poetry in me. Grey eyes sparkling, a beautiful mouth, loose dark hair over her forehead, her body panting against mine as I hauled her up from having let her drop on the floor. Oh! the poetry that ought to have surged through me. What did surge through me?

This one's the right one for me.

Oh! the echoes, if it comes to that, of chapel jokes in my youth about 'waiting for Miss Right to come along'.

The girl said: 'I think one of my heels must have come loose.'

'Oh,' said I.

Was it love at first sight? Certainly it was at first sight. But love? Love, love, love . . . Did I hear nightingales singing, waves crashing, bells tinkling, winds blowing? . . . I cannot say that I did. I just heard one of the flattest sets of words I had ever come across, at regular intervals.

This one's the right one for me.

Her glance went swiftly round the room, and then came back to me. She did not say anything. Laughing made two lines, like brackets round her mouth, flash into existence and out again. The flat set of words might have been signalled to and fro between us – was she thinking I was the right one for her?

'I don't know your name,' I said.

'It's Elspeth.'

I said: 'Mine's Joe.'

To my surprise, she blushed. I said:

'We ought to get somebody to introduce us to each other.' I straightened my tie. 'I'm all for the proprieties.'

'I'm sure we can get somebody to introduce us,' she said. 'If you like.'

We were standing at the edge of the dance-floor, and just then the 'Dark-town Strutters' Ball' stopped. A whirling gust of air caught us.

'What are you two doing?' We turned to find Harry's inquisitive eyes moving shrewdly from one of us to the other.

I said we were looking for somebody to introduce us. A look of great cunning came over Harry's face.

'I'll introduce you,' he said.

I thought: He's guessed! Harry's curiosity was insatiable, but that was not to say it was always wildly off the truth.

'Are you,' I said to Elspeth while we were being introduced, 'by any chance Scottish?'

'No. I'm English.'

Harry was not in the least affected by this attempt at diversion. 'I think you two ought to come and tell Barbara you've met.' He said to me: 'Elspeth is one of Barbara's friends.'

I looked momentarily at Elspeth with fresh eyes. She seemed unconcerned by the revelation. Perhaps, I thought, it might be all right – I did not know what had made me think I might be in for some opposition from Barbara.

I said: 'Didn't Barbara mean us to meet?'

Harry burst into laughter. 'Of course. That's what we invited her for.'

Elspeth turned on him. 'Really!' She was blushing again.

I said to her: 'Don't worry!'

She said to me: 'I'm not, really.'

Harry led us through the doorway into the hall. There we came straight upon Barbara and her mother, who must have been keeping an eye on the dancing.

'What happened?' Barbara asked Elspeth.

'We saw you enjoying yourself,' her mother said to me.

Barbara's mother looked like Barbara, only, like many mothers in comparison with their daughters, more so. Her jaw was longer and squarer than Barbara's, her complexion so much higher in colour that it looked permanently weather-beaten. The look of confidence in her eyes was opaque. Battle-axe, I thought. She said:

'It's the first time I've seen that kind of dancing.'

Her smile told me instantly that she had viewed my performance not as showing the flag for persons of a higher social status but as abandoning it to join persons of a lower social status. How could I make her see the truth? At that moment I caught sight of myself in a big looking-glass on the wall behind her – a smart chap, in a bow tie, grinning. How indeed?

Barbara said to me: 'We're going up to my room to see if we can find a pair of my shoes that will fit Elspeth.'

I said: 'But aren't all your shoes the same size?' I had forgotten that in the romantic hope of making their feet look smaller or smarter or both, women buy shoes of all shapes and sizes.

Elspeth and Barbara exchanged feminine smiles instead of replying to me.

Anyway, I thought, watching Elspeth go up, she would have to come down. I could afford to wait. The fact of which I was convinced was not one that could alter with time.

For want of something to do, I turned to Harry and inquired who the man over there with the heavy jowls was.

'That's Barbara's *bookmaker*,' he said triumphantly, and went away.

The man was now standing next to a fair-haired girl, leaning over her shoulder and quietly putting his hand on her waist. His jowls looked heavier than ever.

I was going to point him out to Barbara's mother, but found that she had gone. I saw Robert coming out of the room where the bar was: with him still was Harry's boss. He called to me.

'Joe, will you come over here?'

Harry's boss and I shook hands. I reminded myself of the rule Robert had formulated for me to obey when I met bosses.

'We've been having an interesting discussion,' Harry's boss said. He was about my height, a tough, muscular little man with a leathery, grey face and a croaking voice: he used to make Robert and me think of a shark. We liked him. In the strictest privacy we used to call him The Shark.

I nodded my head. Robert's rule was for my self-preservation.

'Very interesting indeed,' said Robert.

I nodded my head the other way. The rule was, of course, to try not to say *anything*.

Robert began to say: 'It was about –'

'I was telling Robert,' said Harry's boss, not being the man to let anyone else speak for him, 'that you chaps are more fortunate than we are in getting supplies of people to do research.' He stared at me, showing his teeth slightly – just like a shark.

I tried wagging my head this time.

Harry's boss gave Robert a glance, as much as to say, 'Is your friend dumb?' and continued, undismayed by my handicap, with his exposition.

'You'll hear it said that our present budget is too small, that the country ought to be spending more than three and a half millions on medical research. So it ought. But if we had more money we should scarcely know what to do with it. We've got plenty of problems we should like investigated, but chaps of the right quality to investigate them don't exist.' He aimed a question mid-way between me and Robert. 'How would you cope with that one? I should like to hear what you'd say.'

I said nothing. I thought Robert must be pleased with me.

Robert began: 'Lunn and I took steps some years ago to ensure that bigger supplies of research people were *made*.'

Lunn and I! He really was pleased with me. He really must think I was increasing my reputation with The Shark.

I was so encouraged that from then on I never looked back. Until Harry's boss shook hands again – 'That was a very interesting discussion!' – I did not utter. As we separated Robert gave me a frankly congratulatory look.

Within five seconds of our actually having separated, Harry was at my elbow. A honeyed voice said close to my ear:

'The Shark's in good form, tonight, isn't he?'

I caught a bright sideways glance coming past Harry's snub nose and said nothing.

'You know he's going to put in for another half million on our budget?'

I could not help it – I burst into laughter.

Harry looked hurt. For a moment instead of whirling he seemed to be quite stationary. Then he picked up.

'I must go and find Barbara's mother,' he said busily.

I stayed where I was. In a little while I saw Elspeth looking in the crowd for me. I called to her. When she joined me I said: 'Let's go and have a drink!'

'I think I've had enough already.'

'Let's dance, then! Will you be all right?'

'If we don't do anything too sudden.'

'Nothing easier.'

I took her on to the dance-floor. The lab-assistant had been deposed from his charge of the gramophone, and low soothing music was coming from it now. A voice crooned.

You are
The breathless hush of springtime . . .

'Suits me,' I murmured.

Elspeth did not hear.

We did a gentle circuit of the room, quarter turns all the way. 'Did you know that man was Barbara's bookmaker?' I said.

'No. I'd only just met him. Thank you for rescuing me.'

I had rescued her. I brushed my cheek against her hair.

'What a romantic beginning!' I murmured, this time loudly enough for her to hear.

As I went on brushing my cheek against her hair, I was unable to see her expression. You cannot have everything.

You are the angel-glow, crooned the voice, taking a more improbable flight,

That lights a star . . .

This one, I thought, is the one for me. Just that. Why try to think about anything else?

I had never felt like this in my life before. I had fallen in love before; I had fallen, I have to admit, into bed; I had fallen into ecstasy; and, my goodness, I had fallen into error. But I saw all of these things now as things else. In the conviction that this one was the right one for me, I had the feeling, quite new, that I had this time cut all the cackle and come straight to one single, stark, wonderful hoss. It was a traumatic experience, traumatically satis-

fying. I could have gone on doing the quarter turns all night.
Elspeth said:

'You don't really have to be quite so un-sudden as this . . .'

I dutifully swung into a running turn, which ran us backwards
into another couple.

And now that moment divine, crooned the voice, brought to the
foreseeable misfortune contingent upon apostrophizing one's love
with an inventory, namely having to wind it up,

When all of the things you are
Are mine.

The orchestra went on playing the song over again without the
voice, and we sank back into the quarter turns.

'Isn't this nice?' I said.

Elspeth nodded her head so far as that was possible, seeing that
we were cheek to cheek.

'We must meet again.' It hardly seemed necessary to say that.

She nodded her head again, and that was enough for the time
being. We must meet again, again and again.

Soon after this it was midnight, and everyone crowded into the
room and we all joined hands for Auld Lang Syne. Then Barbara
announced that there was food ready in the kitchen, whereupon
everyone crowded out again at twice the speed. I lost touch with
Elspeth, and expected to find her in the kitchen. When I got there
I saw her trapped on the other side of the room with Harry and
Barbara's mother.

Suddenly, quite close to me, I saw Annette.

'Has Robert left you on your own?' I said.

Her eyes were bright, and when she shook her head the bell of
hair swung to and fro. She had discarded her shapeless jumper and
skirt in favour of a party dress that reminded me of what the girls
of fifteen used to wear at our school dances: it was of a shade that
used to be called apricot. She was wearing no make-up. She looked
charming.

'Who was the girl you were dancing with?' she asked.

'Did I make such an exhibition of myself as that?'

'One always notices anyone who falls down,' said Annette.

I burst into laughter, and Annette looked pleased.

'She's called Elspeth,' I said. 'Why do you want to know?'

'I liked her. I should like to know her.'

I could not resist the indiscretion of saying: 'I hope you'll have plenty of opportunity.'

Annette said: 'Are you going to marry her?'

Her tone was simple, sweet, unoffending. I was taken aback.

'Good God! I don't know . . . I've only just met her. Give me a chance.'

'But, surely that's just what you've had. A chance, I mean.'

I hastily crammed a sausage roll into my mouth.

Annette said: 'I should like you to dance with me before you go. You look as if you know what you're doing. I don't.'

'You could have a few lessons,' I said sharply. I had great faith in lessons.

Annette shook her head and looked away. 'I suppose I'm self-conscious,' she said. I cannot say that she looked specially troubled by the thought.

'Anyway,' she said, 'Robert doesn't dance very much.'

'No.' I was glancing through the crowd to see if there was any sign of Elspeth getting free. And I was distracted by the word 'marry' having been introduced into my thoughts.

Suddenly it occurred to me that Annette appeared to think that I really could get married.

'Yes, let's dance!' I said enthusiastically. 'I'll teach you.'

I danced with Annette. There was now no sign of Elspeth. Perhaps she had gone home. Perhaps she felt a little shaken after all. Perhaps somebody had offered her a lift in a car. After I had handed Annette over to Robert, I made a last tour of the house without finding Elspeth. I decided it was time I went home.

As I said goodnight to Harry, I asked:

'What's happened to Elspeth?'

Harry gave me a quick look. 'I thought she was waiting for *you* to take her home.'

I was on no account going to accept that remark for the start of a conversation with Harry. 'I expect she's already gone,' I said, with such decisiveness that it carried me over the threshold and out into the garden before Harry could try another tack.

The drizzle had stopped, but the bare branches of prunus and lilac still dropped their large drops of water on my head in the darkness. I looked forward to my walk home. I was of the opinion that, unlike most of the guests I had left behind at the party, I was sober.

I thought about Elspeth. I was not dismayed by not having seen her again. I could well do without seeing her again that night, I thought. My conviction that she was the girl for me, the one exactly right for me, was quite enough for me to cope with. For the time being I wanted no more. I walked back up Putney Hill just thinking about it.

3

A Table at the Carlos

I let a couple of months go by before I got in touch with Elspeth.
What was I waiting for? you may wonder. I will tell you. I was
waiting till Sybil's next trip to London was over.

In the days before the war, when I was a schoolmaster, I had
had a robust friend who used to prolong his anguish over the passing of an old love until he had got a new love actually ready to get
into bed with him.

'I must have continuity,' he used to say – somewhat self-
righteously, I used to think.

My own need now was the reverse. I must have *dis*-continuity.
It seemed to me as a changed man, as a man now aiming at marriage,
improper to get in touch with Elspeth while still 'carrying-on', as
my mother would have called it – no doubt did call it, to Harry –
with Sybil. As a changed man I was getting curious ideas of
propriety, I noticed. But there it was. The recurring pattern had to
be broken. I needed discontinuity. And I happened to have previously arranged for Sybil to come up to London in February.

So that accounts for the delay. It also accounts for a final scene
in the bar at Euston whose mournfulness exceeded all previous
mournfulness. This was, I had decided, really the last time I was
going to see Sybil. Is it any wonder I was mournful? Sybil, with
the looks of Marlene Dietrich, with the softest of voices and the
most touching of myopias, was now gone, gone for good. From
now on I was aiming at marriage.

I drank a large whisky and considered the prospect. And I considered Sybil again, too. Marriage, I thought . . . the very word was
like a knell.

I meant to try and marry Elspeth. I bought myself another whisky and told myself to put knells out of my mind, even though this one was metaphorically ringing a New Year in as well, more obviously as an Old Year out.

During January and February I kept out of Barbara's and Harry's, way. This was not difficult because for part of the time I had to go down to one of our major research establishments and do what was called a staff-review. Instead of being able to dwell on the breathless hush of springtime and the angel-glow that lights stars, I had to bend my mind to following professional discussion about shock-waves, aspect-ratios and suchlike; which, I can tell you, takes a lot more out of you than thinking about love. It also, I can tell you with the same authority, puts a good deal more into you, too.

I had noticed, before, the therapeutic value of a stay at one of our research establishments. If you lead a life of sexual disorder, there is nothing like a bit of science and technology for putting you straight. In the first place I found it interesting to think about shock-waves and aspect-ratios just out of natural curiosity. In the second place the people who were doing research on these topics had so little intention of discussing anything else that they gave me less than half a chance to maunder privately about my sexual life. I used to come away from these visits feeling a tireder but a better man. Perhaps only a little better; certainly a lot tireder. Still, only a little better, I felt, is *something*. Good for you, science and technology!

Since nobody else I knew could give me Elspeth's address, I had to ask Harry for it.

'I thought you'd want to know it,' he said, kindly, 'sooner or later.'

I thanked him.

He said: 'I suppose you weren't able to take her up straight away because of being out of London.'

'Yes,' I said, delighted by the thought that his spies at Euston must have failed him for once.

'Elspeth was very disappointed, I think, that night. She was waiting to go home with you. She was up in Barbara's room . . .'

He was looking at me with such an innocent expression, and the speech had gone so smoothly, that a pause elapsed before I tripped, in retrospect, over the test phrase. 'She was waiting to go home with you.'

I tripped, before I knew what I was doing, with chagrin and frank astonishment. I had realized that I was a changed man, but I had not realized I was so changed a man as to be shocked by the thought of a girl being ready to go home with me the first time she met me.

'How did she get home?' I asked casually.

Harry answered in his high, fluid voice: 'We put her up for the night here.'

I felt relief.

In the time between telephoning Elspeth and meeting her I reached a conclusion about myself that could scarcely have been more embarrassing. My reaction to the concept of the girl I proposed to marry being prepared to go to bed with me the first time she met me was the typical reaction of my father and the congregation of which I was no longer a member. I could now only conclude that, having discarded my recurring pattern, which, when all was said and done, was my own invention, I was going to fall back into the conventional pattern of the society in which I had been brought up. Not to put too fine a point on it, I must be going to be *respectable*.

I recalled what I chose to regard as my life of revolt. I had seceded from my father's church, in fact I had seceded from all religious belief; and I had practised my recurring pattern. Altogether a pretty fair score in the way of revolt, as both sides admitted. And now at the age of forty I was thrown back in one sphere at least – I saw no sign of dawning religious belief – to the start. I saw the prospect of courting Elspeth as if we were any two members of the choir, any two respectable members of the choir, that is.

A further thought occurred to me before I met Elspeth again. Supposing Harry had not been lying about her? Horrors! When I sat waiting for Elspeth in the foyer of the Carlos Hotel, where

286

I had asked her to dine with me, one of the questions I most wanted to find the answer to was whether Harry had any grounds for his lie.

The Carlos was an hotel I had frequented since about the middle of the war. It was small and, as far as I could gather, very grand – the sort of place that made Claridge's look rather commercialized: I mean, the Carlos would never have had flags outside, or gypsy music, or anything like that. As a result of my dining there alone when there were air-raids going on, some of the servants had got to know me. And considering how good the food was, I decided it was not as expensive as all that. The Carlos, as I had told Elspeth, not without intent to make an impression, was my favourite hotel.

You may think my attitude to the Carlos does not accord with my having said a little while ago that I was simply petty bourgeois. Not a bit of it. I may have cultivated some of the tastes of persons of a higher social class than myself – who would not cultivate the Carlos, if he had the chance? And I may have modelled some of my behaviour on theirs – I had removed most of the provincial accent from my speech, though naturally I could not do anything about removing it from my physiognomy. But I never really felt that my own social class was any different from that to which I had been born.

Perhaps I can make myself clearer by referring to my political attitudes. I had taken it into my head that the Labour Party were out to try and give the lower classes a better time of it, the Conservative Party to see that the upper classes did not lose one jot or tittle thereby. For that reason alone I could never have voted anything but Labour. (I may say that I kept strictly away from political meetings because the sight of M.P.s tended to put me off voting altogether.)

'The Left is motivated by envy and hope,' Robert had once pronounced, 'the Right by nostalgia and fear.'

Awful as the whole human race was, I stood by the side which at least was moved sometimes, in its envy, by hope.

So there you are. I was sitting in a big high-backed armchair in

287

the entrance hall of the Carlos, not feeling like a lord. If anything, I was feeling like Charlie Chaplin sitting in a chair made for Hamlet. I was waiting for Elspeth. Beside me, on a heavy William Kent-ish table with a marble top, there was a vase of flowers. The time of year was spring. The flowers were mimosa. I did not have to wait long for Elspeth, because she was punctual. She came through the revolving doors, hatless and a shade less pale than I had remembered. We shook hands.

She was nervous. And so was I. A handshake, and a formal handshake at that, was somewhat different from the last physical contact we had exchanged – I glanced at her cheek, thinking that my cheek . . . She caught me doing it, and suddenly we were looking each other in the face again as we had done when I hauled her up off the floor.

'Let's have a drink!' I said.

'I don't drink very much . . .'

I said playfully: 'I only suggested one, anyway.'

Fleetingly the lines like brackets round her mouth came and went. She really was nervous, I thought. As we went past the huge vase of mimosa I saw her notice it with surprise and awe.

'What a lot!' she said.

'And who's paying for it?' said I. 'Us, of course.'

She succeeded in laughing. I was pretty sure she had never set foot in a place as grand as this before. We both sniffed the mimosa with pleasure, and then I steered her into the big drawing-room, where there were more vases of it. At this she laughed naturally.

While we were having a drink I realized that she looked less pale because on the previous occasion she had been wearing a coral-coloured dress whereas tonight she was in dark green. It suited her: I noticed that her eyes were a transparent blue. No jewellery, no scent. I bet she has not got many dresses, I thought, and found the conjecture touching.

We had a drink, and then another one. Some of her nervousness disappeared, but not the air of mild formality. As you will have gathered, I was on my best behaviour. It became apparent to me that so was Elspeth. Our behaviour at the party, whether it was our worst or not, was a thing of the past, I thought – as also was Harry's deplorable suggestion. I had no doubt that Elspeth was somehow moving along on the same lines as me. Our parents, after they had got over the surprise of our being in the Carlos, would have recognized us as their own son and daughter respectively.

I have said 'our' parents. The way Elspeth and I spent most of our time over dinner was in exchanging information about our careers and our families. Her social origins were not very different from mine.

Elspeth was twenty-five years old and working as a school-teacher in Bethnal Green.

'I'm afraid I didn't go to a university,' she said, blushing, and glancing swiftly round the room as if she were ashamed of something.

I too glanced swiftly round the room. 'I doubt if all these ladies are honours graduates of Girton or Somerville, either.'

She grinned, though she still looked ashamed.

'Where *did* you go?' I asked.

'To a teachers' training college.'

'Did it do you any good?'

'It was very hard work.' She paused. 'So it must.'

I said: 'That's a fine Calvinist sentiment! *Your* father doesn't happen to be a nonconformist minister, does he?'

She laughed 'No. He's a school-teacher. We're all school-teachers in my family. You know, at council schools . . . I've gone the highest, by getting into a senior school.' She was amused. Then she said: '*Your* father's a minister, isn't he? I think Barbara told me.'

I nodded my head.

She was thinking something. I asked her what it was.

'Well, only that ministers' sons either become ministers themselves,' she said, 'or go to the other extreme.'

'Oh!' I cried.

She blushed again and let her table-napkin fall on the floor. I felt as if my reputation must be on the floor in the moral sense.

'You don't know me,' I said.

'No,' said she, looking frightened.

A waiter came and picked up her napkin, and for a while we concentrated on our *hors d'œuvres* – in my opinion, particularly good at the Carlos.

I reflected on the concept of marrying somebody whose social origins were approximately the same as my own. I was perfectly happy about it. In fact I had never really thought of marrying either above or below me. I supposed I might have thought of marrying above me, as ambitious men did – I *was* ambitious. But I was ambitious as a writer, as an artist. Had I been a publisher or a politician, it would of course have been a different matter: I had noted that politicians and publishers were great ones for marrying into the aristocracy. But I never saw how it could make me write better novels even if I married a Royal Princess. So why worry? I asked myself.

I looked at Elspeth – she happened to be eating a little mound of shrimps in a curry-flavoured sauce that she had been saving to the end – and thought there was no need to worry at all. She was eating slowly and with pleasure. Nice and relaxed, I thought. The right one for me. From bending forward over her plate, a dark strand of hair had fallen across her forehead.

'Well?' I said, when she had finished the shrimps.

'M'm,' she said.

'It's a nice place, this, isn't it?'

She said 'M'm' again.

While the wine-waiter took over, I looked approvingly and proprietorially round the room. It was panelled in a brightish wood that I took to be mahogany. On most of the tables there were small lamps with old-fashioned pink shades and tapering silver vases with daffodils in them. The curtains were of some dark, unstirring colour. My glance was caught by the flickering flame of a spirit lamp that rose up when a chafing-dish was lifted off it.

When we had got started on our next course, I said:

'How do you come to be a friend of Barbara's?'

'We send some of our children to Barbara's clinic.'

290

'Oh,' I said. Nothing easier to understand after all.

'The L.C.C. always seem to send you a long way from home.'

'What?' I was completely at sea, now. 'They send *you*?' I was trying to work out all sorts of complicated interpretations.

She said: 'No. Barbara.'

I laughed.

'They could perfectly well have found Barbara a job,' she said, 'somewhere near to where she lives, instead of sending her all the way down to our borough.'

I had no views on this. Judged by the heat with which she spoke, Elspeth had.

I said: 'If the L.C.C. had found her a job near where she lives, you would never have met her.' Anyway, no civil servant would be prepared to judge L.C.C. policy on one example.

'I shouldn't . . .'

I looked at her. 'And so you'd never have been at the party . . .'

A smile showed at the corners of her mouth. She glanced away and drank some wine. We paused for a little while. Elspeth said:

'Barbara tells me you write novels.'

In the ordinary way I should have replied: 'Yes, have you read any of them?' in a tone which indicated that a negative answer would not be well received. (I never understood why people expected one to smile, if not actually to pat them on the back, when they disclosed that they had never read any of one's books.) I said:

'Yes.'

'I should like to read them.'

I had met this remark before: the correct riposte was, 'Well, what's stopping you?' I said:

'That's the spirit!'

'Actually,' she said, 'I've just finished –' and she named a book I had brought out after the war.

'What did you think of it?'

She smiled shyly: 'I've never met an author before.'

I was interested by that but did not see how it answered my question. Elspeth said:

'I don't know the kind of thing to say about a book to its author.'

'I should just concentrate on praise,' I said. 'Sustained praise, with a touch here and there of flattery.' I recalled a friend, a woman, who, when I sent her a manuscript for her opinion, used to ask: 'Which do you want to hear, flattery or what I really think?'

Elspeth gave a laugh which seemed to absolve her from the need to reply. Encouraged, I said impetuously:

'The book I'm just about to bring out is much better than any of the others.'

'Oh, I shall get it!'

At that moment I thought of my reputation in her eyes. I have to say that the book I was encouraging her to read was on the same lines as this which you are now reading: it was about myself. Only it was about myself before I became a changed man. The moral tone of the book I was encouraging her to read was consequently nothing like so high as the moral tone of this book – after all, if you are behaving respectably, your moral tone cannot help being high, can it?

You see my point. I was sitting there in the Carlos with Elspeth, behaving in the most respectable manner imaginable, namely in the manner of a man who is taking a girl out to dinner with a view to matrimony. The book of mine which was going to come out in the following month was about a man who took his girl out to dinner with a view to *not* marrying her. A reprehensible view. A reprehensible man. I had difficulty in recognizing the fact that it was me, even me before metamorphosis.

'What is it called?' Elspeth was asking.

I told her, wishing I had given it one of those American titles like *Now Yesterday* or *Here and Forever* that nobody can remember. Elspeth did not write the title down but I knew she would not forget it.

'I shall watch for the review,' she said.

People always said that, rather as if they had some idea that both they and I gained merit by it.

'They may be bad,' I said insincerely.

'I don't think they will.' For all her shyness Elspeth was giving me a sparkling look, quick but direct, appraising but admiring.

'Oh!' I cried. 'I'll let you read a proof copy if you like.'

Elspeth said she would like.

I grinned. 'I suppose you might as well know the worst.'

Elspeth looked down at her plate, which by now was empty, and I saw her forehead go pink. What a wonderful girl! I thought. Just right for me . . . It only remained now for her to think my novel was the funniest, the wittiest, the most touching, the most truthful, and in some ways really the most profound book she had ever read.

'What would you like to eat next?' I asked, happy enough to buy her the most expensive *crêpes* on the menu or even a whole *bombe surprise* for herself.

Elspeth considered the alternatives and modestly chose to have some *marrons glacés*.

'I love chestnuts,' she said when the waiter had gone, 'but I've never tasted *marrons glacés*.' She smiled. 'We couldn't afford them.' She smiled. 'I still can't.'

I made the sort of tut-tutting noise that rich people make in the effort of trying not to hear what the poor are saying, and said:

'Well, they are pretty expensive.' I did not want her to think I could afford to dine at the Carlos every night, though I guessed she would have found somewhere not so grand less of a strain. 'Actually,' I said, 'I don't think I tasted them till the days when I was an undergraduate.' I had explained to her about my mother inheriting a little money which had enabled me to go up to Oxford – those were the days when only a grand slam, so to speak, of scholarships and grants enabled a boy to go up to Oxford without some other source of money. 'We were quite poor, you know. If there's anything poorer than a Methodist minister, I'd like to know what it is.'

'Yes, but you didn't have five brothers and sisters. I mean, your parents didn't have to bring up six children . . .'

'Six children!' I cried. 'They're not Roman Catholics, are they?' Though I no longer believed in God, I was still a hundred-per-cent

Protestant. Generations of nonconformity had endowed me with a blood-pressure that rose at the mere thought of Papism. I could have married Elspeth if she were a Mormon or a Seventh Day Adventist, but not if she were R.C.

Elspeth shook her head. 'Of course not. Actually they were Baptists, though I'm not.' She grinned. 'They really wanted six children.'

'I see . . . That's all right,' I said, though I was not sure I hoped Elspeth would want six children.

'We were very happy, really,' she said, 'though we had to go without lots of things that most children have.'

I saw the force of that.

'Do you know,' she said, 'that until I went to college I never had a dressing-gown.'

The fact she disclosed was poignant, but the portentous tone that came into her voice made me, I am sorry to say, want to laugh.

Elspeth was offended. I could see her saying to herself: 'I won't tell him anything else.' I realized that for me to say something even more poignant, such as 'Until I went up to Oxford, I never even had a pair of shoes,' would only make matters worse. And that would not have been in keeping with my parallel response to her remark, which was, 'I'll give you a wonderful dressing-gown . . . You shall be warm, however chilly the night, for the rest of your life.' This was assuming, of course, that I did not lose my job as a civil servant and have all my manuscripts turned down by publishers.

'Here come your *marrons*,' I said.

Elspeth tried one and her expression melted. My absence of feeling had been shown to be only of the moment and possibly not characteristic. I ate some runny Camembert cheese and the meal ended in delicious harmony.

Afterwards, when we came out of the hotel, it was a dry night, and we walked up through Grosvenor Square to Bond Street Tube Station, where Elspeth went east and I west. On the station platform, before she got into the train, I took her hand again and kissed her goodnight.

Her train moved out. When I turned to go to the adjacent platform, I felt as if the image of her face, smiling as she waved to me through the window, were still lingering on my retinas. Sparkling eyes and a long mouth curled up at the corners: the right face for me. Was it, I asked myself in an effort to be detached about it, a beautiful face, the sort of face that could for instance launch a thousand ships? I supposed it was not. But that did not worry me. I had my doubts about such faces: I suspected that if I saw the face of Helen of Troy her nose would look to me as if it started out of the middle of her forehead. And furthermore I was not looking for a face that would launch a thousand ships. I was only looking for a face that would launch just my ship.

4

Miscellaneous Conversations

I told Robert I had spent an entirely satisfactory evening with Elspeth.

'Who on earth's Elspeth?'

Robert's attitude towards the existence of anyone whom he had not discovered for himself was incredulity.

'The girl I met at Harry's party on New Year's Eve,' I said. 'You saw her. I told you I was going to take her out to dinner at the Carlos.'

'Was it a good dinner?'

'Very good.' I began to describe the dishes we had eaten, in detail as boring as I could make it.

In retaliation Robert gave me what we nowadays referred to, *vide* W. H. Sheldon, as a mesomorphic glare. Mesomorph is the name for the square, all-muscle type of man, and the glare is the blank unchanging expression you see on his face. (The word 'glare' is chosen because the emotion in which mesomorphs most readily express themselves is rage. Undiluted men of action, they burst into rage when action does not produce the desired result. The glare gives intimations of this.) Most of our colleagues in the Civil Service, like men of action in all walks of life, were predominantly mesomorphic, and as a private parlour game Robert and I used to give them marks out of ten for the impenetrability of their glares. Robert's large F.D.R.-like face rather untypically did not score more than about seven out of ten. And my own score was so much less that, in order to keep up in my Civil Service career, I practised my glare regularly in the mirror after shaving.

I said to Robert:

'You ought to pay attention when I mention Elspeth. Because I think it's possible I may marry her.'

Robert's glare disappeared instantly. He said with emotion:

'I hope you do.'

And while he said that his face fell into an expression which I readily identified – it was the expression into which both our faces fell when, for example, somebody whom we loved who had no literary talent announced that he or she was going to write a novel.

'You must meet her,' I said.

'I should like to,' he replied – in a tone with which we accepted the prospect of reading the first 10,000 words of manuscript.

I gave up.

In fact it turned out immediately afterwards in our conversation that Robert was preoccupied about something else. He had been called over to see Murray-Hamilton. One of the senior people at the research establishment at which I had done my staff-review had complained to Murray-Hamilton about something I had said.

'The snitch!' I cried, finding just the word I wanted from the vocabulary of my pupils when I was a schoolmaster.

Robert looked grave.

I asked who the man was.

Robert shrugged his shoulders. 'I don't know. As it was some deputy superintendent or other . . .'

I asked what I was supposed to have said.

'History in this case doesn't relate that.'

I was about to comment angrily when Robert went on: '*I* don't know what you're supposed to have said. I suppose Murray-Hamilton does, but that's not what concerns him. As he sees it, whether you said it or not, even whether you were provoked to it or not, you *offended* somebody. Introduced friction into the machine . . . That's something he takes seriously. He's bound to take it seriously.'

'Oh, blast!' I said. 'Why can't he take no notice for once?'

'He's not the sort of man who could, even if he approved of you in the first place . . .'

That remark shut me up for quite a while.

I had a picture of Murray-Hamilton sitting in his office brooding and reflecting. A new thought crossed my mind. Could it be that what he was interminably brooding and reflecting upon was the awesome difference between Right and Wrong? A book, a large ledger, lay open in front of him. Then I saw Spinks, 'Stinker Spinks', come in – at that I discontinued thought in favour of speech – and I said to Robert:

'I wonder what I really did say.'

Robert had got up and gone to look glumly through the window. He said:

'Probably something sharp and bright.' He paused. 'But that's immaterial . . . The fact of the matter is that you say things that set these people's teeth on edge. You make them feel you're getting at them.'

'Oh,' I said.

'Even your quips are not the sort they're used to – or even take to be quips, for that matter.' He turned on me. 'I've heard you, myself, invite people to think mesomorphic glares are funny, when they have mesomorphic glares themselves!'

'Oh,' I said again.

Robert turned away from me. 'You may have to pay for it, that's all.'

'What do you mean by that?' I asked quickly.

'I don't know,' he said.

That remark shut me up altogether.

Robert went on glumly staring out of the window. He had nothing else to say on the matter, either then, it appeared, or later.

During the next few weeks I had other, different things to think about.

The time came for me to invite Robert and Annette to meet Elspeth. I invited them to dinner with us at my flat. I bought some very expensive *pâté* and spent an additional ten shillings a bottle on the claret. The flat was central-heated and warm, and three hyacinths growing in a pot gave my living-room – I had two rooms

298

– an agreeable smell. It was the first time Elspeth had been to my flat: I should have thought it quite improper to invite her alone. Robert and Annette seemed to me, though they might not have seemed to everyone, to constitute proper chaperonage.

After dinner Robert and Annette sat on the sofa and held hands, at least they began by holding hands. I thought it was a good thing for Elspeth to observe that a man as eminent and as lofty in general purpose as Robert, and a girl as high-minded in the philosophical sense as Annette, made no bones about liking – well, you had only to see them together to see what they liked.

And I must say that Robert knew how to play his part. He instructed both girls on how good a novelist I was. By this time Elspeth had read the proofs of my new novel and declared that she liked it. This, of course, was not enough for Robert. I listened to him with pleasure and satisfaction. Girls do not, more's the pity, want to sleep with a man because he writes good novels; but if they are not averse to the idea of sleeping with him in the first place, then hearing that he writes good novels sometimes appears to help things along. (For this reason the artist's life is not entirely composed of suffering and rejection.)

Robert did me proud. None of us were left in any doubt that my new book was a small masterpiece. Small? You may think that was not doing me as proud as all that. I recommend you to concentrate on the important thing. It is masterpieces that live, whatever the size. Better a tiny masterpiece than the most massive of potboilers. Robert said:

'He may even make a bit of money with it.'

I glanced at Elspeth. She was looking radiantly pretty, in the dark green dress which made her eyes look so blue. The same dark green dress – she probably had not got any other dress . . . Money. I thought of making a bit of money in an entirely new light. How could two live on the income of one? By the earner taking a cut.

'How much?' I asked Robert, poignantly.

He mentioned a sum. Not enough. Nothing like enough!

Elspeth's expression of general enthusiasm and amusement did not falter. No more did it need to. Nor did Annette's falter. No more did hers need to, either. Robert earned much more than me, and Annette never wore anything but the same jumper and skirt.

'Of course,' Robert was saying loftily about my novel, 'it's probably the most original book to come out since the war. And it may well be the progenitor of a whole series of similar books.'

'But the money?' I interrupted. 'What about the money?'

Robert shrugged his shoulders, as one does when a man of talent reveals a petty obsession – which happens to be pretty often, if it comes to that. Of course I wanted my book to be a masterpiece and a progenitor and all the rest of it. I wanted that first of all. But *after* that . . .

The following morning at the office, Robert came in and said:

'I think Elspeth's a nice girl. A very nice girl. Intelligent . . . and comparatively relaxed.' He nodded his head in agreement with his own description.

I nodded mine. I said:

'I need someone who's pretty relaxed. Someone to cushion my . . . fluctuations.'

Robert nodded his head again, probably not so much in agreement with my description of myself as in censure of what I was describing.

'Yes,' he said gravely. 'I think she'll do that for you.'

I was satisfied. In fact I was happy.

Annette, too, was approving, though on different grounds. Next time we met, she said to me:

'I knew I should like Elspeth. I admire her.'

I said: 'She admires you.' I thought that actually Elspeth admired above all Annette's First in Modern Greats.

Annette went on: 'I think I envy her really.'

I said with astonishment: 'What do you envy her for?'

'Her profession, of course.' Annette looked at me, smiling. 'It's a very useful one.'

I had forgotten for the moment that Elspeth was a school-teacher – possibly I was thinking chiefly about the time when she would cease to be one. And I had also forgotten that Annette was still doing nothing, apart from turning her D.Phil. thesis into the form of a publishable monograph and writing occasional reviews for professional journals.

'Oh,' I said. 'I didn't know you'd been talking to her about it.' Nor did I see why, with marriage imminent, Annette had been talking to Elspeth about it.

Annette laughed. 'I haven't.' She looked away and her hair swung girlishly. 'But I think I will,' she said, in a firm clear voice. And then she added, even more clearly and firmly: 'I must.'

5

Approach to Marriage

My novel came out in April. I have observed that it was a book on the same lines as this one you are now reading, so you can judge its quality by inference. Masterly? Oh well, have it your own way! Though I can tell you that *some* people said it was masterly. And what is more, they were paid for *their* critical efforts.

Robert and I followed the reviews with the sort of excitement with which one follows the results of a General Election. I had made a list of the days of the week on which novel reviews appeared, so I duly arrived at the office on any particular morning with a copy of the right paper. Robert, of course, had one as well. We hurried out of the office at lunch-times to buy the appropriate mid-day editions of the London evening papers, and after we came out of work in the afternoons we went up to our club and furled through magazines like *The Sphere* and *The Tatler*, for which, since they were inclined to lag behind in reviewing, we were not prepared to risk the outlay of ready money. And I had a press-cutting agency, which I used to telephone for reviews that Robert and I had missed but which watchful friends had seen in, say, *The Farmers' and Stockbreeders' Gazette*.

It was a thrilling time, more thrilling in my opinion than watching election results come out – though it would presumably not be so in the opinion of a political party leader.

'I think it's going to be all right,' Robert announced when the most important reviews were in.

So I settled back for 'the bit of money' to come in. My publishers appeared to be settling back too, because the book went out of print three weeks after publication. Several weeks elapsed before it came into print again, but everybody said it did not affect my sales; at least, my publishers said that. I trusted the bit of money would come in.

While I was waiting and trusting, the time for Robert's marriage to Annette came near. Now that I was buoyed up by thinking I might manage to get married myself, I was freed from my disfiguring envy of Robert's good fortune. In fact I began to think he might envy me, who foresaw no trouble of any kind with my loved one. For signs of trouble, as far as Robert was concerned, were beginning to appear. They were trivial, of course. Signs of trouble always are to start with.

I sympathized with Annette. The first difference of opinion arose over whether the wedding was to be grand or not. I first heard of it one Sunday afternoon when Annette invited Elspeth and me to tea with her and Robert at her father's flat.

We were eating slices of bread and butter and marmalade. Annette gave Robert a clear-eyed look and said:

'Must I dress up?'

She was awaiting an answer Yes or No. Love and devotion for the person to whom she addressed the question seemed to shine from her face. At the time she asked it she was wearing the usual polo-necked jumper and some wrinkled navy-blue trousers – as it was getting towards summer I presumed it was a thinner jumper, but it looked the same. Her complexion had its delicious cleanly sheen and her bell of hair glistened as if she had just washed it.

'Dress up in what?' said Robert.

'In bridal white,' said Annette. 'You know I don't want to, darling.' She gave him an amused smile. 'I don't see myself as the central figure in a fertility rite.'

Robert burst into a laugh. 'That's just what you'll be, my girl!'

Annette smiled back at him, simply, without inhibition. I was reminded of Robert's observation, when he first got to know Annette and her philosopher friends, that they believed in their new brand of high-mindedness being accompanied by plenty of copulation. To Robert and me, who happened to have been brought up on a brand of high-mindedness that was accompanied by continence, this new combination was surprising. It made us ready to re-consider our former unfavourable judgement on high-mindedness.

'I'm on Annette's side,' I said. 'After all, neither of you have any religious beliefs.' And they had been sleeping with each other for months.

Elspeth said: 'Oh, I'm on Robert's side. It's something that only happens to one once in one's life.' She suddenly faltered and blushed. 'At least I hope it does . . .' She looked down – I realized that I had not breathed a word about marriage to her.

'Exactly,' said Robert, and rewarded her with a dazzling look of friendship. He went on: 'Elspeth is right, you know. At certain points in one's life, the maximum ceremony may well be desirable.'

Annette said to Robert: 'I find ceremony embarrassing.' She looked at him. 'It really is embarrassing to me, you know. Can't we do without it?'

'If you can't bear it, of course we'll do without it,' he said, and gave her a quick, faintly mechanical smile.

Annette's father came into the room.

We had not heard him come into the flat and we were all surprised to see him. He did not usually come back from his house in the country till later on Sunday night. He looked round to see whom Annette was entertaining. It was a characteristic gesture, such as I had often seen grand people make – he was weighing up whether to stay with us or not. He said:

'I should like some tea if there's any left.' He spoke with a mixture of politeness and carelessness that amused me.

Annette's father was different from the Civil Service bosses in our part of the world. Our department had none of the social advantages of being, say, antique, like the Home Office, or chic, like the Foreign Office. In fact I had once caused a bit of trouble by remarking, innocently and truthfully, in what had turned out to be wrong company, that our department, as far as cachet went, was one of the slums of the Civil Service. (You may ask how there can be such a thing as the wrong company for Innocence and Truth. Kindly address your question to Murray-Hamilton and Spinks!)

In the first place, Annette's father looked different from our bosses. He was tall and slender, whereas they were mainly of medium height and broad: he looked as if he might once have played badminton, whereas they looked as if they might have excelled, in fact most of them had excelled, at games where you run about all the time, knocking other people over. And of course his manner was different. Murray-Hamilton and Spinks, for instance, had a manner that was affable and jocular and rather commonplace, though in their different ways neither were commonplace men. Not so Annette's father – scholarly and *dégagé* were the words that sprang to my mind as I watched him.

Annette said to him: 'I'll make some fresh tea for you.' From the way she looked at him it was obvious that she was very fond of him.

He sat down, folding his long legs gracefully. He said: 'Don't, if it's any trouble to you.'

Somehow it made me think of the way he conducted his public life, of the cultivatedly diffuse sort of minute he wrote to his peers – 'Do you think X is a good name?' he would write of some Vice-Chancellor of a university. 'I met him in the Club and thought he might do for us, but you may think differently.' Annette's father, I thought, showed you how the power-game after all really flowered at the top; though I never quite understood, being convinced that in general it was active, opaque, heavily muscled men who got to the top, what phenomenon was responsible for Annette's father flowering there. I used to speculate on two questions. One was, had the upper reaches of the Civil Service in the previous genera-tion been more sheltered, more university life? The other was, was Annette's father only about one-third as *dégagé* as he seemed?

Annette went out to make some fresh tea and her father said to Robert:

'Really I shall have to give up this house in the country. It's an extravagance I can't afford any more.'

He gave a brief circular glance at Elspeth and me, to make sure that we were taking it in. His eyes were somewhere between grey and hazel in colour, very bright without being specially humorous.

Robert nodded his head in statesmanlike agreement.

'On the other hand,' Annette's father went on, 'going down there is my only chance of getting away from the Civil Service. And doing some of the things I really want to do . . .'

He was writing a book on Hellenistic art between two dates of wonderfully esoteric significance.

'But of course,' he went on again to Robert, 'I know I'm not telling you anything you don't know already.' He was referring to Robert's writing novels.

Robert was beginning to say something about senior civil servants having to work too hard when Annette came back with the tea. 'I'm sorry we've only got marmalade,' she said to her father. 'I forgot to go out and buy some jam.'

Her father began to eat a slice of bread and butter, without marmalade. 'I was talking to Robert about giving up the house.' Then he turned to Robert as if the idea had just struck him. 'I suppose you and Annette wouldn't care to live there, or perhaps it's too far out of London?'

Robert's cheeks went slightly pink. 'Clearly, we should have to think about it,' he said. 'I think we probably –'

Annette interrupted: 'Oh no, Father. I don't want a house at all.'

We all looked at her. I cannot say Annette looked in the least perturbed as a consequence. I glanced at Robert: he did.

Annette said: 'I don't want to have servants. It would embarrass me to have servants . . . I don't think we *ought* to have them.'

Suddenly Elspeth spoke for the first time since Annette's father had come in. 'All we ever had was a woman who came in once a week to do the washing.'

'What's that got to do with it?' I said to her.

Elspeth replied: 'I was just telling you.'

Annette said: 'I'm not laying down a principle for other people. It's a personal choice that I shouldn't think of presuming to impose on other people.' She smiled. 'Though I should try to convince them of it if they came to me for advice.'

Her father said: '*Do* they come to you for advice?'

Robert said: 'Yes, that's a good question.'

Annette just went on smiling. The result of that round – Two Civil Servants *v.* Annette – seemed to me a draw.

Robert said: 'It's going to be increasingly difficult to get servants anyway. So I suppose Annette's views may be regarded as bringing her into line with the times.' He said it humorously but he sounded distinctly huffy all the same.

Annette's father said: 'I can only hope the times won't move too fast for me. I shall have to have some servants to look after me when Annette leaves me.' He helped himself to another piece of bread and butter, without marmalade.

Annette said nothing. Nor did anybody else.

In the social class to which I, like Elspeth, had been born, the question of whether one had a woman in to do the washing was decided by whether one had the money to pay her or not.

Annette and the others remained silent for a long time. I had a distinct feeling that a moral choice was floating over our heads.

Moral choices, I thought, are a pain in the neck.

Approach to Bed

I should have prophesied that Annette and Robert would be married in a registry office and then live in a big house. They were married in church and then lived in a smallish flat.

The flat where Annette and Robert went to live was the one which had formerly been occupied by Annette's father. He had sold the house in Berkshire and set up in a big flat at the back of Gorringe's, where he employed two servants. Annette employed none.

Robert said to me: 'We've been rather fortunate, as a matter of fact. This arrangement will mean we shall have a good deal more money in hand for entertaining.' He paused.

'Who's going to do all the cooking and so on?' I asked, feeling very unimaginative.

'Annette will do some. And we shall get people in, professionals, to do the rest.'

I said: 'I see.' I thought I did see. I suspected that Annette and her father were turning out to be distinctly richer than I – or Robert – had thought. And why not? I liked the idea of big dinner-parties, and of anybody I knew being richer than we had thought. The bigger the better. The richer the better!

At this point I have to say that I was not getting any richer myself. As far as making a fortune out of my new novel was concerned, I was still trusting. I had written a book, the most original novel since the war, the probable progenitor of many others like it – I had Robert's word for all this – and yet . . . Furthermore some people who were so revered as to be paid for writing their opinion had said it was masterly, and yet . . . A dent must have been made on the public's mind: what about that dent on the public's pocket?

My desires, my expectations, were modest. For instance, I was not expecting the traffic in Piccadilly Circus to come to a standstill. All I desired was that a fraction of the total public, a small fraction – just a few tens of thousands of them – should go into their booksellers, even into their Free Public Lending Libraries, and utter the title of my work. But how many had done? I have been advised not, for my own sake, to tell you.

'I have kept your book out of your father's way,' my mother wrote to me, 'but I have read it. Shall I send it back to you?'

I judged from his silence that my literary agent must be in America, even though it was the season of the year when American publishers streamed over to London, looking for books. One morning Harry joined me as I strode down Putney Hill to the bus-stop.

'I was having a drink with your agent last night,' he said. 'He'd got an American publisher with him. I asked him if he'd read your book. Nice chap. He said he had.'

'What did he think of it?'

'Actually he said it was the funniest book he'd read in years.'

'Is he going to buy it?' I looked at Harry.

Harry shook his head. 'I'm afraid not. He said it was too British.'

We went on walking.

I considered the verdict. I looked at it from many angles. First angle: how could it be too British when I *was* British, when all my forebears, as far back as any records went, had been British? What did he *expect* it to be? Second angle: the implication seemed to be that Americans would not understand my book, would not understand what it was about. This puzzled me even more. Were Americans unable to comprehend the situation of a young man who sleeps with his girl and does not want to marry her? I should have thought not. Certainly I should have thought not, when I recalled the situation of some of the young Americans whom I had got to know in London during the war. Too British, indeed. I liked that! Third angle: no, two are enough . . .

By the end of the summer I thought it was time to start writing another book. Another book? Yes, another book.

I went to Norway for a holiday, thinking that if I could bring a Norwegian scene into this new book, I could get my holiday expenses off income tax. While I was away I wrote a long letter to Elspeth. I was delighted with the result. She wrote a long letter back. She said she had an idea that she wanted to discuss with me when I got back. I have to admit that the first thought, the first, imbecile, groundless thought that crossed my mind was that it might be marriage.

We met in a public-house in Soho, near to a restaurant where I was going to take her for dinner. With the possibility in view of two having to live on the income of one, I was beginning to consider the Carlos a hasty choice of rendezvous. As Elspeth was a bit shy of going into a public-house by herself, I got there early. It was an unusually hot September evening, sultry and airless. The doors of the public-house were wide open, and the resident smell of spirits was tinged with a visiting aroma of garlic and French cigarettes. On the opposite corner of the street there was a collection of swarthy little men wearing black suits and shirts without ties: they seemed to be doing nothing, as if perhaps they might be dreaming blankly about the eastern shores of the Mediterranean; but I had been told they were engaged with the machinery of betting. They turned slowly to gaze in the direction of my pub. Elspeth came in.

She was wearing a thin summer frock, prettily draped over her small breasts, swirling out across her not so small pelvis. 'Goodness, you're sunburnt,' I said, and kissed her enthusiastically.

She laughed. 'So are you.' There were small dots of perspiration on her upper lip – apart from using lipstick, she appeared to be copying Annette in going without make-up.

'I'm glad you asked me out straight away,' she said, 'before my sunburn fades.'

'Didn't you think I should?'

For an instant she looked me in the eye, and then the corners of her mouth went up. 'How was I to know?'

'You might have,' I said humourlessly, in fact slightly shaken. Marriage, indeed!

We sat down at a table by the door and she said she would like to drink some iced lager. When she took off her short pair of white gloves I noticed the trace of dark gleaming down, all the way up her arms. I wondered how soon I could ask what her idea was.

We drank some lager and put the tall glasses on the table. A huge bluebottle made a buzzing circuit of them and went its way towards some sandwiches under a glass dome on the counter.

'I liked your letter,' I said.

'Yours was very funny,' she said. 'It nearly scared me off replying at all.'

'That's ridiculous,' I said. 'Now yours even incorporated suspense.'

She looked astonished.

'I'm dying to know,' I said, 'what the idea was you were going to talk to me about.'

To my surprise she blushed. 'Oh, it was nothing. I mean, it was only just an idea. *You* know . . . I mean, well, I wondered if it might be a good idea if I changed my digs. I'm always coming up to Putney nowadays, to see you, and Barbara . . .' She broke off, and then suddenly she said: 'After all, you never come down to the Green.'

'You mean you're going to come and live in Putney?' I cried.

'If you think it's a good idea . . .'

With an effort I said: 'I think it's a marvellous idea.'

Elspeth drank some more iced lager. The colour remained rosily in her cheeks.

A marvellous idea. Marvellous or menacing? It transpired that she had already found somewhere suitable and was only waiting to give her new landlady the word that she was ready to move in.

I told Robert about it first thing next morning.

He said: 'It's an encircling movement, old boy.'

'You only say that because you've been caught yourself!'

'I don't think so, you know. I see no evidence for that presumption.' He paused in a dignified way. 'I should have said it was entirely my own doing.' From dignity he passed to moral initiative. 'Anyway,' he said, 'you've been encircled before, haven't you, and got away with ease?'

I regarded this comment as unhelpful.

Robert looked at me. 'And anyway,' he said, 'I thought you wanted to be caught this time, don't you?'

'Yes. I mean, no,' I said. 'Yes. No.'

Robert shrugged his shoulders.

Was it yes, or was it no? Or both? I tried to forget about it. Elspeth came to live in digs in Putney, and the immediate results were happy to say the least of it.

'You reproached me with not coming down to the Green,' I said to her one evening when we were out for a stroll after dinner. 'But it's rather nice to be up on the Heath.' We had an arm round each other's waist.

'You should see Victoria Park on a summer's evening.'

I asked myself what that could mean.

I thought things over. From the beginning I had felt that Elspeth was going along the same lines as me. And what did those lines lead to? An act of will. An act of *my* will.

I decided to ask Elspeth to go to bed with me. No, do not misunderstand me! Above all, do not misunderstand me! I argued that going to bed with her would make my act of will easier. Do you see? In a way, I should be half-way there.

I recalled an event of my young manhood that must have impressed itself on me. One of my friends, son of a high-minded, free-thinking, upper middle-class family, had been sent away for a week-end with his fiancée by his mother – to make sure everything was all right before they married. As I recalled it now, I thought how, in spite of everything, I was a child of my time, of those far-off early 'thirties when any reasonable couple made sure that everything was all right before they married. I was comforted by the thought of myself as a child of my time.

However, when it came to the point, I felt very nervous. How I envied that chap who had his mother to organize it for him!

I broached the subject with Elspeth one evening when we were lying on the sofa together.

'I've been thinking about us,' I said, trying to make it sound as if 'us' were spelt with a capital U.

She lay still, with her head resting on my arm.

'If we're thinking of going on . . .' Shades of girls who had used that phrase to *me* when they meant getting married, as I did now! 'I mean,' I said, 'if we're thinking of getting married . . .' I practically had palpitations at using that word.

'M'm,' said Elspeth, still lying very still.

'Well,' I said, 'don't you think perhaps we ought to make sure everything's all right, first of all?'

I waited.

Quietly Elspeth turned her head and kissed my cheek.

'Do you?' I said, joyously, getting up to look at her.

She whispered something that I could not hear.

I swore to myself there and then that if everything was all right I would let nothing stop me asking her to marry me. I lay down again, putting my arms round her more tightly.

'When?'

She whispered: 'Not now . . . Not tonight.'

'Oh, no, no,' I said. 'We don't want to rush it. Perhaps you ought to come and stay here. At the week-end?'

I thought she nodded her head.

So I found myself with four days to wait. In four days I should be half-way towards having my act of will made for me.

The following Friday evening Elspeth arrived at my flat. I had made it look neat and pleasant, flowers in both rooms, clean sheets on the bed – it was a double bed – all kinds of drink in the cupboard. She was wearing a dress I had not seen before, dark blue with a light blue pattern on it. Her hair smelt delicious when I kissed her.

'I'm sure the hall-porter saw my case,' she said, as she opened it to take out her sponge-bag and dressing-gown.

'I don't see that that matters.'

We went and had dinner in the somewhat indifferent restaurant

313

in the basement of the building. I doubt if we noticed what we were eating.

At last we got to bed, hugging each other closely because the clean sheets felt cold. We kissed each other prolongedly.

I said: 'I'm a bit nervous.'

'So am I,' she whispered, though I thought that hardly mattered so much.

This went on for some time.

'I'm very nervous,' I said.

She whispered: 'Never mind . . .'

I began to get very worried. 'This is bad,' I said.

Elspeth hugged me and caressed me.

Everything was not all right. It was not all right at all. My act of will! I was not half-way towards it – I was making a grotesque progress in the opposite direction! What can I do now? I thought. If everything is *not* all right, there is no point in asking her to marry me, even if my will would stand up to it. I turned away from her and looked at the light of the bedside lamp shining on the ceiling.

I waited. No sign. No sign . . . I saw my hopes crumbling, my dreams come to nothing, my life recurring in the same empty pattern for ever. I turned back to her and buried my face in the curve between her ear and her shoulder.

'I'm no use,' I cried. 'I'm no use to you.'

'You must never say that again!'

Her voice rang out resonantly, firmly. As my lips were against her throat I could feel the resonance through them. I was startled. I was more than startled.

Looking back on it now, I know exactly how I felt. I felt as if I had suddenly thought: Why, there's somebody *else* in bed with me!

Until this moment I had been so preoccupied with myself, or rather with my self, that I had not really thought of Elspeth as a separate, independent person at all. She was the person at the other end of *my* problem, only seen by me so far as she affected *me* . . .

With one fine resonant speech, Elspeth had ended all that. I had got somebody else in bed with me, a living, whole, human person.

I was too startled even to say 'Good gracious!' I felt that it was the biggest surprise in my life.

Well, one of the things about a surprise or a shock is that it is said to take one out of one's self. I lay there with my face against Elspeth's throat. The vibration of this shock went on tingling in my lips.

After a few seconds, I really did say: 'Good gracious!' I felt the blood beginning to bump in my pulses. I had been taken right out of my self, without a doubt – I was a different man!

'Darling,' I said.

Elspeth took her hand away and turned *her* face into the curve between *my* ear and *my* shoulder.

'Darling!' I said. I could not even hear what she replied.

I moved over.

So there it was. Everything was more or less all right. Not the performance of a lifetime, I admit, but you can tell whether everything is all right or not. It was.

After we had had a rest I got out of bed and said:

'I suppose you could do with a nice cup of tea, now?'

Elspeth, deliciously pink in the face, looked up at me – I could not think why she seemed surprised.

The fact was that I was feeling as if I could do with a nice cup of tea myself.

7

A Decision and a Celebration

You may wonder if I immediately asked Elspeth to marry me. Well, no, as a matter of fact, I did not. I had sworn to myself that if everything were all right I would make my act of will. But then, I asked myself, could I say yet that everything was all right? I mean, definitely. One swallow did not make a summer, though I conceded that most people would think it meant they could reasonably look forward to a spell of warm weather.

Elspeth came to stay with me every week-end.

'I miss you in the middle of the week,' she said, 'darling.'

The discussion which followed was about which night of the week was more nearly equidistant from the week-ends.

The weather, in my metaphorical sense, was getting pretty warm; and had my act of will not been hanging over my head all the time, I should have basked in it without restraint. Even as it was, I basked quite a lot.

In our leisure moments, Elspeth and I indulged ourselves in true lovers' speculation and reflections. 'Wouldn't it be dreadful,' she said one day, 'if one of us didn't like it?'

'Dreadful,' I said.

Her imagination took a Gothic turn. 'Wouldn't it be dreadful,' she said, 'if one got married and then found the other person didn't like it?'

'Horrible,' I said impetuously. 'Appalling!'

And then I came to. Married . . . Had somebody said something about getting married?

I realized that Elspeth now saw no reason whatever why we should not get married. This exemplified to me one of the characteristics that most markedly differentiated women from men. Confronted with the prospect of being tied, of being trapped for life, women showed neither reluctance nor caution. How different from men! I thought. Or, to be precise, how different from me! Women's nature seemed to make them ready for the trap. Men had to steel themselves to it. I felt that in my nature the steely element was . . . well, not very steely.

One evening when Elspeth arrived, she said: 'I'm sure the hall-porter knows why I come here.'

This seemed probable. He never did much work, but he kept a very efficient eye on everyone who came in and out. I said: 'Oh.' We had agreed not to tell our friends – in particular we wanted to tease Harry by keeping it from him – but I did not see that it mattered if the porter knew.

'He said "Good evening" in a particularly insolent tone.'

I was surprised. He was a tall, lounging fellow, with a full-cheeked, oval face that made me think of a rabbit's. I had never had any trouble with him.

'I don't see what I can do about it,' I said. 'I can't very well tick him off.'

'No,' said Elspeth, thoughtfully.

I could, of course, put her in such a position that she did not have to suffer this kind of thing. But could I? Could I?

As the weeks passed I had found that I was getting no nearer to my act of will. Half-way there, I had told myself when I asked Elspeth to put our relationship on a somewhat marital footing. I was certain now that Elspeth was the one for me, and I must say she gave me little basis for arguing that I was not the one for her – on the contrary. So why could I not bring myself to the point of asking her to marry me? As I did not like putting the question to myself, I decided to try putting it to Robert.

I told Robert one dull wintry afternoon when we were coming out of the tea-shop after lunch. I felt it was a crucial occasion in my life, a day I should always remember: the only thing I can remember now, apart from what we said, is that a little way ahead

317

of us on the pavement there was a woman in a red coat exactly the same shade as the pillar-box she was just passing. Robert said: 'Annette and I thought you probably were.' He looked at me affectionately. 'I'm glad. You've been looking much better these last few weeks.'

'Better?' I said. 'Was I looking worse before?'

'A more regular life seems to suit you.'

We walked in silence for a few moments, threading our way between people walking two or three abreast. Robert bought a newspaper. I was reflecting on the favourable effect on me of a regular life. Marriage was a regular life.

'The question is,' I said, 'what to do next?'

'Are you going to ask her to marry you?'

'What do you think?'

'You could do worse, much worse.' Robert glanced at me. 'Come to think of it, you *have* done in the past.'

'Considering that was on *your* advice, too,' I said. 'I –'

Robert said: 'I think Elspeth's a very nice girl. Very suitable.' He paused. 'You're very lucky.'

I laughed. 'You make it sound as if my deserts were a broken-down hag aged fifty!'

'I meant you're lucky in the sense that I'd say I was lucky to have found Annette.' A tone of strong feeling came into his voice. 'Someone odd enough to interest you, and equable enough to make you a good wife.'

Actually I did not think Elspeth was at all odd.

We came to Trafalgar Square and waited for the traffic lights to let us cross the road.

'Are you going to marry her?' Robert asked, as buses whizzed past the ends of our noses.

'That's what I can't make up my mind about.'

'Do you want to?'

'Yes. I suppose I do.'

'Then why don't you? I'm sure she'd marry you.'

The lights changed and the buses lined up their radiators across the road. We went in front of them and walked along the south side of the square, dodging the pigeons.

We came to the next road-crossing. Robert said:

'Of course there's the possibility that *she*'ll settle it by marrying *you*.'

'She's much too young and too shy.'

Robert laughed. 'I shouldn't rely on that.'

I was shocked by his cynical tone. He did not seem to realize that I was in love with Elspeth. I sincerely did think that – sweet girl! – she was too young and too shy.

This was a crossing without lights: we got safely as far as the island.

Robert said, on a different tack: 'Well, I suppose you can go on as you are.'

'Don't you see, that would mean I've fallen into my recurring pattern again?'

'I do see that.'

There was a lull in the buses and taxis. 'Come on, jump for it!' I said. We got to the other pavement. Though we had not discussed our objective, I judged that we must be making for the London Library. We went on walking in silence.

Suddenly, 'I really *will* marry her!' I said loudly.

'Good,' said Robert. 'I hope you will.'

We had to cross another road.

'I take it you're going to the London Library?' said Robert.

'I thought you were.'

'I hadn't thought of it.'

'Nor had I. Apart from thinking that's where you were going.'

'I'm perfectly willing to go, if you want to.'

'So am I, if you are.'

'Let's go, then!'

We crossed the road and continued on our way.

My will had hardened. I am not pretending it was steely yet, but somehow I felt sure that from this point I was not going to slip back any more.

I felt so sure that I stopped dead in the middle of the pavement, making Robert stop to look at me with the maximum attention, and said to him again:

'I really *will* marry her.'

This time his expression was quite different. 'Good!' he said, and his large grey eyes shone with pleasure and belief.

As we started to walk on again, he said: 'We ought to have a drink tonight.'

'To celebrate my decision?' I said, grinning.

Robert grinned too, but looked away in order to avoid answering my question. He said: 'Why don't you drop into the club late-ish tonight and join me for a drink? I shall be there with Annette's father and Harold Johnson.'

I recognized this instantly as a real treat for me. Sir Harold Johnson, another high civil servant, had only recently come Robert's way and had made the greatest of impressions upon him. As I gathered it from Robert, Annette's father and Sir Harold Johnson were, as far as exercising power in the outward direction went, among the top half-dozen or so men in the Service. As far as having influence in the inward direction, among those top half-dozen or so men themselves, Sir Harold Johnson had the edge over Annette's father, hands down. The fullness of time was going to bring Sir Harold Johnson to even greater boss-hood.

But this was not all. As far as Robert and I had observed, there was something in the opinion of the general public that senior civil servants, able and admirable though they might be in their jobs, were in their personalities not very exciting. But when it came to the highest bosses of all, public opinion had got it quite wrong. Among the highest of bosses, with Sir Harold Johnson as a case in point, personality could proliferate to a degree that, in the eyes of Robert and me, qualified as grand eccentricity.

To be allowed to meet Sir Harold Johnson was a great treat for me. 'Why not?' I said, enthusiastically.

Dutifully following Robert's instructions I entered our club at half past ten that night. I made my way through its Piazza San

Marco, where there were a few cheerful, but comparatively quiescent members, drinking and chatting; from the doorway of the bar, however, came trumpeting, hallooing noises. I went into the bar.

In the semi-darkness I saw about three groups of noisy men. The noisiest, standing beside the bar itself, consisted of Robert, Annette's father, Sir Harold Johnson and a couple more members of the club. Robert waved to me as I came up. 'Come and join us, Joe!' He and Annette's father and Sir Harold Johnson and the other two men were happily and obviously drunk. They were hallooing with drink – at least Robert and Sir Harold Johnson were.

Robert said, with a don't-careish effort at formality: 'I don't think you've met Sir Harold Johnson.'

Sir Harold Johnson shook hands with me. He was a tall, strong man, like an ex-rowing Blue.

As I looked at him for the first time closely, I was reminded of another public misconception about high bosses in the Civil Service, i.e. that they all look as if they have come from Eton and Balliol. Annette's father did, as a matter of fact. Sir Harold Johnson, I saw, did not. Definitely not. His face, long-jawed with fleshy-lidded bright blue eyes, could not have sprung from one of our oldest families. Though one might have seen its characteristic expression at a racecourse – the expression, with lids momentarily half-dropped and mouth drawn knowingly down at the corners, of a man just about to take a trick – it would not have been *inside* the Royal Enclosure. I took to him immediately.

Robert had obviously taken to him. Handing me a large glass of port that I had never asked for, Robert looked at him and said to me:

'You ought to know he's read all our novels. In fact he's read practically *all* novels.'

I looked at Sir Harold Johnson, staggered, and remained standing beside him.

He looked at Robert steadily.

'Very remarkable, very remarkable,' said Robert, having some trouble with his r's.

321

I drank some of my port.

Robert glanced at everybody else's glasses and turned to the bar to order some refills.

Sir Harold Johnson now looked steadily at me.

'I'm not going to talk to you about novels,' he said. 'I've talked enough about novels this evening.'

I nodded my head.

'I'm interested in your job,' he said. He nodded his head in the direction of Robert. 'You chaps must have a very interesting job. People! Seeing people.'

I began to nod again.

Suddenly his eyelids half-dropped and his mouth drew down at the corners. 'Seeing them as ectomorphs and mesomorphs!'

Robert's voice came over my shoulder. 'It's all right – he's picked *that* up from Huxley's *Perennial Philosophy*!'

Sir Harold Johnson was watching me as if he were waiting to see if I knew he had got endomorphs up his sleeve. I said:

'Yes.'

'Well?'

Another nod was out of the question. I said: 'I think there's something in it.'

His eyes remained steady for a moment, and then a smile seemed to spread slowly round his long jaw. 'What do you think of this?' he said, and, looking up in the air, recited:

> Let me have men about me who are thin,
> Rough-headed men and such as wake o' nights.
> Yond Cassius has a fat and well-fed look.
> He thinks too much – such men are dangerous.

Everyone standing round laughed.

Triumphantly Sir Harold Johnson finished his port and handed his glass to Robert for some more. He swayed.

Annette's father, on whom drink appeared to have had a silencing effect, proposed that we should all sit down. He and the others moved towards some chairs. Sir Harold Johnson stayed waiting for his next drink. Looking down at me, with the cheerful expression of a man who has just taken a trick, he said:

'Was that quotation up your street?'

I said it was.

He did not move. Robert handed another glass of port to him – and another to me. Sir Harold Johnson went on staring down at me. At last he said:

'You know what *you* want to do?'

I shook my head, waiting . . .

'Get rid of your inhibitions!'

8

A Silver Rupee

I did not say anything to Elspeth immediately about getting married, but I felt that she must sense my new internal stability. We spent a most enjoyable week-end. I had told her I was going to tell Robert about us, and she asked me what he said.

'He was very pleased,' I said. 'He told me I was lucky . . .'

Elspeth said, out of the blue as far as I was concerned: 'I told Joan.'

Joan was Elspeth's friend on the staff of her school. I said: 'And what did *she* say?'

'Oh, I think *she* seemed pleased . . .'

The following evening I did a thing that I very rarely did. Instead of walking straight up the hill from the bus-stop, I dropped in at a public-house for a drink on my own. The saloon bar was large but at that time of day it was likely to be deserted. I was prepared to see a workman chatting over a pint of beer with a barmaid, or a couple munching pork pie and potato salad, and to hear the wireless playing what sounded unremittingly like the Light Programme. I glanced round – and saw Harry. He was sitting at a small table, opposite a man who had his back to me.

'Joe!' he called, in his high sweet voice. 'Come and join us!'

I went.

'This is a surprise for you,' said Harry, as I got to the table and his companion turned towards me.

His companion was our hall-porter.

'You know Jamie Gordon,' Harry went on with cheerful effrontery. 'Jamie used to be a lab-attendant at the first anatomy lab I ever attended.'

I looked at Gordon – I had not recognized him at first because he was not in his uniform.

'It's my day off, sir,' he said, grinning. In ordinary clothes he looked slightly less like a big cheeky rabbit, but that was not saying much.

I pulled up a chair to the table. I looked at Harry, and then at our hall-porter. So much for Elspeth and me trying to keep Harry from knowing what we were up to!

'I ran into Jamie,' Harry explained, 'just outside the pub.'

I did not know what I was expected to say to that.

The wireless said: 'This is the Light Programme,' as if it were necessary.

However, when Harry went to the bar to buy a round of drinks, I could have sworn he set up slightly less whirling disturbance in the air.

And when I stood up to leave after we had finished the drinks, he said: 'Come in and see us soon,' in a slightly lower voice than usual.

I could not help smiling. I had caught a glimpse in Harry's small, inquisitive, brown eyes of something I had rarely seen there before – shame.

The next day I told Robert about the incident. Robert had for some time shown a peculiar passion for hearing about Harry's manoeuvres – I could only suspect he was thinking of someone like Harry as a character for his next novel. On this occasion, however, Robert's passion seemed to be less. He scarcely waited for me to finish before he said:

'Did you know that Elspeth had been talking to Annette about her career?'

'No,' I said. 'And I don't see what help Annette could be, anyway.'

'The situation, old boy, is the other way about. Elspeth has been seeing fit to give Annette help, if that's what you choose to call it.' He paused. 'Elspeth has been asking Annette why she, Annette, doesn't become a teacher.'

'What sort of a teacher?'

'The same sort of teacher,' Robert said crossly, 'as she, Elspeth, is.'

You will remember the emotion with which I first perceived that Elspeth was a person who existed in her own right outside the bounds of my egocentric cosmos, that she was a living, whole, human person – and what a delightful one, at that! – separate, independent, and so on . . . Well, it is one thing to perceive that the girl at the other end of one's problem is a living, whole, human person, separate, independent, and so on: it is another to contemplate her taking separate, independent action in one's friends' affairs.

Robert had been taking it as settled, now that Annette was married to him, that she would give up exercising moral choice over careers and occupy herself with social duties on his behalf. His projected series of grand dinner-parties, I was happy to note, had already begun. Elspeth and I had been to one of them – wonderful food from Fortnum's and the men all in dinner-jackets. (Annette, somewhat startlingly, had worn her wedding-dress.)

'What are you going to do about it?' I asked him.

Robert shrugged his shoulders. 'I don't know.' He looked away. 'I think perhaps you might have a word with Elspeth.'

I thought perhaps I should have to.

In general I was convinced that 'speaking' to people was liable to do more harm than good. In this particular case, it suddenly occurred to me after I had left Robert, it might also bring worse things to light. Suppose that in their state of admiring and envying each other, these two girls had *exchanged* suggestions – suppose that in return for Elspeth's suggestion Annette should become a school-teacher, Annette had suggested that Elspeth should take a degree in philosophy. I saw myself married to a wife who kept going out every evening to lectures at a Polytechnic. What a thought! What a marriage! I decided not to 'speak' to Elspeth. Undesirable ideas are best left unwatered by discussion.

And so Elspeth and I came to Christmas, nearly a year since we first met. We were each going to spend the holiday with our families – should I ask her before or after? I had not made up my mind. It was to be one or the other, anyway. I was now so certain that I was going to marry her that I had been to my tailor's and ordered a new overcoat and new evening-clothes, on the grounds that if I did not get them before I was married, I should never be able to afford them after.

On the last evening before we went away, Elspeth came to stay at my flat. She was just thinking it was time to start cooking the dinner when, to our embarrassment, the doorbell rang. We straightened ourselves up and went to the door. It was Harry.

We were surprised. Since the occasion when I had found him drinking with Gordon, the hall-porter, Harry had kept out of my way. Elspeth had seen Barbara from time to time down at Bethnal Green, but we had not been invited to their house.

'Can I come in?' Harry said.

'Of course.'

Harry's face looked less pink than usual. 'I've got something for you,' he said nervously. 'I expected I'd find Elspeth here too.' He was carrying a parcel. 'Just some Christmas presents for you both.'

The presents were a bottle of whisky for me and a bottle of scent for Elspeth. It was the brand of whisky I liked best and the most chic and expensive kind of scent. Both Elspeth and I were touched.

'Let's open the whisky!' I cried.

Elspeth laughed at me. 'Let's open the scent!'

While Elspeth took the scent into my bedroom, I poured out some large drinks. Harry was satisfied. He sat down fatly on the sofa, his face as pink again as ever.

'Barbara was sorry she couldn't come,' he said. 'She's gone to listen to somebody giving a paper at the B.M.A.'

If I knew anything about it, Barbara had never been consulted. 'M'm,' I said.

Elspeth came in and we smelt the scent. 'I'll sit by you,' she said to Harry. He sprang up politely, and a whirling gust of air set up.

We started to drink. Harry, in high spirits now, seemed determined to show us how affectionate and uninquisitive he was. I

327

have to say that he succeeded. You see, for the present he really was affectionate and uninquisitive.

We invited him to stay for supper. He accepted. We had a huge dish of eggs and bacon. By the time we were drinking our coffee our rapprochement was complete, in fact perfect.

In a gust of boundless, selfless, uninquisitive concern for our happiness, Harry said to us:

'*When are you two going to get married?*'

I saw Elspeth blush, and my confusion was so unbearable that I looked down at the table and could scarcely form an intelligible reply. In fact I cannot remember what I did reply. Somehow we managed to pass the hiatus over. But I swore to myself that I would ask Elspeth to marry me *immediately* I got back from the holiday. 'I really can't let that happen again,' I kept saying to myself, not only that night but every time during the following week at home when I remembered it.

Actually Harry, when he left us that night, said to me while he was putting on his overcoat:

'I'm glad you didn't take it amiss when I said that.' He wagged his globe-shaped head with boyish satisfaction. 'I thought I'd chance my arm.'

At home my mother, though occasionally permitting herself an oblique reference to 'your Elspeth', made it clear that nothing would persuade her – not that she had any need to fear persuasion from me – to mention my marrying Elspeth. With my father I had no private discussion. His clerical duties, i.e. preparing his sermons, delivering them and visiting his parishioners, resulted, as always, in his being either *incommunicado* or not.

I had resolved to ask Elspeth to marry me immediately I got back. I did.

Elspeth came round to my flat on the evening of our return to London. I still kept remembering Harry's kindly, hopeful, selfless, uninquisitive question . . . We were washing up after dinner, or rather Elspeth was washing up while I changed the living-room back from dining-room to sitting-room. We were conversing while

Elspeth stood at the sink and I moved to and fro. The emotion I was feeling!

We were supposed to be talking about our plans for the week-end. Above the rattle of crockery in the sink, Elspeth was shouting to me:

'I think we ought to stay in, just by ourselves, this week-end.'

'I think,' I shouted back, 'we ought to get married as quickly as possible, don't you?'

'*What?*' Something splashed into the water. She sounded amazed. I felt amazed.

I went into the kitchen – it was a very small kitchen. 'I think,' I said, 'we ought to get married as quickly as possible, don't you?'

She had turned from the sink to look at me. Her pale complexion was suffused with carmine, her sparkling blue eyes seemed to have gone smaller. Looking at me she saw the truth of my generalization, that when somebody says something and you cannot believe your ears, they certainly have said it.

Her lips were moving, the lines at the corners of her mouth flashed in and out. 'Well, yes . . .' I rushed to embrace her.

There was a flap, which came down from a cupboard to form a table, that served as an obstacle between the door and the sink. 'My darling!' I cried, putting one hand on her waist and rubbing my hip with the other.

We kissed each other.

'My darling!' 'My darling!' We kissed each other again. She was fumbling to take off her rubber washing-up gloves.

'Darling, I love you,' I cried. 'I want us to be married as quickly as possible.'

She looked at me. Tears were coming into her eyes.

'For ever,' I said.

'Oh yes, that's what I want, too . . .'

I lifted the flap so that we could get past. 'Let's go and sit down!'

She managed to get the gloves off and left them on top of the refrigerator.

We went and sat on the sofa and kissed each other many times. 'Isn't it wonderful?' I said.

Elspeth nodded her head.

'I love you,' I said.

She touched my lips with the tip of her middle finger.

'I do so want us to be married.'

'Yes . . .' she whispered.

After a while she looked down at her lap. 'But you didn't ask me,' she said.

'Didn't ask you what?'

'Well, if I'd marry you.'

'Oh dear! I wanted to come to the point as quickly as possible.'

She looked back at me. The corners of her mouth showed a fleeting grin.

'I thought,' I said, 'you *would* marry me . . .'

She was smiling.

'Didn't you think I'd marry *you*?' I asked.

She stopped smiling. 'Yes, I did to begin with, but I began to wonder . . .'

'But I always meant to.' I took hold of her hand.

'Darling.'

This kind of conversation went on for some time, but gradually it became less romantic and more practical. I wanted to settle where and when we were to get married. I wanted to be married by a registrar.

'The alternative,' I said, 'if we were to be married in a church, would be to be married by my father. We should have to tell him, and he'd volunteer to do it. I really couldn't face that.'

Both Elspeth and I were unbelievers. If we asked my father to marry us, I knew he would conclude that somewhere in us lay the seed of belief. I did not like the idea of unbelievers taking advantage of believers any more than I liked the idea of believers taking advantage of unbelievers.

'At a registry office,' I said, squeezing Elspeth's hand, 'we can get married sooner.'

Elspeth squeezed my hand in return.

In the end we decided to get married at a registry office without telling anyone but the witnesses. An exciting, romantic atmosphere came back into the conversation. (Perhaps I ought to say that in our romantic excitement we innocently overlooked the construction that some people – I will not say what sort of people – put on marriages that take place in a hurry.)

Next morning I set about making arrangements to marry Elspeth. I had some surprises. When I asked the registrar how soon we could get married, I learnt that for £3 6s. 9d. I could get married in two days' time.

And then I took Elspeth to buy a wedding-ring. Robert and I had a habit of looking in the windows of jewellers' shops. (I thought we were odd until I did a day's count of the relative numbers of men and women who were doing the same as us.) Robert had a particular taste for sapphires. I chose diamonds that were not pure white, especially pinkish ones. The rings we were used to staring at often cost thousands of pounds, though of course I knew there were presentable rings to be had for hundreds or even tens of pounds. I had no idea that wedding rings were to be had for units of pounds.

'It's incredible,' I said to Robert, 'you can get married in no time at all, for next to no money!'

'Society sees to it that getting married is made easy.'

'I'll say it does.' We used to entertain ourselves with the concept of The Pressure of Society. As far as getting married was concerned, it seemed to me now that you had only got to make the smallest first move, and the pressure of society rushed you through the next before you knew what you were doing. No wonder some bridegrooms looked white as a sheet on their wedding-day – finding themselves at the ceremony perhaps a good six months, perhaps a good six years, before they meant to.

Four days later Elspeth and I got married. I did not look specially white in the face nor did Elspeth. But Robert and Annette did.

Elspeth and I arrived at the registry office about ten minutes late, because we had begun our preparations by spending too long over titivating my flat for the reception. It was decorated with large branches of mimosa which we had been keeping cool in the bath-room till the last moment. There was a bottle of champagne and a luscious cake from a French shop in Soho. The guests, our witnesses, were Robert, Annette and Elspeth's school-teacher friend, Joan.

Anyway, we arrived at the registry office, and there in the waiting-room we found Robert, Annette, and Joan. I had never seen Joan before, and expecting her to be the plain partner in the alliance, was surprised to find her quite as pretty as Elspeth. We were ten minutes late. Annette looked pale. Robert looked chalky.

The ceremony seemed to be over in no time, and Elspeth and I were delighted with the result. The thin gold ring was on her finger – never, on any account, to be taken off, I told her. We got into a taxi and embraced each other all the way home. Married! Married for good! I got out of the taxi first, and while I was paying the driver saw Elspeth pause, before she got out, to pick something off the floor.

'Look what I've found!' she cried, holding out her palm for me to see what was in it.

It was a small coin, silver, stamped *1 Rupee*.

The taxi drove away leaving us standing there, smiling with delight. It was an omen. It was too fantastic to be anything but an omen.

'Darling, keep it!'

'Of course I shall,' Elspeth said, putting it in her bag.

Hand in hand we went quickly to the lift, so as to get up to the flat before the others arrived. When we opened the door the smell of the mimosa was overpowering.

The reception was a success. The guests ate some of the cake and drank all the champagne, and then did not go away. It is diffi-cult to know what to drink after champagne at five in the after-noon, if your host has not got more champagne: they all said they would like some tea. I did not hurry them, I was so happy. I was triumphant, if it comes to that. They had all said I could not get married, but I could. I had done it.

Suddenly, looking at Robert, I realized why he had looked

chalky. When we were ten minutes late he must have thought I was not going to turn up. Silly fellow!

As soon as they were gone, Elspeth carried the telephone into the room and we began sending telegrams to our families and ringing up our friends. While Elspeth was talking on the telephone, I was drafting the notice of marriage for *The Times* and the *Daily Telegraph*. I felt in this case it ought to appear surrounded by a special border like that on a greetings telegram. Or possibly just encircled by a wreath of laurels. They had said that I could not get married, that I had missed the boat. Not a bit of it. I was on the boat. I looked at Elspeth. What a boat! My boat . . .

Elspeth was ringing Harry and Barbara.

'It's Barbara,' she said, handing the receiver to me. 'She wants to congratulate you.'

'Well she may!' I whispered to Elspeth. Then I said: 'Hello, Barbara. What do you think of the news? Isn't it wonderful.'

'It really is. Congratulations, Joe.'

'I've pulled it off. What do you think of that?'

'Splendid,' she said.

'I've got married after all.'

At that I heard Barbara laugh. 'Yes, you have, Joe,' she said. 'But you have to remember *getting* married is very different from *being* married.'

'What!' I cried. And then added: 'Well, of course it is. I can see that all right.'

'You have my congratulations, all the same,' she said.

I handed the receiver back to Elspeth. 'It's your turn to talk to her now,' I said with my hand over the mouthpiece.

I did not listen to what Elspeth was saying to her. Of course there was a difference between *getting* married and *being* married. Or was there? What the hell did Barbara mean?

Part Three

I

Newly-Wed

We awoke next morning before the alarm went off, and I stretched out to find the catch on top of the clock which prevented the bell from ringing. There was scarcely any light coming through the gap in the curtains. The air in the room seemed close and scented. I rolled quietly back into my place.

Elspeth was stirring. As it were in sleep, her hand came on to my waist and her breasts brushed across my chest. I kissed her on the eyelids.

'Darling,' she murmured.

'My wife.'

She stretched a little, away from me, and then came back. 'I feel so sleepy . . .'

I whispered 'So do I', more not to disturb the warm drowsy atmosphere than to express the whole truth. In one way I felt sleepy: in another I was obviously not. Our first morning married. My thoughts drifted round the idea for a few moments, and then began to circle round another idea. I put my hand on the small of her back and pressed.

Everything was so quiet that I could hear the clock ticking.

We stayed for a while, just touching each other. I kissed her again.

'I feel so sleepy,' she murmured in a different way.

I whispered: 'I'll go very, very gently. So that it won't wake you up.'

I felt her kiss my shoulder.

With Elspeth lying drowsily, I acted according to my stated intention; but of course the fallacy in it began to assert itself, and

337

soon she could no longer seem to be asleep. As I did not suppose either of us had ever thought she could, I was not specially conscience-stricken – after all, what nicer way was there, I asked myself on her behalf, of coming awake.

In due course we both came fully awake. Our first morning married . . . I had time now to consider it at leisure. When I thought I must be getting a bit heavy, I raised myself on my elbows and looked at Elspeth. She smiled at me. Her dark hair was strewn across her forehead and I caught a glimmer of light from her eyes. I thought of a quotation, something about on such a morning it being bliss to be alive, and kissed her enthusiastically under the chin from one ear to the other. Having read physics at Oxford and not English Literature, I was never able to lay my hands quickly and accurately on quotations; yet I never felt it held me back.

'Goodness, it's warm in here,' I said, pushing off the bed-clothes. I switched the light on.

Elspeth said: 'We forgot to take the flowers out of the room last night.'

This explained why the air smelt so scented to me when I woke up. I smelt it now. 'A good job, too,' I said.

Elspeth laughed and put her arm round my neck. 'I don't mind, darling,' she said. 'You can't be having baths all the time.'

All the time. I made no comment on the implications of that. 'Just think!' I said, looking into her eyes, 'you're here to stay . . .'

Although I was looking into her eyes, I noticed she was yawning. I exclaimed.

Elspeth blushed. 'It wasn't a yawn, really.'

'I'd like to know what else it was.'

She glanced away with an expression so melting, as if I had touched some secret she was keeping, that I kissed her again.

After that I said: 'Now I really must get up and have a bath. Do you realize what time it is?'

Though it was our first morning married, we had both got to go to work as usual. The alarm clock, with its bell put out of action,

338

had given a frustrated click a quarter of an hour ago. I jumped out of bed, gave Elspeth a parting slap, and went to the bathroom. We were already late.

I was late getting to the office. I sent for Froggatt, in order to put the news of my changed status into the official grapevine. To my mind it was worthy of an office notice, being much more piquant than the records of transfer and promotion which formed the typical content of Froggatt's communications. Anyway, *I* was transferred, *I* was promoted. Transferred to respectability, promoted to the ranks of decent ordinary men. Married!

Froggatt looked at me with his drooping, bloodhound eyes and permitted his long face a momentary gleam of amusement.

'May I be the first person here to congratulate you?' he said, in the musical lugubrious tone wherein he combined to perfection that mixture of superficial deference and underlying opposite which characterizes the Executive Class.

'You may,' I said. I was delighted to see his feeling for his status – 'the first person here' – peeping through his genuine congratulation. 'Thank you.'

'I take it you'll inform Accounts.'

'Accounts,' I said.

'You'll have a different code number for tax purposes now,' he said. 'As I'm sure you know.'

I tried to look as if I did know.

'In fact you'll get a rebate for the whole of the present tax-year, won't you? As from last April.'

I had often been irritated by Froggatt's getting at loggerheads with the inhabitants of the snake-pit, but at moments such as this I forgave him. This kind of support was just what an S.E.O. was for.

'If you like,' he said, 'I'll notify Accounts. Then they can get in touch with you.'

'Excellent.' In the past Accounts' getting into touch with me had usually meant they were going to try and disallow the taxi-fares on my claims for travel expenses.

When Froggatt had gone, I reflected on how my absence of

interest in money had been shown up. Robert was always telling me that I did not think enough about money; and for Robert to tell was for Robert to reproach. Apropos of income tax, I did know that the possibility of claiming a full year's rebate brought the national marriage rate to its peak in March, but I had never thought of taking advantage of it myself.

I felt deflated, even chastened. I saw that one of my many moral defects was now going to have greater significance. I liked money very much when it came to me. The trouble was that I never thought hard about how to make it come to me. With a wife to keep I had clearly got to think about how to make it come to me. How many times as cheaply could two live as one? I asked myself. Just under half was my estimate.

I rang up Accounts instead of waiting for them to ring me.

After that I deliberately sat for five minutes trying to think hard about money. I wished it did not happen to be the day when Robert had seen fit to stay at home to correct the proofs of his new novel, because I could have done with his advice, despite its reproachful tone, on how to make money come to me. I reflected on the hastiness with which I had persuaded Elspeth to give up being a school-teacher, not that she needed much persuasion or that I felt the least inclined to change my mind. I wanted no more of being roused by an alarm clock so that she could set out for Bethnal Green; and I wanted to come home in the evening certain of finding her there already, possibly already cooking something delicious for dinner. You may think it had not taken me long to accept the decent, odrinary man's idea of married life. That is what I thought.

It was clear to me that as a civil servant I could never make money come to me. Robert and I used to comment with surprise on the fact that we had never been offered any bribes, even during the war when we had in our gift, so to speak, civilian jobs for people who were liable for military service. The nearest we came to it was when Air Marshals came to see us about jobs for their sons which would, in the national interest of course, keep the boys away from flying. What was the bribe there? The mateyness of an Air

Marshal's manner, the glances, as between equals, from his glaring *beaux yeux*. Not, as Robert would say, a bribe and a half, that.

I supposed there was promotion to be thought of. With Murray-Hamilton and Spinks in the saddle, not, as Eliza Doolittle said, likely. Anyway, I could not be promoted without doing a different job.

Which left me with my art as a source of money. I thought of the excellent press my last novel had got; and then I thought of my publisher's most recent half-yearly statement of royalties. Robert still insisted that the book was a minor masterpiece. My publisher's half-yearly statement of royalties insisted on a minor balance. Of course I consoled myself again with the fact that it is masterpieces, minor or not, that last. The difficulty, as I saw it now, was how was *I* to last? I was nearly at the end of another novel, in the same vein as the previous one. I was pretty happy about it. I had written just what I wanted to write, and I had hit off exactly what I wanted to say – that, in case anybody would like to know, is how original works are written. Robert had identified it as yet another minor masterpiece.

Now, what was to be done? I had been told often enough. I had plenty of friends who were willing to tell me, friends who were in a position, were I to do what they told me, to help produce the result I desired. By that I mean friends in the film industry and the magazine industry. They admired my talent. While having to say that my minor masterpieces were not the slightest use to them, they had not the slightest doubt that I had the talent to provide just what they were looking for. Now you see what I am getting at. What I was required to write was not just what *I* wanted to write, but just what *they* wanted me to write. In other words, crude words, I was required to prostitute my art.

With only the slightest change in tone, in attitude, in subject, I could provide just what was wanted – so ran the argument. With only the slightest change, I could be a prostitute. I was not surprised by the argument, since one of the underlying themes of women's magazine stories, and obviously one of the dearest themes to their readers, was that all women, with only the slightest change, could be prostitutes. Let them try it! was all I could say, speaking as their artistic counterpart.

Speaking as their artistic counterpart, I can only say I believe it is nothing like as easy as it sounds to prostitute oneself. One has to have the talent for it, and if one is born without that talent, one had better stick, so to speak, to monogamy. One's talent, be it for communicating truth or untruth, is nothing like so flexible as people think. I could not decide which people struck me as the more unrealistic, writers who were not born with the talent for pleasing all men planning to write best-sellers, or writers of best-sellers planning to go somewhere, such as a purifying island in the South Seas, to write a serious work of art. If only one could be born all things! I thought. I knew it was no use my setting out to prostitute my talent because my talent would not stretch that far. No, I repeat, it is not as easy to be a prostitute as everyone thinks. In fact, it is jolly difficult. When I saw those girls on the streets, I took off my hat to them. They were doing something I could not do.

My meditations on how to make money come to me were at an end. Robert was wrong in thinking I was incapable of thinking hard enough about it. What I was incapable of, to my regret, was thinking on the right lines. I felt very discouraged. I pressed the bell for my P.A. to bring in my morning's work. While I was waiting for her to come, I wrote on my scribbling pad: 'Go to bank.'

I needed some cash with which to take Harry and Barbara out to dinner. We had invited them earlier in the week, without telling them that by then we should be married. Our reasons were sentiment. We could never forget that it was under their roof that we had met for the first time – tenderest recollections moved us, of dancing at their New Year's Eve Party, of 'The Dark-town Strutters' Ball' in which I hauled Elspeth up from the floor and first looked into her eyes – 'This is the one for me!' And then later, supreme cause for our gratitude, Harry's crucial question, asked out of selfless, uninquisitive affection for us: 'When are you two going to get married?' There was no argument between Elspeth and me about whom we should take out to dinner on our first day married. Thank goodness for Harry and Barbara! was how we expressed our feelings towards them in anticipation of seeing them.

It happened that before they arrived, Elspeth and I expressed our feelings towards each other. We mixed ourselves some martinis and then set about bathing and changing – a procedure fraught with the likelihood of expressing marital feeling. I was standing in my vest and shorts, getting a clean shirt out of a drawer, when Elspeth came from the bathroom, holding a towel in front of her. The towel gave her a delightful air of modesty and unconcern.

'That looks nice,' I said as she went past.

She pretended not to hear.

'It would be wonderful just to see a bit more,' I said, and kissed her on the shoulder.

She turned to look at me. Without make-up her complexion had a glossy sheen: there were damp curls of hair on her temples.

'Darling!' I put my arms round her.

'The towel's damp.'

I took it away.

Her cheeks went pink. 'Darling, you know what time it is?'

'Indeed I do.'

I pushed her quietly backwards to the bed. 'You're wonderful!' I whispered, leaning over her.

'Harry and Barbara'll be at the door at any moment.'

'I'm practically at it, now.'

'Darling!'

We had to be quick. At any moment the doorbell might ring and we could not pretend we were out. I began to sweat. A race against time. A race against time.

We won it.

'Oh!' I said.

Elspeth was quiet.

'Well . . .' I murmured. For a few moments we were both quiet. I glanced at Elspeth – just at the moment to catch her yawning. We burst into laughter.

'Good Heavens! Just look at the time!' On the chest of drawers

I saw the remainder of the drink I had been carrying round with me while I got dressed. I drank it. I handed Elspeth hers and she sat up and drank it. We kissed each other; and then we began to rush into our clothes.

'They'll be here any minute.'

We saw each other in a mirror, looking pink in the face. I was knotting my tie.

The doorbell rang.

'There they are.' I put on my jacket, kissed Elspeth's bare arm, and ran to let in Barbara and Harry.

Harry and Barbara stared at me briefly: I suppose I stared briefly at them – after all, there was no reason why I should not. 'Come in!' I cried. 'You wonderful pair . . .' I was still thinking, Thank goodness for Harry and Barbara! I kissed Barbara on the cheek and shook Harry's hand. They followed me into the living-room. They congratulated me again on my new status.

I was just pouring some drinks for them when Elspeth came in. All three of us now stared briefly at her. She looked sparkling – in my eyes her whole outline seemed to shimmer – and the moment I caught her glance I knew that our expression of marital feeling, in combination with a couple of martinis, had produced one of those bursts of hilarity-cum-elation that are impossible to hide.

'I'm afraid we've had a drink already,' I said, as I handed glasses to Harry and Barbara.

'So I see,' said Barbara with a smile.

Elspeth came and stood beside me and I felt her elbow brush against mine. Barbara saw it and went on smiling. There was nothing wrong with Barbara's smile, and yet somehow it contrasted with Elspeth's and mine. I looked at Harry, to see how he was reacting.

'Is that some of your new manuscript?' he said, with an artlessly innocent glance sideways at a sheaf of papers on the table.

'Yes,' I said.

Harry turned his head to look at it steadily and longingly. He was wearing a new very dark grey suit, and his great girth, encased in almost black and momentarily unrotating, seemed to have a faintly sinister quality that was missing when it was light and on the move.

'Yes,' I repeated, in a disinterested tone. 'That's the first draft of Part I.'

Harry waited. He waited for me to ask him if he would like to read it. I let him go on waiting. I had no intention of letting him read a word of it before publication.

'You do work hard,' said Barbara.

'Have to,' I said. 'If I don't work, I don't eat.'

Barbara finished her martini. Smiling, she handed me her glass.

'I suppose now I'm married,' I said, 'I can still go on eating if Elspeth works – happy thought . . .'

'Is Elspeth going to go on working?'

Though my back was turned to her, I could tell this must be a key question in Barbara's catechism – I recognized the 'I-know-you-better-than-you-know-yourself' sort of tone. I swished the stirring rod vigorously in the jug so that the ice cubes clinked and clattered.

I turned back with Barbara's drink. With her left hand she was fingering her big topaz and diamond brooch. With her handsome topaz-and-diamond-coloured eyes she was giving Elspeth a look of friendly interest. As she took the drink from me she switched the look to me.

'I'm delighted that you've got married,' she began, 'and I hope you'll both be very happy – I'm sure you will – but I'm still not sure I quite understand . . . Tell me, Joe, what did you get married *for*?'

I gave the contents of the jug a splendid swish and said:

'Whadda ya think?'

Barbara's expression did not change. On the other hand, Harry's did. I just happened to notice him give her an odd glance – he looked momentarily hunted . . . I thought I knew why. I guessed it. My answer did not go for his marriage. Poor old Harry!

Barbara tasted her drink. 'You've made this very dry.'

'You've got to catch up with us.' I glanced at Elspeth's complexion, which was now radiantly pink.

Barbara laughed. 'I doubt if we shall!'

We took them to a restaurant where we could dance. Elspeth and I danced together.

'I'm afraid we're in disgrace,' I said. 'They're rather cross with us.'

Elspeth giggled.

'I know we've not behaved in good taste, but between friends it oughtn't to matter. Look at the times when we've called on Robert and Annette, and they'd practically only just –'

Elspeth giggled again.

I went on – 'And we didn't take umbrage like this.' I thought about Robert and Annette. 'In fact I envied them. I wished it were us.'

Elspeth rubbed her cheek against mine. 'Never mind darling, I don't think you've done the wrong thing.'

I laughed and looked at her. 'With a bit of luck I'll do it again before the night's out.'

Elspeth moved slightly away from me. 'Oh no . . . !'

'Poor old Harry and Barbara,' I said.

'"Tell me, Joe,"' said Elspeth, '"what did you get married *for*?"'

The music stopped and we returned to our places. I ordered another round of brandies. I was beginning to feel tired, and I noticed that shadows were beginning to appear under Elspeth's eyes. Harry and Barbara did not look tired.

Elspeth and Barbara began to talk to each other, and Harry talked to me. First of all he gave me a quick, bright glance, and then said:

'You must be thinking about your future, now.'

His baggy eyes were sparkling, I thought, as if he were in possession of some peculiarly private information. Looking inordinately shrewd, he said: 'Your long-term future.'

'Oh, I suppose you mean children . . .'

Harry grinned. 'I think some of your father's congregation think you've thought of that *already* . . . So your mother tells me.'

'Really!' I said. 'Oh, oh, oh!'

Harry said, slightly unconcernedly now: 'I meant you must be deciding whether you're going to stay on with Robert or not.'

Just to lead him on, I said: 'Yes.'

Harry looked away, diffidently. I waited. He looked back. 'Are you going to move away?'

I said: 'I don't think so.'

Harry drank some brandy. I noticed that Elspeth and Barbara seemed to be getting on very well together. I said to Harry:

'Why do you ask?'

'I was just wondering.' He paused. 'It must be very difficult for you.'

'Why difficult?'

'Difficult to see what there is for you, if you stay on.'

I was just on the point of drinking some more brandy myself. I halted, angrily. And then I saw that Harry's expression was unreservedly friendly and thoughtful.

I did not reply. How in God's name, I asked myself, did he know about my relations with Murray-Hamilton and Spinks? Had he managed to get to know Spinks? And if he had heard something about my future, what?

Harry was waiting for me to comment. I said:

'As long as Robert stays on, everything remains static, and that suits me.'

'And if he goes?'

I did not say anything.

Harry nodded his head as if I had.

I glanced at Elspeth. My wife – another mouth to feed in the future. And children, we were hoping to have children. In the long-term future more and more mouths to feed. That was what the phrase long-term future meant to me.

Harry looked at me. 'Anyway, you've got plenty of friends to make useful suggestions.'

I was touched.

At that moment the band stopped. Harry looked at Barbara, and said it was time for them to go home.

Our celebratory part was at an end. At the last moment, when we saw them into a taxi, there was a recrudescence of our sentimental regard for them. Thank goodness for Harry and Barbara! A little later, when we called a taxi for ourselves, we suddenly felt the evening had been a success.

'Goodness, I'm tired,' said Elspeth, leaning her head on my shoulder.

'So am I.'

She giggled. 'I'm a bit drunk, too.'

We embraced.

'What a pity,' I said, thoughtfully. 'Too tired and too drunk . . .'

Elspeth laughed.

When we got home we went straight to bed. We lay in each other's arms. My faintly regretful mood persisted. 'Too tired and too drunk . . .'

'We'd better go to sleep,' Elspeth murmured.

I waited a little while and then I whispered: 'I don't think I *am* too tired and too drunk . . .'

'I know . . .'

My regretful mood dispersed in no time. 'Darling!' I said.

I was not too tired and too drunk. I was just at the point when fatigue and the effects of alcohol counterbalance each other in such a way that one can go on and on, as it seems, indefinitely. There is a tide in the affairs of a man, I kept thinking as I went on and on, which, if taken at just the right point, like this, leads to a remarkable fortune. I felt uplifted by it, exalted. I got more than a bit above myself.

'This,' I said to Elspeth, 'this, this is what I married you for.'

'Oh,' she said. 'Oh.'

At last, at long last, I had opportunity to think over what I had said. I felt that I had taken advantage of Elspeth's ignorance about the tide in the affairs of a man. And not a bad thing, at that, I decided.

Elspeth was asleep.

2

Oil-Cloth on the Tables

At the beginning of March I thought Robert was looking more
pre-occupied than usual. It was always on the cards that Robert's
looking pre-occupied in my presence was the result of further snip-
ing from Spinks and Murray-Hamilton, but this time I judged that
it could not be so. During the last few weeks I had not been to a
meeting of any kind and had conducted no interviews.

Often when Robert was troubled by something he was provoked
to confide it through being stirred by something else. In this case
I happened to stir him by reporting a conversation between Elspeth
and me. It was a conversation I thought Robert ought to know
about. It had taken place the previous Sunday morning.

Elspeth and I had had an enjoyable breakfast in bed. We were
lying side by side. I was thinking that I ought to be reading the
Sunday newspapers. Elspeth yawned.

I raised myself on one elbow to look at her.

'Tired?' I said.

A look of amusement shone in her eyes.

'What?' I asked.

'You've got black circles.'

'They'll go when I get up.' I smiled at her.

'What are you smiling about?'

'I was just remembering the first book about Married Life that
I managed to get hold of when I was a boy. It said one of the most
important problems that faced a newly married couple was: "How
often?"' I laughed.

Elspeth laughed.

'Ridiculous,' I said.

'M'm,' said Elspeth.

I went on laughing. 'As if you arrive at that sort of thing by argument!'

Elspeth went on laughing.

Then she said: 'How often did it say?'

I was still laughing till that moment.

'How often did it say?' she said again.

'I don't remember. I don't think it said. It couldn't, anyway.'

'Oh,' Elspeth looked up at the ceiling. 'I read something like that that did say. You know, what a bride ought to expect . . .'

'Good gracious!' I was so surprised as to be gormless enough to add: 'How many was it?'

Elspeth said: 'Once a night for the first year, twice for the first six months, and three times a night for . . . you know, just the beginning.'

'Oh! Oh!' I cried.

'What's the matter?'

'What's the matter? Why, it's mad. *What* a programme! It'd be killing!'

Elspeth was silent.

I looked at her. 'Is this what you were expecting from *me*?'

Elspeth blushed.

'Oh!' I cried again, and lay down.

Then I said: 'You must have read it in a woman's magazine.'

Elspeth said: 'I don't think I did . . .'

'Well, it must have been written by a woman. No man could possibly have written it.'

Elspeth had nothing to say.

For a little while I too had nothing to say.

I jumped out of bed. 'I know how to settle this.'

'What are you going to do?' Elspeth asked suspiciously.

'Look it up.'

'You can't,' I heard Elspeth saying, as I went to a bookshelf in the living-room. I took down a book which was the record of a statistical inquiry that had recently been published and that, at the time, was being much talked about. *Sexual Behaviour in the Adult Human Male*. To my mind it was a pretty satisfactory inquiry, since it disclosed principles that had always been obvious to me, namely that people's range of possible sexual behaviour was much wider than it was officially supposed to be, and that people did not do what they publicly said they did. I furled over the pages now for an equally truthful disclosure of detail.

'Here it is,' I said, taking it to show Elspeth. 'Total outlet, active population – age forty, that's me; average 2.3 times per week.' I was delighted with the information: I even felt I might claim a small pat on the back. I repeated loudly: '2.3 times a week!'

Elspeth looked nettled, and tried not to see the graph at which I was pointing.

'Now, let's see,' I went on. 'Robert's forty-five. 1.8. Think of that! Poor Annette . . . Just think of one point eight per week!'

'I'm not going to,' said Elspeth. 'And I think you ought to stop thinking about it.'

I was sitting on the bed beside her, with the book in my lap. She raised herself and turned over a wad of pages before I could stop her.

'Thought-control,' I said.

She was not listening. She had caught sight of what was on the new page. 'I don't remember this bit,' she said, in a tone that was different.

'Two point three,' I said, slipping my arm round her back.

She pretended not to hear me. My attention was caught by the lobe of her ear, peeping between two dark curls. The hand with which she was holding the book was touching me.

Of course, deliberately, I only reported to Robert the first part of the conversation to begin with, up to 'once a night for the first year, twice for the first six months, and three times at the beginning'.

'Good God,' he said.

He was standing between the top corner of my desk and the

window, where the leads from my telephone and buzzer dropped to the skirting.

'I thought you ought to know,' I said. 'I didn't want you to be living in a fool's paradise.'

'That's the most daunting piece of news I've heard for a long time,' he said, and moved heavily towards my easy chair, catching his feet in the wires and bringing the telephone and buzzer crashing to the floor. I picked them up and stood by the window while he sat down. I let him suffer for a little while.

'Extraordinarily daunting,' he muttered. And then: 'What did you say?'

'Oh,' I said, putting on the tone of loftiness and confidence in which he normally addressed me, 'I saw my way through it quite rapidly.'

'What did you do?' he asked, for once in the tone in which I normally addressed him.

'I checked it in the standard work of reference.'

'What in God's name is that?'

I went on with the account of my conversation with Elspeth. Robert agreed with me that it must have been written by a woman. 'Or a man who ought to be a woman,' he said, impatiently waiting for me to come to the figures.

I watched him when I came to the 1.8. Instantly his eyes flickered with a recognizable glint, secretive, prudish and triumphant.

I laughed without saying anything.

Robert laughed without saying anything.

We were both silent for a while. Our laughter died away, as did our feeling of being daunted. It was at this moment that Robert's mood changed over unpredictably. He suddenly came out with what had been troubling him.

'Annette's going on with this idea of taking Elspeth's job when Elspeth gives it up.'

I stared at him. Elspeth had been keeping it dark from me.

'You poor old thing,' I said.

Robert shook his head gloomily. 'It's a moral choice,' he said. 'She sees it as a moral choice.'

'You poor old thing,' I repeated.

When I got home that evening, I reproached Elspeth. She said:

'I did tell you once and it upset you. Anyway, nothing very much had happened. I shall have to finish out my term's notice – we couldn't work an exchange in the middle of term. Whether Annette will get my job isn't decided.' Elspeth paused. 'She still wants it. She's been going ahead to try to get it.'

I asked how far she had gone ahead.

'She's got on to the L.C.C. about it, and she's having an interview with the headmistress. There's a terrific shortage. They'll let her come "on supply", if not as a permanent member of the staff. She's having her interview with the headmistress next week.'

I decided to talk to Annette.

Elspeth arranged a meeting that she considered would look unarranged. Sometimes when I had a light afternoon at the office I left early and met Elspeth out of school. I met her the afternoon Annette had an interview with the headmistress.

I arrived at the school gates just before Elspeth and Annette came out. It was a cold blustery afternoon with patches of icy drizzle carried in the wind. The darkness of the sky made the hour of the day seem later than it was. A few yards further down the road stood a man in white overalls holding a pole with a circular sign on top of it to stop the traffic while children crossed the road. The children, as far as I could see, were well-fed and warmly dressed: and the prams that some of their mothers were pushing looked as new and grand as anything one saw in Hyde Park.

Suddenly a burst of emotion took me unawares. The impetus to make the change from what I remembered from my boyhood, when my father worked in a working-class place where under-fed mothers pushed their babies about in little carts made from orange-boxes mounted on broken wire-spoked wheels, had come from Socialists: and I *was* a Socialist. I had always felt that I was a Socialist by birth, by social origin. My burst of emotion – I may say it was as unusual to me as it was unexpected – came from feeling that I was *right* to be a Socialist. At the thought of feeling I was right to be anything whatsoever, I exclaimed, 'Good gracious!'

I saw Elspeth and Annette come through the gates. I kissed Elspeth. And then I kissed Annette.

'Tea now,' I asked them, 'or when we get back?'

They glanced at the dark sky and hugged their overcoats round them. 'Now,' said Elspeth. 'Now,' said Annette.

I said: 'We'll go to a Lyons or an A.B.C.'

Elspeth said: 'We won't, darling. We don't have Lyonses or A.B.C.'s down here.'

I felt ashamed of my ignorance and Annette burst into laughter. 'Lead us somewhere!' I said to Elspeth.

As we walked along I said to Annette: 'How did things go with the headmistress?'

'Very well.'

'Do you mean she'll have you?'

Annette smiled. 'If I decide I want to go.'

So she had not decided? I advised myself to hold back from argument.

Elspeth led us to a café behind a large window that was too steamed-up for us to see what was inside. It turned out to be a big place, the inner half a step lower than the outer, filled with tables covered in old-fashioned oil-cloth. All the tables were made to take six persons at least.

The girls settled down and I went up to a counter with its back to the large window. There was a burly man in a white apron behind the counter: on a shelf to one side of him was a small wireless set, playing popular jazz. The tea cost twopence a cup less than the lowest price at which I had previously been led to believe it could be profitably served in a café. I thought the burly man in the white apron must be a good chap. I bought some solid-looking buns.

The girls, like all the girls I had ever known, ate heartily.

'What a nice place!' said Annette. 'If I come to work down here I shall come here for tea every day.'

'What on earth for?' I asked.

'I feel at home here.'

I said: 'It can't be very like any home *you*'ve been used to.'

Annette laughed. 'Not in the material sense. The material sense isn't important to me.'

'It would be to most of the people sitting at these other tables, if they were offered the chance of having their tea every day in the sort of surroundings you're used to.'

'Exactly. One makes one's choice for one's self.' Her tone was light but firm. I noticed, now that she had loosened her overcoat, that she had gone back to the dark knitted jumper she used to wear all the time before she married Robert. 'One makes it for one's self, not for anyone else. If I go on having my tea every day in the sort of surroundings I'm used to, I shall still be choosing to do it.' She bit a piece of bun.

'I see,' I said. I also saw that we were discussing a great deal more than choice of locale for tea-eating. 'And what about these people?' There were a couple of elderly men, dressed very shabbily, sitting at separate tables nearby. 'Don't you think they'd think they were lucky if they found themselves in a position to have any choice?'

'Yes.'

'In fact, if we get down to talking about things that really matter, isn't the kind of choice, in particular the moral choice, that preoccupies you and your friends, one of the perks of the leisured classes?'

Before she could answer, I went on. 'In fact, really getting down to business and talking about the pattern of one's career, for example – do you think that I've ever felt I had much choice about what I was going to do next? Because I certainly haven't.' I glanced at Elspeth, rallyingly. 'Do you think Elspeth has, either? You may argue that I actually have done, but all I can say is that it's never seemed like that to me. The only option I have had was to take the one thing that was offered me or to starve. You may say, of course, that I had a choice there.'

Annette smiled: 'I suppose I should.'

'Well, I can tell you, that isn't how it seemed to me.'

We stopped arguing for a moment. The tea was good as well as cheap. The sound of the jazz was cheering.

'I wonder why those two poor old chaps are having their tea here, all by themselves,' I said.

Elspeth looked at them. 'I suppose their families have migrated to one of the new estates up the line, Hainault or Woodford, or somewhere. They're probably too old to move . . . And yet I'd have thought somebody would have asked them in for a cup of tea.' She answered my question: 'I don't know.'

'The school seems crowded,' Annette said to her.

'Do you really think of coming to teach here?' I asked.

Annette looked at me. 'If I do I shall cease to be a member of the leisured classes, shan't I?' She laughed. 'At least I shall have no leisure.'

I did not like the sound of that. Poor old Robert! Poor old thing! Out of the corner of my eye, I saw Elspeth become more attentive. I said:

'You'll have made your choice, anyway.'

'And I shall feel, as a consequence, that I'm really doing something useful.'

'And that will satisfy you?'

'I shouldn't have put it that way – but yes . . .'

'At the expense of poor old Robert's feeling homeless?'

Annette was not piqued. 'At the expense of Robert's being a bit put out,' she said in her light firm tone.

'Sometimes when you talk about moral choice,' I said, 'you make me feel it's something I've missed. More than that, as if it's something I lack. As if my moral nature were coarse, and insensitive, or even as if I were in some way morally blind. At other times' – I paused – 'I feel it's something I'm just as well without. Exercise of moral choice is one of the perks of the leisured classes, for one thing. For another thing, it often seems, to people who aren't preoccupied with it, to come pretty close to self-indulgence.'

Annette suddenly blushed. I went on. 'You mean your statement

"One chooses for one's self" to be a scientific observation of what happens. But it often rings with a note of *approbation*, which makes it sound like the statement of someone who is exclusively preoccupied with his or her *self*.' I shook my head. 'You see what I mean.'

'I do. And if it did, I should agree with you.'

'Are you sure,' I said, 'that you don't want to come and work down here in order to avoid what, for some reason I don't understand, would be the greater effort of running a house and home for Robert?'

'I don't think it's right to have servants,' Annette cried. 'And I don't want to have to do myself the things they do – I can do more valuable things.' She raised her voice a little. 'And some things *are* more valuable than others. Some ways of living are more valuable than others.' She paused. 'And value,' she went on, 'if it means anything means value here and now.'

I drew back. I had been lectured before on the super-significance of 'here and now'.

'The value of our way of living, here and now, arises from the personal choice we make, here and now,' Annette said.

'Ergo, the succession of here-and-nows,' said I sarcastically, 'is a succession of personal choices.' Which made the future, I thought, a poor look-out for Robert.

'I was not going to say that at all,' said Annette. 'I was going to say, ergo – if you commit me to ergo – our way of living is just as valuable as we succeed in making it. Our lives are what we put into them.'

'Cor!' I said, but it sounded unconvincing – which was no surprise to me, because I agreed with what she said. The concept of moral effort was as dear to me as it had been to my nonconformist fore-bears.

There was another pause. Elspeth was the first to speak.

'I suppose I'm going to do the opposite thing to Annette,' she said. 'It seems funny, doesn't it?' She glanced at me. 'It isn't going to make *me* feel immoral, darling, to live on your moral earnings.'

Annette laughed. I gave Elspeth a look of praise. That's the sort of girl you want to marry! I thought.

After a moment, Annette said: 'Perhaps I shall let Robert choose for me.'

I smiled at her. 'Perhaps . . .'

Annette moved her head suddenly, so that her bell of hair swung to and fro.

'I don't think I shall,' she said. 'Let's talk about something else!' She took off her overcoat, letting it fall across the back of her chair.

Elspeth said to me: 'I should like some more tea.'

I picked up our empty cups and went to the counter. As I walked away, Annette set her elbows on the oil-cloth and said animatedly to Elspeth: 'When you come here alone, do you talk to people sitting at the same table?'

Suddenly an idea that had been lurking at the back of my mind came to the front. I could have said: That's broken my dream! Annette, twenty years ago, would have become a Communist.

As I waited while the burly man in the white apron poured the tea, I gazed through the steamy window in the direction of the street; but I was back in the thirties, at Oxford . . . thinking of intelligent, upper-class girls, choosing to join The Party.

Those days had gone, and I was confronted with the difference. Annette was a Socialist of sorts. She had little use for the Labour Party, which she regarded as worn out. 'They've got no theory for *now*,' she had once informed me. 'They had a theory fifty years ago, but it's no use for now and they know it. They're just hoping to muddle through without.' And she had less use for the Communist Party: she was completely disillusioned with revolution.

'Oh dear!' I said to myself, as I carried the cups of tea back to them. I was confronted by the fact that I was a generation older than they were. Was that difference the root of my feeling irritated by Annette? When I remembered that I had been equally irritated by intelligent upper-class girls, especially pretty ones, choosing to join The Party, I thought not.

What irritated me was something that had irritated me throughout the whole of my life – the peculiar kind of self-concern that always seemed to go with the deliberate making of moral choices. I had never liked it. I never should. I thought of Robert, who liked it as little as I did.

'Poor old Robert,' I said to myself. 'He's had it.'

3

An Official Visitor from America

One afternoon my P.A. rang me.

'I've got someone to speak to you, Mr Lunn, who says he knows you. I think he's an American. Do you know a Mr Thomas Malone? He says he met you in Washington. I've got him on the line now.'

I could not remember anyone named Thomas Malone, not anyone special, that is. It sounded the sort of name that a lot of people might have. I said:

'If he says he knows me, I suppose he must. Put him through to me.'

I heard her say 'Here's Mr Lunn for you, Mr Malone', and then a loud, exuberant, American voice said to me:

'Hello there! Is that Mr Lunn? This is Tom Malone here. How are you?'

I said I was very well.

'Remember me?' he said. And then he announced the name of his office.

At that I remembered who he must be. Three years earlier I had been over to America on an official trip, and for one of the jobs I had to do he was my opposite number. Without being able to recall what he looked like, I did remember that we had got on well.

'Remember that night at the Statler?' he asked, even more exuberantly.

We must have got on very well. I had a weakness for hearty evenings, for being a man among men.

'Wish I could!' I said facetiously, while trying to think which one it was.

'That's the boy! I can hear you haven't changed.'

What is commonly called a warning instinct made me say quickly:

'Oh, but I have. Wait till you see me!' I thought I had better put him wise to my change of status as soon as possible. 'Since you last saw me I've got married.'

'Then you look better than ever, I guess.' He laughed. 'Am I going to have the pleasure of meeting Mrs Lunn?'

'Certainly you are,' I said, recalling that on the evening of the party at the Statler I had not had the pleasure of meeting Mrs Malone, very definitely not. I had gathered that Mrs Malone was at home looking after their five children. I said: 'How long are you staying?'

He said he was planning on staying through Wednesday – today was Monday – when he was going to Paris. 'I've got to drop in on NATO and SHAPE.' He had also got his plans for London, these including an evening with me, and a morning looking round what he chose to call our 'outfit'. He wanted to meet our bosses – I may say that after his fashion he was quite a big shot, himself. 'I may even tell them how good you are at your job!'

To my chagrin Robert was not in London. It was just my luck, I thought, for Robert to be hearing about people with whom I had made a negative hit and then to be missing when I could produce somebody with whom I had made a positive one. Positive, I thought and not afraid to say so!

Tom – I had to call him Tom, since Americans give one no alternative between calling them by their Christian names and calling them Mr – had already got hold of Robert's name. Also of the name of Murray-Hamilton. He had not previously met either of them.

I was free to fit in with his plans. Elspeth and I would take him out to dinner that evening. The next day he could have a look round our outfit and meet Murray-Hamilton. I put down the telephone receiver and pressed the buzzer for my P.A. to come in so that I could tell her about it. I felt excited. The telephone seemed to have transmitted to me a gust of euphoria.

When Elspeth and I met Tom Malone that evening his state

was clearly euphoric. I could not say whether I should have recognized him or not. He was short and stocky, about the same height as me and a stone and a half heavier – that stone and a half being composed of muscle, powerful active muscle – and he had the sort of square, snub-nosed, grinning Irish-American face that seems to be made for expressing a mixture of blarney and ruthlessness. It was obvious, from the moment we met, that he liked me. I could not for the life of me think why.

It was obvious that he liked Elspeth, too. Every glance he gave her was so filled with life and energy that I felt ashamed of lapsing from my duty as a host – the trouble was that since getting married my list of girls, from whom I might have rustled up one for an occasion such as this, seemed to have dispersed. So soon, I thought, so soon . . . How sad I felt to have lost them! And yet, how cosy I felt to be just with Elspeth!

'You didn't tell me your wife was so young and pretty,' he said to me, while we were drinking some preliminary whiskies.

'Did I have to?'

'Well' – he gave Elspeth and me a vigorous, blarneying look – 'no!'

Elspeth blushed. I was delighted.

When we had settled at our table in the restaurant and were looking at the list of things to eat, Tom said:

'If you won't raise any objections, I'm going to buy the champagne.' He glanced at us to make sure he was carrying us. 'O.K.?'

'Champagne!' we cried enthusiastically, meaning that it was O.K. – actually it usually gave Elspeth and me stomach-ache.

I was amused. We had brought him to an expensive restaurant. Up to now I have omitted to tell you that Tom Malone was both clever and quick on the uptake. I may also take this opening to observe that in my experience there is nobody like an American for summing up on the spot exactly how expensive a restaurant is. 'Lots of champagne!' he said.

I decided he should have caviare if he wanted it. He chose smoked salmon.

The evening was a great success, and I was pleased for more reasons than one. Honesty compels me to admit that in the first place I had felt relief at having Elspeth to get me out of spending another evening like the one at the Statler. Much as I had enjoyed it – it really was one of those nights when one cannot remember next morning what happened – I just did not want another. Not here. Not now.

'You take him out tonight on your own, darling,' Elspeth had said when I had first told her Tom Malone was here.

Let me explain why she said it. A few months earlier, just after we got married, I had happened to make, in passing and yet not unaware that she would pick it up, one of my favourite generalizations, that married men had a tamed look. Elspeth took it amiss. She took it touchily, I thought.

I did not start an argument with her about the truth of the generalization: it stood up to the test of experiment to the extent of enabling me, when I was interviewing our scientists and engineers, to judge whether they were married or not and get the answer right eight times out of ten. I could never understand why people took it amiss. They would not have expected a man with a full belly to have the same look as one who did not know where his next meal was coming from.

In my opinion, based on observation, when a man was satisfactorily married a certain look went out of his eye. A certain, identifiable look. (Its disappearance had enabled me, only a few weeks earlier, to guess that a candidate who came up before an annual promotion board had got married since we saw him the previous year. When he asked me how I guessed and I innocently told him, he said with a furious glare: 'I happen to be rather tired at the moment because we've just been moving house!') That tamed look . . .

It was women who took the generalization the most touchily.

'I suppose you think you'll look tamed?' Elspeth said.

'Why not?'

'You'll think it's my fault.'

'I shan't *notice* it. That's the point.'

'I don't like to think other people will.'

'*They* notice next to nothing.' I changed my tone. 'And anyway, darling, I think it's worth it . . .'

At that Elspeth's tone changed. But not her intention. From then on she encouraged me to have hearty evenings out with my friends, to keep up my minor taste for games-playing, and so on.

So you can see how it came about that Elspeth asked me if I would like to take Tom Malone out for an evening on my own. And I am afraid you will also be able to see why I declined.

While we were eating some particularly succulent fillet steaks, I looked at Tom and wondered if he regretted the kind of evening we were having. Sybil! – I suddenly thought of Sybil. She would have been just the girl for this evening. She would have liked Tom Malone and Tom Malone would have liked her. I wondered where she was, and I felt glum. And ashamed of myself . . . However cool and remote she was, I had no excuse for just quietly letting her go, with hardly a word, when I decided to get married. Dear Sybil, who had never done me a scrap of harm, in fact had always done me a power of good.

However, Tom Malone did not appear to be regretting the kind of evening. On the contrary.

Incidentally, just to finish off my case about being tamed, let me add that all men who are satisfactorily married – and most men are: I was astonished by the number of letters I got from men from whom I would never have expected it, writing to congratulate me on my marriage, who said with obvious truthfulness: 'I can only hope you and Elspeth will be as happy as we have been' – all such men have a recognizable, tamed look; but this does not mean that they all do not have an eye for a pretty woman, far from it. A certain look, which identifies an unmarried man, goes out of their eyes. But other looks can come in. I would not have needed to glance twice at Tom Malone to know that he was a married man. I did not need to glance at him twice to know that, were I out of the way, he would have made a pass at Elspeth.

I thought Elspeth was looking remarkably pretty. She was pressing her knee against mine.

Tom said to me:

'Next time you come to Washington, you must bring your wife with you.' To Elspeth: 'Have you ever been to the States?'

Elspeth shook her head. As scarcely ever having been out of the country caused Elspeth exaggerated feelings of inferiority, I intervened quickly.

'I'm afraid the Civil Service don't pay for wives to go to Washington with their husbands.'

'Why shouldn't *we*, if we invite you? Why don't we do that? You did us a lot of good last time you came. It would be worth it to our outfit just as much as to yours.' Tom looked at us with blarney and ruthlessness in his bright blue, slightly bloodshot eyes. 'Come on, let's say we're gonna do it! O.K.?'

'O.K.!' we both cried, caught up by the spirit of the moment.

'As soon as I get back to Washington, I'll have us send an official invitation. Who do we send it to – Mr Murray-Hamilton?'

'That would be correct,' I said. I could not subdue a wish that for once Murray-Hamilton should hear good of me, even though I knew – Robert had told me often enough – that I stood the best chance of survival in my job if Murray-Hamilton heard nothing of me, neither ill nor good. (Why, I asked myself, should people who think ill of one become even worse disposed to one if they hear a good report?)

'Then that's as good as settled,' said Tom. 'Here's to Mrs Lunn in Washington!' And he finished his glass of champagne.

I did not see it ever happening, but that did not stop me finishing my glass.

'We need another bottle,' said Tom and beckoned the wine waiter.

Elspeth now appeared to be blushing all the time.

By the time we left the restaurant it was nearly midnight. We were all floating in euphoria. Tom and I went and stood out in Jermyn Street while Elspeth got her coat: we needed air.

'It's been a very, very swell evening,' he said. 'London's a wonderful town. Wonderful people.'

'Glad you liked it.' I glanced up the street, thinking about taxis and home. 'Which way do you go from here?'

'Got 'ny ideas?'

He was giving me a knowing, encouraging grin. How could I possibly pretend to misunderstand him? I looked round quickly for Elspeth to save me – she did.

'Ready?' she said, coming down the steps to us.

Tom burst into laughter. So did I. Elspeth said to him:

'Are you coming back to have a drink with us?'

Tom said: 'Well, no, I'll stroll back to my hotel. It's only just down Piccadilly.'

We said our goodnights, and then Elspeth and I got into a taxi. I put my arm round her.

'What an extraordinary man!' Elspeth said. 'What do you think he's going to do now?'

'I hate to think.'

I felt Elspeth kiss my cheek and I heard her whisper: 'I don't . . .' She kissed my cheek again.

'Good gracious!' I whispered. 'Surely you don't mean in a taxi?' I knew that was just what she did mean; but I thought it well, now that I was married, to start being a bit stuffy about such matters.

'It's quite a long way to Putney,' she whispered.

On the following morning neither Elspeth nor I had stomach-ache from the champagne. 'You look very well,' she said to me. I was relieved. I did not want to take Tom Malone over to see Murray-Hamilton looking as if some of the things I was supposed to be accused of were true.

My P.A. had arranged for us to see Murray-Hamilton at eleven o'clock, and at a few minutes to eleven I got a telephone call from the policeman on the front door to say that Tom had arrived. I said I would go down to meet him, to save him coming up to my office first.

'Hello there!' The exuberant call rang through our foyer. Tom and I shook hands vigorously. He looked spruce and freshly shaven. 'All set?' he said.

We began to climb the staircase – Murray-Hamilton's office was on the first floor.

'Did you get home safely last night?' I asked.

'Fine,' he said. 'London's a wonderful town. Wonderful people.'

I glanced at him. He glanced at me, with his Irish grin – and caught his toe on the edge of the stair. 'Since I last saw you I haven't missed a minute of it.'

I glanced at him more closely. 'You don't mean,' I said, 'that you haven't been to bed?'

'Not to sleep,' he said. 'How do I look?'

I laughed. 'No different,' It was true. His blue, slightly bloodshot eyes looked bright and clear. His step was powerful and energetic. Looking at me, he laughed with satisfaction. A great gust of his breath came across to me. Brandy. Pure brandy. He was drunk.

'I'm looking forward to meeting your Mr Murray-Hamilton,' he said.

I could well imagine that he was.

It embarrasses me to describe the meeting of Tom Malone and Murray-Hamilton. In fact I seem, presumably for the sake of my own peace of mind, to have forgotten a good deal of it. I remember crossing Murray-Hamilton's large room and seeing Murray-Hamilton sitting brooding and reflecting behind his huge mahogany desk. A particularly handsome Ministry of Works picture glowed from the wall behind him. Our feet made no sound on the carpet.

'It certainly is a pleasure to meet you, Mr Murray-Hamilton,' said Tom, striding forward to shake his hand. 'And I certainly consider myself fortunate to have Mr Lunn here to introduce me to you.'

'Sit ye down,' said Murray-Hamilton, banishing his brooding look in favour of an affable smile. He handed Tom a cigarette, and then lit it for him – I wondered if the match would ignite Tom's breath.

They began to talk. They began to talk about Tom's work, and about ours. Tom talked loudly and forcefully and with sustained emotion. I tried to keep out of the conversation. Things could hardly be worse, I thought. The brooding, reflective look was creeping back into Murray-Hamilton's eyes.

In due course Tom referred to my last official trip to Washington. At that I realized things could be worse.

Loudly, forcefully, and with sustained emotion, Tom Malone told Murray-Hamilton how wonderfully I had represented our department, how wonderfully I had represented *him*, Murray-Hamilton. Do you wonder my memory begins to give out?

Tom paused – I wondered if I had ever seen a man so drunk.

Tom went on. He told Murray-Hamilton what a grasp I had of my job, and what a technique I had with which to do it. And he ended up by telling Murray-Hamilton I was the best interviewer of scientists and engineers in the United Kingdom.

I really do not remember anything else till I had got Tom Malone out of the room. I do not want to remember anything else.

When Tom and I got outside we went steadily down the staircase. At the turn we met Spinks, Stinker Spinks, going up. Spinks and Tom Malone turned to eye each other; Tom missed his footing, and with a succession of bursting laughs bumped down to the bottom of the staircase on his backside.

He was a damned good chap, Tom Malone.

4

Robert's Troubles

I did not give Robert an account of Tom Malone's visit – for once I thought he might be allowed to preserve his disbelief in the existence of anyone whom he had not found for himself. I was haunted by my picture of Murray-Hamilton sitting at his desk, the ledger open before him . . . on opposite pages he recorded Right and Wrong.

Robert had a new novel coming out. Also he had Annette to cope with. In case you have not had the opportunity to study the artistic temperament, perhaps I ought to say that it was the former which occupied him the more.

Robert had a fit of gloom. He was always in a hypersensitive state just before a book came out – a state from which he was readily thrown into apprehension if not gloom. And this essential state appeared not to be seriously altered when, as the centre-piece of his excellent press, he had the middle page to himself in *The Times Literary Supplement*. Very useful, indeed. People do not appear to read it, but they do appear to know it is *there*. For instance, the *T.L.S.* circulates officially, along with *Nature*, the *Economist* and others, through the offices of the upper echelons of the Civil Service. Within a fortnight of Robert's getting the middle page, he had been invited out to lunch by first Murray-Hamilton and then Spinks.

'What did Stinker Spinks say to you?' I asked.

Robert was markedly offhand. 'Actually he was rather interesting, when off his normal beat. It appears that he's got quite an important collection of Roman coins. I didn't know about it. He talked quite interestingly about them.'

'Do you think he'll invite *me* out to lunch when *I* get a middle in the *T.L.S.*?'

Robert said: 'I think he might, you know. Murray-Hamilton definitely won't, I can tell you that. But Stinker might. There are moments when his desire to be near to success, even somebody else's, is even greater than his envy of it. I think he might ask you.' He paused. 'If you have this ambition, peculiar as it is, you ought to be warned that his club gives you a very poor lunch. An execrable lunch.'

When we went to our own club it was obvious that Robert in their opinion was doing well. No body of men responds more quickly to a change in the barometer of one's prestige than one's club, especially to an easily visible movement in the upward direction. Members who have not spoken to one before, speak to one: members who have spoken to one before, offer one a drink: members who have offered one drinks before, suggest one goes up to dinner with them: and members with whom one has dined for years say they are going to buy one's book. It is difficult not to let it go to one's head.

The first weeks after publication passed. And once again gloom, this time a different kind of gloom, supervened. The reviewers who had put Robert's book at the head of their columns were now, with equal hebdomadal panache, putting somebody else's book there. Robert came into my office and sat heavily on the corner of my table.

'I feel,' he said, 'as if I might just as well have dropped it into the sea.'

I understood how he was feeling.

Why worry? you may ask. How right you are – please go on! Why be a writer? Why be Robert or me? Why not be two other chaps? Robert and I sometimes considered your last suggestion as the one, true way out of our dilemma.

'I might just as well have dropped it into the sea,' Robert said again.

The poignance of the concept kept me silent. Attention, attention . . . all artists are endlessly craving attention. A neurotic lot – not like everybody else.

Robert found little to console him in his domestic situation. Annette was still holding to her moral choice. Speculating on what he might do, I took it into my head that he might get Annette's father to take his side.

Then one day I happened to meet Annette's father. I called at Robert's flat on my way home from the office, to collect some of my manuscript which Annette had been reading. To my surprise, the door was opened by Annette's father.

'Come in,' he said cordially. 'I'm here on my own.' Tall and stork-like, he walked ahead of me down the corridor. 'I'm staying here while my flat is being re-decorated. It's rather more agreeable than getting a room at the Club.'

I was touched by his unusual cordiality. Tall and stork-like, he preceded me down the corridor – to the kitchen.

'I was just going to have a whisky,' he said, 'to save myself trouble, though I should prefer to have some tea. Perhaps as you're here we might make some tea?'

In the kitchen he turned to look at me with a sparkling, encouraging look in his eye. It was the most intimate sign of recognition he had ever given me. I felt that he was almost offering me his friendship. Actually, I realized, he was inviting me to make tea for him.

'The first step,' I said, 'is to put on the kettle.'

'I believe that is so,' he said, with an amused glance round the kitchen which indicated little intention of doing it himself. I filled the kettle and lit the stove.

'At least it is,' I said, 'for people of our class.' I did not see why he should not get something of what he was asking for. 'In schools for the lower classes,' I said, having picked up the information from Elspeth, 'the child's first instruction is, "First empty the pot!"' In case he did not follow, I added: 'The implication being that the pot has not been emptied after being used.'

To my surprise he bestirred himself to the extent of looking for

Annette's tea-pot. It was on the window-ledge. He picked it up, weighing it, and then with a negligent gesture handed it to me.

It was full.

I burst into laughter. I could not help admiring him. I had demonstrated that I did not give a damn. No more did he. He smiled with sub-fusc satisfaction.

'I wonder where Annette empties it,' I said.

He stroked his moustache and gave me a swift glance from under his eyebrows – he had long eyebrows that curled outwards. 'She used to empty it in the lavatory – after we'd once suffered a slight contretemps after emptying it down the sink.' He took the tea-pot from me and went out of the room.

When he came back the kettle was boiling and I had got cups and saucers for us.

'Shall we have tea in here?' he said. 'It will save us trouble, won't it?'

'I think Annette and Robert have their tea in here,' I said.

'Very sensible of them.' He got a bottle of milk and some butter out of the refrigerator. 'There doesn't seem to be very much to eat,' he observed as he shut the door. 'We must be going out for dinner.'

I opened a bread bin and took out half a sliced loaf wrapped in waxed paper. We sat down at a small table and began our tea.

'I wonder where we're going for dinner,' he said. 'I know Annette's first choice of place to go out to for dinner is a coffee-stall in the Fulham Road.'

'I didn't know there was a coffee-stall in the Fulham Road.'

'They're getting harder to find,' he said, with a touch of gloom. 'We're always having to go a long way . . .'

I tried to find a happier topic.

'This is superior tea they have,' I said.

'Very good.'

He got up and looked in some of the cupboards.

When Annette and Robert moved into the flat they had had the kitchen completely done up by one of the classy kitchen firms that had made their appearance since the end of the war. The tops of the stove and sink and the benches of drawers were all on the same level, while the hanging cupboards also were perfectly aligned. Some of the cupboard doors and drawers were painted bright yellow, the rest white, while the benches and our table were covered with the latest thing in plastic surface materials. The kitchen was much envied by Elspeth.

Annette's father opened a hanging cupboard which, as far as I could see, was empty except for a small jar on the lower shelf. He brought the jar out.

'Marmite,' he said. 'Annette used to eat a lot of it when she was up at Oxford. She believes it to be highly nutritious.' He spread some on a slice of bread and butter, and then passed the jar to me. 'I don't know if you know it? I rather like it.'

I said: 'You'll need something pretty nutritious if you're going out to a coffee-stall for your evening meal.' I thought of the pork chops which Elspeth had ordered for us. What a satisfactory marriage mine was!

'That's what I thought,' he said.

I waited a moment and then said directly:

'What line are you taking over Annette's becoming a school-teacher in Bethnal Green?'

'I would have thought she might find a teaching-post nearer home.'

We stared at each other.

After a pause he said: 'Of course, she's changing, you know. I mean, since her marriage.' He could see that I was expecting some revelatory comment. 'She dresses better, don't you think?'

'I suppose I do.' It occurred to me that at dinner-parties which succeeded the first one, when she had appeared in her wedding-dress, Annette had worn a black frock which Robert had chosen – Elspeth thought it was cut too low at the front, but I thought it was all right.

'I always thought when she was at Oxford,' her father said, 'she looked as if she had just landed by parachute.' He could not resist glancing at me slyly.

I laughed.

'Oh yes,' he said, pretending not to have heard me, 'I can see Robert's influence.' He gave me the same glance again; and this time I saw a gleam, light and clear, of malice.

I stopped laughing. The full measure of his detachment had for the first time really struck home to me. He was clever, cultivated, cordial and humane; he was unusually free from envy and stuffiness. He was also free, I thought, from serious concern with anyone but himself, dazzlingly free . . .

And I had taken it into my head that Robert might be hoping for his intervention! I had made a frightful ass of myself. I knew Robert could not possibly have hoped for such a thing.

Annette's father spread some Marmite on a second slice of bread and butter. 'I do recommend this,' he said.

Out of sheer moral disadvantage I took some. A look of amusement was glimmering in his eyes.

'What do you think of Robert's new novel?' he said. 'You and he write very different kinds of novel, don't you?' He paused. 'I think it's very interesting that you should have such a high opinion of each other's books. It does you both credit.' He leaned forward a little. 'And it *interests* me.'

We engaged in literary conversation.

Meanwhile I was reflecting on a matter that had not occurred to me before. I knew that every shrewd man considered it was a good idea to marry his boss's daughter. To a really shrewd man it is so self-evident as not to require consideration – he just does it automatically. What I had not reflected on before was what the boss thought about it.

I kept thinking of the gleam of malice, light and clear, that Annette's father had let out of the corner of his eye.

5

Several Points Illuminated

Annette moved into Elspeth's job.

One day when I happened to see Barbara – it was a day when I was going to the office by Tube and we met on the station platform – I asked her how Annette was getting on at the school.

Barbara was going down to her Bethnal Green clinic. 'I suppose you see Annette quite often now,' I said.

'Yes, we're getting to be quite friends.'

'How's she doing?'

'Very well indeed.' Barbara looked down the railway line. It was a cold June morning and there was a drift of mist in the cutting. 'I think she's made an excellent adjustment.'

'That's fine,' I said. 'What has she adjusted?'

Barbara smiled. 'You know what I mean.'

'You mean she's adjusted herself to the children,' I said, modelling my tone on that employed by Robert on such an occasion – that tone of a bright boy successfully taking part in a guessing competition.

Barbara said: 'She's made an excellent *overall* adjustment.'

'Over all what?' I burst into laughter. 'All right. I won't go on. You mean that you think her "moral choice" has made her feel cheerful.'

'I do.'

'And what about poor old Robert?'

Barbara began to say something, but I did not hear it because the train came into the station. We got in and sat down side by side. After a while I could not resist teasing her.

'I suppose it was "adjustment" you had in mind when you warned me that it was easier to get married than to be married.'

She nodded her head.

'What does it mean,' I shouted, 'actually?'

She thought for a moment. We were crossing the river: it looked pretty in the morning light.

'Learning to live with each other. Making allowances for each other's different desires.'

'Most of the time we seem to have the same desires.'

Barbara looked at me. The train stopped in the next station.

'Do you really find that?' she said.

I thought about it. It was true. I said:

'I suppose we must be easy-going, that's all.'

Barbara was smoothing a crease in her skirt – she was wearing an expensive-looking dark grey suit. Just before the train started again she said:

'And you have no feeling that you're *missing* something?'

'Well, no . . .' What could we be missing? Children? There was not time yet for us to have had any. I was at a loss. I said: 'Missing what?'

Barbara leaned towards me.

'Have you had many quarrels?'

'No.'

Instantly I knew that I had failed to recognize a key question, and as a consequence, worse still, had truthfully given the wrong answer.

'You mean,' I shouted, 'we ought to quarrel?'

'It's very unusual not to.'

'Why ought we to quarrel?' I put my ear close to her mouth to be sure of hearing her anwer.

'It's one of the commonest ways of relieving the tension of marriage.'

I was confronted with the possibility that my marriage had no proper tensions.

I was silent. I got out my newspaper. It was *The Times*. Since getting married I had started to take *The Times* and to wear a bowler hat. I felt that such a radical change in status as getting married ought to be marked in my case by an appropriate change in outward habit. Elspeth did not mind my taking *The Times*, but she hated the bowler hat, on the explicit grounds that it did not suit me. I suspected that implicitly she considered it was a symbol of tameness. Actually I thought I looked ridiculous in it. (Come to that, I thought all other men looked ridiculous in bowler hats. Just think detachedly of a human face, and then of a bowler hat on top of it!)

Throughout the day I considered the fact that Elspeth and I did not quarrel. If there were tensions in our marriage we were not releasing them. And if there were no tensions there must be something seriously lacking. I meant to discuss it with Elspeth when I got home.

When I got home – delightful experience! . . . Elspeth was there – Elspeth opened the door for me. A delicious smell of cooking came out. I realized exactly, now, what it meant in romantic novels when it said 'He kissed her hungrily.' Elspeth, by a marvellous combination of instinct and intelligence, was turning herself into a first-rate cook. The time was just long enough after the war for food to be getting varied and plentiful again, even though some of it was still rationed. Publishers were racing each other to bring out new cookery-books: I used to give them to Elspeth as presents.

After dinner we sat on the sofa, enjoying the pleasures of digestion before we did the washing up. I was holding her hand.

'Men are carnal,' I said, as a more highbrow way of expressing the fact that the way to a man's heart was through his belly.

Elspeth stroked my hand consolingly.

'I must say it's wonderful being married,' I said.

Elspeth gave me a quick look.

'It's specially wonderful being married to you.' Luck had come my way after all, and all at once.

Elspeth said: 'You never asked me.'

I was caught. I could not think what on earth she meant.

'You never asked me to marry you.'

'No more I did.'

377

She looked at me closely. 'Don't say you don't remember!'

I frequently got into trouble for not being able to remember cardinal events in our married life. 'Of course I do,' I said. 'You were washing up, and I was in this room.'

She relaxed. 'Near enough . . .'

I touched the wedding ring on her finger. 'Ought I to have asked you?'

'Yes.'

'Didn't you know I was going to ask you?'

'I wasn't sure . . .' She faltered. And then she picked up. 'I thought it was getting time.'

I laughed and then kissed her.

I touched her wedding ring again. 'Poor baby, you didn't get an engagement ring, either.'

She blushed.

'When I get the Book of The Month in America, I'll buy you a great big diamond.'

'I don't want a great big diamond.'

We were silent. Suddenly she laughed. I asked what was the matter.

'I just thought of you buying yourself all those new clothes before you got married.'

I thought the best thing I could do was to laugh.

And then I picked up. I kissed her cheek. 'You're not doing so badly.'

She turned quickly and kissed me.

We were silent again. 'It *is* wonderful . . .' she said.

At that moment I recalled my conversation with Barbara, *Was* it wonderful? *Was* it?

I said: 'Darling, do you think we ought to quarrel?'

Elspeth looked at me in some stupefaction. 'What for?'

I then reported my conversation with Barbara. Elspeth listened with attention, and at the end said:

'I don't agree.'

I was relieved. In fact I was pleased, terribly pleased. I confided:

'I don't like quarrelling.'

'Nor do I,' said Elspeth.

I said: 'I don't quarrel easily, and when I do, I mean it. Unfortunately I can't make up and forget it. I remember it.'

'I've hardly ever quarrelled with anyone. And when I did it upset me for months.'

I said: 'In that case, I think we'd better go on as we are. It seems all right to me.'

'I don't want to quarrel with you, darling, ever.'

I said: 'Then, don't let's!' I was very happy about this outcome.

Elspeth sat quietly, thinking about it. After a little while I became discursive. I explained to Elspeth a fact which had first occurred to me several years ago, that some people seem to need to quarrel. 'It seems to provide the friction, the stimulus,' I said, 'which makes them feel they've really been brought to life.' I recalled one of Robert's former loves – the one who hit him with the whisky bottle.

'In fact,' I wound up, 'it seems as if, for some people, a clash of wills is inseparable from sexual excitement.' I paused. 'I should have thought it must be very tiresome for them. And tiring . . .'

We were silent. I was thinking that my generalization was profound and that the tone in which I had stated it was admirable.

Elspeth said: 'I've remembered – I think that book was by an Indian . . .'

I was caught again. I simply could not work it out: I had to say 'Which book?'

Elspeth said: 'That one that gave you and Robert such a shock. What did he call it? Daunting?'

'An Indian!' I said. I suddenly thought of millions of bright-eyed, birdlike little Bengalis, perpetually on the boil. But I was not willing to give an inch. 'An Indian *woman*,' I said.

Elspeth laughed. She looked at me sideways. Her eyes were sparkling.

I jumped up. 'Come on!' I said. 'It's time to wash up.'

Elspeth got up. 'I've been waiting for you all this time.'

We went into the kitchen and did the washing up. If our marriage was missing something, we still had plenty to keep us satisfied.

The following morning, whom should I meet, as if by chance, but Harry. I was sure he had been lying in wait for me somewhere on the route to my usual bus-stop. He fell into step with me.

'Lovely morning, Joe,' he said.

I agreed that it was. The lilacs and laburnums were in flower in people's gardens. It was some time since it had rained, and the dust on the road gave out a faint familiar scent – it reminded me of being somewhere abroad, where roads were always dry – the South of France on a dazzling spring morning, in the days long before the war . . . Some little girls in purple blazers passed us.

Harry said: 'It's nice to see you again.'

I nodded my head.

It was difficult to say whose fault it was, that we had seen so little of each other recently.

Somehow Elspeth's and my getting married had estranged us from Harry and Barbara. 'You could scarcely think it really could be that, when it was they who brought us together,' Elspeth had said.

'The movements of the soul,' said I, 'are not necessarily to be explained mechanically.'

As this speech had a somewhat dowsing effect on Elspeth, I added: 'Actually, it's one thing to bring people together, and another to know how you're going to take the outcome.'

The light had come back into Elspeth's eyes.

So, when Harry said it was nice to see me again, I felt it as unintended reproach, and yet there was nothing I could do about it.

'Why don't we have lunch together?' I said, doubting if it would do any good. Harry and Barbara, in their married state, had looked at Elspeth and me in ours, and something had – well, made them turn their heads away.

'Yes, we will,' said Harry.

He swung along beside me – he walked with short steps, seeming, compared with me, to be balancing forwards on his toes.

'I hear you saw Barbara yesterday morning,' he said.

I smiled, 'Yes,' I wondered if it was to discuss this that he had waylaid me, and decided not. Harry was too innately wily to come straight to the point, even when there was not the slightest reason for not doing so.

'She's a strange girl,' he said, looking in front of him.

I was touched.

'I'm very attached to her,' he said.

I was touched again.

He turned his head – I was aware of an odd glance coming round his snub nose – and said: 'She has a good deal to put up with from me.'

I said mildly: 'Yes.' It seemed fair enough.

'Even if I didn't see myself as others see me, I should realize that,' he said. He seemed to be laughing.

'Yes,' I said again, now completely mystified.

Harry said nothing else. In a little while we came to the bus-stop.

We climbed to the upper deck of the bus and settled ourselves in two seats at the front.

'Well,' said Harry, speaking now in his high, fluent, conversational tone. 'What do you think of Robert's new novel? I've scarcely seen you since it came out.'

The scales of mystification fell from my eyes. Though there had been a break in our conversation, and though Harry's tone was different, the subject was still the same. Before I could answer, he said:

'I enjoyed it tremendously.'

I knew what he had waylaid me for.

You may remember that although Robert did not see much of Harry – in my belief because he had not found Harry for himself – he used to question me about Harry with such interest that I suspected he must be thinking of someone like him as a character for a novel. Well, there was a character in Robert's new novel who resembled Harry in some important respects, in particular being globe-shaped, whirling, and impelled by curiosity – while differing in others, such as social origins, profession and so on.

'I enjoyed it tremendously,' Harry repeated, just to make sure the point had gone home.

I said nothing. I should have loved to question him about what he thought of Robert's character – it would have taught me a lot about Harry and a lot about literary art. For Robert's vision of Harry, as far as it actually was of Harry, was different from mine. I tended to see Harry as a sort of non-sexual voyeur, whose ferreting out of details about everybody's lives somehow fed his sense of power. Robert saw his own Harry-like character in a more Dostoievskian light, as wildly whirling in the flesh and pretty wildly whirling in the soul as well, held in control only by a strong will – a will stronger than I would at first sight have given Harry credit for. Yet every so often the will of Robert's character failed him, and an act of a most peculiar kind so to speak escaped him. It was an act of what Robert chose to name 'motiveless malice'.

The vision fascinated me, partly because I had seen nothing of such acts in Harry's conduct of recent years, partly because it evoked an extraordinary recollection from my boyhood. Harry had told a school-girl whom I was going out with that I was writing love-letters to another girl. It was untrue: there was no basis for it: Harry had absolutely nothing to gain. The girl dropped me, refusing to tell me why, and I was unhappy for weeks – during which time Harry had listened to my confidences and gone to great lengths to console me!

Such an act of 'motiveless malice' provided Robert with a dramatic turn – completely invented, of course, since in life his own path and Harry's scarcely ever crossed – in the central plot of his novel.

Suddenly I heard, to my stupefaction, Harry saying:

'I enjoyed it most of all for the portrait of that young economist.' This was the character I was thinking of.

'It was splendidly done,' Harry said. 'I know what it's like to be that sort of man.'

I turned to look at him and in his expression saw strong emotion. His eyes were shining. 'Yes,' he said. 'Robert understands us very well . . .'

Then, just as suddenly, his mood changed. His shining glance shifted obliquely and his tone of voice went up.

'I think,' he said, 'Robert understands me better than you do, Joe.'

I looked through the bus window as if I had noticed something specially interesting about the traffic.

'Don't you?' he asked triumphantly.

'I think that's for you to say.' I went on looking through the window.

For a little while Harry looked through the window, too.

'Yes, Joe,' he said. 'Let's have lunch together – let's make it soon!'

6

A Surprise and a Shock

Throughout the next months I worked hard on my new novel. I was beginning to have the highest hopes of it. I had made a dent in the public's consciousness with my previous book. It seemed reasonable to believe that another small masterpiece, banging on the identical spot, would make the dent deeper. Why not? The public's consciousness is not like a tennis-ball.

'You're bound to make a bit of money sometime,' said Robert. 'I rather fancy it may well be this time.'

I was not, of course, expecting to make a similar impression in America. My sense of humour had not become the least bit un-British, as far as I could see, during the last year. When I read through my manuscript, it made me laugh. When Robert read through my manuscript, it made him laugh. But what was the good of that? *We* were British.

'One thing's certain,' Robert said, still in his optimistic mood. 'Courtenay will be delighted with it.'

Courtenay Chamberlain was my publisher.

I said: 'I think he will.'

This encouraged Robert still further. 'If you don't get an excellent press for this, I shall be very surprised. Very surprised indeed. And, well . . . you may well make a bit of money.' He grinned. 'And so will Courtenay.'

I grinned, but not quite so much.

Anyway, in October, having given the manuscript its last cuts and titivations, I sent it on its way to Courtenay. Another small masterpiece. (Actually, by now, I was getting a bit sick of reading it, but that did not make me feel any less inclined to accept Robert's opinion of its quality.) I registered the parcel.

Then Robert and I sat back to wait. In these days Robert seemed to be enjoying a remission from his gloomy, apprehensive, pre-occupied state of the last few months. For one thing my affairs were clearly going much better. For another his own affairs, I judged, were troubling him less. All the same, I was completely unprepared for what he said to me one morning when he came into my office.

Robert was sitting on the corner of my table, stirring a cup of tea which our P.A. had just brought in. We had been talking about a visit we were going to make to one of our research establish-ments, and he had lapsed into gazing idly through the window.

'By the way,' he said, turning to me, 'it looks as if Annette's going to have a baby.'

For a moment I was too surprised to think, and then, I am ashamed to say, I thought something unworthy about him.

'Good gracious!' I said. 'That's wonderful news.'

'It's not a hundred per cent certain yet, but I shall be very surprised if she isn't.'

I began: 'Did you –?'

Robert gave me an authoritative look. 'It's unintentional as far as both of us are concerned.' He paused.

I paused. 'What does Annette think about it?'

'She seems very happy about it.'

'What about her doing a job? It will affect that.'

'I realize that.' Robert thought about it. 'In some ways it's a little awkward, happening at this particular point in time.' He glanced at me sideways. 'But she's quite certain that she wants to have it . . . And I don't need to tell you that I want her to have it.' He looked at me full face. 'I want it very much.'

I was moved by his emotion. 'Then I'm very, very glad indeed.'

'I think it will be all right.'

I laughed with relief. 'All women want to have babies, anyway.'

'Some less than others.'

We were thoughtful.

I told Elspeth that evening. 'You must admit it's a surprise,' I said.

She glanced at me oddly. 'Yes, darling.'

'What's the matter?'

She began to smile. 'It's a bit alarming, isn't it?' she said. 'Think about us . . .'

That point had not struck me. 'We shall be all right.' I hugged her. 'You're a wonderful wife.'

We were silent for a little while.

'It makes all the fuss about whether she ought or ought not to become a school-teacher look rather academic,' I said.

Elspeth said: 'Why?'

I said: 'Well, she won't be able to, now.'

'Not at all. She can have time off to have the baby and then go back again. Time off,' she repeated emphatically, 'with pay!'

I did not argue. That was as might be.

And then I thought: Suppose I made a bit of money with my new book, should Elspeth and I think about having some children? I began to long for that bit of money.

And that reminded me that it was time I heard from my publisher about my new small masterpiece.

Another fortnight elapsed, and then one morning I had a telephone call from my literary agent. Robert was in my office at the time, sitting on the corner of my table.

My agent was ringing me with news from Courtenay.

'What is it?' said Robert, beginning to turn pale.

I tried to listen to both him and my agent.

'Doesn't he like it?' Robert asked incredulously.

I put my hand over the mouthpiece. 'He thinks it's wonderful. But he can't publish it.'

'Why on earth not?'

My agent rang off.

I turned to Robert.

'He thinks it's too improper.'

Robert went on turning pale.

Part Four

I

Learning the Law

Two days later I had lunch with Courtenay.

Courtenay was an excellent publisher. The discouraging thing about him was that there was a startling physical resemblance between him and me – discouraging to me because, though we looked startlingly alike, I was an artist and he was a businessman.

Let me give you an example. The first time we met, Courtenay asked me to have lunch with him at his club. Being young in those days and unused to clubs, I was pleased and impressed. We sat down at a table and ordered what we were going to eat.

'What would you like to drink?' Courtenay asked. 'A glass of beer or something?'

'Thank you,' I said shyly, 'I should like a glass of beer.'

Courtenay called the wine-waiter and ordered a glass of beer for me and a bottle of wine for himself.

You see what I mean about being a businessman? And yet he was not insensitive, far from it. Later in the meal, when I was finishing my glass of beer and he his glass of wine, a rueful look came into his eyes, large, light-coloured eyes that Robert, with a more romantic vision than mine, used to refer to as sad and lemur-like. Courtenay put down his glass not quite empty and said to me consolingly:

'It was only cat-piss, really.'

We looked, I can tell you, surprisingly alike. He was the same size and shape as me; he had the same large rounded forehead as me and the same sort of curly hair, now turning grey like mine. He looked very lively and, worse still, he looked – painful though it is to say it, artistic integrity compels me – dapper . . . I looked at him and I thought of myself. I was an artist and he was a business-man. I wore a bow tie; he wore a bow tie and a carnation. One day, when we were washing our hands in a club lavatory, he suddenly looked intently into the mirror above his wash-basin, and said in a rueful tone:

'Joe, why do I look such a cad?'

Far was it from me to give him an answer.

He was an excellent publisher. To be an excellent publisher you have to be a businessman. I had no intention of leaving Courtenay.

On the other hand, the morning I met Courtenay for lunch I was not what my Civil Service colleagues might have called happy in my relationship with him. I felt amazed and injured. My small masterpiece *improper*? (Or, more accurately, perhaps too improper to be published.) It seemed to me incredible. It was no more improper – if you want to be able to judge for yourself – than this book you are now reading! (To be accurate, just about the same.) I went to Courtenay's club looking pale, I have no doubt, but feel-ing proud.

I was early and had to wait in the foyer. I meant to reproach Courtenay as soon as he came in, not to wait until after lunch. Businessmen, I had learnt, went in for lunch first, business after-wards, a form of etiquette that I, as an artist, found intolerably digestion-destroying. In the past I had put up with going through the whole lunch, with wine, waiting for Courtenay to say what he thought of my new manuscript. Nowadays I used to ask him before he got his overcoat off. Lunch first, business afterwards – O.K. But Art before either!

Through the glass doors I saw Courtenay coming vigorously up the steps. He was not wearing an overcoat. A carnation glowed in his smartly cut lapel. He shook my hand.

'It's a very good book, Joe,' he said, warmly. 'Very good.'

I stared at him.

'But I can't risk publishing it.'

Before I could say anything he got me moving up the staircase to the bar.

Courtenay got some drinks and we settled down in a corner by ourselves.

'So you think it's improper?' I said.

Courtenay gave me a shrewd glance. 'Who said I said that?' Though his eyes might normally, according to Robert, look sad and lemur-like, they could give a shrewd glance that was positively levantine.

I told him my agent said he said that.

Courtenay then did look sad. 'How you both misunderstand me,' he said. He looked at me straight. 'Do you think I'm a prude, Joe? Do you honestly think I'm a prude?'

I said I did not think so.

'You, Joe, can write anything you like,' he said, 'and I should like it.' He began to smile. 'In fact, in this book you have . . .' He went on smiling. Then suddenly he stopped smiling. 'But if I print it, I shall have the Home Office down on me like a ton of bricks. It won't do, Joe . . . Publishing's a business, you know. Something you artists sometimes don't fully understand. The firm's got to make money, not lose it. If I brought this book out I'd risk losing a hell of a lot of money.' Then he added. 'And it's not *my* money . . . It's the firm's money.'

I cannot say my heart was wrung as much as his by that thought. I said: 'But surely it's not as improper as all that? I've read books much *more* improper.'

'So you may have. So have I. They've been published and nothing has happened to them because the Home Office hasn't been interested in them.' He drank some of his gin-and-tonic and then gave me his levantinely shrewd look. 'But we've just heard that the Home Office is going to start getting interested.' He glanced round as if he might be making sure that nobody was eavesdropping. 'Apparently they're just about to open a new drive . . .' He paused. 'In case you should be thinking that some other publisher might be ready to publish your book, I'm afraid that won't be so. The word's going round . . .' He drank some more gin-and-tonic and said modestly: 'I just happened to be the first one to hear.'

This left me for some time with nothing to say.

'I suppose,' I said at last, 'I shall have to alter the book?'

'I sincerely hope you will,' he replied.

I remarked. 'You sound doubtful . . .'

'I am, Joe, I am. I don't know how much you'd have to alter it to make it pass.'

'There must be some standard of reference,' said I.

Courtenay shook his head. 'The Home Office, or the Director of Public Prosecutions, can set the standard more or less where they like. Since the war everybody's noticed that it's been going down. Now they're going to put it up. We shan't know how high they're going to put it' – he made a gesture with his hand – 'till they put it.' He rested his hand on my arm. 'It's got us publishers worried, Joe. Definitely worried.'

'No more worried than it's got one of us writers,' I observed.

'For instance,' said Courtenay, 'they could take *The Decameron* out of circulation tomorrow if they felt like it.'

'But you don't publish *The Decameron*.'

'No.'

'And I,' said I, 'am nothing like as improper as Boccaccio.'

'I know.' He patted my arm. 'Have another drink, Joe. I wish I could help you, old boy.'

With a lively step he went to the bar. When he came back with two more drinks, he said:

'Of course I'm not entirely without any suggestions for you, Joe. Don't think that! I want to publish that book, Joe. I believe in it.' He looked at me. 'My suggestion is that you should talk to our solicitor about it. I rely on him. Will you do that, Joe? He'll explain the law to you, and then even make some suggestions about how to . . . tone the thing down so as to get by with it. You just twist the book a bit' – he grinned – 'and we'll twist the Home Office.'

I said all right, I would see the firm's solicitor.

We drank the rest of our drinks without making any further headway. And I must say I did not feel very much like eating any lunch afterwards.

In his businesslike way, Courtenay arranged for me to see the solicitor on the next afternoon.

The solicitor had his chambers in an old rabbit-warrenish sort of building. However, the room in which he himself worked when I finally got to it reminded me agreeably of a tutor's room in a college. It was a square room with a tall sash-window that looked out on to a green stretch of grass. The walls were panelled and painted white – as in college rooms, they looked fairly dirty – and they were ornamented with old county maps in Hogarth frames. An electric fire was glowing in the fireplace.

When I entered the room the solicitor got up from his desk – I saw my manuscript on it – and smiled at me in a pleasantly composed way. He was tall, slender, nicely filled-out. I judged him to be about fifty. His neck was long and cylindrical, and he had a smooth oval face. His hair appeared to have gone white prematurely. Altogether he was a nice-looking man. Beautiful teeth, I noticed, when he smiled. Nice grey eyes.

'Ah,' he said, shaking my hand and speaking in a warm unaffected voice. 'I want to tell you how much I've enjoyed and admired your book.'

I must have looked startled.

'You see,' he said, giving me his pleasantly composed smile again, 'I want you to see right from the start, that I'm not pi.'

π? For a moment I was startled again. Then the language I had never spoken at a prep. school came back to me. 'Oh, pi,' I said, nodding my head. 'Yes, not pi . . .'

'H'm – h'm.' He sat down again.

Actually I would not have thought at first sight that he *was* pi – or not pi, for that matter.

I sat down in a big leather armchair beside his desk.

He clasped his hands beneath his chin and began.

'The first think I have to explain to you, Mr Lunn, is that the law relating to Obscene Libel is –'

'*Obscene Libel!*' I cried.

He smiled. 'Libel, in this case, does not mean what you think it means. The word derives from *libellus*, meaning "little book".'

Little book! That was just what I had written. A charming, attractive little book, a masterly little book!

'But obscene!' I still cried. 'That means repulsive, repellent. There's nothing repulsive or repellent about what I've written.'

'Not to you, clearly. Not to many people, I dare say.' He spoke slowly and evenly all the time. 'But that is not relevant, I'm sorry to say. One of the questions we have to ask ourselves in the first instance is: Might it seem repulsive, repellent, to the Director of Public Prosecutions?'

'How am I to know? I've never met him. Anyway, there's always *somebody* to whom *something* is repellent.'

'I was referring to the D.P.P. in his official role.' He smiled a little.

'What's that?'

'That of advising the police whether or not to take action over a particular book.' He paused. 'Though I must tell you the police are not bound to take his advice.'

'I see,' said I.

'Not,' he went on, 'that it need necessarily be the police who set the Act in motion in the first place. Any person, any private person, can set the Act in motion.' He paused again. 'But we are straying away from the point. I have to explain to you that in connexion with the Act there is no definition of what is obscene.'

'Oh,' I said.

'Nor is the punishment for "publishing an obscene libel" anywhere defined or limited.'

'Oh,' I said again.

'Of course,' he went on, 'there are, as it were, *some* signposts.' He smiled at me.

'M'm?' I said.

'In the absence of a definition of obscenity, we have a test for obscenity. You probably know it? That of Chief Justice Cockburn in 1868.'

I shook my head. He nodded his.

'In any case, I should have felt bound to remind you of it,' he said.

'It goes thus: "The test of obscenity is whether the tendency of the matter charged as obscenity is to deprave and corrupt those whose minds are open to such immoral influences and into whose hands a publication of this sort may fall" . . . Let me anticipate' – he held up his hand in a pleasantly composed way – 'a claim that I'm sure you must be going to make, that you, as the author, had no intention to deprave and corrupt any of your readers.' He smiled at me, shaking his head. 'In the court, this is ignored. The intention is judged entirely from the book itself . . . I can go further. In the court the author has no *locus standi*, as we call it. He may neither give nor call evidence.'

It dawned on me that he must be the most composed person I had ever met.

'And lastly,' he went on, 'two final points, before we get down to work on your book, in which, I'm afraid, we shall have to make radical alterations if we are to meet the Home Office in its new mood – in what we have reason to believe will be its new mood – two final points. With reference to Chief Justice Cockburn's test. There is no certainty in *theory* as to the meaning of the words "deprave and corrupt" nor to which class of persons they apply.' He paused. 'Nor is there any certainty in *practice* either.'

There was a short silence.

'Well, thank you,' I said. 'It sounds to me as if you've covered the lot.'

'Thank you for saying so.' He turned slowly to look out of the window. The light glimmered on his beautiful teeth. The contrast between his white hair and smooth uniformly brownish complexion was striking. He turned back to me.

'In our work we shall have two signposts on which we can rely,' he said. 'The one, my knowledge of previous indictments. The other' – his voice became more resonant – 'our own good feelings.' He nodded his head. 'It is the latter which in the long run will make the more important signpost. Incomparably the more important. I'm confident that if we rely on our own good feelings, all will be well.'

Something made me feel inclined to reserve my judgement.

'Now,' he said, beginning to turn over the pages of my typescript.

'To begin with I think we'd better look for isolated passages that might cause us trouble.' He glanced up and smiled. 'I can reassure you. They are fewer than might be expected. If I may say so, that is a tribute to your talent.'

As he appeared to mean it, I smiled back.

'Here is the first point. I see here a word consisting of the letter "f" and three asterisks.'

'Good gracious,' I said. 'That word's printed in full about ten times a page, in—' I named an American war-novel that everybody had read.

'In that work,' he said, 'you will recall that the word was *mis-spelt* . . . I'm afraid your device leaves it open to the correct spelling, when no doubt might be left in the mind of the Home Office.' He held up his hand. 'Now, please don't think I'm being pi! I'm not suggesting you should remove it. Indeed, I'm not. We all know the word is sometimes used, even if we do not use it ourselves. What I'm suggesting is that you may keep the letter "f" and add four, or perhaps five asterisks.'

'That might certainly leave some doubt in the mind of the Home office,' I said.

'With five asterisks we might have no trouble at all. And our good feelings would be spared.'

I said: 'I think I'll cut the whole remark out.'

'That would be meeting the Home Office more than half-way. I'm glad, Mr Lunn.'

He went on turning over pages. 'And now,' he said, looking down, 'I have to notice that here you've mentioned a member . . .'

'Member?' I said, startled. 'Member of what?'

His head remained down. 'I was hoping you'd take my meaning without further explanation. I was using the word "member" in the sense of . . . "organ".'

'Oh dear,' I said. I felt as if I were going to blush. Then I said: 'Where have I mentioned it?' I went and looked over his shoulder at the manuscript. 'But I *haven't* mentioned it,' I said. 'Show me where!'

'Ah, that is merely a tribute to your literary skill. It is not mentioned by word, but I have no doubt that the Home Office would feel it was *there*.'

'If two people are making love,' I said, 'it's bound to be there! Home Office or no Home Office.'

'H'm, h'm,' he said thoughtfully. Then: 'Making love . . .' He looked up from the manuscript. 'I wonder if your good feelings tell you that kissing might serve your purpose just as well?'

'I can tell you,' I said, tapping the manuscript, 'it wouldn't serve *theirs*!'

There was a long pause.

I said: 'I suppose that scene will have to go out.'

'That's excellent, Mr Lunn. I'm very glad indeed to hear you say that. I can see that ours is going to be a very fruitful partnership.'

There was a pause. He quietly turned back the pages of my manuscript, so that the book was closed.

'I see that I can now safely leave isolated passages to you, Mr Lunn.' He smiled. 'I wish that were the end of our troubles. If the law were concerned only with isolated passages, I can assure you it would be. However, the law is so framed that there is no certainty as to whether the test of obscenity is an isolated passage or the book's dominant effect. We now have to consider the book's dominant effect.'

'The dominant effect,' I said with authority, 'is that of a work of art.'

He said: 'In declaring a book "obscene" according to the law, it is very doubtful if a judge or jury may take that into consideration.'

'Oh,' said I.

He smiled. 'I hope I'm not tiring you with so many explanations. I think I can make quite shortly the statements in the light of which we have to consider your book for the purpose of judging its dominant effect. Obscenity, as you know, has always been confined to matters related to sex or' – he completed the sentence hurriedly – 'the excremental functions. Furthermore, we say something is obscene, we know it to be obscene, if it arouses in us a feeling of shock, of outrage.'

I was really irritated.

'In your book there is a good deal about matter related to sex,' he went on. He smiled friendlily. 'Now didn't your good feelings tell you that the dominant effect of the way you had presented them might arouse a feeling of shock, of outrage, in some persons who might read it?'

'Not till there was some question of the book not being published.'

He shook his head in a way that signified composed disappointment in me. 'I'm afraid it may arouse that feeling. It well may. The characters in your book make love to each other. There appears to be no likelihood of their generating children thereby – in fact you go to no lengths to conceal from the reader that they are not married. What is the dominant effect of the passages in which these actions are recounted?' He answered the question himself, after first posing another one. 'Do we see them in a light of immodesty, of shame? . . . Undeniably we don't.' He paused. 'The dominant effect of these scenes is of pleasure.' His lips formed the word as if it were spelt with a capital P. 'Of undivided Pleasure! Of complete Enjoyment!'

'That was what I had in mind,' I conceded honestly.

He said: 'Suppose, then, a jury were directed to imagine a typical young person – tempted to sexual activity, and asking desperately, "How do I stand?" and "Where do I go from here?" – searching for an answer to his problem in your book.' He paused. 'What answer do you think he'd find in your book?'

I did not say anything. He was making me feel shy again.

'The answer he'd find would be Yes, a thousand times Yes, wouldn't it?'

I said: 'I think a thousand's a bit much.'

'You may be right . . . But twice would be enough.' There was almost a tremor in his composure. 'Or even once, more's the pity!'

I looked out through the tall sash-window. The grass looked very green, the daylight very limpid. Not like his imagination, I thought.

'You now see what I mean by the dominant effect, Mr Lunn.'

'Indeed I do,' I replied.

He smiled very composedly, very friendlily now. 'I'm glad you've been so understanding,' he said. 'Obscenity is a very difficult thing to make clear to authors. And the task of making it clear is specially difficult for anyone like myself, who, as you now see, is not in the least pi.'

I nodded my head.

He picked up my book to give it back to me. 'This is an excellent book, Mr Lunn. When you are rewriting it, just let *good* feelings be your guide. Then the Home Office will let it go by. In affairs relating to sex, remember modesty, concern for the conventions, awareness of sin; above all don't give us a dominant effect of undivided pleasure, complete enjoyment, as you have done!' He smiled. 'Think of that typical young person whom the jury might be directed to imagine! . . . Keep him *clean!*'

He stood up, and I stood up. As he shook my hand he said:

'When I look into your face, Mr Lunn, I can see that you *can!*'

2

Was It a Help?

When I bore the news back to Robert he was very distressed. By that time I was beginning to feel more than distressed.

'Altering isolated passages is child's play,' he said.

I nodded, thinking of the infallible device, i.e. excision, that I had already hit upon.

'But the dominant effect . . .' Robert shook his head.

'I don't see,' I said, 'how I can produce a different dominant effect with those characters and that story.'

At the thought of them Robert bowed his head. He was no doubt dwelling on undivided Pleasure, complete Enjoyment.

'The trouble is,' he said, 'that the dominant effect is . . . *you*.'

I did not quite like the sound of that.

'It's you,' he said, 'who shines through the whole book.'

Shine! That was better.

'If only,' I said, 'I could shines a bit more *cleanly!*'

'That,' said Robert, 'is the disability we've got to get round, somehow – the disability, I may say, *vis-à-vis* the Home Office. I personally don't agree with either Courtenay or his solicitor that the book is obscene, and I doubt if anybody we know would.' He paused. 'But it isn't anybody we know who's going to set the Act in motion; or anybody we know who's going to decide whether the Act shall take its course.'

'In some ways it would be a help in these circumstances,' I said, 'if you did think it was obscene, and then I could alter it so that you didn't.'

Robert glanced at me. 'Yes. I see that.'

'Or,' I said, 'if the dominant effect is *me*, I could ask *you* to rewrite the book.'

'I think you can take it,' said Robert, in a slightly sharper, loftier tone, 'I should treat the subject rather differently.'

I had nothing to say to that. We remained silent. I was concentrating on how *I* might rewrite the book so that, in the circumstances of there being no definition of what was obscene, it could in no circumstances be pronounced obscene.

Robert interrupted me.

'I wonder how this business started,' he said. 'I bet you when Courtenay first read this book he didn't think it was anything worse than mildly improper, in an amusing, amiable, acceptable way.'

'I didn't even think it was improper!' I cried. 'I just thought it was natural.'

Robert went on: 'Granted that, when he put it to this egregious solicitor you saw, he got the answer he did get, I still don't see why he sent it to the solicitor in the first place.'

'He heard the Home Office were going to start a new drive.'

'That's as may be. But I wonder what made him associate a prospective Home Office drive with your book . . .'

I shrugged my shoulders. I was too preoccupied with my own actual problems to be drawn into Robert's speculations. I was trying to think of the typical young person whom I was to try not to deprave and corrupt – remembering that nobody really knew, least of all cared to say, what being depraved and corrupted entailed.

'And I wonder how it's done, anyway,' Robert was saying. 'I suppose people at the Home Office get together with people in the Department of the Director of Public Prosecutions, and then they tip off Chief Constables to start reading books.'

'*My* book!' I said, thinking of my innocent, natural, small masterpiece in the hands of a Chief Constable.

Robert said: 'I think I'll make it my business to have lunch with Courtenay. It can't do any harm to find out how he got the word from the Home Office, and it might do some good.'

There were occasions, it seemed to me, when Robert sounded more like a civil servant than an artist. However, I did not say anything.

Two days later Robert had lunch with Courtenay. When he got back, he came straight into my office. Without taking off his overcoat he sat on the corner of my table and said:

'I've found out how Courtenay heard the Home Office were going to start a new drive against books. He didn't hear direct. He was told by an intermediate person. And your book was specifically mentioned at the time . . . Who do you think that intermediate person was?'

I looked at him. Having declared our thoughts to each other continually over the last twenty years, there were occasions now when we just read them. I said instantly:

'Harry.'

Robert nodded.

'Good God!' I said.

Robert went on nodding.

'But why?' I said. 'And how?'

Robert paused and then said with heavy detachment – and very faint knowingness:

'I suppose "motiveless malice" . . .'

I pondered this.

'Incidentally,' said Robert, 'have you let Harry read the manuscript?'

'I have not.'

'How could he have read it?'

'He has a drink sometimes with my agent. I suppose he got a few pointers out of him, harmlessly enough, and then' – I thought of one of Harry's favourite phrases – 'pieced it together . . . Nobody has more skill, or more practice, at piecing things together than Harry.'

We paused. Suddenly I had a new idea. I said:

'I suppose Harry didn't fabricate the rumour about the Home Office?'

Robert shook his head. 'That would be carrying motiveless malice to inconceivable lengths. No. I should think he did pick up something, probably from some bird in the Home Office who belongs to his club. It's very much a place for senior civil servants, especially youngish ones who're on the way up.' He continued my education by naming some of them.

I brought him back to Art. I said:

'But it doesn't follow that because Courtenay heard the Home Office were going to start a new drive that it was going to be directed against me for one.'

Robert shook his head.

There was a pause.

Robert said: 'I'm afraid the result of my researches isn't relevant to the immediate literary problem that confronts you.'

Now I shook my head. The result of his researches was not relevant to what I proposed to write; but it was relevant to what I proposed to do. I meant to see Harry without delay. I told my P.A. to ring him up.

Harry invited me to lunch at his club. It was not a club I liked at the best of times – like most men I cared only for my own. And this was far from the best of times.

In outward appearance Harry's club seemed to me to combine gloom with stodginess, its most imposing feature being a huge staircase of considerable grandeur and practically no illumination. And somehow my invariable recollection of the club was of having coffee, after a poor meal, in an alcove on this staircase. In fact there were no alcoves on the staircase itself, but that did not affect my invariable recollection. This was the club, as Robert observed, where senior civil servants had seen fit to swarm, as for instance bishops and vice-chancellors swarmed at the Athenaeum, or men of unusual talent and exceptional goodwill swarmed at mine.

When I arrived Harry and I went straight up to lunch – partly because we were late and partly because his club, like several others which prided themselves in not moving in an ungentlemanly way with the times, had no bar. (My invariable recollection of another club, much superior socially to Harry's, was of having to have drinks before meals standing up, more or less *under* the stairs.)

I dodged the club's soup by asking for potted shrimps, which were imported in blue cartons from a reliable contractor.

'I'm afraid,' said Harry, 'I don't belong to this club for its food.'

Not feeling called upon to express an opinion on that, I said:

'On the whole civil servants don't notice what they're eating. They're too busy thinking.'

Harry's eyes brightened. 'What are they thinking about?'

'What Action they ought to Take, of course.' I could never understand how the idea had got into circulation among the general public that civil servants were characterized by their capacity for doing nothing. The lower orders of the Civil Service may not get much of a chance, but the bosses are indomitable men of action. Confronted with a new fact, the first response of any moderately senior civil servant is to say 'What Action ought we to Take?' or of a boss as grand as Annette's father to ask 'Is there anything we ought to do about it?'

Harry laughed – a high-pitched, fluent laugh.

'By the way,' I said, 'did *you* tell Courtenay Chamberlain you had reason to believe the Home Office would object to my novel?'

'Yes,' Harry said immediately.

I looked at him. His small brown eyes looked at me unwaveringly. And yet he blushed. The whole of his face – which was quite a lot, I can tell you – was suffused with bright carmine. I do not think I had ever seen him blush so deeply before.

'Why?' I said.

'Because I did have reason to believe it,' said Harry. The blush was fading upwards into where the scalp showed through his thinning dark mouse-coloured hair.

'Will you explain to me how?'

'With pleasure, Joe,' He was trying to recover himself. 'You have a right to know.'

I gave him my mesomorphic glare.

'The Home Office are going to switch their policy,' he said, 'in the direction of cleaning things up. That's definite. I heard it from someone in this club who's in the Home Office. He didn't actually tell me in so many words, but I pieced it together.'

'I see no reason why he should not have told you in so many words.'

Harry jumped. 'I wanted to be discreeter than that,' he said.

'Discreeter?' said I.

The wine-waiter belatedly put two glasses of sherry in front of us. I drank some. Harry drank some – he had apparently given up abstention for this occasion.

'I immediately saw the danger to you,' he said.

'Danger?' I said. 'What danger?'

Harry drank a little more sherry to wet his lips.

'I knew this chap had read your previous books.' Harry tried to smile. 'He enjoyed the last one very much, thought it was very funny – *and* true.'

'Yes?'

'I wanted to find out what line the Home Office might take if you brought out another book that was . . . more so.'

'More what?'

Harry drank some more sherry.

I said: 'What reason have you to believe my next novel is what you choose to call "more so"?'

Harry looked at me brightly and blandly. 'Well, *isn't* it?'

'That,' I said, 'is a matter of opinion.'

'Exactly!' said Harry. 'Of course I haven't read it, so I don't know . . . But why do you think your agent's so enthusiastic about it?'

'Because it's an excellent book.'

There was a pause while we finished our shrimps.

Then I said: 'So you wanted to find out what line the Home Office might take if I brought out another book that was more so?'

Harry looked menaced. 'I thought it would be interesting to know.'

'And what was the outcome?'

'He thought yours might well be the sort of book that a Chief Constable might pick on.'

I have to admit that my confidence fell.

'So you see, Joe . . .'

I said nothing for a moment. Harry looked round for the wine-waiter. He had ordered one of the best bottles the club stocked: there was no sign of it.

A waitress brought us some veal croquettes.

We began to eat. I said:

'So instead of telling me all this, you went and told Courtenay?'

Harry said: 'I happened to *see* Courtenay!' He gave me an unhappy look. 'I've seen so little of you recently. We don't seem to see as much of each other as we used.'

I glared at him.

'I can see you're angry with me,' he said.

'You weren't expecting me to be pleased with you, were you?'

'I *was*!' Harry cried. 'You've misjudged me!'

My glare changed, against my will, to a look of amazement.

'I thought I'd chance my arm for your sake,' Harry said. 'Suppose the book had come out and you'd been prosecuted.'

The wine-waiter poured out two glasses of claret at last. We waited for him to go away.

'I'd have told you if I'd seen you,' Harry went on. 'I can see you think I was trying to make trouble. You don't know how difficult things are for me.' He paused, his face bright with emotion. 'I know I've sometimes chanced my arm in the past and it's caused trouble. But this time it wasn't like that, Joe. If you're thinking it was what Robert calls motiveless malice, you're mistaken! I *had* a motive . . . And it was to *help* you!'

I felt as if my head were beginning to spin a little.

I proceeded to eat some more veal croquette with an unusually wet-looking brussels sprout.

'I'm not the sort of man you think I am,' said Harry.

I had never before felt so closely confronted with what is referred to as the mystery of personality. What for certain was at the core

406

of spinning Harry? And how could I for certain tell, bearing in mind relativistic notions, if he set me spinning myself?

'Not quite, anyway,' he said. 'Not always.'

Something made me want to laugh.

Instantly there was a gleam in Harry's eye.

'Isn't this food awful?' he said. 'But the wine's good.' And he drank some wine.

I said: 'I'm in a hell of a mess over the book, Harry. I just don't know how to alter it. Courtenay's solicitor's opinion makes it simply impossible – and Courtenay won't publish unless his solicitor is satisfied.'

Harry nodded his head sympathetically. 'How's Elspeth taking it?'

'She's very upset.'

There was a pause while we finished our veal croquettes.

'Yes,' said Harry. 'That's a pity.' A look of special unconcern came into his face. 'Last time we saw her we thought how well she was looking.' He had picked up the menu card and was looking at the list of puddings.

He handed the card to me.

'She isn't going to have a baby, is she?'

I said: 'No,' with what I meant to be equal unconcern.

Harry smiled sweetly. 'It's all right, we were just wondering.'

I said: 'Give us a chance! We've only been married a year.'

'Yes,' said Harry, pacifyingly. 'That's just what I said to your mother.'

'To my mother!'

I thought it would probably be difficult to estimate, now, which of our heads was spinning the faster.

'Now don't get me wrong, Joe!' Harry smiled shrewdly at me round his snub nose. 'Your mother doesn't necessarily think you ought to have started one yet. I think she's being got-at by members of your father's congregation.'

'Those old tabby-cats!' I said. 'When we got married they suspected Elspeth was going to have a baby and thought she ought

407

not to. Now we've been married a year without having one, they think she *ought* to.'

Harry smiled. 'It's the way of the world.'

'Too damned symmetrical,' said I.

And yet I was wondering too. *Ought* we to be going to have a baby? I had not thought of it in that light before. Could it be that the pressure of society was getting me mobilized for the next step?

In due course Harry and I finished our meal and then, it seems to me in recollection, we drank some tepid black coffee in an alcove on the staircase.

Somehow Harry had composed our quarrel. There was no doubt about it. I did not know if I could possibly believe what he had told me, and I was suddenly feeling more hideously got-down than ever by the prospect of changing my novel. Yet I was glad he was there.

In my reflections I heard him saying again:

'You don't know how difficult things are for me.'

3
Dark Days

I completed my work on the isolated passages – I found what I thought might be mistaken for several more. This kind of work was what Robert and I called literary carpentry, and we both enjoyed it. For example, it never failed to give me pleasure to see how, if one began using one's blue pencil at any point on the page of a manuscript and stopped at almost any other point, the thing still read on. (Would that more novelists, especially American naturalistic writers who produce 900 pages of 'total recall', would discover this innocent professional pleasure!) My pleasure in this case was mixed with a good deal of regret for some pleasing, natural scenes. And when I happened in my spare time to read a Deep South novel in which, as you might expect, there was printed a lavish description of a rape, my pleasure was mixed with a lot of bad temper.

However, I thought it wise to show my manuscript with its first alterations to Courtenay's solicitor. In the first place I felt that a pat on the head from him would be encouraging: in the second I had hopes that somehow the excision of isolated passages might have reduced the dominant effect.

Courtenay's solicitor was indeed pleased. I went to see him to collect the manuscript from him.

'This is a step in the right direction, Mr Lunn. Surely a step in the right direction.' His smiling grey eyes and his shapely lips remained steady. 'I see that you've removed several major isolated passages that must surely have given the Home Office cause to think . . .'

'Cause to think? As if they didn't know!'

And then, thinking of the pleasing, natural, isolated passages that had gone, I thought of the passage in the Deep South novel that, in contrast, had been allowed to remain. My bad temper got the better of me. I pointed out the contrast to Courtenay's solicitor.

He nodded his white-haired head smoothly.

'But, Mr Lunn, I don't think there'd be any harm in your writing about rape.'

At this my bad temper broke out. 'Thank you for nothing!' I cried. 'I don't want to write about rape. I couldn't anyway – I've no experience of it!'

I saw him looking faintly perturbed by my anger, so I changed my tone.

'Actually,' I said, 'I don't think I could get any experience of it. I'm rather shy, by nature. I like to be encouraged . . .'

'I wasn't suggesting you should write about rape. I was only illustrating the major contention that you'll remember my putting to you last time we discussed this matter.'

'I see what you mean,' I said. 'I'm allowed to describe sexual activity if it's a crime. What I'm not allowed to describe is a simple, natural ***** that both parties enjoy.'

He nodded his head slowly, as if, for instance, I had at last seen that a straight line is the shortest distance between two points.

'Exactly. That is what I have been trying to put to you in essence. Though of course it's a question of degree. No one, not even the Home Office in its strictest mood, would expect an author not to refer to the phenomenon you mentioned. Refer to it, of course. But in describing it there must be limits to how far an author may go.'

I was reminded – I am sorry to say I was reminded – of a favourite recollection that Robert and I shared, of overhearing two office girls sitting in front of us in a bus.

'I'm not going out with *him* any more. He wants to go too far,' said one.

To this the other said: 'I agree with you, I really do. If you let them go as far as they want, where would they stop?'

410

The concept of far-ness had exercised Robert's imagination ever since. What was too far? Or not far enough? And finally what was the farthest you could go?

'I think,' said Courtenay's solicitor, 'we should all agree that in this first draft you go a good deal too far for the Home Office.'

I said: 'I see.'

'That is what governs the dominant effect.' He handed me back my manuscript for the second time. 'I now look forward to read-ing this excellent book again when good feeling has kept you from going a fraction of an inch further than is absolutely necessary.'

I was dismissed. My alterations had clearly not altered the domi-nant effect at all. Far from feeling that I had been patted on the head, I felt that I had been kicked in the b**.

It took me some time to realize what the total effect of this interview had been. 'I just can't alter the dominant effect,' I said to Robert.

'I have to admit,' he said, 'that I can't see how the concept of far-ness can be applied to it in any way that would help you.'

'The only thing I can see for it is to scrap the book altogether.'

'I think that would be very foolish of you,' he said sharply.

I said nothing. I felt that Courtenay's solicitor, the Home Office, the Director of Public Prosecutions, and the typical young person into whose hands my book might fall, had between them got me down altogether.

I put the book aside.

'I'll come back to it in a little while,' I said to Elspeth, 'when I feel less persecuted.'

But I did not believe I could ever come back to it.

In the weeks that followed I concealed from Robert that I was not working on the book any more. I could not conceal it from Elspeth. She said nothing to me about it. I could see that she was taking it to heart in a way I had never bargained for. After all, was it not she who was the stable, relaxed person who everybody had said would cushion my fluctuations of feeling?

I started to wake up in the middle of the night. In the first moment I would feel as if I had awakened naturally, and then suddenly, like a shutter dropping, the cause would come to me. My masterpiece, my small masterpiece . . . dropped into the sea, before it had ever been out in the air and light. I can't see how to alter it, I thought, I *can't* alter it.

One night I realized that Elspeth was awake too. I turned my head on the pillow, and I felt her hand take hold of mine.

'What is it?' I whispered.

Her fingers gripped mine.

'Tell me . . . !' I said.

'I'm worried for you. I know what it means' – she meant my book – 'to you.'

I squeezed her fingers in return. 'Please don't worry, darling . . .'

There was a pause.

'It can't be helped,' I said.

Suddenly her whisper carried strong emotion. 'If only I could *help* you!'

I smiled in the darkness. 'Darling, that isn't a thing to worry about. You couldn't be expected to re-write the damned thing.'

'If only I could!'

I whispered lightly, 'One novelist in the family's enough.'

She did not reply.

'Cheer up . . . !' I whispered, and to show that I was being play-ful I began to stroke her face.

I felt tears rolling down her cheeks.

I thought: Oh dear!

I went on stroking her face and then I began to kiss her. It suddenly struck me that it was difficult to know who was trying to comfort whom.

Those were indeed dark days. I simply did not see my way out of them. And my sufferings as an artist were not alleviated, I remember, by my current activities as a civil servant. Not only did I have to go to the office and behave as if there were nothing the matter: I had to put up with one of the chores I would most gladly have let Robert in for if I could. It was interviewing, for some temporary jobs in one of our explosives research establishments, a string of organic chemists.

Organic chemists had come to be my *bêtes noires* – they seemed to me to be characterized by a peculiar combination of narrowness and complacency, having changed neither their techniques nor their opinion of themselves since the days of World War I. Organic chemistry had seen some truly glorious days at the beginning of the century, and the 1914–18 war, with everybody thinking mostly about explosives and poison gas, had been a chemists' war. But after that had come the glorious days of atomic physics; and World War II, with everybody thinking mostly about first radar and then atomic bombs, was a physicists' war. To the sort of young men I had to see the point had not gone home. On they went, sticking together parts of molecules, by their crossword-puzzley techniques, to make big molecules: then, by more crossword-puzzley techniques, they verified that they had made what they thought they had made: and then they started all over again.

When asked if they used techniques nowadays invented and used by physicists, they said to me rebukefully:

'I rely on classical methods.'

And when invited to discuss the way their parts of molecules behaved in terms of electronic structure, they said very rebukefully indeed:

'I'm afraid I'm not a theoretician.'

Some of them, it seemed to me when I got particularly desperate, might never have heard the electron had been discovered.

(In fairness I have to say that since then – I am writing about 1951 and it is now 1960 – my opinion has changed. Young organic chemists have changed, to the extent of whipping at least one 'modern technique', nuclear magnetic resonance, smartly out of the hands of the physicists.)

Anyway, it was in 1951 when I had to see a string of rebukeful, classical, non-theoreticians, in a dark February when I felt more like hiding in a corner and seeing nobody. However, the chore at last came to an end.

One weekday morning I found myself, instead of interviewing anybody whatsoever, looking into the window of an antique shop in Sloane Street. I had already stopped to look into the window of several others, but I should have been hard put to say exactly what I had looked at. I was wandering. There was nothing I wanted to do or, for that matter, to look at. Elspeth had gone to stay for a few days with her mother, who was ill, and I had taken a day off from the office. I found it a consolation to be walking instead of sitting still, and I had calculated that I could rely on the contents of antique shops to have a slight but certain fascination for me – it was not often, I thought, you came across a work of art that seduced you with its colour, symmetry, and balance, and at the same time offered you the opportunity to sit on it, eat off it, or keep things in it.

I lingered in front of the windows, hunched in my overcoat, though for February the morning was unusually sunny. When there was too much reflection from the plate glass, I put my face close to the pane and cupped my hands on either side of my eyes; so that I could peer into the calm, uninhabited depths of the shops, calm with the sheen of lamplight on velvet and brocade, uninhabited because all the things for sale were so expensive that nobody was inside buying anything.

On a small table at the side of one window there was a marquetry box that caught my eye. The door of the box was left open to reveal that it was a miniature chest of drawers. 'It couldn't be prettier,' I said half-aloud. I thought it would do for Elspeth to keep her jewellery in.

Suddenly I was pierced by superstition. If I bought Elspeth the box, we should both come out of our desolation. The gods would be placated. The Home Office would be placated. Elspeth would be happy again. I stared at the box. I pushed open the door of the shop.

The owner of the shop quietly but expeditiously brought the chest out of the window and set it down for me to see. I asked how much it was. Oh, oh, oh!

'It couldn't be prettier,' I heard myself saying. I should not have been surprised to hear myself telling him the whole of my story. I went on staring while he pulled out the drawers one by one, to show me that the bottoms were made of oak and had no worm-holes.

'As far as we know,' he said, courteously giving me what I took to be the old malarkey, 'it was made between 1750 and 1780. You might say it was a copy of the kind of cabinet that came in in the latter part of the seventeenth century.'

I managed to get out of the shop without buying it.

In the street again I was dazzled by the sunshine, and I stood still for a moment, recovering from the price.

I was startled when I heard someone say: 'Joe, what are *you* doing here?'

It was Annette. There she stood, in a tent-like overcoat.

'If it comes to that,' said I, 'what are *you?*'

'The school's shut for scarlet fever. I've just been shopping at MacFisheries.' There was one a few yards farther down the street.

I said: 'Surely there's one nearer to where you live.' It seemed incredible that she had taken to shopping at all.

'I prefer this one.' Her tone was so indisputably that of a connoisseur of fish-shops that I did not argue.

I tried to raise a smile. 'I must say London's comforting. One's always running into people one knows.'

'When I first saw you, you were looking as if you were lost.'

I took hold of her elbow. 'Let's go and have some coffee!'

I knew where there was a Kenya café. When we were settled over our coffee and chocolate biscuits, I told her what I had just been doing when she met me.

'I think you ought to buy it,' she said.

I was not surprised by one woman's advising me to buy a present for another woman, as this was the recognized policy of what Robert and I usually referred to as the Trades Union of Women. I said:

'But it's sheer superstition! You can't act on superstition.'

'That's just what you can do,' said Annette. 'One doesn't take

415

the gods seriously.' She took off the head-scarf she was wearing and shook out her bell of hair.

I watched her, slightly mesmerized. Her clear light brown eyes seemed to shine with amusement. 'All choices aren't necessarily moral ones, you know.'

I was suddenly reminded of a conversation I had had with her and Elspeth in a steamy café in Bethnal Green. 'Oh, aren't they?' I said – was she taking the mickey out of me?

Annette said: 'I wish Robert's superstitious feelings could be bought off in a similar way.' Her light-eyed smile disappeared. 'He's terribly apprehensive lest anything should go wrong with me or the baby.' She looked at me earnestly. 'He's so persistent with his apprehensions that they become catching.'

'Don't I know that!' I calculated that her baby must be due in about four or five months.

'I hope Robert will get over it,' Annette went on. 'After all, I want to have at least three more.'

'Three more what?' I said. I could scarcely believe she meant babies.

She did mean babies.

'Good gracious!' I said. 'How you've changed!'

'I don't think so.'

I thought for a little while and then inquired with some diffidence: 'How have you fixed on four?'

'That isn't so interesting,' she said, 'as *why* we've fixed on four.'

'All right,' I said, willing to please. 'Tell me *why* have you fixed on four?'

'We think the degree of possessiveness we feel about each other will be less in a family of six than in a family of two.'

'I should think it couldn't help but be,' said I. But then I asked: 'What about your degree of love, though? In particular that of you and Robert for each other?'

In my opinion, loving people takes energy, takes time. If you start to love more people, those you already love have got to accept a cut.

Annette said: 'One has to make up one's mind whether it's worth it or not. I think it is.' She paused and then her tone suddenly changed. It became tender, almost shy – it reminded me of some other occasion, when she had seemed much younger. She said:

'I was never sure Robert wanted me, until he married me. And now I'm terribly possessive about him.'

I was touched. Then I asked:

'What about teaching? Do you intend to go on teaching as well?'

'Naturally.'

This really did give me something to think about. I guessed it must have given Robert something to think about, too.

Our waitress, seeing me apparently inactive, came over and asked me if we would like more biscuits or coffee.

Annette said to me: 'Of course, Barbara thinks I ought to go on teaching.' And she laughed to herself.

I laughed to myself.

'You know,' said Annette, 'that she's pregnant too?'

I did not know. 'Good gracious!' I said again. 'I thought they'd finished procreating.' Their youngest child, as far as I recalled, must be about seven.

'She and Harry thought they'd like to start again.'

I said nothing.

'I don't know if it was our example,' Annette said with a sort of comfortable amusement.

'I have a theory,' I said, 'that people's marriages interact when they come up against each other.'

Annette laughed. 'Everybody will be having babies!' She finished her coffee.

I suddenly thought: What about Elspeth and me? I felt, I have to admit it, that we were being left out of something. So much for that old Pressure of Society, dammit! I felt envious of Robert and Annette, envious of Harry and Barbara, envious of everybody who was going to have a baby.

Annette put on her head-scarf and then picked up a string bag in which there was a parcel of what I presumed to be fish. I noticed that her face looked thinner, as if the flesh were drawn down from her chin. She said thoughtfully:

'I shall have to get a taxi.'

We went out into the street. The morning was still calm and sunny, and there was a faint smell of wood-smoke diffusing from where a gardener must have been burning leaves in Cadogan Place.

'It's like spring,' Annette murmured. I thought of my book, unprinted; of Elspeth, unable to help . . .

Two stringy superior-looking women who were passing glanced with distaste at Annette's head-scarf – they were hatless, their grey hair being beautifully arranged and dyed, in one case purple and in the other steely blue. They got into a large Rolls. I stopped a taxi for Annette.

'You go and buy that chest for Elspeth!' she said happily, and drove away.

I stood alone again on the pavement.

I went back to the shop. You may think I was in the grip of neurosis. Maybe – but not quite so far in the grip of neurosis as not to reflect that, if I were going to try and buy off the gods, I was not necessarily bound to pay Sloane Street prices.

The box was back in the window. Compulsively I pushed open the shop door. Courteously the owner made his appearance from the depths of the shop, and, when he saw that it was me, got the box out of the window again and placed it in front of me. I stared at it.

I admired it, said how much I should like to have it, and observed how costly I thought it was. Then I uttered the formula:

'Is that the lowest you'll let it go for?'

'Let it go' was a dealer's expression. What an expression! I thought as I waited to hear this dealer reply. Two things might now happen. He might say Yes. Or he might say – you think he might say No? Then you have not bothered to learn the ritual. The alternative to Yes is the antiphonal formula: 'I'll go and look in my book, and see what I gave for it.'

With a thrill I heard him utter the antiphonal formula. While he retired to wherever he kept his book, I waited patiently, quietly opening and shutting the drawers of the chest.

He was willing to 'let it go' for £8 ros. od. less than he had originally asked. I bought it.

Afterwards I stood outside the shop, holding the chest in my arms while I waited for a taxi, and feeling a peculiar emotion. The price I had paid for it was enough to make anyone feel peculiar, yet it was not the price that caused me to feel so peculiar.

In my arms I was holding a present. A present for Elspeth, a present for the gods, a present for the Home Office . . . ? I scarcely knew which. I only knew that somehow the dark days had reached a turning-point. Whether they were going to turn lighter or even darker was a different matter.

4

The Turning-Point?

Elspeth was due to come home. The present was awaiting her.
Now that I came to consider it with detachment, I was not sure
whether I liked it or not.

And yet, as I moved round the flat, making everything look tidy
in readiness for her, I thought I did like it. With a large gin-and-
tonic in my hand I sat on the edge of the bed and looked at it, on
top of the chest-of-drawers. In the shaded lighting from behind me
the scrolly patterns of acanthus leaves, composed of golden-brown
woods splashed with malachite and mother-of-pearl, seemed to
glisten with some inner radiance of their own.

'It couldn't be prettier,' I said to myself. 'Elspeth will love it.'

You can see from this that I was not certain about something.
I was not certain that the gods would love it. I had not seen my
way yet through my literary difficulties. My manuscript remained
in the cupboard where I had put it on its most recent return from
Courtenay's solicitor.

Superstition, neurosis . . . Not for nothing was I the son of a
non-conformist clergyman, I thought. Behind the words superstiti-
tion and neurosis, in my mind, lurked the word self-indulgence.

'I shall be glad when Elspeth comes,' I said to the warm, empty
room.

Elspeth came. I told her about the present for her, but not about
the superstition and neurosis. I told her it was to put her jewellery
in.

'It's beautiful!' she cried. 'Oh darling . . .' She kissed me and
thanked me.

It did look beautiful.

We sat down side by side on the edge of the bed with our arms round each other. After a while she said:

'But I haven't got any jewellery to put in it.'

I smiled into her eyes. 'You shall have, my darling.'

I noticed that her eyes looked tired. At the same time they seemed to be searching in mine. I knew what she was thinking. The dark days . . . The marquetry box had not diverted her.

'Buying it was a turning-point,' I said. 'I felt sure it marked a turning-point.'

She looked down at her lap.

I noticed the thin gold wedding ring on her finger. I touched it.

She put her head on my shoulder.

We began to talk about other things. I tried to keep my spirits up and I could tell she was trying to do the same.

In the middle of the night I woke up. The shutter suddenly dropped. Nothing had changed.

I lay very still. Nothing had changed at all.

'Darling . . .' Elspeth whispered.

I did not reply.

Elspeth could tell I was awake. 'Darling,' she whispered, 'speak to me.'

I turned and put my arms round her but I could not speak.

'I wakened every night while I was away,' she said, 'wishing I could help you.'

'My darling,' I said. 'This is where we were the other night.'

'But it's *where I am!*' she cried.

I did not say anything.

'When two people are married to each other,' she said, 'they should be a help to each other. You're a help to me, but I'm not to you . . .'

I held her more tightly. 'That's silly,' I said gently.

'We've been married a year and I'm no use to you.'

A sudden recollection came to me that was too poignant to be borne. *You must never say that again* – I heard her voice. Before I could manage to get any words out she said:

'You must wish you'd never married me!'

I was staggered by the incredibleness of the remark, of the *situation* . . . It had never occurred to me that she might feel like this. My discoveries in our married life had been first that she was a living, independently existing person, and next that she was a living, independently acting person. Love, contrary to a lot of what is said about it, does not teach you to know everything about the loved one. It makes you more sharply aware of some things, but it definitely makes you miss others. I ought not to have missed this. I was deeply ashamed of myself for not having seen it.

'My darling,' I said, 'I love you. I shall always love you. You're my wife. I wouldn't have it any different . . . I couldn't imagine it any different now . . .'

I felt tears coming into my eyes.

I went on talking to her. I was speaking to her from the bottom of my heart. As the things that lie at the bottom of one's heart are few in number and very simple, I suppose I must have become somewhat repetitious. I would not have had my life any different: I could not imagine it any different now. I loved her. I wanted to give her confidence, unshakeable for the rest of our lives. And she listened to me.

Had things been such that the question could have been put to me at the time, I should have answered that I was thinking only of her soul and mine, that I was expressing truly spiritual love. I think I was. I was genuinely surprised, after a while, by being reminded that the soul and the body are one. I had not noticed the body, but it was clearly there.

When we next started to talk we had the light on.

I was looking at Elspeth's face. 'My darling . . .'

'Yes?' She did not smile at me.

There was a pause. I heard my watch ticking on the bedside table.

'What are you going to do about your book?' She still wanted to know.

I looked at her. 'I've thought what to do,' I said. 'While I was in the bathroom.'

Her blue eyes looked at me steadily.

'My life,' I said, 'is obviously a series of acts of will. So I've just got to make another. Tomorrow I'll start writing the whole thing again, and then *not* send it to Courtenay's egregious solicitor. I'm going to ask Harry to get his Home Office friend to read it instead. With a bit of luck that could settle it.'

Her glance wavered, and suddenly, hesitantly, she smiled.

I remained bending over her, looking at her. The liberating idea actually had come to me in the bathroom.

But now I began to say something else to her – and until I had begun it I had no idea I was going to say it.

'My darling,' I whispered. 'I love you . . . You're my wife. I shall always love you. I want us to have –' I did not finish the sentence. Instead I blurted out: 'I want you to make me a dad. As soon as possible!'

With a quick movement she turned her head away on the pillow. I heard her breath drawn in, and she burst into tears.

'What is it?' I cried, trying to see her face.

'Darling . . . *Yes* . . .'

At last she turned back to me. I got my handkerchief from under the pillow and dried her face.

'You'd better dry yours,' she said.

I stroked her hair for a long time while she looked up at me. Again I heard my watch ticking.

'Fancy all this happening in the middle of the night,' I said.

She appeared not to have heard me. Suddenly I noticed a faint flicker at the corners of her mouth.

'What are you thinking?' I said.

'I was thinking if only you'd said what you've just said half an hour ago . . .'

I burst into laughter.

We both laughed. And then went quiet again. Somehow we

found ourselves staring at the marquetry cabinet, which seemed to be glistening radiantly at us.

'Like the flowers that bloom in the spring,' I said, 'it obviously had nothing to do with the case.'

'It's beautiful,' Elspeth said firmly. 'I shall always be fond of it. Thank you for it, darling.'

5

The Stream of Life

When I told Robert that Elspeth was pregnant, he was stirred, I could see, to strong emotion.

'I'm very, very glad,' he said. 'That's the best news we've had for a long time.' Startlingly he shook me by the hand.

'I think it's pretty good news too,' I said. (I must say it did strike me that fertility must be the predominant state in which the human race existed – hence, when you come to think about it, its history.)

Robert was also stirred to strong generalization.

'There's no doubt that having children,' he said, 'does make one feel part of the Stream of Mankind, in a way that one wouldn't otherwise.' He nodded his head loftily in agreement with himself.

To one who was classed MISC/INEL for the Stream of Mankind this came as a most poignant, hope-giving thought.

I nodded my head vigorously in poignant hopeful agreement with him.

'It's a very good thing,' Robert went on in the same tone, 'for a writer.'

'Anything that's good for a writer will be good for me,' I said, trying to please.

Robert's eyes glinted. 'Though it's fair to say that the majority of writers have achieved it without its having done their books any noticeable good.'

The moment I laughed he switched to lofty seriousness again.

I said nothing. In fact, thinking of my own small masterpiece no longer caused me such pain as it had in the days when I saw no way out of the dilemma presented to me by Courtenay's solicitor. I had spoken to Harry.

We had met again, for lunch yet again at Harry's club. Harry had insisted. There were not veal croquettes this time. There were chicken croquettes.

I put my proposition to Harry. I said: 'Presumably the chap who let you know the Home Office were going to start a fresh drive must be pretty close to the policy-making machine.' I saw a hunted look come into Harry's eyes. 'If you ask him to read my book, when I've re-written it, he ought to be able to let us have some sort of authoritative opinion.'

'I see that,' said Harry. The hunted look was disappearing.

'We could then tell Courtenay, and that would eliminate the necessity of having to get it approved of by his egregiously pi solicitor – which seems to me next door to impossible . . .'

Harry's small bright eyes became even brighter.

'You think I might,' he said, 'chance my arm . . . ?'

I had never thought I should live to see the day when I would hear Harry refer to 'chancing his arm' with a *frisson* of pleasure.

'That's what I should like you to do, if you will, Harry.'

Harry gave me a look which indicated that he had a good idea what I was thinking. However, he was prevented from saying anything by an interruption. Two men were passing our table and we both happened to look up. One of them was Harry's boss.

Harry's boss stopped, gave us a shark-like smile, and then, glancing from me to Harry and back, said in his croaking voice:

'Hello, Lunn. I've just been reading your last book.'

And at that he moved on.

'A man of action,' I said to Harry, 'but not of comment.'

Harry grinned.

We went on with our chicken croquettes.

'Of course we know,' Harry said, 'my chap in the Home Office definitely did like your last book.'

I nodded my head.

'Joe, I *will* chance my arm! I'm sure I can manipulate it. I'll get him to read the manuscript and let us know if the Home Office would be likely to do anything about it or not. He wouldn't need to tell me in so many words.' A light came into his eyes. 'I could piece it together.'

'I'm sure he wouldn't,' I said.

'There's only one other thing . . .'

I looked at him, wondering what on earth that could be.

'There'd be no objection,' Harry said diffidently, 'to my reading it first?'

I burst into laughter. 'None at all, my dear Harry!'

I felt liberated. I knew I could get down to work again on the book with the prospect of getting a sensible opinion on it from an authoritative person. Thank goodness, I thought, for the Civil Service.

And so life had perked up again.

Soon after that Elspeth had told me her own liberating news.

As Robert remarked, there was reason for feeling part of the Stream of Mankind. Indeed calling it the Stream of Mankind seemed to me putting it in too abstract a form. I felt there was a sort of clubbiness in the air: Robert and Annette were due to have their baby in the late summer, Harry and Barbara in the autumn, and Elspeth and I at the end of the year. We were all in it together.

I happened to say to Barbara that as far as we were concerned, the Stream of Mankind was in no way drying up.

'Parents,' she said firmly, 'have to have two children merely to replace themselves, and three to make a positive contribution.' She smiled. 'My dear Joe, you've got a long way to go yet . . .' All the same, her voice sounded softer. I noticed it was distinctly musical. I wondered why I had never noticed that before.

'Do you see me,' I said, 'having three children?'

'I don't see why not.'

I smiled at her without answering. And well I might! How things had changed!

Congratulating myself on my saintliness, in not pointing this out, I asked playfully:

'Or even four?'

'I expect Elspeth'll have some views on that,' she replied, smiling away the underlying Trades Union of Women tone.

'Naturally,' I said, like a well-trained member of the federation of employers.

After a few months the sort of clubbiness that had come into the air surrounding our close friends and us became even more clubby.

In the past I had been unequivocally in favour of the State running a free medical service, without considering whether I in particular stood to gain a great deal from it. If I, who happened to be well most of the time, helped to subsidize people who were ill, it seemed to me fair enough. Elspeth, a sterner Socialist than I, had come out even more strongly on this side of the argument: a free National Health Service was her idea of doing good; and given the opportunity of doing good or doing bad, she inevitably chose to do good.

One day, apropos of having the baby, she said to me:

'Of course I shall have it on the N.H.S.'

I said: 'Of course.'

And we discovered that she had been enrolled into one of the most gigantic, engulfing clubs in the country, that of mothers having babies on the N.H.S. At first Elspeth quailed, but conscience kept her to it, and soon she was overwhelmed. Month after month she had check-ups, did exercises, went to classes, and brought home vitamin pills and orange-juice. The effect of it all became so hypnotic that I began to feel like a co-opted member of the club myself. Elspeth told me some prospective fathers had sympathetic morning sickness. As I felt very well in the mornings, I offered to show willing by joining in the relaxation exercises.

At the time predicted, Annette had her baby. Robert, after going about for a few days so pale as to look green, turned up at the office looking as pink as if he had drunk half a bottle of brandy. The child was a boy, perfect in all respects, and Annette was extraordinarily well.

'Of course, having a child makes one feel part of the Stream of Mankind,' he said, too inflated to remember that he had said it to me before, 'in a way that one doesn't otherwise.'

Who was I to deflate him?

His speech sounded wonderfully lofty and detached, but I had intimations – and I was pretty sure he had intimations – that he was going to be an absurdly devoted father. Strongly affectionate and subtly power-loving, he was just cut out for it. Furthermore, if Annette's theories about the size of his family won the day, there was going to be plenty of scope for him.

It was a little while after this incident at the office that another, rather different one, occurred. I was chatting with my P.A. when she happened to say:

'I wonder if we're going to see you going to America later on in the year.'

'Oh?' I said.

She saw my surprise. 'I thought you knew . . .' She blushed at the thought of her indiscretion and explained: 'It's that Mr Malone who came to see you that time, you remember him –'

'Indeed I do!'

'He's written to Mr Murray-Hamilton about a conference they're going to have in Washington. And I *thought* he'd mentioned your name to go to represent the ministry.'

It was clear that she did more than think that Tom Malone had mentioned my name – the grapevine must have told her. I did not press her for further indiscretion.

About three weeks later Robert was discussing our annual Staff Promotion Review.

'I'm afraid I may have to leave you to cope with the last part of it single-handed,' he said, and paused. 'I shall probably have to go to Washington.'

'*You?*'

He looked at me. I told him why I had said '*You?*'

Robert was apologetic. He admitted that Tom Malone actually had mentioned my name. 'As a possibility, but no more,' he said. 'He knows as well as you know that he can't formally ask for a particular individual to be sent.'

I saw that.

Robert said: 'Anyway, Murray-Hamilton couldn't be induced

by me or anyone else to send *you*.' He paused and softened his tone. 'I didn't tell you all this because I thought there was no point in worrying you more than was necessary.'

So that was that. The incident, unlike the ledger for Right and Wrong, was closed.

I turned my mind to other things. The Stream of Life was carrying me on.

6

Still Darker Days

At the predicted time Barbara had her baby. Harry confided to me:

'You know, I adore very young babies.'

'Good gracious!' I said. I thought I should adore mine the more the older they got.

Harry looked knowing. 'There are quite a lot of men who do, you know.'

This had never occurred to me before. It seemed to me incredible that I must constantly be passing quite ordinary-looking men in the street, in Oxford Street for instance, whose natures were stirred to the depths by the sight of newly born infants.

On the day of their child's christening Harry and Barbara gave a large party. Elspeth and I went.

'There'll be no jiving this time,' I said. She was getting quite large.

Elspeth grinned affectionately. 'I think it'll be all right, provided you don't throw me on to the floor again.'

I grinned affectionately back. 'The Dark-town Strutters' Ball.' 'This is the right one for me! . . .' I remembered that statement which had expressed for me the poetic climax in human experience, falling in love. The fact of the matter was that, utterly flat as the statement was, I still had nothing whatsoever to add to it.

'Well, even so, we're not going to,' I said finally.

Elspeth smiled in a complacent way.

Everybody was of the opinion that her child was going to be a boy. Her doctor, her mother, the woman at the clinic, and even Barbara, committed themselves with a single practised glance to this opinion – the woman who came to clean our flat said: 'I can tell by where you carry it, dear. That's a boy, mark my words.' Talk about clubbiness! I, now thoroughly enclubbed, went along with the rest.

We enjoyed the party, even though we did not jive. I had just finished rewriting my novel, and that had brought me temporarily to a state of invulnerable high spirits. In the sense that the dominant effect was *me*, the book remained of course the same. In the sense that the dominant effect derived from specific expressions of feeling that might bring a blush to the cheek of a young policeman, it was toned down – rather skilfully, I thought. I handed the manuscript over to Harry on the day after the party. I then had to wait.

Immediately after that the Promotion Review began. Robert went to Washington.

The Promotion Review went on. Robert found official reasons for staying in America.

The Promotion Review ended. And then, late one afternoon, my P.A. came in and said:

'I've just heard from Mr Murray-Hamilton's P.A. that there's a Parliamentary Question on the way over. Mr Spinks has told her to mark it first to Mr Froggatt, and then to you.'

I presumed it to be a question addressed by some Member of Parliament to our minister about something he thought was wrong. P.Q.s were a rare occurrence in our office. (Far be it from me to say that this was because we rarely did anything wrong. It was just that our work was not the sort that immediately evoked grievances among the public.) I regretted that Robert was not there to cope with it, and said:

'Tell Mr Froggatt to bring it in as soon as it arrives.'

Actually this order was unnecessary, as everybody dropped whatever he was doing when a P.Q. came in – anyone who thinks civil servants are not sensitive to what is said about them in Parliament does not know anything about it.

It was next morning before Froggatt came in with the file.

'It's the usual thing,' he said lugubriously. 'If you don't get what you want, kick the civil servant who you think's to blame.' He looked at me in a thoughtful way. 'I don't know what the public would do if they hadn't got us as scapegoats.'

Suddenly his long fiddle face and large slightly aggrieved-looking eyes struck me as exactly what you would expect to see actually on a scapegoat.

I nodded my head sympathetically.

'I think you'll find all the relevant papers are there,' he said.

The file began with a short letter from the Right Honourable Mr Adalbert Tiarks, M.P., to our minister, saying he would like our minister to advise him on the reply to a letter, which he enclosed, from one of his constituents. This is what the letter said:

Dear Mr Tiarks,

I do not expect you will remember me though I remember you, as I was the office-boy when you gained your first post with our firm as Assistant Sales Manager, North-West Sub-Region. In these circumstances I trust you will not think I am presuming to write to you. It is about my son Wilfred. I trust when you hear the facts that you will agree that it is a case of injustice as I do.

My son Wilfred has got his B.Sc. in chemistry with honours and has just taken his Doctor of Philosophy. Thus he is a highly trained scientist. He read an advertisement for highly trained scientists to work for the Government and applied for it. He got his letter for interview at the Ministry and went up with high hopes, as he is always reading in the newspapers that there is a grave shortage of highly trained scientists. He told me when he came home that he thought he had failed. He had.

The reason my son thought he had failed was the unfairness of the chairman of his interview. The chairman told my son that he was not a chemist himself and asked in a manner which upset my son if my son knew something about electrons which Wilfred says do not come into his studies, as he has been making chemical substances that have never been made before. My son is convinced that if he had been interviewed by a highly qualified

433

chemist like his professor he would have got through with flying colours. Instead of that, because of the Ministry's chairman, he is debarred from working for his country and may have to have his call-up for the Army.

I trust you will pardon this letter for being so long, for I do feel it is a case of injustice that it is only right to write to you about it. It has been a great strain to his mother and me to keep Wilfred at college, and so it is a great blow to us when his hopes are shattered thus. Is it therefore the Government's intention that a boy like my son, who has got his Doctor of Philosophy, should be debarred from serving his country through the unfairness of a Civil Servant?

Yours truly,
R. T. Longstaff (Mr)

P.S. I have not mentioned that I am writing this letter to Wilfred.

The letter was touching, but I have to admit that my predominant response to it was not sympathy for a father. It was a peculiarly unwelcome kind of concern for myself.

The file had been marked first to Froggatt so that he could attach all the relevant papers. There they were, attached. An application from W. Longstaff for a post as Temporary Scientific Officer; a couple of professional references, one from his professor and the other from his supervisor of research; a copy of a letter from us calling him for interview and another saying that we had no appointment to offer; and on top, the last object to be attached by my P.A. – a rectangular index-card covered with my own handwriting.

While I was checking them, there was a telephone call. It was from Spinks, Stinker Spinks.

'About that P.Q. you should have on your desk at the present moment –'

'Yes,' I said. 'I have it.'

'Murray-Hamilton will be in Glasgow till the end of the week.

I've just telephoned him. He'll want a suggested draft reply from you on his desk without fail next Monday morning.'

I said: 'Yes.' *Suggested* . . . anybody but Spinks would just have said a draft reply. I put down the receiver and looked at the index-card. It was filled up with notes about W. Longstaff made by me during the course of his interview.

'Tallish stringy white-faced schizoid-looking individual with unusually handsome eyes. 2:31/2:5. Got a II(i) chem, took to organic "because it's more orderly". Ph.D. without a single fresh idea of his own but has given satisfn to his prof classical synthesis. Not the sort of soma for creative energy. Tight constrained meagre temperament. Thoroughly second-rate but will prob get on through nagging persistence. Passionately anxious to come to us thereby avoid military service. Proposing get married – "prefers cycling". Reads *Daily Tel* "because it's unbiased". Cripes! P.T.O.'

I read it with sarcastic ill-humour. The aim of my notes was to recreate the man for me when I read them. Reading these notes I remembered W. Longstaff. He was awful.

I turned the card over.

'Board more unanimous not to have him at any price than I'd expected. P.H.S. wanted us to send protest to D.S.I.R. about his being given Ph.D. Grant in the first place. Cripes again.'

I must say I read that side with a diminution in ill-humour. W. Longstaff was awful, but it did not follow that my colleagues would inevitably see his awfulness. They had! And furthermore P.H.S. was one of our cleverest, toughest, youngish organic chemists.

The telephone rang again. It was Stinker again.

'A letter has just come in for Murray-Hamilton from W. Long-staff's professor. I'm sending it over by hand.'

'Thanks,' I said.

'Also I've just heard from the Minister's principal private secretary – the Minister's personally interested in this case.'

'Perhaps *he* remembers R. T. Longstaff as an office-boy.'

Stinker laughed. He at least had a sense of humour – but nothing, let me repeat, nothing else.

I sat waiting for the professor's letter, not surprised by the fact that, in the Civil Service, it never rains but it pours. The Civil Service is devised, rightly, to provide an elaborate system of cross-checks and cross-references: let there be a break at some point or other in the network and switches are tripped all over the place.

The professor's letter, I thought when I got it, was designed to trip me. It was from W. Longstaff's professor of organic chemistry to Murray-Hamilton, and it began characteristically 'Dear Sir, I am at a loss to understand why, etc . . .'

I could have made his loss good in no time at all, I reflected. Unfortunately that was not what I was officially required to do. I was required to draft a reply from Murray-Hamilton to the Right Honourable Mr Adalbert Tiarks, M.P. I wished Robert were at home to draft it instead of me.

I knew, of course, exactly what line the department should take – it was perfectly obvious, not to say laid down in the rubric anyway.

Justice to W. Longstaff had been done. Murray-Hamilton would accept that without much trouble. Justice to W. Longstaff must now be seen to be done. W. Longstaff must be interviewed again by a board, (i) whose chairman did not ask him any unkind questions about the electronic structure of the molecules he synthesized and (ii) whose constitution was such that his professor was not at a loss to understand how it arrived at its verdict.

To settle (i) make Robert the chairman.

To settle (ii) co-opt the professor on the board, so that he would be a party to the decision.

It was perfectly simple, perfectly straightforward.

(And W. Longstaff, being awful, would be turned down again.)

Why, you may ask, did I find it so hard to draft a reply for Murray-Hamilton? Why did I wish Robert were at home to draft it instead of me? What inhibited me?

Every time I put my pen to paper I thought of Murray-Hamilton, brooding, reflecting. No matter what I wrote on my minute paper,

I knew what was written on the great ledger . . . I had done Wrong.

Of course I managed to write something in the end. And I thought it wise to send Robert a letter by airmail, saying what was going on.

On the following Monday morning, when Murray-Hamilton must have been studying what I had finally managed to write, the door of my office suddenly opened and Robert came in.

His face was white. 'I got your letter and caught the overnight plane back,' he said.

His face was white but not white from fatigue.

'Gawd, do you think it's as bad as that?' My spirits were plunging so fast that I could not keep up with them.

Robert flopped down on my table.

'If I judge the situation aright,' he said, 'it's probably worse.'

I stared at him. He had fallen into one of those moods of heavy silence that always indicated despair.

At last he roused himself.

'Look,' he said, 'I shall have to tell you this. I haven't told you before because I didn't want to worry you unnecessarily. I thought you'd got enough on your hands, with your book sub judice and Elspeth pregnant . . . For some time now Murray-Hamilton has been proposing to eliminate this directorate altogether, or rather "roll it up", as he calls it, with the establishments division . . . They'll find something else for me to do, probably with wider scope, where they can give me my head a bit more . . . But there was absolutely nothing I could do to make him change his mind about you. He wanted the changes to eliminate you altogether.'

I could not say anything.

Robert gave an odd wry smile to himself as he went on. 'He's a very pertinacious man. But so am I. Also he's a humane man – outside keeping you in the Civil Service he'd do anything to help you. But I told him his humaneness wasn't much use . . . Anyway, before I went to Washington I thought I'd just about argued him into the position of letting you have some sort of role in the new organization . . .'

He stopped. He did not need to tell me anything else.

437

In the end he stood up and said, not looking at me:

'I suppose you've not had any news about your book yet?'

I shook my head.

He went towards the door. 'I'd better go over and tell Murray-Hamilton I'm back.'

7

Help

That evening I had to tell Elspeth.

'What is it, darling?' she said when I came into the flat.

'You'd better sit down while I tell you,' I said.

As she already knew about *l'affaire* Longstaff, there was not much more in quantity to be said.

We sat side by side on the sofa. The flat seemed absolutely silent. There was a faint smell in the air of the dinner cooking, possibly burning.

'So there it is,' I said.

Elspeth put her arm round me.

'Try not to worry, darling . . .' she said. 'We shall be all right . . .'

I looked down at my hands. All right – you and I and the little one! I thought bitterly.

'We shall be all right,' she repeated. 'I can help you, darling.'

I looked at her.

'We can earn a living together,' she said. 'You can write. And I'll go back to teaching. I can work. I can help.'

I could not speak.

'So you see . . .' she said.

I put my arm round her and pressed my face against the side of her throat. 'My darling, my darling,' I kept on saying.

We remained like that for what seemed like hours. I cannot tell you if the smell of burning got stronger. I noticed nothing.

The telephone rang.

'What's that?' I said.

'The telephone,' said Elspeth.

I got up and staggered across the room to answer it.

A light, high voice said gaily:

'The coast's clear!'

'What?' said I.

There was a hiatus. The voice said: 'Is that you, Joe?'

'Yes, it is.'

'This is Harry. The coast's clear!'

'What coast?'

Harry laughed. 'Were you drunk, or fast asleep or something? I'm talking about your novel. The coast's clear. I've just heard . . . You can go ahead. Have it printed. It's O.K. by the Home Office.'

'Good God!' I said.

'And may I say,' said Harry, 'I think it's excellent, Joe. It's your best book.'

At last I understood. By this time Elspeth was trying to share the earpiece with me.

Harry said: 'I don't know what you and Elspeth are up to – you sound *non compos* to me . . . I'm going to ring off, and you can ring me back when you feel up to it.'

With an especially fluent, honeyed, triumphant Good-bye he rang off.

'Well!' I looked at Elspeth.

Her eyes were shining. 'Ring up Annette and Robert!' she said.

We rang up Annette and Robert.

And then we stood, facing each other. I put out my arms and Elspeth moved towards me.

'Whoops!' She put her hand on her stomach.

'What on earth?'

'It's all right. Just the baby moved.'

'The darling baby, the darling you!' I embraced both.

Then we noticed the smell of burning.

After we had eaten our dinner, we thought about Murray-Hamilton and the Civil Service again. We spent the night in each other's arms, not sleeping much because of the strange combination of misery and joy.

Next morning Robert came straight into my office to hear all over again such detail as I had heard from Harry.

'It couldn't be better,' he said. 'I wasn't able to do anything at all with Murray-Hamilton. Incidentally you'll be interested to know that in the new organization there's going to be no place for your old enemy Stinker Spinks. He's a permanent, so he can't be sacked, but I think you'll find he's moved off into distinctly outer darkness.'

'Well, poor old Stinker!' I cried. Detestable though he was, at that moment I really did feel sorry for him.

Robert looked at me. 'I wasn't able to do anything with Murray-Hamilton; but it occurred to me, last night after your news had cheered me up, that we're not entirely without resources. You could appeal, of course; but as a temporary you wouldn't really stand a chance. No. I think we've got to try to circumvent Murray-Hamilton. There are higher bosses than him, and they haven't all consigned you to the wrong side of the ledger.' He paused. 'I'm going to talk to Harold Johnson about you. I know him better now . . . In fact some little time ago, with you in mind, I got him on the subject of temporaries.' Robert's eyes sparkled momentarily. 'As usual with him, when you press the button you get a powerful – and possibly surprising – response. He took my point. And characteristically observed there's no reason why temporaries should be treated like dogs.' Robert paused again. 'I think I'm going to talk to him again. I don't know why I shouldn't tell him that I think you're doing good work and these people are trying to *get* you.'

I said: 'I shouldn't think he could reasonably intervene.'

'There you're wrong,' said Robert. 'Justice is an absolute fetish with all these people. If it struck him in that way, he could perfectly well, as a personal matter, have a look at the papers.'

In spite of my anxiety I could not help thinking of Sir Harold Johnson. 'You know what *you* want to do?' Pause. 'Get rid of your inhibitions!' Suppose, though, he did send for the papers and saw the record of what happened when my control over my inhibitions momentarily lapsed, what then?

441

Robert decided. 'I'm going to try it, anyway. Something tells me the tide has turned.'

Well, Robert tried it.

I am now at the stage in my story where you do not want another long scene in which Robert told me the result of his trying it. Sir Harold Johnson did not send for me, of course, so I did not have a scene with him. He sent, of course, for the papers.

We had some anxious days of waiting. And then Robert came into my office and I read the look on his face. I shall never forget it, because, just as he was about to speak, two men came into the room. Both were wearing raincoats, and one was wearing a bowler hat. The one who was not wearing the bowler hat was carrying a surveyor's tape-measure.

Neither of them said a word to us or to each other. I recognized them at once as from the Ministry of Works. They had a way of setting about their business, as if nobody else were in the room, at which I never ceased to marvel. It was utterly beyond reproach. I could only imagine that in training them for this kind of activity the Ministry of Works put them through a most rigorous assault-course from which only star recruits ever passed out. Dazzlingly oblivious of us, the one with the tape-measure measured my carpet, and the one without the tape-measure watched him. They went out again.

My fate. I was to be moved to another department, well away from Murray-Hamilton, to what was an Assistant Secretary's post. I was to hold this particular post in my present rank, with the prospect of taking on the rank of the job in a year's time.

'He's a fair-minded man,' said Robert magisterially, 'and used to doing as he sees fit to do.'

'I don't feel I can say anything impartial,' said I.

'What I don't understand,' said Robert simply archiepiscopally, 'is that somehow or other you must have made a favourable impression on him.'

'You * * * * * *!' I cried.

Robert only said: 'I'm inclined to think your troubles are now over.'

8

Scene from Married Life

I rang up the hospital – it was just after midnight – and an Irish
nurse told me the news.

'You've got a beautiful little durl.'

'Little what?'

'A beautiful little durl.'

I realized she must mean a beautiful little girl. A little *girl?* They
had *all* said we were going to have a boy.

'Are you sure?' I asked. 'My wife's name is Lunn. Mrs Lunn.'

'That's right, Mr Lunn. You've got a beautiful little durl.' From
her tone I could tell she was now thinking me as stupid as I was
thinking her.

'How are they?' I said, playing for time.

'They're both fine.'

If I was going to ask her to make sure they had not made a mistake
with the babies, I must do it now, I thought. I felt embarrassed.

'If you're quite sure . . .' I began.

'Sure, an' I'm sure. That's right, Mr Lunn.' She wanted to get
off the line. 'You can come and see them tomorrow night. Now
you can have a good night's sleep, Mr Lunn. Cheerio.'

I put down the receiver and burst into happy laughter. Of course
we had got a beautiful little girl. I was delighted. I got back into
bed again, but I was much too excited to begin a good night's sleep.
For one thing I had to adjust myself to a new idea – as, in due
course, would all those know-alls. Yet the new idea was entrancing. A beautiful little girl . . . Fathers had made fools of themselves
over daughters since the beginning of time, and I found myself
ready to make a start.

The following morning I enjoyed sending telegrams to relations and advertisements to *The Times* and the *Daily Telegraph*. I thought of the people who would read them – how many of them would remember that as little as two years ago they had written me off as far as getting married was concerned? How many of them, now that they could be seen to have been wrong, would realize they had been wrong?

None.

Time had passed. Like Communists whom we had seen reverse their attitudes at regular intervals, they had never been wrong: what they had believed at any particular point in time was a historical necessity for that particular point in time – and therefore right. Happy persons! Fortunate human beings! However, do not think I bore them any ill will. I felt too happy a person, too fortunate a human being myself – deserved though my fortune might be! In the New Year I was going to move to a better job, away from Murray-Hamilton and Spinks. And in the spring my second little masterpiece was going to come out after all.

That evening I went to see Elspeth and the baby. It was the first time I had visited a maternity ward. I, and all the other fathers, were collected in the hospital corridor till the clock struck seven, when we all charged along to the door of the maternity ward – and then slowed up. The floor was softly polished; the beds looked white and fresh; the air was warm; there were flowers on a big table in the middle of the room; and in all the beds round the walls were women looking radiant.

I found Elspeth and skidded across the floor to her.

'You look wonderful!' I cried. Her dark hair, which she had had cut specially short for the occasion, was brushed over her forehead; her eyes shone; the brackets at the corners of her mouth were flickering. I kissed her and the smell of lime flowers wafted into my nose. 'You really do look wonderful, darling.'

'Why not?'

I looked at her. 'Where's the baby?'

'There, all the time.' She pointed to a small box, which I had not noticed, hooked on the end of the bed.

I looked at my first-born child.

Then I looked at Elspeth. 'She looks like your mother,' I said.

'I,' said Elspeth, 'thought she looked like yours.'

I stood looking at the child for a long time. Her eyes were shut, and I thought she was breathing terribly fast – I did not know all babies breathe terribly fast. I touched her hand and she opened her eyes. I caught a glimpse of deep violet-blue . . .

'Oh, she's going to be pretty!' I cried, and tears came into my eyes. I glanced at Elspeth and saw that she was smiling with some satisfaction.

I went and sat down beside Elspeth and held her hand. I stroked her wrist. I began to kiss her wrist.

'Is this allowed?' I whispered.

She glanced around the room and I did the same. In all the white beds were women looking radiant, and beside them dark-clothed men were sitting holding their hands, intently whispering to them. I heard Elspeth breathing.

'Good gracious!' I whispered.

She shook her head in a way that signified 'I know . . .'

I swallowed.

Elspeth put her hand on my hair. 'It's understandable.'

I looked up at her. 'Now I come to think of it, I suppose it is.' I glanced again at the dark-clothed men, intently whispering. 'All those poor bastards must be feeling the same.'

'Sh! . . . Don't use that word here!'

I began to laugh but was checked by one of the babies beginning to cry. Elspeth said: 'It's all right. It's not ours.'

The first baby started off the others. A posse of nurses came and whisked the boxes containing the offenders out of the room. I went and had another look at ours.

She still had her eyes shut. She was still breathing terribly fast. After all, I thought, I am going to be able to feed this darling little mouth. I touched her again, and she opened her eyes.

I went back to Elspeth feeling very strange emotion. Elspeth said:

'While I think of it – will you leave me some small change before you go? I've got nothing to pay for my newspapers with.'

I got some money out of my pocket. She pointed to where her handbag was and asked me to put the money in her purse.

I opened the purse. Inside it was a banknote and something folded in tissue paper.

'What's this in the tissue paper?' I said.

'Can't you guess?' She smiled quietly. 'Open it!'

I undid the paper. It contained the silver rupee we had found in the taxi on our wedding-day.

I sat down beside her. 'Have you carried it about with you all the time?'

'Of course,' she whispered.

I held it in the open palm of my hand, so that the light shone on it.

'It was for luck,' I said.

I could only just hear her – 'That's what it's brought us, darling . . .'

I looked at her. 'It *has* . . .'

We went on looking at each other. Then I touched it to my lips and carefully folded it back again in its tissue paper. Very carefully.

In a little while it was time for me to go.

'Fathers,' enunciated a clear, authoritative, feminine voice from the doorway, 'not able to come in in the evening, may come in for a quarter of an hour at nine o'clock in the morning!'

When I got outside I started to walk instead of catching a bus. The night seemed very dark, but not exceptionally cold – like the night, I thought, of human ignorance. I was pleased with the concept as a simile, but could not see any special application for it at the moment. I felt illuminated, myself. I was in possession of the most important piece of knowledge, which seemed to energize my whole being with light and warmth. It sent my body striding along the twilit street, and my imagination circulating among the peaks of Art. I could have seen it written in stars across the night sky . . .

You want to know what it was? It was:

MARRIED LIFE IS WONDERFUL

I dropped into an unfamiliar public-house for a glass of beer. A man standing beside me at the deserted bar said: 'You don't belong round here, do you?'

I told him what brought me there.

'Is it your first?' he asked.

I said it was.

He gave me a long look. 'Then *your* life is just beginning,' he said.

On the point of saying 'Then I can't think what I've been doing up to now', I said:

'I expect it is.'

At that moment, for no reason that I could find, I suddenly thought again of the official letter telling me I was MISC/INEL. What nobody knew, except me, was the effort I put into trying to be EL. That, I thought, was the theme of my life. MISC/INEL, trying to be EL. In this simple statement were embodied the poetry, the dynamism, the suffering of one man's existence.

I finished my beer and left the pub.

Next morning, in the lift on the way up to my office, I met Froggatt.

'I hear we have good reasons to congratulate you on a certain matter,' he said in his leisurely tempo. He was smiling.

I said he had.

He asked me if we were still living in a flat.

I said we were.

'Ah,' said Froggatt, as the lift came to a stop, 'then you'll be looking for a house, now.'

Now I am not intending to make anything of this incident. But when I got to my office and thought about it, I saw it, as Froggatt might have said, in a certain light.

I had got a wife; I had got a baby; and now it appeared that I had got to get a house . . .

I sat in my chair and expressed myself in a phrase everybody was using in those days. 'Can you *beat* it?'

Instead of ringing for my P.A. I meditated. The conclusion I reached was that this side of the grave there is simply no end to anything. Simply no end.

Well, so be it.

PENGUIN DECADES

Penguin Decades bring you the novels that helped shape modern Britain. When they were published, some were bestsellers, some were considered scandalous, and others were simply misunderstood. All represent their time and helped define their generation, while today each is considered a landmark work of storytelling. Each is introduced by a modern admirer.

50s

Scenes from Provincial Life/William Cooper (1950) Nick Hornby
Lucky Jim/Kingsley Amis (1954) David Nicholls
The Chrysalids/ John Wyndham (1955) M. John Harrison
From Russia with Love/Ian Fleming (1957) Christopher Andrew
Billy Liar/Keith Waterhouse (1959) Blake Morrison

60s

A Clockwork Orange/Anthony Burgess (1962) Will Self
The Millstone/Margaret Drabble (1965) Elaine Showalter
The British Museum is Falling Down/David Lodge (1965) Mark Lawson
A Kestrel for a Knave/Barry Hines (1968) Ian McMillan
Another Part of the Wood/Beryl Bainbridge (1969) Lynn Barber

70s

I'm the King of the Castle/Susan Hill (1970) Esther Freud
Don't Look Now/Daphne du Maurier (1971) Julie Myerson
The Infernal Desire Machines of Doctor Hoffman/Angela Carter (1972) Ali Smith
The Children of Dynmouth/William Trevor (1976) Roy Foster
Treasures of Time/Penelope Lively (1979) Selina Hastings

80s

A Month in the Country/J. L. Carr (1980) Byron Rogers
An Ice-Cream War/William Boyd (1982) Giles Foden
Hawksmoor/Peter Ackroyd (1985) Will Self
Paradise Postponed/John Mortimer (1985) Jeremy Paxman
Latecomers/Anita Brookner (1988) Helen Dunmore

DECADES 1950s

The 1950s was the decade of post-war glamour, Barbie dolls, Pop Art and the Cold War. Britain celebrated the coronation of Elizabeth II and welcomed the Angry Young Men. The teenager was invented, rayguns were the toy of the moment, and Marilyn Monroe and Elvis Presley changed the face of modern culture forever.

Scenes from Provincial Life/William Cooper (1950)
'The joy of Cooper's novel … lies in its readability and freshness. It's funny and candid and surprisingly, disconcertingly modern' – Nick Hornby

Lucky Jim/Kingsley Amis (1954)
'*Lucky Jim* remains unchallenged as the archetypal British comic novel … the themes of class, education, true feeling versus social convention, duty versus passion, honesty versus pretension, have rarely been more skilfully or amusingly explored' - David Nicholls

The Chrysalids/John Wyndham (1955)
'It seems amazing now that anyone could have received *The Chrysalids* as a novel written about the future, when, like *Nineteen Eighty Four*, it is so clearly a novel about the time - and place - in which it was written' - M. John Harrison

From Russia with Love/Ian Fleming (1957)
'Intelligence is the only profession in which a fictional character is many times better known than any real practioner, alive or dead. The fictional character is, of course, James Bond' – Christopher Andrew

Billy Liar/Keith Waterhouse (1959)
'*Billy Liar* is the work Keith Waterhouse will be remembered for … what makes the book unique is its mixture of laddish humour and exorbitant fantasy. And the hero, of course – a rebel in the cause of comic realism' – Blake Morrison

He just wanted a decent book to read ...

Not too much to ask, is it? It was in 1935 when Allen Lane, Managing Director of Bodley Head Publishers, stood on a platform at Exeter railway station looking for something good to read on his journey back to London. His choice was limited to popular magazines and poor-quality paperbacks – the same choice faced every day by the vast majority of readers, few of whom could afford hardbacks. Lane's disappointment and subsequent anger at the range of books generally available led him to found a company – and change the world.

'We believed in the existence in this country of a vast reading public for intelligent books at a low price, and staked everything on it'
Sir Allen Lane, 1902–1970, founder of Penguin Books

The quality paperback had arrived – and not just in bookshops. Lane was adamant that his Penguins should appear in chain stores and tobacconists, and should cost no more than a packet of cigarettes.

Reading habits (and cigarette prices) have changed since 1935, but Penguin still believes in publishing the best books for everybody to enjoy. We still believe that good design costs no more than bad design, and we still believe that quality books published passionately and responsibly make the world a better place.

So wherever you see the little bird – whether it's on a piece of prize-winning literary fiction or a celebrity autobiography, political tour de force or historical masterpiece, a serial-killer thriller, reference book, world classic or a piece of pure escapism – you can bet that it represents the very best that the genre has to offer.

Whatever you like to read – trust Penguin.